D0295941

The Shogun's Queen

www.penguin.co.uk

A daguerreotype of Lord Shimazu Nariakira (1809–58).
The earliest surviving Japanese photograph.
It was created by one of his retainers, Ichiki Shirō.

The Shogun's Queen

Lesley Downer

BANTAM PRESS

LONDON · TORONTO · SYDNEY · AUCKLAND · JOHANNESBURG

TRANSWORLD PUBLISHERS
61–63 Uxbridge Road, London W5 5SA
www.transworldbooks.co.uk

Transworld is part of the Penguin Random House group of companies
whose addresses can be found at global.penguinrandomhouse.com

Penguin
Random House
UK

First published in Great Britain in 2016 by Bantam Press
an imprint of Transworld Publishers

A CIP catalogue record for this book
is available from the British Library.

ISBNs 9780593066867 (cased)
9780593066874 (tpb)

Typeset in 11/14.5pt Sabon by Falcon Oast Graphic Art Ltd.
Printed and bound by Clays Ltd, Bungay, Suffolk.

Penguin Random House is committed to a sustainable
future for our business, our readers and our planet. This book
is made from Forest Stewardship Council® certified paper.

MIX
Paper from
responsible sources
FSC® C018179

1 3 5 7 9 10 8 6 4 2

To Arthur

Hana no iro wa	The cherry blossom falls, its colour lost
Utsurinikeri na	In the long rain of time.
Itazura ni	So too
Waga mi yo ni furu	Age takes my beauty as in vain
Nagame seshi ma ni	I gaze my life away.

Ono no Komachi, poetess, ninth century AD

What a city was Edo (now called Tokyo) in the days of the Shogun! The great straggling city swarmed with men-at-arms, some of them retainers of the different nobles, others Ronin, desperadoes who had cast off their clanship and ruffled it on their own account, ready to draw on any or no provocation . . . I shut my eyes and see picturesque visions of warriors in armour with crested helms and fiercely moustachioed visors – processions of powerful nobles with their retinues marching along the cryptomeria avenues of the Tokaido, the road by the Eastern Sea.

Algernon Mitford, second secretary to the
British legation in Japan, 1866–70

United States Steam Frigate Susquehanna
Off the Coast of Japan

To His Imperial Majesty, the Emperor of Japan,

THE undersigned, commander-in-chief of all the naval forces of the United States of America stationed in the East India, China and Japan seas, has been sent by his government of this country, on a friendly mission . . .

From Commodore Matthew C. Perry to His Imperial Majesty,
the Emperor of Japan, 7 July 1853

Contents

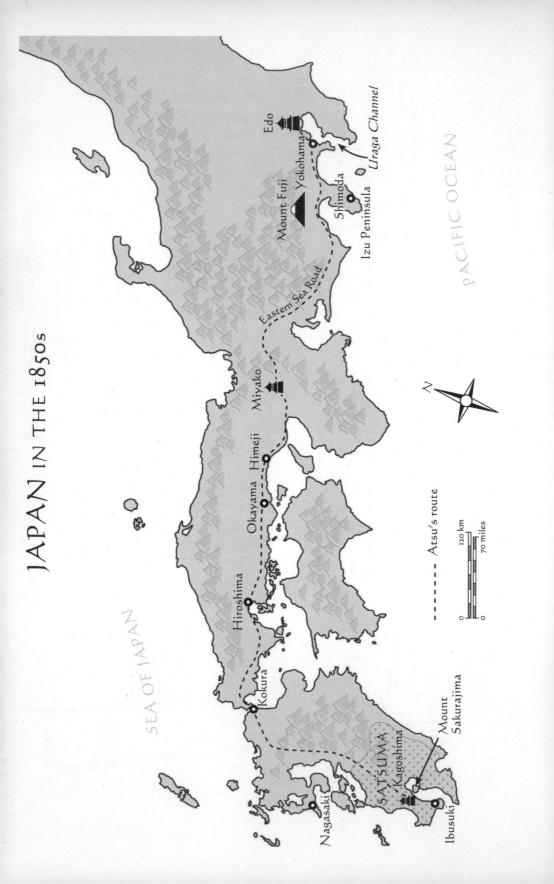

JAPAN IN THE 1850s

SEA OF JAPAN

PACIFIC OCEAN

Uraga Channel

Edo

Yokohama

Mount Fuji

Shimoda

Izu Peninsula

Eastern Sea Road

Miyako

Himeji

Okayama

Hiroshima

Kokura

Nagasaki

SATSUMA

Kagoshima

Mount Sakurajima

Ibusuki

N

------- Atsu's route

120 km

70 miles

0

0

PLAN of the WOMEN'S PALACE in EDO CASTLE

千代田城大奥之図

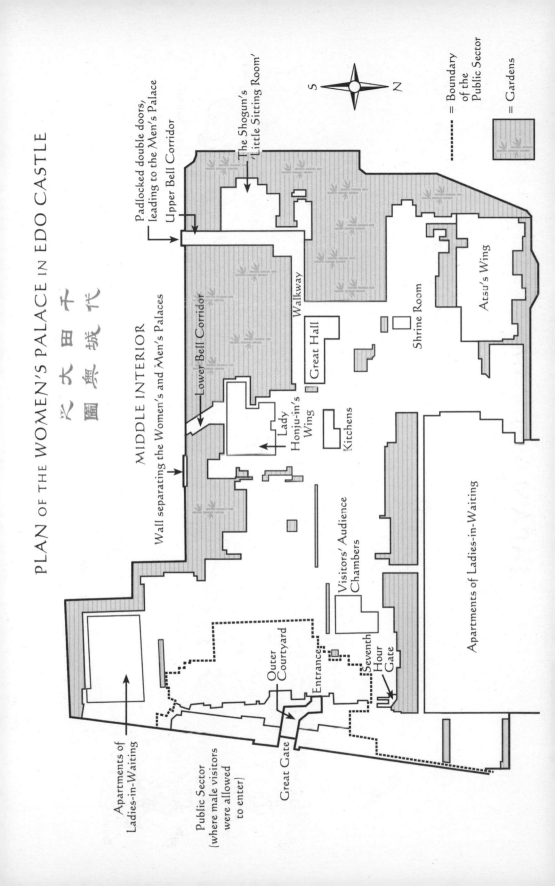

S — N

= Boundary of the Public Sector

= Gardens

Padlocked double doors, leading to the Men's Palace

Upper Bell Corridor

The Shogun's 'Little Sitting Room'

MIDDLE INTERIOR

Wall separating the Women's and Men's Palaces

Lower Bell Corridor

Walkway

Great Hall

Shrine Room

Atsu's Wing

Lady Honju-in's Wing

Kitchens

Visitors' Audience Chambers

Apartments of Ladies-in-Waiting

Apartments of Ladies-in-Waiting

Outer Courtyard

Entrance

Seventh Hour Gate

Great Gate

Public Sector (where male visitors were allowed to enter)

Cast of Characters
(* indicates that they existed in real life)

* Atsu, known in childhood as Okatsu, later Imperial Princess Sumiko of the House of Fujiwara and the Midai, then Lady Tensho-in

KYUSHU

* Tadataké Shimazu, Lord of Ibusuki, Atsu's father
* Atsu's mother, Wife Number One
* Atsu's brother
Haru, Atsu's maid

* Kaneshigé Kimotsuki, later Lord Tatewaki Komatsu, a young Satsuma retainer
* Takamori Saigo, a young Satsuma retainer

* Lord Nariakira Shimazu, Prince of Satsuma
* Princess Teru, his daughter
* Lord Narioki Shimazu, his father
* Lady Yura, his father's concubine
* Lord Hisamitsu Shimazu, Lord Nariakira's half-brother and son of Yura
Toshikyo, Lord Nariakira's page
* Komin Kawamoto, retainer working on daguerreotype
* Koan Matsuki, retainer working on daguerreotype

Elder Maki, chief lady-in-waiting at Crane Castle
Lady Umé, Lord Nariakira's concubine

Lady Také, Lord Nariakira's concubine

Retainers, concubines, ladies-in-waiting

MIYAKO (the Imperial Capital, modern-day Kyoto)

* Emperor Komei, known as the Son of Heaven
* Prince Konoé of the House of Fujiwara
* Princess Konoé of the House of Fujiwara
* Lady Ikushima, Atsu's chief lady-in-waiting and adviser

EDO (modern-day Tokyo)

* Iesada Tokugawa, nicknamed Masa, the thirteenth shogun
* Ieyoshi Tokugawa, the twelfth shogun, Iesada's father
* Yoshitomi Tokugawa, nicknamed Yoshi, Lord of Kii
* Lord Keiki of the House of Hitotsubashi
* 'The Evil Dragon of Mito', Nariaki Tokugawa, Lord of Mito, Lord Keiki's father

* Lord Abé – Prime Minister Masahiro Abé, Chief Senior Councillor of the Tokugawa shogunate, 1845–55
* Lord Hotta – Prime Minister Masamuné Hotta, Chief Senior Councillor of the Tokugawa shogunate, 1855–58
* Regent Ii – Naosuké Ii, Great Elder of the Tokugawa shogunate, 1858–60

* Governor Inoué of Shimoda
* Governor Nakamura of Shimoda

Members of the State Council

WOMEN'S PALACE (the Great Interior)

* Lady Honju-in, Iesada's mother, the Lady Dowager

* Lady Shiga, also known as Oshiga, Iesada's concubine
* Lady Tsuyu, concubine of Lord Ieyoshi, Iesada's father
Chief Elder Anekoji
Middle Elder Omasé
Lady Hana, lady-in-waiting in the Great Interior
Lady Maru, lady-in-waiting in the Great Interior
Yasu, Atsu's maid who accompanies her to Edo
Chiyo, Atsu's maid who accompanies her to Edo

Doctor Taki
Doctor Moriyama

Ladies-in-waiting, companion priests, lower-ranking ladies, dwarf entertainers, concubines of previous shoguns, bath attendants, carpenters' foreman, carpenters, palace guards, boating attendants

* Princess Tadako, first wife of Iesada (deccased)
* Lady Hideko, second wife of Iesada (deceased)

FOREIGNERS

* Townsend Harris, Consul General of the United States of America
* Hendrick Heusken, his Dutch secretary and interpreter

Preamble

Year of the Dog, third year of the Kaei era, a yang metal year
(February 1850 – January 1851)

Japan has been at peace for close on two hundred and fifty years, ever since Ieyasu Tokugawa unified it in 1603 and took the title of Shogun – Barbarian-Quelling Generalissimo. His descendant, Ieyoshi, the twelfth shogun, now fifty-seven, governs with the help of a council of ministers from his castle in the glittering city of Edo in the east of the country. In the official capital, Miyako, another personage lives hidden away inside his rundown palace – the emperor. He has no temporal power but performs religious functions. He spends his days conducting rituals to placate the gods, to ensure good harvests and keep Japan safe and healthy.

Japan is made up of some 260 princedoms each under its own daimyo – clan lord – and with its own army. Each has a degree of autonomy but all are under the overlordship of the shogun. The 'inside lords', the daimyo who fought on the side of the shogun in 1603 in the great battle which ended years of civil war, have their domains mostly in the north and east of the country and hold the reins of power. The 'outside lords', who fought against the shogun, have lands mainly in the south and west. Paramount among these is the fabulously rich Prince of Satsuma, ruler of one of the most powerful domains at the far south-west tip of the country.

Within the domains there is the occasional power struggle. Nevertheless, under this system Japan has maintained peace and stability for nearly two hundred and fifty years and developed a glorious culture.

For most of this time foreigners have been largely prohibited. Chinese traders come and go and there is a tiny colony of some twenty Dutch merchants, all men, who live on an artificial island off Nagasaki. Once a year, most years, a Dutch ship arrives with goods to sell and takes away goods for export. No other foreigners, certainly no westerners, are allowed to approach the country by ship and those who do are driven away; and any Japanese who are shipwrecked abroad are not allowed to return, on pain of death, though in recent years this edict has been less stringently enforced.

But there are shadows hovering over this precarious stability, ships looming on the horizon threatening to invade, barbarian nations eager to share in Japan's fabled riches. And as the third year of the Kaei era comes to an end, no one dare assume any longer that life will continue in just the same way for ever . . .

Prologue

*Third day of the twelfth month, Year of the Dog, Kaei 3
(15 January 1851): Crane Castle, Kagoshima, in the Satsuma domain*

'Halt! Who goes there?'

Lanterns flicker outside the wooden walls of the palanquin. Feet stamp, metal clangs on stone.

The palanquin hits the ground with a bump.

Inside it is pitch dark apart from the thread of light that rims the door. The traveller looks down at her small white hands, twisting them apprehensively. She left home at cockcrow and the sun has long since set. She has been sitting in this cramped wooden box all day with her legs curled under her, pitching back and forth on the shoulders of the bearers. She's chilled to the bone and exhausted but she'd far rather stay huddled for ever in her miserable conveyance with its nauseating odour of lacquer than step out and face these hostile men.

The gruff shouts drum into her head. She smells smoke and tallow, hears the crackle of torch flames.

She braces herself, pats her hair into place and smoothes her kimono skirts, badly creased by now. She's never been away from home before. She wonders what will happen when the door slides back, what these sentries – she assumes they're sentries – will do when they discover who she is and why she is here.

She takes a breath, tries to still the beating of her heart. 'My name is Okatsu, daughter of Tadataké Shimazu, Lord of Ibusuki,' she says, as clearly and loudly as she can. Her voice sounds high-pitched and tremulous in the night air. The last thing she wants is for these men to discover that she is only fourteen years old or – worse – that she is afraid. 'I have a letter for His Lordship,' she adds in as firm a tone as she can manage.

The sentries suck their breath through their teeth and confer in mutters. 'If you'd be so good as to hand it out, Your Ladyship, we will ensure it reaches him,' says a wheedling voice in deferential tones.

'I have been instructed to deliver it directly into His Lordship's hands,' she says sternly. She has rehearsed her words again and again during the long journey here. 'I am charged to see that His Lordship, and only His Lordship, opens it. I request to be admitted into His Lordship's presence.'

'Apologies, Your Ladyship. We have orders to check the identity of all visitors before they enter the precincts.'

The door to the palanquin rattles. Before she can utter another word it slides back. Faces peer out of the shadows, as hideous as demon masks in the lantern light. She blinks, dazzled by the sudden glare.

The sentries' eyes widen. There's a long silence, an intake of breath. 'Well, what do you know!' says one, shaking his head. 'A child!'

'And what a beauty!' says another.

The lanterns and faces close in. A cold wind swirls.

She shrinks back. On her knees, swaddled in futons, she feels small and vulnerable. She is a lord's daughter, she reminds herself. She draws herself up. 'I require to be admitted into His Lordship's presence,' she snaps with as much dignity as she can muster.

The men grunt and back away and the door slides shut. Once again she's cast into darkness. Footsteps retreat across the court-yard, staves clang on cobblestones. She bites her lip. Will they arrest her, lock her up, take her hostage? Her father and His Lordship are bitter enemies. The sentries may suspect she is a decoy, that she plans to assassinate His Lordship, that the letter is poisoned.

She curls her fingers around the hilt of her dagger. Like all women of the samurai class, she carries it tucked into her sash at all times and she knows how to use it, to fight if necessary or, if she is captured, to kill herself.

Winding her way along the coast, dozing in her palanquin, she's been trying not to think about the events that have brought her on this freezing winter's night from her peaceful home in the seaside town of Ibusuki to the towering gates of Crane Castle in the city of Kagoshima. Now images flash through her mind – the gatherings, the raised voices, the doors slamming late into the night.

She screws her eyes shut as she remembers that fateful day when soldiers arrived to arrest her father, shouting as they slammed their staffs against the door. He was lucky, he'd been put under house arrest. But several of her friends' fathers had been sent into exile and two were executed. She blinks back tears as she thinks of it.

And there was worse to come. Her father's closest friend, a much loved uncle, had been ordered to commit ritual suicide and her father had been commanded to witness it. She pictures her father's face when he came home that night, his shoulders slumped. He'd brought back her uncle's white linen underrobe, black with blood. He gathered the whole family together and held up the robe so that everyone could see it. She hears his voice, hoarse and ragged, ringing in her ears. 'Take a long, hard look,' he'd croaked. 'This is the price of justice and loyalty.'

'Justice and loyalty . . .' No one tells women anything and especially not fourteen-year-old girls, but she's worked out that there is a power struggle between His Lordship, the veteran Prince of Satsuma, and her father's cousin, Lord Nariakira, His Lordship's son. Lord Nariakira is Okatsu's favourite uncle and her father his most loyal ally. There is no doubt which side of the struggle she and her family are on.

She shuffles and grimaces as blood comes flooding back into her legs, numb from kneeling for so long.

A couple of months have passed since that terrible night. The maple leaves had fallen and there was a dusting of snow on the ground. Then – just yesterday – her mother had come in search of her. Okatsu had been in her room, bent over her books. Her mother took her aside, her elegant face pale and drawn. She had a task for her, she'd said hesitantly. She was to go to Crane Castle, the seat of His Lordship the Prince of Satsuma, to deliver a letter.

Okatsu was startled that her own mother would send her into a hornets' nest, into the enemy camp. But when she tried to ask, her mother raised a finger.

'Not a word,' she said.

Okatsu understood. The less she was told the less she'd be able to give away if she were captured and tortured. She drew herself up, proud that she'd been entrusted with such a vital mission.

'I have faith in you, Okatsu-*chan*,' her mother had said, handing her a scroll box. 'I know you will do your best.'

Okatsu had been taken aback to see tears in her proud mother's eyes. As she'd stepped into her palanquin at dawn that morning the whole household had lined up to see her off. Even her father and brothers were there to wish her a safe journey, as if they weren't sure they would see her again.

There are footsteps outside the palanquin. The sentries. The young lady may enter but she is to leave behind the attendants and guards who have come with her from Ibusuki. The bearers take her in her palanquin up to the great entrance hall of the castle. There she gingerly unfolds her legs, first one, then the other, and steps out into the dark hallway.

A bevy of stern-faced women sweeps out of the shadows, exuding musty perfume. They grip her elbows and usher her through long corridors and into a side chamber. Muttering, they remove her heavy kimonos one by one until she is naked and shivering. She grits her teeth, trying not to recoil as they poke bony fingers into every crack and cranny of her fourteen-year-old body. She is of samurai stock, she reminds herself. She must not disgrace her family by showing the slightest humiliation or fear. The women take away her dagger and remove her hairpins and her hair falls in a glossy black curtain around her bare body. They check that she has no other sharp objects then tell her brusquely to dress herself and give her a ribbon to tie back her hair.

Guards carrying torches that blaze with huge yellow flames walk ahead of her through a maze of gloomy corridors. She follows, aghast at the lack of ceremony. She'd been expecting a chamberlain or, at the very least, a maid to escort her. Footsteps echo on the wooden floors, cobwebs hang from the lintels. The walls dwindle away into darkness above her. Men, heavily armed, line her path, silently watching. She holds the precious scroll box tightly in both hands and walks boldly, keeping her head modestly bowed, but her heart is thundering. Each step she takes is one step closer to the dragon's lair where she must face the enemy, the old lord.

They come to a chamber that smells of candle wax and tobacco smoke and dust. Without even an usher to announce her, the guards push her unceremoniously inside and the door slams shut behind her.

She looks around wide-eyed. Candles on tall gold candlesticks light the corners. Servants and bodyguards kneel along the walls.

There is a wheezing cough. At the far end of the room an old man squats like a toad on a dais, his head poking from the stiff brocade of his robes. He licks thick crusted lips as he stares at her, his small eyes half hidden in the folds of his face. Okatsu has never seen anyone so grizzled and wrinkled and jowly. So this is His Lordship, the Prince of Satsuma, the tyrant who ordered the arrest of Okatsu's father and the death of her uncle.

She kneels, face to the floor. As she looks up, an expression of lust crosses his face. A tremor runs up her spine.

His mouth creases into a smile. 'Well, now. What have we here?' he quavers in a thin dry voice. 'A gift, is it, a peace offering from my errant kinsman and subject Tadataké? Quite right. He's caused me trouble enough.' He leans forward, the leathery flesh of his neck wobbling, narrows his eyes to slits. 'And such a pretty little creature,' he says, leering. 'Such soft white skin. A perfect little doll! Who would have thought my cousin's ugly son could have sired such a beauty? A most acceptable gift.' He licks his lips.

Okatsu draws herself up, shaking with indignation. Even if he is her liege lord and master, how dare he treat her with such scant respect!

'If I may be so bold, my lord,' she says, trying to stop her voice from trembling, 'you are misinformed. I am a messenger. I have a letter for you.'

'Have you indeed? Don't be afraid. Bring it over here. Show me.'

On her knees she edges towards him, holding out the scroll in both hands. Through the heavy silk of her kimono skirts she feels the tatami like ice under her legs. She smells the old man's breath, hears him wheeze. His eyes are fixed on her.

'Let me see it,' he says thickly. He stretches a hand out, clamps thick fingers around her wrist and wrenches her towards him. Taken by surprise, she loses her balance. Her legs fly up and her skirts fall open and she sprawls face down on the floor.

Flushed with mortification she tries to sit up, but before she can move the old man is on top of her. His flabby body presses her to the ground, his hot breath blows around her ears. Probing fingers squeeze her buttocks, her waist, grope for her budding breasts.

She gasps for breath. Desperately she wriggles this way and that, trying to escape. Her face is crushed against the tatami. She twists her head to one side, shoots a glance at the servants and guards who stand blank-faced along the walls. They look away. She realizes with a shock of desolation that no one will help her. No one dare risk His Lordship's wrath by interfering. No one cares what becomes of an annoying child sent for His Lordship's entertainment. She is on her own.

The old man is heaving his clothes up, shoving her legs apart. She feels cold air strike her bare legs as he pushes himself between them. She is struggling to breathe under the weight of him.

She is trained in the martial arts. She wonders if she dare try to fight him off. But he is her lord and master. She is not permitted to oppose his will. She is shocked and dismayed that her liege lord should behave in such a way.

She frees one hand, heaves herself up, tries to push him off. She hears the tear of silk as he wrenches at her skirts. She is determined not to cry. 'My lord,' she pants. Her voice comes out as a sob. She takes a breath and shouts as loudly as she can, 'Please. Please stop. Please let me go. You demean yourself!'

He gives a start. There's utter silence. 'Demean myself?' she hears him wheezing. 'Demean myself? Are you not honoured, child? I am your lord. How dare you oppose my will!'

She is about to answer when the door slides open. An overwhelming smell of perfume and face powder swirls into the room. 'Nari-*sama*!' shrieks a woman's voice.

The old man pushes Okatsu aside and scrambles to his knees, panting.

Okatsu gasps for breath. She sits up and wipes her face, her hands shaking. She smoothes her hair and brushes off her skirts. She has never in her life been so humiliated. Then she turns towards the woman and her heart sinks. This must be Lady Yura, His Lordship's chief concubine.

She is said to be so beautiful that no man can resist her. Okatsu has heard that she practises black magic, that she cast a spell over the old lord, that she has anyone killed who stands in her way. People say that she had Lord Nariakira's children killed so that her bastard son could inherit the princedom in place of Lord Nariakira, the rightful heir.

The woman is dressed in brilliantly coloured silk kimonos with a lavish design of pine trees, bamboo and snow scrolling across the skirts. Her delicate oval face, heavily powdered, shimmers alluringly in the candlelight but the black-rimmed eyes that glare at Okatsu are icy cold. Her perfumed hair is wound into a glossy coil and studded with tortoiseshell combs and jewelled hairpins. When she opens her scarlet lips to speak, her black-painted teeth turn her mouth into a bottomless chasm. She is infinitely more terrifying than the old man.

'You thought I'd leave you alone with some whore?' she snarls. She has the accent of a Satsuma carpenter's daughter, not a lady of high rank.

Okatsu is still trembling. 'I am not a whore,' she shouts indignantly. 'I am Okatsu, daughter of Lord Tadataké of Ibusuki.'

His Lordship waddles back to the dais and squats on his brocade cushion, pushing strands of oiled grey hair into place with a liver-spotted hand. His face is red and puffy. He's panting loudly.

'Now then, Nari-*sama*. The moment I go away . . .' Lady Yura raps her fan across his thick knuckles.

'I am a messenger. I have a letter,' Okatsu says insistently.

The concubine gives her an icy stare. 'What nonsense,' she says with a toss of her head. 'What do you mean by coming here?'

Okatsu looks around for the scroll box. It has skidded across the floor. She picks it up, holds it out to the old man. He casts a timid glance at Lady Yura. Then he turns to Okatsu, bushy eyebrows raised. 'Demean myself?' he mutters. He shakes his head. For a moment a flicker of something – shame, maybe, injured pride – crosses his face.

'Please take it, sire,' Okatsu says.

'Don't touch it,' hisses the concubine. 'You know this is a trap.'

Okatsu gazes straight at the old man, holds out the scroll box in both hands. He harrumphs, wipes his face with a handkerchief, then reaches out and takes the box gingerly, as if it's red hot.

Okatsu sits like a statue, trying to conceal her relief.

Grunting, the old man opens the box, takes out the letter and unrolls it. Okatsu hardly dares breathe as he holds it up to the candlelight. She doesn't know what it says but it can't be welcome news.

He runs a stubby finger down the lines of characters, frowning. His face blackens and his eyes bulge. The flesh between his eyebrows protrudes. Then his jowly cheeks sag. He nods heavily and looks up, his eyes bleary. 'So that's the way it goes,' he mutters.

Lady Yura takes the letter between long white-painted fingers and her eyes open wide. A scowl creases her powdered forehead. Okatsu peeks at the two of them, trying to guess what they are thinking.

Finally the old man calls for a writing desk and paper, a brush, block of ink, ink stick and water dropper. A servant grinds some ink for him and slowly, laboriously, licking his thick lips, he writes an answer. The servant sprinkles sand over the ink. The old man rolls up the letter, seals it, presses his stamp to the sealing wax, calls for a scroll box and holds it out with an exaggerated bow to Okatsu.

She is on her feet, faint with relief, eager to be gone, when the concubine calls for tea. Reluctantly she has to stay yet longer and make uncomfortable small talk.

Finally Lady Yura summons a guard and whispers in his ear. He leads Okatsu into a labyrinth of corridors, running ahead, holding a single candle. She hurries after him, clutching the precious letter, wondering where he is taking her, what secret instructions Lady Yura has given him. The beetling hallways look entirely different from the path she took on the way there. She prays to the gods to keep watch over her, hopes that she doesn't end up down a well or in a dungeon or at the end of some dark corridor with her throat cut.

She hardly dares take breath till she sees the entranceway and her palanquin outside with the guards and ladies who've come with her from her home.

The old women are waiting to return her dagger and hairpins. 'It's late,' says one, her mouth cracking into a black-toothed smile. 'Won't you spend the night here in the castle?'

Okatsu bows politely and orders her bearers to set off straight away on the long journey through the night. She doesn't manage even the glimmer of a smile till she's back in her father's mansion.

Safely back in Ibusuki, Okatsu mulls over that disturbing encounter. At her lessons, bent over her books, all she can think of is the old man crushing her under his weight and the icy cold eyes of the concubine, glaring at her. Over and over again she runs through all that happened, ponders how it might have gone. At least she is not dead, not even hurt, and she still managed to fulfil her task. She wonders why – why she was sent on such a perilous mission, and what has been achieved. Above all, the letter pricks her curiosity. She wants to know what it said and what the old man's answer was.

And so the Year of the Dog comes to an end and the Year of the Boar, the fourth year of the Kaei era, begins. On the first day of the first month, every person in the country becomes one year older. Okatsu turns fifteen. Nearly two months more pass and the plum trees are in full bloom when her mother runs in one morning to tell her that Lord Nariakira is here, asking to see her.

In the grand reception room the rain doors have been pushed back and light filters in through the paper screens. Lord Nariakira is warming his hands over the brazier.

He's a handsome man with a thoughtful face, tall and powerfully built with a broad chest. Usually he wears ceremonial kimonos with huge starched shoulders that stick out like wings but even in loose informal robes he still fills the room with his presence. He has piercing eyes that seem to take in everything, and a proud jut to his jaw. His stern face softens when he sees Okatsu.

Everyone else is in awe of him but he's always been kind to her. He says she's like a daughter to him. Whenever he comes he always has stories to tell her, marvels to show.

'Come and sit here with me,' he says. He speaks in grand lordly language, quite different from the earthy Satsuma brogue.

A servant lights a long-stemmed pipe for him. He takes a long slow draw and a thread of blue smoke curls towards the bamboo ceiling. He taps the pipe out in the tobacco box. 'I wanted you to be the first to know,' he says. 'My father has abdicated. I am the Prince of Satsuma now.'

Okatsu smiles at him joyfully. So the power struggle is over. They can live in peace again.

'There is a lot of work to be done,' he says, his face grave. 'But first I must thank you. You are a brave young woman, braver than most men could ever be.' He picks up his pipe again. 'I understand you met my father and that concubine of his, Lady Yura.'

Okatsu lowers her eyes. She's ashamed of what transpired, how close she came to failing in her mission.

'My father is a cruel and ruthless man. The whole princedom has suffered under his rule – farmers taxed to the hilt, samurai on starvation-level stipends having to take odd jobs, good, hardworking people forced to live in penury. I would have stood by, let his reign run its course. After all, I am the next in line. But then my children started dying.'

He pauses, stares into the glowing embers of the brazier. The rain doors rattle and an icy draught sweeps through the room.

Okatsu nods, remembering the funerals, the tiny coffins, Lord Nariakira tearing his hair, wild with grief, as one by one his sons had died. The whole princedom had gone into mourning.

'Not one survives,' he says. 'Not one.' His voice is a hollow whisper, as if he is speaking to himself.

He looks up, his face dark. 'Children die. It is a fact of life. But to lose all four, that was too cruel.' He groans, thumps the floor with his fist. 'It was not chance or fate. It was a curse. That woman cast spells on my children to make them die.'

Okatsu gazes at him, perplexed. 'Do you really think that, Uncle?' she asks.

Everyone talks about spirits and magic and spells, about ghosts and goblins and long-nosed tengu, though Okatsu has never seen any herself. When children are born dead or families fall into ruin, people say it's the doing of the spirits. If the dead can't rest in peace they hover around the living, causing harm. That is why it's so important to tend the ancestors' graves and make offerings and pray to them.

But Lord Nariakira is different. He's taught her to think for herself. He's told her about the red-haired men who live on a man-made island outside Nagasaki. He admires their culture and their way of looking at the world.

Every year a ship comes from their country, Holland, bringing barbarian instruments and books of barbarian knowledge, which he collects and studies. He's shown her books of charts and maps and diagrams, covered in dense illegible squiggles which, to her intense admiration, he can read. Sometimes he lets her peer through his 'mirror of distant hopes', a long metal tube fitted with lenses which brings the stars so close you can almost touch them. It makes the moon look so big you feel you could step out and walk on it, and she's seen that far from there being a rabbit pounding rice cakes up there, as everyone says, the surface is actually grey and pock-marked.

Lord Nariakira knows there's no rabbit on the moon, so how can he believe in curses and spells?

He starts as if he's forgotten she's there and gives a sigh. 'I am not a superstitious man,' he says. 'But you have to believe the evidence. When my children started dying one after the other I sent one of my most trusted chamberlains to investigate. He discovered a serpents' nest of evil – priests making images of my sons and placing curses on them, hermits practising black magic . . .'

'And you believed it, Uncle?'

'There was no other explanation. The only question was, who was hiring them? Who stood to gain from my children's deaths? It did not take much to work it out. It was Lady Yura.'

Okatsu pictures the toad-like old man and the hard-faced woman at his side and shudders.

'A vulgar, venomous creature.' Lord Nariakira's voice is a growl. 'She ensnared my gullible old father and poisoned him against me. She wanted to have her bastard son made prince in my place. If I had no heirs, you see, I would not be a fit successor for my father. So she had to have my sons killed.

'It had to stop. I had to topple my father, take power myself. But he moved more quickly than I expected. He guessed I was plotting a coup and made the first move, swooped on my supporters.'

Okatsu holds her breath. She hears the soldiers hammering at the door, remembers her uncle being led away in the middle of the night. She sees the bloodstained robe, hears her father's voice croaking out those fateful words: 'This is the price of justice and loyalty.'

'Six of my followers killed themselves before they could be arrested,' says Lord Nariakira. His face is hollow and his voice hoarse. 'You know what my father did? He had their corpses taken and strung up on crosses. One he had sawn into pieces. Fourteen of my men committed suicide, seventeen were sent into exile. The rest were put under house arrest or died in jail.

'But in the end the old man brought about his own downfall. No one could stand by and watch when such atrocities were being carried out. When news reached Edo of his bloody purge the Council of Elders decreed he had to go. The question was how to deliver the news, how to persuade him to leave peaceably, without civil war engulfing our domain.'

He looks at Okatsu gravely. 'That was where you came in, my child.'

'The letter?' Okatsu whispers.

Lord Nariakira nods. 'The messenger had to be a girl, so young that my father wouldn't suspect treachery, but so beautiful that he'd be curious to see her. It had to be someone who knew nothing of the negotiations in Edo and wouldn't give anything away. She also had to be fearless, someone who wouldn't flinch or run away.

'You were the only person who could do it. We all knew your intelligence and courage. I asked your father to authorize you to carry out this task and explained the risks to him in full. No one knew what my father would do if he was presented with an ultimatum.'

'And you never breathed a word of it to me,' Okatsu gasps, cold with horror. 'No one did. You sent me into a monster's lair. Do you know what your father tried to do to me? How could you send me to that terrible place knowing what those people are like?'

He looks at her, his face gentle. 'Did he try to touch you?'

She nods, looks down, her eyes filling with tears.

'He is well known for that. He thinks it is his right as a clan lord. But I hear you resisted.' A flicker of a smile crosses his face. 'That was brave of you. He must have been astonished. No one ever defies him. I knew you would stand up for yourself. That was why he accepted the letter.'

For a moment he looks abashed. But she is a fifteen-year-old girl and he is the lord of the realm. 'It was for the good of the princedom,' he says loftily. He narrows his eyes, looks at Okatsu as if she of all people ought to understand.

'No one cared what became of me.' Even as she hisses the words she knows it's true. They all of them, men, women and children, have to be prepared, even eager, to die to serve the greater cause – their lord, their domain. That is a samurai's duty.

'It was best not to tell you,' he says gently. 'Your innocence was your best protection.'

She swallows hard, opens her mouth to protest. He holds up his hand. 'I knew you could do it,' he says. 'I had faith in you and you repaid it amply. We are all in your debt.' His face is unruffled. He stares into the distance. He has far greater matters on his mind than the well-being of one young girl.

She shakes her head, gives a sigh. 'At least tell me what the letter said.'

'It was from the chief senior councillor, Prime Minister Abé. "Your tyranny has gone on too long," he wrote. "Your people suffer under your cruel reign. Your position is no longer tenable. The only honourable course is for you to retire. We shall take all necessary measures to ensure that our decree is observed. His Majesty intends to present you with a prized set of tea utensils on the occasion of your retirement to congratulate you on your long reign. We shall appreciate receiving your acceptance of this gift."

'If he had refused to accept the letter it would have been an act of rebellion. The government would have had to send troops to remove him.'

'But if he had refused it he would have had my head cut off,' Okatsu whispers. 'Isn't that what they always do, execute the messenger?'

Lord Nariakira smiles. 'You were not in danger. He is too easily seduced by a pretty face. No, Lady Yura was the real threat. But I knew your youth and innocence and purity would win them over. And you see,' he continues smoothly, 'our ploy worked. He obeyed the government's decree. He abdicated and appointed me prince of the domain. My father's oppressive reign is over and it is thanks to you.'

There's no point arguing any further. Curiosity overcomes Okatsu's anger. 'What became of him?'

'He is in retirement in Kagoshima. He lost his princedom but he still has his concubine. The irony of it is that she got her revenge. I have no sons. Unless I can produce an heir her bastard son will become prince when I die. Let us pray to the gods that that will not be for many years.

'You have proved yourself, my child. You have justified my faith in you. I hope I shall never have to call upon you again to do anything so dangerous.'

His eyes move to the open doors. Okatsu sees the pale winter sky, the black sands of Ibusuki's beach, the sea sparkling not far away.

'The world is changing,' he says. 'I have told you about the Hollanders.'

Okatsu nods, remembering the mirror of distant hopes through which she saw the moon's pocked surface.

He looks at her sternly. 'They are not the only nation who wish to encroach on our lives. There are others far less benign.

'Ten years ago barbarous hordes from a distant land called Britain descended on the mighty empire of China. They rampaged along the coast, looting and raping, and threatened the emperor's capital, Peking. They forced the Chinese people to buy their opium, a terrible drug that saps the body and the spirit, turns people into ghosts.

'Our country too is in danger. Barbarian vessels have been sighted approaching our shores. Thus far we have repelled them but they will return. We have had warnings from the King of Holland himself. The western nations take land, carve out empires for themselves. They have conquered much of the world and now they have turned their sights on us. So far we have managed to keep them at bay. But our princedom, our whole realm, may soon face a crisis greater than we can even imagine.

'All that you and I have been through, the sorcery, the killings, may turn out to have been an insignificant dispute compared to what is to come. We must be on our guard. We will need strong rulers in place, men able to make vital decisions, in preparation for that day. We need to be ready.'

His face is grim but Okatsu feels an unaccountable thrill of excitement. The world is changing. Her beloved uncle is prince of the domain, a new era is beginning – and it's an era in which she feels sure she will have a role to play.

PART I

The Barbarians Arrive

1

Okatsu

Twenty-third day of the sixth month, Year of the Ox, Kaei 6, a yin water year (28 July 1853): Ibusuki, in the Satsuma domain

Ibusuki was a beautiful place, a land of gold and sunshine where the sky and ocean were perpetually blue. It was a spa town, famous for its health-giving waters, where people came to be buried in the steaming black mineral sands along the beach. Whenever the wind changed the pungent rotten-egg smell of sulphur wafted through the streets. Cranes swooped, birds twittered, monkeys roamed the flower-clad hills, palm trees swayed and the purple cone of Mount Kaimon, more perfect than Mount Fuji, rose misty on the horizon.

The governor of Ibusuki, Tadataké Shimazu, was a minor lord, not important or rich enough to be entitled to a castle, but he had a large and splendid mansion set in expansive grounds which dominated the samurai section of town. Here one hot summer's morning his daughter Okatsu knelt gazing out at the gardens, drumming her fingers on the tatami.

Two and a half years had passed since that memorable night when Okatsu visited Crane Castle. She was seventeen now, tall and long-limbed. She was not a classic beauty. Her skin was white, white as porcelain, but her face was oval rather than melon-seed-shaped and she didn't have the long jaw and bland expression of the beauties in the woodblock prints. Her nose was a little too pronounced, her mouth full, almost sensual, more suited to a geisha than a lord's daughter, and her sparkling black eyes were unusually large and expressive.

The strangest thing of all was that she was still unwed. Most of her childhood friends had married at fourteen or fifteen and moved in with their husbands' families. She met them in the street from time to time, babies proudly tied to their backs. Her oldest brother too had taken a young bride who'd recently moved into the house. But Okatsu still had unblackened teeth and unshaved eyebrows and wore girlish kimonos with long fluttering sleeves. If her parents waited much longer to arrange a marriage for her, she thought, she would turn into that most pitiable of creatures, an old maid.

She snapped her fan open and started to whisk it to and fro. The scent of sandalwood mingled with the smell of leaves and flowers and moist earth and the faint perfume of her blue and white cotton yukata.

A bell rang out, sounding the fourth hour. The rain doors that formed the outer walls and the gilded screens that divided the rooms had all been taken out, turning the mansion into one vast airy pavilion. She shuffled impatiently and glanced across the open rooms to where the servants swept and dusted on the far side of the house and the cooks prepared a meal in the kitchens. No one was paying any attention to her. If she was careful she'd be able to slip out.

Haru was kneeling beside her, sewing placidly. She had been Okatsu's maid since childhood and was her accomplice in everything. She gave an imperceptible nod. She knew exactly what was on her mind.

Okatsu rose to her feet and strolled languidly towards the front of the house, making believe she was going nowhere in particular. She'd nearly reached the shadowy vestibule when a dainty figure came pattering across the tatami.

'Okatsu-*san*!'

Okatsu gave a guilty start. It was Wife Number Three, one of her father's concubines, a perfectly coiffed geisha with a brisk down-to-earth manner.

'Going out, are you?' asked Wife Number Three. 'It's very hot out there, you know.'

Okatsu's heart beat uncomfortably hard. She knew exactly what Wife Number Three meant – that a clan lord's daughter did not go out in public. 'I'm just going for a stroll,' she replied. 'There's a festival today.'

Wife Number Three looked her up and down through narrowed eyes. 'I was young myself once,' she said with a smile.

As Okatsu stepped outside, the wave of heat nearly knocked her off her feet. Haru was at her heels, holding a parasol over her head. A young girl of good family certainly couldn't be out on her own.

The street was packed with people – bent old women, swaggering young men with their hips thrust out and their sashes slung fashionably low, pedlars, flower sellers, geisha, burly workmen and a woman with a monkey clinging to her back. Shouts filled the air and succulent aromas rose from roadside stalls where men with chequered headbands grilled octopus and squid.

Okatsu pushed her way through. She glanced behind her one last time to make sure no one had followed her, then turned down a narrow lane just wide enough for one person. Haru had slipped away discreetly, gone to wait at her aunt's house.

When she was out of sight of the crowds Okatsu picked up her skirts and ran. Soon she had left them far behind. She smelt sulphur and heard the crash of breakers, then scrambled up a ridge of black sand dotted with pines and palm trees and ran down the other side on to the beach.

The sea stretched blue in front of her, turning a deep shade of sapphire as it rippled towards the opposite shore of the bay. Trees tangled in foliage tumbled almost to the water's edge. Seagulls shrieked and soared and a cormorant swooped with a flash of black feathers.

Okatsu kicked off her sandals, feeling the sand hot between her toes, and ran to the hidden cove she knew so well. She was late. He would be wondering where she was.

But the cove was empty. There was no one there.

'Kaneshigé-*sama*,' she called. Her voice echoed around the rocks. 'Hurry. I don't have much time. I'll have to go back soon.'

She gazed around at the little beach, the waves lapping on

the shore. They'd spent so much time here over the years.

Kaneshigé. The salty smell, the roar of the surf, reminded her of how he used to tease her and chase her across the sand when they were little, and bring her seashells he'd found or strands of seaweed. Even when they'd reached the age where boys and girls were no longer allowed to spend time together, they had found ways to meet. They'd tell each other what they were doing and what they were studying. Her hopes and dreams, her picture of the world, had grown larger than if she had just sat at home sewing, as girls were meant to do.

All these years that her parents had never arranged a marriage for her, she'd always clung to the secret hope that they might marry her to Kaneshigé. After all, their families were friends – though they both knew that that was not the way things worked. In the end they were just pawns. Sooner or later they would be married off in political unions.

Kaneshigé was still a good friend of her brother. But no one could ever know about their secret meetings. If anyone had found out they would have been in terrible trouble. Her father might even have been ordered to kill her.

Time passed, the shadows moved. She paced up and down in the shade, filled with foreboding. It was unbearable not knowing where he was. Supposing he never came? Supposing his parents had found out about their meetings and forbidden him to leave?

Then she heard the pad of footsteps and a slender figure appeared on the ridge. For a moment he was silhouetted against the deep blue of the sky, the sun lighting his face, his robe tucked casually into his sash, his legs bare, his two swords glinting. She jumped up, laughing joyfully.

'Kané-*sama*.' It was her pet name for him.

'Okatsu-*san*.' He leapt down on to the sand.

She ran to greet him and threw herself into his arms. Even to meet him, let alone embrace him was a shockingly improper way for any young woman to behave, especially the eldest daughter of the lord of the town. She knew that perfectly well. But she loved him too much to care. No one ever came to the cove. There was no one here to see them, no one would ever know. He held her tight and she closed her eyes and pressed her lips to his. She breathed his smell, felt his thin young body against hers. His heart was pounding. He was panting. He had been running.

She drew back and looked at him, ran her eyes across his face – the down on his upper lip, his dark eyebrows and full mouth. 'I wanted so badly to see you,' she murmured.

He barely heard her. His eyes were burning, his face alight. 'You won't believe it!' he cried. 'Have you heard?' She had never seen him so alive. He was brimming over with excitement.

She stared at him. 'Heard? Heard what?'

'They're here. They've come. Barbarian ships, heading for the capital!' He blurted out the words. 'Barbarians. We're under attack!'

She clapped her hands to her mouth. 'Barbarians . . . ? You're not fooling me?' She looked at him. He was deadly serious. 'But . . . But when?'

'A fleet of ships, pitch black, as big as mountains, bigger than any ship could ever be. Fishermen in Shimoda saw them first. They couldn't believe their eyes. There was no wind at all, their boats were becalmed, yet the ships were speeding across the water as if demons were on their tails, spewing out smoke. At first they thought it was pirates or ghost ships or dragons, but then they realized. Barbarians, heading for the capital. They dropped their nets right then and rowed to shore as fast as they could and raised the alarm.'

Okatsu stared at him, trying to take it in, her heart thumping. She'd had a sixth sense all morning that something was out of place, something wrong. But were they really being invaded, just as Lord Nariakira had predicted? 'Barbarians?' she repeated. 'Who told you?'

'I was on my way over here to see you when the first messenger galloped in. His horse was lame, just about dead. The gods know how many horses have died to get the news here. Don't you see?'

'See what?' she whispered.

'It takes twenty days for the news to reach us,' he said, his eyes flashing.

Okatsu nodded, trying to grasp what he meant. He was right.

The port of Shimoda was three hundred and fifty *ri* away, a month and a half's journey on foot and at the very least twenty days on a succession of foaming horses, galloping night and day at breakneck speed.

'Those ships passed Shimoda twenty days ago. Twenty days!' He was shouting. 'The gods only know what's happened since then. They could have reached Edo, sailed into Edo Bay, attacked the castle, burnt the city and be heading down here and it'll be days before we hear anything of it.'

'Edo,' Okatsu breathed. 'They could have reached Edo.'

The birds had stopped singing, even the crash of the breakers seemed to pause.

Edo. To them in their tropical southern princedom Edo was another planet, as distant as the moon. It was further away even than Shimoda, four hundred *ri* to the north-east, almost two months' journey on foot. The one thing she knew was that it was the capital, the hub of the country, a vast city spreading *ri* upon *ri* around the castle, where Lord Nariakira regularly went to pay homage. She'd heard he spent much of his life in Edo. It was said he had palaces there and a staff of hundreds. For the barbarian ships to push that far was like shooting a poisoned arrow into the heart of their country.

'Barbarians,' she murmured in tones of disbelief. 'Barbarians.' Perhaps if she said the word often enough she could defuse the threat. 'But in that case . . . we're finished. We're all dead.' It was just as Lord Nariakira had warned. These were not gentle Hollanders. These were other beings, those nameless hordes who'd rampaged across China. Barbarians like those didn't come in peace. They threatened their lives, their world, everything they knew.

Things were spinning around her. The world was turning upside down. But she couldn't help feeling curious as well. She wished she could catch a glimpse of these exotic creatures with her own eyes.

'Do you think that was what it was, that light we saw in the sky?' she gasped. A shiver ran down her spine.

It had been half a year ago, on the third night of the first month, when the plum blossoms were coming into bloom. It was cold but not so cold that they couldn't meet. They'd crept down to the beach that night after the New Year festivities were over. They'd been gazing at the heavens, as they often did, picking out the Northern Dipper and the stars and planets, hearing the roar of the breakers.

Suddenly they'd seen a ball of light with a long fiery tail that skimmed the horizon, brushing the bottom of the Dipper. It shot up into the sky, flashed over the town and disappeared towards the south-west, leaving a brilliant trail across the sky. If Okatsu had been superstitious she might have thought it was a dragon or a flying fox or a mountain demon on some sinister mission.

'Look! Over there!' Kaneshigé had cried. 'A flying star. Have you ever seen anything like it?'

She'd taken his hand and held it, awed that they were seeing it together.

Back home the women were staring in amazement. These were samurai women, ready to pick up their halberds at the slightest provocation to drive off an intruder. But confronted with something supernatural, they quivered with fear. They'd run around in a panic, twittering about what it might portend. Surely the heavens were issuing a warning.

She'd laughed at them. 'Don't be silly,' she'd said. Now she had a terrible suspicion that they'd been right. Perhaps the comet really had been an omen. Perhaps it had been a portent of disaster, a warning that barbarians were on their way.

'Lord Nariakira will have received the news by now,' she said shakily. 'The messengers will have stopped at Kagoshima before they came down here. He'll be on his way. He'll know what to do. I must go. He'll be asking for me.'

He tossed his head and laughed. 'Nothing matters now,' he said. 'We can do as we please. It's all over.'

Okatsu smiled hesitantly. She didn't know if he was right or not. All the same, if barbarians really were about to destroy their world, then the rules that kept them apart were trivial in the face of such a momentous upheaval.

He was gazing at her. 'I know one thing that matters – you,' he said. 'You're so beautiful.' He ran his finger through her hair and down her cheek and she thrilled to his touch.

He took her in his arms. She could feel their hearts, pounding in unison. He pushed her down on the sand and pressed his lips to hers. She shivered as he ran his hand down her body. Hunger for him rose in her and she forgot her worries and fears as the world began to dissolve.

Suddenly there was a noise like thunder, distant at first then coming closer, so loud that it couldn't be ignored. The ground was shaking.

She pushed him away. 'I must go,' she gasped.

Hastily they sat up, pulled their clothes together, brushed off the sand and raced to the top of the ridge. The road was full of men and horses, galloping towards the town in a blur of dust and hooves, manes and tails flying. At the head of the cavalcade was a huge black charger with a familiar figure bent low over the withers, pounding along the road.

With a shock she realized that they were standing in full view of the horsemen. She shrank back into the trees. 'They'll see us,' she gasped.

'They can't. They're going too fast,' said Kaneshigé.

The horsemen slowed abruptly as they reached the crowds of people. Okatsu heard heralds shouting, 'Get back, out of the way. On your knees! His Lordship, make way for His Lordship.'

Lord Nariakira gazed around, eagle-eyed. Okatsu felt a jolt. She was sure his gaze had fallen on her, that he saw everything, knew everything – though surely he had more on his mind than an errant niece.

'I must go,' she gasped. 'He'll be looking for me.' Yet still she lingered. She clung to Kaneshigé's hand, unwilling to say goodbye.

'Let's meet tomorrow, at the usual time,' he said. 'I'll be here, waiting.'

Okatsu gazed at him, wild-eyed. She couldn't be sure any more if they'd meet tomorrow or when they'd meet or if they'd ever be able to meet again.

Careless of who might see them he took her in his arms, snatched a last long kiss. Then the air filled with noise as fire bells started to jangle and the great temple bell to boom, sounding the alarm.

2

Okatsu picked up her skirts and pushed her way through the crowds. Everywhere she looked she saw fearful faces. Rumours were spreading like wildfire. People clutched each other's sleeves, mouthing the words, 'Barbarians! The barbarians are here. They've come, they've invaded!'

'Evacuate the town,' shouted voices. 'To the mountains, flee!'

'Prepare to fight,' bawled others.

Back home the courtyard was crowded with horses and men. Okatsu was slipping inside when she bumped into her mother. The older woman glared at her, her face pale.

'Where have you been?' she demanded breathlessly. 'How could you, Okatsu, at a time like this? We've been looking everywhere for you. Look at the state of you, sand on your skirts. His Lordship is here. Something terrible has happened. Hurry. He wants us all to assemble. He has something to announce. We must go straight away.'

On the men's side of the house, clouds of tobacco smoke mingled with the sharp scent of chrysanthemum petals, burning to keep mosquitoes at bay. Okatsu's father, grandfather and brothers puffed long-stemmed pipes while maids ran in and out with trays of chilled barley tea. As Okatsu and her mother entered, the room fell silent. Okatsu lowered her eyes and took her place with the other women kneeling along one side.

Lord Nariakira knelt formally, holding his fan of office. He was in the place of honour in front of the alcove, his face stern. His clothes were sweat-stained and strands of oiled hair hung around his face but he was no less imposing for that. His page was beside him and his men – some young and muscular, others ancient and white-haired – knelt around him.

Okatsu glanced at him, heart in her mouth, searching for some sign – a frown, a knowing look – some hint that he'd seen her earlier. She couldn't put it out of her mind, that moment when he had turned and looked towards them. She was sure he had seen her standing with Kaneshigé on the ridge. But if he had he revealed nothing. He was imperturbable, at his grandest.

Brow furrowed, he glared around the assembled gathering.

'Grave news,' he announced, pitching his voice against the clamour of the bells. 'My men have ridden night and day to deliver it and I have come straight here to alert you.'

The men glanced at each other. They leaned forward, listening for all they were worth.

'You will have heard the rumours by now,' he said, his voice low and menacing. 'Tojin, barbarians. Barbarians have arrived. They have sailed along our coast and landed on our shores. The crisis we have been expecting for so long is upon us.'

'Barbarians.' The word echoed around the great hall. The men stared around wildly, some aghast, others frowning and resolute, drawing their breath through their teeth in a chorus of hisses. All these years they'd lived in peace, without fear of invasion, and now . . . now . . . barbarian hordes swarming across the water to attack their country. 'Barbarians.' With that word everything changed. The world seemed to tilt on its axis.

Okatsu's father looked up from under his bushy eyebrows. 'Where, my lord?' he asked.

'They have dropped anchor at Uraga, in Edo Bay. The capital is under threat.'

Okatsu put her hands to her mouth. 'The capital,' she gasped. 'So it's true. They've reached Edo.' Her small personal worries faded into nothingness in the face of events of such magnitude.

'Quiet, Okatsu,' her mother murmured.

'You mean we have been invaded?' her father asked.

'We do not know that yet,' said Lord Nariakira. 'My messengers have flogged their horses to get to me so quickly. It seems fishermen at Shimoda saw them first and sounded the alarm. There are rumours aplenty. A whole fleet, they say, each vessel bigger than any ship anyone has ever seen, like floating fortresses, bristling with cannon, moving at demonic speed. All no doubt hugely exaggerated. I shall find out the truth soon enough and discover how the government is responding. The one thing we know for now is that they are here.'

'Barbarians,' muttered Okatsu's father. Okatsu had not seen him so grim since the night he had brought back her uncle's bloodied robe. He could take on any human enemy without flinching, but this was a more than human threat. 'We have to assume their intentions are hostile.'

'It seems so. We know they threatened our tributary, the kingdom of Ryukyu.'

Okatsu's father nodded heavily. Okatsu had heard him talking about it. Not long before, foreign vessels had approached the Ryukyus, the chain of islands south of their princedom. The king there paid tribute to His Lordship, who had sent warships to turn the intruders away. They'd left, but everyone had been shaken by the encounter.

'If they came so close that time they were bound to come again,' boomed Lord Nariakira. 'And this time it will not be as easy to rid ourselves of them. We must not forget what happened to China eleven years ago – her cities attacked, her citizens killed, the emperor forced to bow to their demands. These barbarians filled their coffers by forcing China to buy their opium. They've seized land too, a small island off the coast called Hong Kong, which they use as a base to send troops and traders into that hapless country. We must not suffer the same fate.'

'They've been baying at our doors long enough,' growled Okatsu's father. 'We'd always suspected we'd be next in line.'

'The government is warning us to prepare for war,' said Lord Nariakira. 'We must mobilize our forces and arm ourselves for battle, bolster our defences, shore up the sea walls, install cannons, prepare our men to protect our land.'

'I wish we had a spy in Edo, inside that secretive court of theirs,' muttered Okatsu's brother. 'They must be in a panic. I doubt if they have the faintest idea of how to deal with the barbarians.'

Barbarians here, on their doorstep, threatening to invade. Okatsu's heart beat harder, her breath came more quickly. She felt a shiver of excitement. She'd always been curious about the Hollanders. Now she might see them for herself, these creatures from another realm.

Before she could stop herself, in that great hall full to the rafters with venerable grey-haired warriors, she'd raised her voice and asked, 'Are these the barbarians who attacked China or are they from some other country? Why are they here? What do they want?'

Okatsu's father and brother and their men and Lord Nariakira's entire entourage, from the downy-cheeked pageboy to the grizzled retainers, swung round and glared at her. She closed her mouth abruptly and lowered her head. She'd done it again. She'd forgotten. On those rare occasions when women were allowed to appear in public, they had to keep silent.

Okatsu's mother drew her breath through her teeth and slapped Okatsu on the arm. 'Enough,' she hissed. 'How dare you, Okatsu, at a time like this, in front of everyone? You shame us all.'

Okatsu's father bowed his head. 'My apologies, my lord,' he said in tones of mortification. 'I will deal with this child later.' He glowered at Okatsu through lowered eyebrows.

Lord Nariakira turned his fierce eyes on Okatsu and his face softened. 'No need for discipline, Tada-*dono*,' he said to Okatsu's father. 'She is a sharp one, that daughter of yours. She always gets to the crux of the matter.'

Sweat beaded his forehead. A retainer handed him a handkerchief and he dabbed impatiently.

'These are good questions,' he said, addressing Okatsu. 'Tojin – barbarians – come in many stripes and colours. Our students of western knowledge devote themselves to learning about them and their culture. These newcomers are not Dutchmen. If they were, they would have obeyed our laws. They would have landed at Nagasaki, as the Hollanders do. But they have not. They have encroached uninvited into our sacred waters, and from that alone we can have no doubt that they intend us ill.

'From all I hear, they are not British either. We know a great deal about the European nations, of which the country called Britain is one. Their culture is ancient and sophisticated, though they have developed in a different way from us. We practise the arts of peace. Over the centuries we have developed poetry, painting, literature, philosophy. To my knowledge they have none of those, or if they do, they take no pride in them. They have never shown their arts to us. They have no understanding of the world of the spirit, of how the wise man should conduct himself. What they have developed are the arts of war. In their command of the material world they are far in advance of us.

'The ships that approached our tributary, the kingdom of Ryukyu, belonged to them, to the countries of France and Britain.

'But these are different. The King of Holland warned us several times that ships from the country called America were heading for our shores. From what I hear, this is an isolated country a long way from anywhere. If you look on the globe you can see it. It is huge in size but small in population and importance. It has but a short history. It has only recently been colonized by the Europeans. A few of our fishermen have been shipwrecked there. The government allowed them to return without punishment and they brought back fascinating news.

'Some seven years ago, two American warships had the effrontery to sail into Edo Bay.' He glared around the assembly. 'They wanted to trade with us, or so they said. Our government in Edo answered that we trade only with the Dutch and only through Nagasaki and sent them packing. But I always knew they would return. I am told that the American captain tried to climb into one of our barges and a young samurai pushed him bodily back into his boat.'

There was a roar of laughter. The grizzled warriors thumped the tatami, guffawing. 'That barbarian captain,' rumbled voices, 'took a tumble! Slunk off with his tail between his legs. Thought they could force their way in here, those barbarians. We showed them!'

Lord Nariakira rapped his fan on the tatami for silence. He was not laughing. Okatsu caught a gleam in his eye. She wondered if secretly he was as excited by the news as she was.

'These are not demons,' he went on. 'There is no need for foolish superstition. But they are strong, far stronger than us. Their ships do not use wind or oars to move. They have engines powered by steam, which is what enables them to move so fast. If these vessels really are as huge as we hear, then they are far bigger than the Holland ship that arrives every year.

'As to what they want and why they are here, they have yet to inform us of that. No doubt they will say they wish us to open our doors to trade, as a preliminary at least. But we should not be fooled. These newcomers do not come as friends. If they did they would not make such a show of force. We need to arm ourselves, prepare our defences. This is not a time for hesitation. It is a time to act.'

Lord Nariakira's page lit a pipe and handed it to him. He took a puff. Threads of fragrant smoke seeped from his nostrils. He again smacked his fan of office on the tatami, then straightened his back and stared around the room. The bells boomed out louder than ever.

'The time has come to take a step I have been contemplating for quite some time. I have discussed it with my cousin, Lord Tadataké.' Okatsu's father nodded. 'As you all know, I have lost my sons. I have only one child, a daughter, and she is very young. I much value your Okatsu-*san*.'

All eyes turned to Okatsu. Her cheeks blazed all the way up to her ears. The room seemed to rock around her. She clenched her fists, tried to calm her breathing, still the thunder of her heart.

'She is an exceptional young woman, beautiful and talented. We all know her forthright personality. At this time of crisis I need a child, an heir, someone to talk to, plan with, someone closer to me than my chamberlains and advisers. Okatsu-*san* has always been like a daughter to me. Now I wish to make her my daughter in earnest. I intend to adopt her. She will come to Kagoshima, to Crane Castle, to live with me there.'

'Crane Castle? Your daughter?' Okatsu laughed in disbelief. Then she remembered where she was and clapped her hands to her mouth.

Her mother's hand was on her back, pushing her face to the floor. 'Will you never learn to behave?' she muttered.

She heard her father's voice: 'We are much obliged to Your Lordship. We are grateful for the honour Your Lordship does us in taking this worthless child into your household. I hope she will conduct herself well and not bring shame on us.'

Okatsu looked up at Lord Nariakira. He was smiling down at her, his eyes twinkling.

'Well, Okatsu-*san*,' he said. 'Will you come and live with me in Crane Castle?'

'May I . . . May I think about it?' she stammered. 'I need time.'

Her mother interrupted. 'Your Lordship's kindness is never-ending,' she said firmly. 'We are forever indebted to you. Our Okatsu will move to Crane Castle whenever Your Lordship so desires. I will order the maids to prepare her trunk immediately.'

Okatsu bowed, overcome with shock. She had to think, work out what it meant for her.

She had always known that Lord Nariakira was fond of her, that they had a special bond. But it had never occurred to her that he would take her to live in Crane Castle. She knew her parents must have arranged her adoption long ago. This was just the public announcement of it. It was not a surprise that no one had discussed it with her. Children, especially girls, were chattels, to be given away at will. No one discussed anything with them – not their marriage, not their adoption.

So that was why her parents hadn't looked for a husband for her. They'd known all along of Lord Nariakira's plans for her, or at the very least they'd guessed. They'd set her aside for him. They must wonder why she hesitated even for a moment. She knew she should be excited, honoured, thrilled. She would be the daughter of the Prince of Satsuma, most likely his heir. It was an unprecedented honour.

But Crane Castle. It was like being condemned to a lifetime's imprisonment. Her father's mansion was cosy in comparison to that gloomy place. In Crane Castle she would be a great lady, a princess, but she knew very well that she would lose her freedom. The consorts and concubines and daughters of men like Lord Nariakira were seldom seen out in public, and when they were they were always accompanied by their ladies.

The most terrible thing of all was that she would never see Kaneshigé again. They would be torn apart for ever. Bitter tears filled her eyes and she lowered her head quickly so that no one would see them. She had to get a message to him. They had to make a plan, or at the very least say goodbye. Tomorrow would be too late. They had to meet tonight.

As soon as she could, she slipped out of the gathering and ran to her room. She took a brush and ink stone and feverishly started to grind some ink.

3

Okatsu listened out for the thunder of hooves as Lord Nariakira and his retinue galloped away. The alarm bells were ringing more insistently than ever. The town elders had gathered at the gates, waiting for Okatsu's father to explain the news. Squadrons of men filed into the courtyard where her brother was issuing orders, sending some off to track down all the arms they could find, others to reinforce the sea walls and install cannon.

In the women's section of the house the cooks prepared food and drink for the huge influx of visitors. Okatsu's mother was sorting out her belongings, deciding what she would need to take and what she could leave behind. Okatsu sat by her, whisking her fan, trying to hide her impatience, waiting for a chance to escape.

The shadows were growing deeper and the servants were running around with tapers, lighting candles. Okatsu folded her fan, rose to her feet and hurried towards the gates. She no longer cared whether anyone tried to stop her. They couldn't imprison her. She heard her mother calling but she paid no attention. She rushed outside with Haru close behind her.

The street was full of people talking, arguing, exchanging information, discussing what might happen. The easy certainties of the old life had disappeared. She brushed between them, picked up her skirts and ran down to the beach. Barely a day had passed but it felt as if an entire lifetime had gone by. She was a different person now than she had been that morning.

The trees along the ridge cast long shadows. The sea stretched pale and pearly before her. She took off her sandals and padded across the black sand to the cove. It was empty. Kaneshigé's family too would be deep in discussion, deciding how to confront this new and fearsome enemy. It would be more difficult than ever for him to slip away. She couldn't bear to think that he wouldn't manage to come for this last meeting.

Then she heard footsteps. She looked up and saw him on the ridge, edged in gold, with the setting sun blazing pink and orange behind him. She felt a great surge of love and tenderness. Their whole life together – the secret meetings, the talks, the discussions, lying in each other's arms, the plans of how they might run away together, the laughter, the joy, all the happy times they had spent – rose before her eyes.

'You got my message,' she said, her heart full of sadness.

He jumped down, took her in his arms. 'So I was right,' he crowed. 'It wasn't a false alarm. The barbarians have sailed straight into Edo Bay, they're threatening the capital!' He shook his head. 'The place is in uproar. It was a tough job leaving the house, making my way through the streets. Everyone was stopping me, everyone's talking, trying to find out all they can. People are saying there are a hundred warships and a hundred thousand barbarians, but that can't be right. The townsfolk must be climbing the hills around Edo to get a good look at the huge black ships.' He kicked at the sand. 'No one knows anything down here. We had a message from His Lordship to raise troops immediately. That was all he deigned to tell us.'

The sun had dropped behind the headland and a breeze had blown up. He pulled her down next to him on a rock and reached for her hand. She gripped his, feeling the familiar touch of his palm on hers. She wanted to remember that feeling for ever, to hold on to the precious memory. She couldn't tell him her news, not yet. She wanted to enjoy these last few moments of closeness with him first.

'We'll fight them, of course,' he said. 'We've formed a brigade, we're making plans. We'll defend our shores. We'll drive them away, even if we all die.'

She gazed at him, knowing that this could be the last time she'd ever see him. The evening light fell on his face – his smooth golden skin and slanting cheekbones, his large dark eyes and full-lipped mouth intense and determined. They'd grown up together, turned almost without noticing it from chubby children into adolescents. And now he was a man. He had that hawk-like look she'd seen on her father's face, gazing steadfastly into the future. Only samurai had that look. Townsmen kept their eyes fixed on the ground, worrying about money. But samurai were above all that.

'It's time,' he said. 'I don't want to be a scribbler like my father. I don't want to spend my days grinding ink. I didn't learn swordsmanship just to spar with my friends.' His eyes lit up. 'It's up to us now, we young men. All the old men do is talk. We'll fight the barbarians off.'

He lifted her hand to his lips. 'And if the world's going to end, I'll make sure I'm here with you.'

She closed her eyes, grimacing. It was too late now, too late for such sentiment. In his excitement about the barbarians, she still couldn't bring herself to tell him her news. She didn't know what to say, how to phrase it, how to broach the subject.

'It won't end though,' he added. 'We'll win. We'll drive them away.'

Okatsu looked at him, imagining how handsome he would look in armour. He was fearless. She hoped he wouldn't get himself killed. She wished she could find a way for them to spend their whole lives together.

He held her close and pressed his lips to hers. 'We're still here and still together.' She could feel his breath on her face.

She drew back. 'No, no. I can't,' she whispered. 'Not now.'

'You said you had something to tell me.'

She took a deep breath. 'I have to go away,' she whispered, staring at the sand. She stirred it with her toe and a little crab ran out.

He frowned. 'Go away? You mean marry? Go into service? Why has it been decided now? What has it to do with the barbarians?'

She shook her head, blinking away tears. 'I have to enter Crane Castle.'

There was a long silence.

'That's not so far away.' His voice was softer. He squeezed her hand. She loved the feeling of his hand in hers. 'It will be harder to meet, but we'll manage. Even ladies-in-waiting leave Crane Castle from time to time.'

'No, not service. I'm not going into service.' She hesitated. 'His Lordship is making me his daughter. He's adopting me.'

'His daughter?' He released her hand and looked at her quizzically, bewilderment written on his face. He knew very well that, as His Lordship's daughter, she'd be entirely out of his reach. She would inhabit a different realm. They would no longer be part of each other's worlds.

He drew back, stiffened. His face was set in a frown. 'My congratulations. It's a great honour for you.' His voice was brittle. 'I suppose I should call you "Your Highness" now.'

'Stop, stop.' Okatsu was afraid he was going to get down on his knees on the sand and give an ironic bow.

He straightened his back, took on that stern glare and icy tone her father adopted when he was confronted with an impossible situation. She knew that look, like a suit of armour, giving no hint of weakness, protecting him from hurt.

A moment ago they'd been so close. Now they were a million *ri* apart.

'His daughter?' he said, his voice harsh with pain. 'Is that what he calls it? Is that really what he has in mind for you? You're seventeen, you're beautiful. No one could ever be more beautiful. Perhaps what he's really planning is to take you as his concubine.'

Tears filled Okatsu's eyes. 'That's a terrible thing to say. He's like a father to me.'

He smiled ruefully, nodded, sighed. His voice softened. 'You're right. We all know he values your company. You've been like a daughter to him for a long time.' He took a breath. 'So when are you going?'

'Straight away,' she whispered.

'So this is goodbye . . .' His voice trailed off.

She wished she hadn't spoken. It would have been better never to have had this last meeting, just to have disappeared, sent him a letter. Seeing him, sitting here, feeling the touch of his skin, the scent of his hair, it felt the same as it always did, as if nothing had changed, as if they'd always be together. He was all she'd ever wanted and now, of her own volition, she had to give him up. It was too terrible to bear. Hot tears spilled down her cheeks and her shoulders shook with sobs.

'Well, we knew it had to happen,' he said. 'They were bound to marry us off to someone some time. We've been lucky, we've had more time together than we could ever have hoped for.'

He held her tight, pressed her face to his shoulder, stroked her hair. Then he released her, jumped up and started to prowl up and down the beach.

'Why now?' he shouted into the air. 'Why now, Your Lordship? Why do this now? What has this to do with the barbarians?'

'He has no male children,' she said weakly. 'He needs me to be his daughter.'

'Who does he think he is, playing with people's lives?' He thumped his fist into his palm. 'Maybe he's chosen a husband for you. That's it, that's what it is. There's some vital alliance he needs to cement with marriage. Who knows what his plans are? He thinks he's a god himself.' He stared wildly at the setting sun and the ocean, then turned back to her. He sat down again. 'Life is long. Maybe the gods will be kind to us. Maybe we can meet again.' He gripped both her hands. 'We could run away,' he said. 'People do, people that care about each other.'

Okatsu shook her head. 'How would we live? We have no money. We'd be hunted down. His Lordship needs me at this time of crisis.'

She held his hands tight and screwed her eyes shut, wishing she could turn back time, make everything as it had been before she'd heard the news. But when she opened them again, nothing had changed.

The sky had grown dark and the sea was iron grey. In the distance she could see a glow in the sky where Sakurajima, the great volcano that loomed above Kagoshima, Lord Nariakira's capital, spurted ash and fire. She'd have to leave soon.

She couldn't bear it. She put her arms around him and buried her face in his shoulder. 'There will never be anyone else. I wish I didn't have to go. I wish I could stay with you for ever.' She hesitated, took a breath, whispered the words. 'I love you.'

He drew back, looked at her, ran his hand through her hair, across her cheek. 'That hair, those eyes, the way you laugh. How could there ever be anyone but you?' He put his lips to hers and she closed her eyes and let everything fade away till there were only the two of them and the sand under their feet and the waves lapping on the shore.

'One last time,' he said. She nodded, speechless. He took off his robe and spread it in the lee of the rocks. She wept as their bodies came together. She felt his heat, the sweat on his skin, his pounding heart, the bones of his chest pressing against her.

'Okatsu-*san*,' he murmured. 'I am yours. You are mine. Nothing will part us. We will always be together in our hearts.'

Finally they drew apart and pulled on their clothes. They both knew they had to go.

He'd been gripping her hand tightly. Now he released it.

'This is for you.' He took his dagger from his sash and held it out to her. It was beautiful. The hilt and sheath were marked with the crest of his family, the Kimotsuki – two cranes with their wings extended to form a circle. 'Please keep it.'

She raised it to her forehead in both hands and bowed. 'I'll treasure it,' she said, swallowing hard. Tears were running down her face and she was glad that it was dark and he couldn't see them. She could hardly speak. 'I'll keep it with me for ever. I'll always think of you.'

As she tucked it into her sash she remembered her sandalwood fan in the collar of her yukata. She held it out to him. 'Have this to remember me by.'

He tucked it into his sleeve and took her hand as darkness closed in further around them. The moon had risen. It hung low in the sky, huge and white, making a sparkling white path across the water. Bats flittered and squeaked.

He smiled. 'You never know. The barbarians are turning everything upside down. Maybe something will happen to bring us together again.'

Then he jumped up. 'Race you to the end of the beach!'

She picked up her skirts and ran after him through the shallows. He gave her a head start and she ran for all she was worth, then he easily caught up with her and grabbed her in his arms. For a moment they stood, laughing and panting, with the water lapping at their ankles. Then she buried her head in his shoulder, smelling his scent, feeling the warmth of his skin. She held him tight, never wanting to let him go.

He broke away. 'The world's changing. If it doesn't work out, remember, you can always come back to me. If anyone causes you trouble, send for me. I mean it. I'll be here, waiting.'

He turned away into the darkness and she heard his voice above the ripple and roar of the waves. 'Okatsu-*san*, Okatsu-*san*. Don't forget me.'

She gave a sob and closed her fingers around the hilt of the dagger and said softly, 'I won't, I swear it. I won't.'

4

Princess Atsu

Twenty-eighth day of the sixth month (2 August 1853): Kagoshima

The cavalcade swung into Kagoshima and wound along the sea-front where the great volcano Sakurajima spewed out ash and smoke across the bay. Then the vast procession turned up the main thoroughfare and headed for the castle – heralds, standard bearers, retainers, guards, umbrella bearers, shoe bearers, grooms and a long baggage train, filling the broad city streets.

Right in the middle, escorted by ladies in gorgeous silks walking alongside and ornate women's palanquins in front and behind, was a spectacular black and gold conveyance like a miniature palace with a lacquer carrying beam: a 'princess palanquin'.

The lone occupant of this sumptuous vehicle sat, her legs tucked under her, gripping her fan, contemplating her new destiny and her new name: 'Atsu', 'Princess Atsu'. At least it was not too far removed from the name she'd known all her life, Okatsu.

She still felt like Okatsu. How could she not? She stroked Kaneshigé's dagger tucked into her sash, brushed her fingers across the Kimotsuki crest on the hilt, pictured his face, remembered his touch. Every lurch and swing of the palanquin, every rise and fall, took her further away from him. She sighed and whisked her fan, stared unseeingly at the delicate paintings adorning the walls of the little box. She had no tears left to weep.

She told herself how lucky she was. She was going to Crane Castle, to live as a princess, as her beloved uncle Lord Nariakira's daughter. 'This is the way it is,' she reminded herself sternly. 'No one chooses how their life will be, least of all a girl.'

But no amount of thinking could take away her sadness. Without Kaneshigé the world seemed a bleak and empty place.

Atsu, as she now was, had stepped into her little box first thing in the morning and was still there late in the afternoon. Inside it was as hot as an oven, full of noxious odours of polish and paint and lacquer. She pushed aside the bamboo blind covering the small window. She had never seen so many people, all craning to catch a glimpse of her. Some were wide-eyed, some smiled, some gawped open-mouthed as if she were a curiosity at a travelling fair. She smelt dust and sweat and sewage, heard the murmur of voices like breakers crashing on the beach and the crunch and shuffle of straw-sandalled feet moving along the stone-paved road. In her lavish kimonos she felt like a present gift-wrapped, tied up in bows and ribbons, served up in a jewelled casket. She sighed and let the blind fall back again.

At least she still had Haru. Her mother had argued that Haru should stay behind, that she wouldn't know how to do her hair in the proper styles for a princess or which kimonos to lay out for which occasions. But Atsu had persisted and finally her mother had given in. So Haru had been promoted. She was now personal lady-in-waiting to Lord Nariakira's daughter, no less, and rode proudly in the palanquin behind, with maidservants of her own walking alongside.

The procession had reached the castle and was winding along beside the towering black outer walls when Atsu heard the thunder of hooves. There were bells ringing and shouts: 'Clear the way! Clear the way! Urgent message for His Lordship!'

The ground trembled. The horses were nearly upon them. Atsu's palanquin swayed to the left, then to the right, then hit the ground with a bump. The door slid open and a painted face appeared, eyes wide and panic-stricken. It was the chief lady-in-waiting, sent from Crane Castle to escort her.

'What is it?' Atsu demanded, leaning forward. 'What's happened?'

'So sorry, Your Highness,' the woman squeaked breathlessly, twisting her thin hands. 'There are riders approaching. Please remain seated.'

A moment later three horses charged past, heads drooping, nostrils flared, froth specking their heaving flanks, exuding the pungent smell of equine sweat. Noses to their necks, bottoms high, clinging to the reins for dear life, were three messengers with lacquered dispatch boxes bouncing on their backs, leggings and jackets flying. A fourth horse brought up the rear, staggering under the weight of its giant rider. Atsu caught a glimpse of a heavy brow and flushed cheeks as the man thundered past, lashing at his horse, and disappeared in a cloud of dust.

In all the upheaval of packing and saying goodbye she'd almost forgotten the dreaded tojin in their ships, installed like a canker at the heart of their country. It was surely news of them.

She could hardly wait to reach the castle. The moment the palanquin had been set down and the door slid open she jumped out, gazing around the vast courtyard at the imposing wooden buildings surrounded by verandas and the tree-covered cliff behind. The previous time she'd been here it had been a freezing winter's night and she'd been visiting the enemy stronghold, huge and dark and forbidding. Now she looked around with pleasure and excitement. So this was to be her new home.

Women in elegant kimonos had lined up to greet her. 'This way, madam,' they said, hurrying her towards the vestibule.

Haru was behind her, eyes bright and plump cheeks flushed, hair coiled high in the style of a lady-in-waiting at the castle of the Prince of Satsuma. With her there, Atsu felt bolder.

'I wish to greet His Lordship before I go to my quarters,' she said in as firm a tone as she could manage. 'Please show me to him.' She frowned, bracing herself for a fight.

The chief lady-in-waiting tittered nervously. She was tall and bony with a long angular horse-like face. 'I'm so sorry, but that's not possible, my lady. He's holding audience.'

'Then show me to the audience chamber.'

The horse-faced woman turned pale under her make-up and widened her eyes in horror. She put a painted hand to her mouth. 'But, but . . .' she stuttered. 'As Your Highness is aware, it is prohibited for women to enter a men's gathering, especially when affairs of state are being discussed.'

'Indeed,' Atsu replied and without further ado cut between the ladies-in-waiting and into the shadowy vestibule of the castle. She walked towards the hubbub of male voices she could hear in the distance. The chief lady-in-waiting ran after her, panting and fluttering long white hands in agitation.

The uproar grew as they approached the audience chamber. The chief lady-in-waiting dropped to her knees and slid open a door and Atsu stepped into a hall lit with lanterns and huge candles on stands. It was crowded with samurai on their knees, some in formal starched costumes with huge winged shoulders, others in working clothes or riding clothes or sparring outfits, as if they'd dropped everything and rushed in. They all to a man turned and glared at this intrusion in outraged disbelief.

At the front of the room Lord Nariakira held court on a low stage with his pageboy next to him and his entourage of retainers to each side. He was dressed in bulky formal robes, his hair pulled back from the sides of his head and fixed in a small knot on top of his balding pate. 'Princess Atsu,' he said, a twinkle in his eye. 'So here you are. I have been expecting you. Welcome.'

She gaped at him. Had he really been expecting her to burst uninvited into the audience chamber? She'd thought she was acting freely but it seemed he knew her so well he had guessed what she would do. She had the uneasy feeling that he was the puppet master and she the puppet, obediently doing whatever he required.

He ran his eyes around the assembled gathering. 'This is my daughter,' he said quietly. 'Treat her as you would me.'

He raised an eyebrow and a chamberlain ushered Atsu to the stage, where the pageboy and retainers shuffled aside to make room for her. The four messengers were on their knees facing them.

His Lordship crossed his legs informally and narrowed his eyes. 'Takasaki-*sama*. You were saying?'

One of the messengers bowed and sat back on his haunches. Atsu stared at him. His hair was tied in a rough knot like a countryman and his jacket and baggy trousers were dirty and torn.

'They've gone, my lord. We watched them sail away.' Despite his ruffianly appearance he barked out the words like a Satsuma warrior. 'But they warn they will be back in the spring with more ships, more men and more weapons.'

'At least they give us fair warning,' boomed Lord Nariakira. 'We will not be taken by surprise again.'

'What do they think they're up to, those fellows in Edo?' growled a voice. 'In my day we'd have massacred the lot of them like the worms they are.'

Atsu made out a fierce weather-beaten face and white hair twisted into a topknot.

Lord Nariakira nodded to the old warrior. 'Not so easy, my friend, not so easy.' He turned to the messengers. 'You say they are from America. So what is their demand – to occupy land, take tribute? Or do they wish to trade? Yamada-*sama*, what do you have to tell us?'

'They brought a letter, my lord.' A second messenger moved forward, a young man with wide eager eyes. He was unshaven and his hands were rough and dirt-engrained but Atsu could see by the size of them that he too was a swordsman. 'From their emperor. Our people tried to stop them from setting foot on our soil. We ordered them to sail away and when they refused, not to leave their ships. We tried delaying tactics, sent low-level officials to deal with them. We had messengers galloping up to Edo requesting instructions. But the barbarians refused either to go away or to hand over their letter. They said they were under orders to deliver it only to the person of highest rank, the direct representative of our leader.'

Lord Nariakira's thick eyebrows came together in a frown.

'They used threats, my lord,' said the messenger. He turned pale under the dirt on his face and trembled as he spoke. 'They bombarded the town of Uraga and reduced several buildings to matchwood.'

The grizzled warriors filling the great hall glared and muttered to each other.

'We had no choice but to give way,' the messenger mumbled. 'After much discussion we permitted their leader to come ashore at Koriyama.'

'The effrontery!' Lord Nariakira exploded. 'These people know nothing but brute force. They terrorize us with their cannons on our own sacred soil so they can impose their will on us. It is beyond endurance.'

'I would have cut a few down if I had not been under orders, Your Lordship,' the first messenger barked. 'It was all I could do to hold myself back.'

'They want to demonstrate their strength,' said Yamada, the second man. 'I took a job as an oarsman on a government launch. I rowed out to their ships several times. There are four, two battle-ships, two smaller craft. They are monsters, my lord, fifteen times the size of our largest gunship and more powerful by far. They are steam- and sail-driven. They steamed into Uraga far faster than any of our ships can move.'

Lord Nariakira nodded.

'They easily outgun us,' said the messenger. 'I counted seventy cannons on the command ship, all higher calibre than any of ours. They threatened to destroy our fleet if we intercepted them and they are certainly capable of it. When they fired their cannons to announce that their leader was leaving the ship my heart jumped nearly out of my chest. The noise was louder than a peal of thunder right overhead. The trees shook and the birds flew away.'

The giant rider Atsu had seen had been kneeling silently. She recognized the square jaw and huge barrel chest. He was a good head and shoulders taller than anyone else in the room. He bowed. 'I found a job as a carpenter,' he said. He was surprisingly softly spoken. 'We built the pavilion for the meeting. Three hundred and twenty barbarians came ashore, in blue uniforms. I counted them. Many more stayed on the ships. I'd say there are a thousand altogether, maybe more.'

More than a thousand. More than a thousand barbarian warriors massed in Edo Bay, within striking distance of the castle. It was a chilling thought.

Atsu leaned forward eagerly. 'From all you say these barbarians are a grave threat. What do they look like? Do they look human like us?'

The retainers turned and stared at her, glaring at her from under their brows. If a woman was going to intrude into a men's gathering, at the very least she ought to keep silent, even if she was Lord Nariakira's newly adopted daughter. She lowered her eyes and flushed to the roots of her hair.

Lord Nariakira nodded. 'An excellent question. Go ahead, Saigo-*sama*. Tell us.'

'They are human, Your Highness, but deformed-looking,' said the tall young man. 'The first thing you notice is their noses, huge and misshapen, like a drunkard's nose. They have round eyes like pigs and bushy eyebrows and snarling red mouths as if they paint them with rouge and corpse-grey skin and bristly red hair. They are a bit like monkeys. They have hair all over their bodies, curled into rings. You can see it sticking out from their clothes at the wrists.'

There were snorts of laughter, then silence. The situation was too grave for merriment.

'And they are huge. When their leader came ashore he had a flag bearer marching in front of him. I am tall, my lord, but this flag bearer was taller, much taller. And there were two men with shiny black skin, even bigger, marching one on each side of him.'

'I have heard of these black-skinned men. Foreigners use them as slaves or servants,' said Lord Nariakira.

'The two black-skinned warriors carried weapons far more powerful than our flintlocks and matchlocks and muskets. There were musicians too, making the most hideous screeching noise. We all put our hands over our ears except for the poor officials, who had to be polite. They wear tight tubular uniforms that encase their bodies, with gold fastenings. There were two young ones – they didn't look so hairy – carrying scarlet boxes which contained the letter, and a line of men behind forming an escort. His Lordship the Prince of Izu and His Lordship the Prince of Iwaki graciously received them. Once they'd handed over the letter they went back to their ships and raised anchor almost immediately. As Your Lordship has heard, they say they will return next spring for our answer.'

'We shall have to wait to hear their demands until Edo deigns to inform us,' said Lord Nariakira, grim-faced. 'We must build up defences immediately in preparation for their return.'

'If they are as powerful as we hear we will have to give in to these demands of theirs, no matter how demeaning they are,' said a thin man with a pinched, severe face, wearing glasses.

The white-haired warrior barked, 'Never. We'll fight to the last man to defend our sacred land.'

Lord Nariakira turned to Atsu. 'Daughter. You have heard these reports. Do you have any thoughts on the matter? What is the best course for us to take?'

He smiled encouragingly. The grizzled warriors shuffled and coughed and stared stony-faced, trying to hide their contempt for a seventeen-year-old girl and her opinion.

Atsu's face burnt and her heart pounded. She was aware of how hot the room was. Her mouth felt dry. She thought hard.

'I am just a woman and I am young,' she said. The room fell silent as she began to speak and she felt her confidence grow. 'I know I ought not to be here. But these intruders threaten our entire realm. Not just Uraga, not just Edo, but us here in Satsuma, even though we are far away. I've always thought of Satsuma as my home. I seldom even think of the rest of our country. But now we must. All the princedoms must unite in one mighty force. This is the only way we can defeat the barbarians.'

'Join our armies?' hooted a voice. It was the elderly warrior, black eyes flashing under his snowy eyebrows. 'Fight side by side, shoulder to shoulder with our ancient enemies? That is the foolish opinion of a girl. We can never do that.'

'Princess Atsu is right, old friend,' said Lord Nariakira gravely. 'The barbarian menace forces us to move away from those old enmities. We have no choice. We have to band together in the face of this common threat.'

There were shouts of outrage. Fists thumped the tatami.

Lord Nariakira waited till silence fell. 'I have been in communication with Chief Senior Councillor Lord Abé,' he said quietly. 'He intends to write to all the daimyo, both inside and outside lords, to ask our opinion as to the best course of action. Such a move is unprecedented. It has never been necessary before. And if we are to unite we will need a strong leader.'

The fourth messenger, a wiry, compactly built young man, had been waiting on his knees. Now he spoke up. 'I have just come from Edo,' he said. 'Your Lordship may wish to hear the latest news. I carry dispatches from Your Lordship's stewards. The city is in panic. Some people flee, some try to arm themselves. Swordsmiths make their fortunes. People buy second-hand armour at twice the normal price, stock up on food and supplies. The price of rice has doubled, tripled, quadrupled. People who live near the coast are evacuating children and old folk. The streets are crowded with people running back and forth carrying furniture and possessions. The priests pray and make offerings day and night, begging the gods to save the country. They ring bells, beat drums. They have sent messengers to invoke the great gods at the holy shrine at Ise.'

'No doubt they are in a panic at the castle as well,' said Lord Nariakira. 'Well done, men. You will be well rewarded. Now go and wash and sleep. I shall receive your reports later in more detail.'

The second messenger, Yamada, the eager-faced young man, bowed. 'There were artists at Uraga, drawing the scene,' he said. 'I took the liberty of buying some prints for Your Lordship.'

He laid out some pictures. One showed a monstrous ship with a dragon's head at the prow with bulging eyes and a ferocious grin and a funnel in the middle pouring out smoke. The artist had recorded the dimensions of the ship and the distances it had travelled.

'This is their leader.' The messenger brought out two more prints.

The first was of a snarling face with hair a startling shade of red, covering the head and chin and cheeks and bristling out at the back of the neck. The creature had a bulbous nose and huge slanting eyes with eyebrows that reached nearly to its hairline, much as Saigo had described. In the second picture the face was less bestial but still far from human. The men passed the prints around. There were snorts of laughter.

Atsu gazed at the pictures, feeling the world rocking around her. So these were the barbarians who had invaded their country. Who would have believed that such creatures could even exist, let alone right here on their shores? Perhaps one day she'd see them with her own eyes.

Lord Nariakira turned to Saigo, one eyebrow lifted quizzically. 'And they really look like this?'

'More or less, yes,' the big youth muttered, flushing. 'These pictures sell like grilled octopus on festival day. Everyone in Edo is snapping them up.'

Lord Nariakira smiled at Atsu. 'Our broadsheet artists like to give their imaginations full flow,' he said. 'They give the public what it wants to see. Otherwise who would buy their work?'

Atsu nodded. He had met tojin, he knew the Holland men, he knew what they really looked like.

Lord Nariakira gazed across the gleaming pates, shiny black top-knots and fierce faces that filled the candlelit audience chamber, all frowning with determination. He gave a sigh. 'I wish I could have been there,' he said. He threw back his shoulders. 'I have no doubt they will be back in the spring, as they threatened. We have at most half a year to make preparations. We must be ready.'

5

'Father,' Atsu said, trying out the new form of address. It felt surprisingly natural. 'Father, I understand that those pictures Yamada-*sama* showed us are not realistic. But even if they're not fire-breathing dragons, we have nothing to match those warships of theirs. It makes me afraid. The thought of our peaceful lives coming to an end fills me with horror.'

It was the day after she'd arrived. Lord Nariakira had taken her, travelling in palanquins with retainers and guards walking alongside, to his summer villa on the coast. It was a lovely low building like a country cottage, made up of interlinked pavilions surrounded by little bamboo trellises, almost on the water's edge. She knelt on one of the verandas, gazing out at a tiny enclosed garden with a pond with carp splashing in it, framed by miniature trees and a stone lantern and pink and red hibiscus. Palm trees, bougainvillea and oleander spread across the hillside and the jagged cone of Sakurajima rose across the bay. Butterflies fluttered, brilliant scarlet, emerald and blue, cicadas chirruped, birds darted and swooped.

She had never been anywhere so beautiful but its beauty filled her with sadness. She yearned for Kaneshigé, wished he were here, that she could enjoy this earthly paradise with him.

She glanced at Lord Nariakira, hoping he couldn't read her mind. He was frowning thoughtfully.

'That ship, that fire-breathing warship,' he said. He looked at her out of the corner of his eye in the way he did when he had something to tell her or one of his extraordinary western contraptions to show her. 'I've seen this coming for a long time and I have been making preparations of my own. Soon I shall have a fire-breathing warship too.'

He took a puff on his pipe. He was in a casual robe, his sash slung low around his hips in the way men wear them to accentuate their prosperously swelling bellies, though in fact he was lean and muscular; there was no belly there to swell. His fifteen-year-old page, Toshikyo, knelt beside him.

'The powers in Edo do not permit the clan lords to build ships,' he said. 'They do not want us to become too powerful. But with the barbarians at our backs they will quickly realize we need all the defences we can find. I am putting pressure on them to lift the ban on shipbuilding and when they do, I shall be ready. I am nearly ready now.' He waved his arm towards the great volcano. 'I have a shipyard at the foot of Sakurajima. My scholars and engineers are studying the Hollanders' shipbuilding techniques. They have been aboard the Dutch ships and examined them minutely and translated all the manuals. We have a full set of Dutch technical drawings. I even have a model paddle steamer already built there. We understand the theory and we have the materials. The moment the government lifts its ban we shall get to work. If all goes well I shall have a steam-and-sail-powered ship within the year.'

He leaned forward and lowered his voice to a conspiratorial mutter. 'We are a long way from Edo here, my dear daughter. You cannot get much further. It is difficult for them to keep a check on us. In a word, they have not the slightest idea of what we are about. We are so far away we can do anything we like.'

He chuckled and clapped his hands and retainers came running. He rose to his feet. 'But we are not here simply to enjoy the scenery. There is much I have to show you.'

It was mid-morning and the sun was blazing out of a dazzling sky. Lord Nariakira strode between the palm trees and tropical foliage towards a group of square grey buildings. Some were two storeys high, others long and low, and some had tall cylindrical constructions on the roofs belching out smoke. From inside came roars and booms.

Outside one building was a row of shiny metal cylinders as big as felled tree trunks, lying side by side, some on wooden stands.

'My foundry,' said Lord Nariakira. 'We make muskets, rifles and cannons here.' He ran his hand lovingly along the biggest metal cylinder of all. 'A 150-pounder, one of the most powerful cannons ever made. I shall have a line of these along the seafront. If the barbarians try to attack they will have a fight on their hands.'

His eyes flashed.

Atsu shook her head dubiously. 'It sounds to me as if those black ships have weapons even more powerful than anything you can produce, Father.'

'The secret is to know our enemy,' he said grandly. 'There is much we can learn from the barbarians.'

He led the way into another building. Atsu looked around, wide-eyed with excitement. Open furnaces blazed along the walls, casting a harsh white glare. Men with grizzled topknots flung baggy-sleeved indigo jackets hastily over their loincloths and dropped to their knees on the ashy ground. Their eyes widened as they saw Atsu. She flushed and lowered her head. It would take time to get used to being a woman in a man's world.

'My glassworks,' Lord Nariakira boomed, thrusting out his chest with pride. He threw his arms wide. 'The largest, most advanced in the country.'

Atsu wiped away the sweat that bathed her face, keeping a good distance from the furnaces. She could feel the heat on her arms and legs, smell it in her nostrils.

A wizened man took off his jacket, revealing a bony sunken chest, and bowed.

'Chubei, our master glassblower,' said Lord Nariakira.

Atsu gasped as Chubei took a rod out of one of the kilns to reveal a wobbly egg-shaped ball glowing fiery white at one end. It changed from white hot to angry orange to dull red and as it cooled he spun it, then put the rod to his mouth and blew. The ball ballooned larger and larger, the walls grew thinner and thinner and with a few more twists a goblet magically appeared. Chubei waited for it to cool, bowed and presented it to her. It was as light and perfect as an egg, and as delicate.

She turned it this way and that, sending shards of light dancing across the walls. 'Did we learn glass-blowing from the barbarians, Father?' she asked.

'Generations ago. We have made it our own now.'

Atsu laughed. Glass didn't play much of a part in her life. There were glass beads, glass bottles, her father's spectacles and the tiny glass *bidoro* pipes that made a chirruping sound when you blew into them, but that was all. 'It's beautiful,' she said. 'But I don't see any use for it. I don't see how it can help us defend ourselves against the barbarians.'

Lord Nariakira showed her a storeroom stacked with bowls and cups and goblets of dark red or deep-blue glass, etched with designs of leaves or bamboo. Atsu had never seen such colours – reds more intense than the sunset, blues deeper than the blue of the sea.

'The westerners put panels of glass in their walls to illuminate the inside of their houses,' he said. 'We like shadow, they prefer brightness. Imagine that, sunshine pouring into your house, filling the darkest corners with light! In England they built a palace bigger than Crane Castle entirely of glass, a house made of light. But it matters little what it is for. First you make it, then you find the use for it. I have something else to show you.'

They climbed a neatly swept path lined with vines and creepers and giant trees to a tall narrow building at the top of the hill. Atsu smelt fumes before they even got there, a caustic metallic odour unlike anything she'd ever smelt before. She wrinkled her nose.

Inside the smell was even stronger. Sunlight poured in through panes of glass set in the roof.

Two men were on their knees to greet them. From their clothes and hairstyles and proud bearing both were samurai. One was tall and gangly with glasses. He looked pale and unhealthy, as if he hadn't seen the light of day for months. The other was brawnier but he too looked in need of a good meal. His broad-sleeved jacket and full hakama trousers were threadbare, the top of his head stubbly and his hands stained with ink.

Filling half the room was a huge wooden box with a metal tube protruding from one side, akin to His Lordship's 'mirror of distant hopes'. Atsu could see the curved glass of the lens glittering inside. The contraption wobbled precariously on a three-legged stand. She'd never seen anything like it in her life.

'Now, tell me what this is for!' said Lord Nariakira with his most inscrutable smile.

'I can't imagine,' Atsu said, laughing.

'This is the very latest barbarian invention,' he began, almost trembling with excitement. 'It may not look like much but you will be amazed at what it can do. I told you about the Nagasaki merchant Toshinojo Ueno who sells saltpetre and has a gunpowder-processing plant. He deals with the Hollanders all the time. Money-grubbing fellow, like all merchants, and he has made a fortune for himself. But he is clever too. He studied with the Dutchmen, learned Dutch science and technology, and some unusual merchandise passes through his hands.

'A few years ago he called on my steward and said, "I have something that will interest His Lordship." My steward took one look and sent a messenger to me post haste. I said, "Buy it, no matter what." I paid well over the odds but I got it and I can assure you, it is the only one in the country.

'Kawamoto-*sama* has been working day and night translating the manuals.' The scholarly-looking man blinked nervously behind his glasses. 'He studied at the Institute of Barbarian Learning. He reads several western languages. He's nearly finished with the translation, is that not so, Kawamoto-*sama*? But it is another matter altogether to get this device to work using only the printed instructions.'

'We've been experimenting for months but we still haven't cracked it,' said the man with the stubbly head, twisting his thin fingers. His hands looked chapped and raw. Atsu saw now that they were stained not with ink but with something else and wondered if it could be the substance that was giving off the noxious smell.

'Show Princess Atsu how it works,' said Lord Nariakira.

The men drew their breath through their teeth. 'It's a

complicated process,' said Matsuki, the stubbly-headed one. 'And very delicate. This is a manual, my lady.' He took a book from a shelf and, holding it in both hands, placed it on a tall table. 'Westerners do everything upside down,' he explained, showing her. 'Their books begin at the back.'

She leafed through the intricate drawings and pages of incomprehensible script, written sideways. It looked more like wriggly snakes or mosquito larvae than writing, not elegant or beautiful at all.

Kawamoto had tied back his sleeves. He opened the door to a small, very dark side room and brought out a shiny silver plate. Holding it by the edges in gloved hands, he polished it and held it up in front of Atsu. 'Can you see yourself, my lady?'

She smiled. She could see herself perfectly – her white skin, her oval face, her black hair coiled into a knot. The image was far smoother and more perfect than in any of the bronze mirrors she had at home. 'It's marvellous,' she said, covertly patting a stray hair into place.

'You could call this a mirror with a memory,' said Lord Nariakira, gesturing grandly at the large wooden box. 'It preserves the image you see in the mirror.' He was frowning gravely but she could see excitement tugging at the corners of his mouth. 'It is called a "silver plate true copy". It is not like an artist's drawing. It makes a perfect picture of reality.'

'But how does it do it?' Atsu asked, staring from the mirror to the contraption and back again.

'It is all to do with the silver plate. It is coated in a chemical substance that is sensitive to light. It enables it to retain the impression of light and shadows.'

Atsu laughed with excitement. 'And could you even make an image of me?'

He beamed. 'Of course. Let us see if we can capture the image of your lovely face.'

The two men ushered her to a seat on a platform where the sun shone directly on her face and set the box opposite her with the lens pointing straight towards her. Matsuki went into the darkened room and brought out a covered wooden tray.

'Inside is a plate just like the silver mirror,' he said. 'We keep it in this sealed tray that protects it from every bit of light.'

They slid the tray into the box. 'We have never yet succeeded in this, my lord,' said Kawamoto, casting a nervous glance at Lord Nariakira. 'Forgive me if we do not succeed today.'

Lord Nariakira nodded. 'Proceed,' he said quietly.

Matsuki took a deep breath. 'My lady,' he said. 'When I say "Hai!", please stay perfectly still and don't move a muscle. Don't blink and if possible don't breathe.'

Atsu smoothed her hair and composed her face.

'Now remember,' said Matsuki. 'Perfectly still.'

The two men glanced at each other. 'Hai!' said Matsuki.

Atsu stared straight ahead, doing her best not to blink, not even to breathe, for what seemed like an eternity. Everyone else seemed to be holding their breath too. Then Kawamoto said, 'Thank you, my lady,' and she relaxed and looked around. She had been far too busy holding her breath, keeping her eyes open and sitting perfectly still to notice what they did with the wooden box.

Matsuki was rushing into the darkened room, carrying the frame. Noxious smells poured out.

'The westerners have been working on this for years,' said Lord Nariakira. 'I have some excellent examples I bought from the Hollanders. Kawamoto-*sama*, show Her Highness what we are trying to achieve.'

Kawamoto laid a flat package wrapped in black fabric on the tall table and opened it. It was an oblong plate like the silver mirror. He tilted it this way and that, keeping it close to the black fabric. Atsu leaned over, expecting to see her own reflection as she had before.

Suddenly she caught a glimpse of something – not her reflection but someone else's. There was a pair of eyes staring at her. She looked behind her, half expecting to find someone crouching there, listening to their conversation.

Lord Nariakira clutched his stomach and laughed till tears ran down his face. 'Tilt it again,' he said. 'Take another look, Atsu.'

Kawamoto tilted the plate away from the sun. Atsu saw the face clearly now, not black but etched in shades of grey and silver on a silver background – a picture made of light. The eyes were looking straight at her, as if the person was there in the room with them.

She scrutinized the plate. It was definitely a man, not a monster, though he didn't look quite human. The face was distorted, bulbous and puffy with coils of pale hair over the ears and snaking across the top of the head. The nose was as big as a tengu goblin's, the eyebrows so low they hung over his eyes and, as far as she could see, there was no neck at all. His clothes were bunched up, with tight tubular sleeves encasing the arms.

Then she realized. She was looking at the face of a barbarian – not a caricature like the drawing the messenger had shown them, but real. She gazed and gazed, her heart thumping with excitement. 'A barbarian,' she cried.

'This is Daguerre-*sama*,' said Kawamoto. 'He is French. He is a brilliant man. He invented this machine. He is the god of the silver print.'

He brought out another silver plate and tilted it this way and that until a curved street came into view, lined with spindly houses with pipes like a forest of spears sticking out of the roofs. There were trees along both sides of the road. When Atsu looked closely she saw a couple of small people. It was as sharp and clear and real as anything she had ever seen, but it was not the world she knew. It was like a scene in a dream or the dragon king's realm under the sea. She stared, mesmerized. She was gazing into another world – the land of the barbarians.

Lord Nariakira rubbed his hands in delight. 'You see? It is a mirror with a memory. You wanted to see barbarians. This is their country. This is what they look like.'

Matsuki emerged from the noxious-smelling darkened room, holding another silver plate. In the excitement of seeing the barbarian Atsu had almost forgotten that the two men had tried to preserve her image in the same way. She rushed over to look, her heart pounding.

Matsuki laid the plate on the black cloth and tilted it one way, then the other, but no matter which way he turned it, it stayed black and sooty. Then she noticed some blurry white flashes in the middle.

'There's something here, my lord,' said Matsuki with great enthusiasm. But no matter how much he tilted it, that was the best they could do.

Atsu sighed. 'I wish I had an image of my mother and father to keep with me so that I could see them as I picture them in my memory.' There were tears in her eyes. Only the previous day she'd said goodbye to them and not long before had said goodbye to Kaneshigé too. How much had changed since then. She dared not say a word but secretly she wished she had a silver print of Kaneshigé's handsome face to keep with her for ever.

She gazed again at the two silver prints. Brilliant though the barbarian undoubtedly was, his face was disturbingly strange and unworldly, different from anything she'd ever seen before. 'I wish I could take a ship and visit the barbarian lands myself,' she said.

'One day we shall but at the moment the government forbids foreign travel. There is a fisherman from Tosa called Manjiro Nakahama who was shipwrecked and rescued by whalers and lived in America for nine years. Recently he returned. He was lucky. The government had eased their policy and decided not to execute him. He speaks the language of the Americans. He has been of great use to the government. He has also helped me with my projects.'

Atsu nodded, trying to absorb all she could.

'You're so fascinated by these barbarian inventions, Father,' she said. 'Yet you want to drive the barbarians away.'

Lord Nariakira thought for a moment. 'We love nature,' he said. 'We enjoy cherry blossom, autumn leaves, winter snows, the harvest moon. The western nations want to rule nature, to use it to make weapons to increase their strength and power. We can use their inventions to make ourselves as powerful as they are. I'm happy to live alongside them. But unfortunately that is not what they want. That will not satisfy them. They want to rule over us, exploit us, pollute our sacred land with their presence. If they can they will take over the entire world with their ships and cannons. They have to be stopped.'

He looked at her gravely. 'You are my daughter now,' he said. 'I know you will help me.'

Atsu nodded. She couldn't see yet how all these extraordinary inventions – the glass-blowing, the silver prints – would help defend them against the barbarians, but she was sure that somehow they would. For all his bluff exterior, Lord Nariakira was a devious man and a ruthless one. She knew he would stop at nothing to get what he wanted. She wondered what schemes he was dreaming up and what part he had lined up for her.

6

'Adopted daughter, he tells us.' Lady Umé narrowed her eyes. She was only a year or two older than Atsu, a strapping young woman with broad shoulders and big hands ending in pink-tinted nails. Atsu was sure that, painted nails or not, if they ever tried sparring, Lady Umé would win. 'Adopted daughter indeed.' She curled her plump lip. 'Strange how dear Nari-*sama* is so much more interested in his so-called daughter than his devoted concubines.'

Atsu pursed her lips and stifled a sigh. She was kneeling with Lord Nariakira's two concubines on the luxurious tatami in one of the grand rooms of the women's quarters. The walls were painted with scenes of mandarin ducks, a symbol of connubial bliss that seemed sadly at odds with the endless sniping that went on here. Caged birds sang and insects chirruped and a lady-in-waiting picked out a melody on a four-stringed koto.

Everything felt so odd and out of place. The castle was vast. The women's wing alone was bigger than Atsu's father's house in Ibusuki and the rooms seemed too big for the number of people in them. There was no sign of His Lordship's consort and no children running around.

Atsu felt like a fish out of water. She missed her parents and Kaneshigé terribly and on top of that she had to put up with these sharp-tongued concubines. They were like unhappy ghosts, endlessly moaning, 'We resent you, we resent you.'

She sighed. 'I didn't choose to come and live here,' she said. 'I think we should try to find a way to get on. We are going to have to live together for the rest of our lives.'

Haru had helped the maids unpack her trunk and arranged her belongings in the room the concubines had allotted her, the smallest and darkest of the private rooms. Besides her favourite books, her mother had slipped in some of the latest novels. Atsu picked up Kyokutei Bakin's *Eight Dog Chronicles*, an enormous volume, and buried her nose in it.

'I wonder if you noticed my family's residence on your way here?' Lady Umé had started prattling again. Atsu stifled a groan and put her book down. 'It's hard to miss. It's the biggest house on Millionaires' Row, across from the castle. It takes up half the street.' Lady Umé wriggled her shoulders and tossed her head. She wore the brightest silks Atsu had ever seen. 'My father is Nari-*sama*'s chief adviser, so it was natural for him to offer me to him as a gift. I can't imagine why your father would have offered you. I can't imagine why Nari-*sama* would have the slightest interest in a small-town girl from Ibusuki.' She screwed up her face as if the thought of that remote provincial town left a bad taste in her mouth.

From the moment Atsu had set foot in the women's wing, Lady Umé had made it clear that this new addition to their ranks presented a far more serious threat than any barbarians lurking on the horizon. Atsu had endured being tripped up and having food spilt on her kimono and her hem trodden on – all, naturally, pure accidents for which Lady Umé offered profuse apologies. The best response was to smile and wait for her to tire of tormenting her.

There was a flurry on the other side of the room where Lady Také had been sitting, quietly sewing. She clicked her tongue. There was a spot of blood on her thumb.

While Lady Umé was large and boisterous, Lady Také was faded and wispy. She was nearly as old as His Lordship and the ladies-in-waiting treated her with deference. She had a delicate fine-boned face and must have been a beauty when she was young.

Elder Maki, the horse-faced chief lady-in-waiting, hissed at one of the junior attendants who slid over on her knees with a damp cloth.

'It's so lively when Nari-*sama*'s here,' Lady Také said with a sigh, dabbing at her thumb. 'But so dreary when he goes.'

Atsu sat up, startled. 'Goes where?'

'Ara!' Lady Také said, lifting her painted eyebrows. 'Don't they teach you anything in Ibusuki?'

Lady Umé gave a hoot of laughter then clapped her powdered hands to her mouth.

'Certainly not about His Lordship's private affairs,' Atsu said as gently as she could.

Lady Také sighed again. 'Edo, my dear. That's where he lives. Her Ladyship is there and his children – well, little Princess Teru, at any rate. That's the only child he has now – apart from Your Highness, of course.' She raised her eyebrows still higher and glanced at Atsu out of the corner of her eye with barely concealed mockery. 'You heard about His Lordship's children, I think.'

Atsu nodded. 'Yes, so terrible,' she said.

'Six, no less. All passed away,' Lady Také said breezily. Clearly none had been hers. 'He has a whole household of concubines there too, you know. We're just here to amuse him when he deigns to come down to his country estate.' She hunched her shoulders and bent over her sewing with a sniff, lips moving wordlessly.

Of course. Atsu had forgotten that Lord Nariakira had another home in Edo. She tried to hide her consternation. Had he adopted her just to abandon her here for months or years with his concubines? With him here to protect her they restrained their spite but once he was gone she would be at their mercy.

'He didn't come down till he was twenty-six,' said Elder Maki brightly. 'That's why he doesn't talk like us.'

Atsu had noticed that he had a grand accent but she'd thought that was just the way lords spoke. Best not to say anything, she decided.

'Do you remember when he first came, my lady?' Elder Maki asked dreamily, a faraway expression on her bony face.

'My, how could I forget?' said Lady Také, her eyes glistening. 'It was eighteen years ago now, at cherry blossom season. What a figure he cut! So handsome, so dashing, so brilliant. He was His

Young Lordship then, heir to the princedom. My father presented me to him as a welcome gift. The nights we spent!' She gazed into the distance, a wistful smile on her withered lips.

'And I was Your Ladyship's attendant,' said Elder Maki, laughing softly. Her angular face had turned quite pink under her make-up.

'That was a long time ago,' snorted Lady Umé. 'He soon stopped coming down – until he found someone young and fresh to liven the place up.' She broke off abruptly and glared at Atsu.

'Such a cultured, elegant life we had,' Lady Také retorted. 'Singing, dancing, painting, tea ceremony parties, poetry-writing competitions – and then Your Ladyship arrived.'

Lady Umé frowned and curled her lip. They glared like cats about to claw each other's eyes out.

'When will His Lordship go back to Edo?' Atsu asked hastily.

'After New Year's,' said Lady Také, sighing again. 'That's when he always goes. We're left like two peas in a pod, rattling around with only each other for company.'

'And how long does he go for?'

'A year or so.'

Atsu brushed away tears. So she'd been torn away from her childhood love, from her happy life with her family, only to be incarcerated in the women's wing at Crane Castle with these dreadful sour-voiced concubines for company.

There was a cough. Haru was kneeling with the other junior attendants, her round face rigid, her jaw tight with anger at the contemptuous way the concubines spoke to her mistress.

Atsu picked up her book again, chewing her bottom lip, and stared at the first page and let her thoughts roam far away. It was the only way she could bear to live here with these women – to think back to those happy days in Ibusuki.

It was quite true, what Lady Také had said. Atsu knew little about life outside Satsuma. As a girl she hadn't been taught that sort of thing, though both Lord Nariakira and Kaneshigé had made sure she knew more than the average young woman. Kaneshigé had studied at one of the academies Lord Nariakira had set up throughout Satsuma for samurai and commoner boys. He knew she was hungry for more than just sewing and the instructional manuals and women's classics she was supposed to read. He would often bring books for her and talk to her about the Confucian classics he was studying and all that he'd learned about the Hollanders' ways and technology.

She pictured him, tall and slender, silhouetted at the top of the dunes, then running down to hug her, holding a pile of books. Once he had brought a map of Edo. He'd spread it on the sand and they'd pored over it together. To her Edo was a magical place, a city of dreams where brilliant men and elegant women lived. She'd gazed transfixed at the map with the perfect cone of Mount Fuji, mystical and beautiful, etched above the network of streets.

Together they'd traced the maze of canals that wound round and round like a snail's shell, so convoluted that no enemy would ever be able to find their way to the centre. Right at the heart of the city there was a blank. Whatever was there was blotted out by a large round emblem of three hollyhock leaves in a circle – the heraldic crest of the House of Tokugawa, the most powerful princes in the realm.

'Edo Castle,' Kaneshigé had said in a hushed voice, with an air of transmitting secret knowledge, as he tapped the emblem with a long tanned finger and sat back on his heels. 'There, where that crest is.'

They both knew it was forbidden to enquire any further. There was so much power concentrated there you'd burn your eyes if you looked too long and hard. It was safest not to try to imagine the castle, not to question or probe or even think too much about it. It was a secret place, the throbbing centre of the world, far too important to be depicted on a map that anyone could see. The best thing was to keep well away from the hollyhock crest, obey orders and ask no questions.

Atsu remembered her mother telling her that in the Tokugawa lands people sliced cucumbers lengthwise. If you cut them across, the pattern of seeds looked a bit like the crest, and it would never have done to go sinking your teeth into it.

That was the way to ensure a quiet life. But it was difficult for a couple of curious, lively young people like them.

Kaneshigé had pointed out the area where the Satsuma mansions were, in the far south-west of the city, a good distance from the castle. The Satsuma were the enemies of the Tokugawa, he'd explained, which was why the Satsuma mansions were so far away. All the same, he'd added with a flash of his dark eyes, they were the most splendid mansions in the city. The Satsuma mansions, of course, belonged to Lord Nariakira. That was where he lived when he went to Edo.

Then it occurred to her. Lord Nariakira would be going soon and would be away for at least a year. Surely castle discipline would relax while he was gone. Atsu smiled to herself. Suddenly she didn't feel so despairing. There was a ray of hope. Kaneshigé had said that Crane Castle was not so far from Ibusuki. Perhaps they might be able to meet. She sent up a silent prayer to the gods who help lovers. But then she remembered. The gods did not control her destiny now. Lord Nariakira did.

7

A few days after she had arrived, Atsu set out to explore her new home. She wanted to find the chamber she had visited three years earlier when she'd come to deliver the fateful letter to Lord Nariakira's father. She was curious to know what had happened to the old man and his fearsome concubine.

'You're not supposed to leave the women's wing unless His Lordship summons you,' Haru said sternly. 'Remember you're a princess now. It's not dignified to wander around.'

'His Lordship won't mind,' Atsu said, pursing her lips.

Haru shook her head. 'You should hear how the servants whisper, ever since you insisted on entering the audience chamber. They close their mouths when I'm nearby but I catch enough to know what they're saying.'

Atsu tossed her head. 'What do I care what servants say? I'm seventeen, I'm not a child any more. What good is it to be a princess if I can't do as I please?'

Haru clicked her tongue. 'It will be me that will be in trouble, not you, my lady. Elder Maki will tear me to pieces. You've only just arrived. You don't want to give the wrong impression.'

Haru was right. The moment Atsu left the women's wing Elder Maki came rushing up, panting, 'I'm sorry, my lady. May I help you?'

'Thank you, Maki-*sama*,' Atsu said firmly. 'I don't need anything.'

As she stepped through the door, Elder Maki was behind her,

gasping, 'Shall I fetch something, madam?' Ladies-in-waiting fluttered around, twittering. Atsu brushed between them, thanking them and shaking her head firmly.

She hadn't realized the castle was so huge. As they walked the corridors, she heard the squeak of 'nightingale floors', installed to ensure that not even the stealthiest assailant could creep in undetected. Maids and attendants dropped to their knees as she passed. The rooms were more lavish than she'd ever seen, with coffered ceilings and wall screens gleaming with gold, painted with picturesque scenes of farmers ploughing their fields. The wealth was breathtaking.

Outside the women's wing, the castle overflowed with people and bustle. Messengers rushed in and out, merchants arrived with trains of bearers laden with goods, petitioners brought gifts and elders lined up impatient for the latest news of the barbarians. Atsu glimpsed mysterious wires strung between the gatehouse and Lord Nariakira's private apartments that carried messages, so he had told her – another of the curious western inventions he was so fond of. Besides candles and lanterns there were also lamps that shone with a pale flickering glow, lit not with oil or wax but with some substance that hissed and gave off a strange smell. But there was no sign at all of the toad-like old lord and his painted concubine or even a room that remotely resembled the dark chamber where Atsu had knelt apprehensively, holding out the rolled-up scroll, where she had had to fight him off. She sighed. It was probably better not to see it.

Outside, the wooded crags of Castle Hill rose behind the buildings. In front gardeners were at work weeding the flower beds, cleaning the ponds, trimming the bushes and smoothing the gravel. A burly young man with a towel knotted around his head was tying the branch of an ancient pine to some wooden scaffolding.

Atsu recognized the giant messenger, Takamori Saigo. Laughing with joy, she ran over to greet him, amazed at the size of him, his bullet head and stocky body, in contrast to his gentle demeanour. Haru scuttled after her, holding a parasol over her head.

'So you're a gardener as well as a messenger!' Atsu said.

Saigo flushed dark red under his tan and dropped to his knees on the black volcanic soil. 'Lord Nariakira graciously allows me to be of use to him, my lady.' He took a handkerchief from his sleeve and mopped his brow, beating off the mosquitoes that buzzed around them.

'I hear they're erecting defences along the seafront,' Atsu said, waving her fan.

'We're the best defended princedom in the country. His Lordship's made sure of that,' said Saigo.

Now that Atsu was a princess, the difference in standing between her and Saigo was so great that they hardly even counted as man and woman any more. He was a mere low-ranking samurai, she told herself, and that meant she could talk to him freely.

'These tojin, these barbarians,' she said, burning with curiosity. She wanted to know all she could about these malformed creatures who had descended uninvited into their lives. 'You've seen them yourself with your own eyes. Are they really as different as you said?'

He stared at the ground then raised his head. He had a frank, open face. Atsu liked the way he paused and frowned before speaking, as if thinking out his answer. It was a relief to talk to someone she could trust rather than the backbiting concubines and obsequious ladies-in-waiting who populated the women's wing.

'Look at it this way, my lady,' he said slowly. 'We have four castes – samurai, merchants, artisans, farmers.' He counted them off on his thick dirt-stained fingers. 'But we never intermarry.'

'Of course not.' Atsu laughed at the very idea.

'We're different castes but we're still the same people. But the western barbarians aren't just another caste. They're different creatures, like monkeys.' He paused. 'This may be distasteful for a lady's ears but . . . you can smell them, especially when you're down-wind of them. They eat animal flesh.' Atsu gasped in disbelief and wrinkled her nose. 'You can smell the meaty smell even from far away. And they're big, bigger than us. Bigger than me, even.'

He grinned like a boy. Despite his size and solemn demeanour he was only a few years older than Atsu.

'But they don't really look as dreadful as in those pictures Yamada-*sama* showed us, now do they?' She couldn't stop the teasing inflexion in her voice.

Saigo knitted his brow. 'They're as much like those pictures as geisha you see on the street are like woodblock prints of geisha, or real women are like prints of beauties.'

Atsu nodded. Woodblock prints didn't look much like real women at all. They were meant to be beautiful, to capture the essence of whatever they depicted. They weren't like silver prints. They didn't set out to capture what you saw with your own eyes.

'The westerners may look like monkeys, but they're far cleverer and far more dangerous. They've overrun the empire of China and turned it into their dominion.' He looked up at her, his brow creased. Sweat trickled from the towel knotted around his head. 'We young men are readying ourselves for war. His Lordship has authorized us to do whatever we can to defend our shores. We call ourselves the Satsuma Brigade. We are ready to pick up our swords and muskets, whatever weapons His Lordship wants us to use.' He hesitated and dropped his eyes, shuffled as if the volcanic soil was digging into his knees. He took a breath. 'Men . . . recruits, that is, from Your Highness's part of the country, are enlisting too.'

Atsu frowned, wondering why he seemed so awkward. 'My brother, you mean?'

'Your brother, yes, and many more.' He reeled off a list of names. Then he lowered his voice and added, 'One of our best men is Kimotsuki, Kaneshigé Kimotsuki. He's the most militant of all.'

Atsu gave a start, her cheeks blazing. Her heart beat uncontrollably. Fifteen days had passed, a good half a month, since she had last seen Kaneshigé. She'd counted every day. She glanced around fearfully. If she was not careful she would give them both away by her discomfiture. She could hardly breathe.

'Is he here in Kagoshima?' she whispered.

'They rode over for a meeting a few days ago, my lady,' he said. 'That was when we met. We have become firm friends.' He looked at her steadily, as if to remind her of where she was, who she was now. She smiled. With him here in the castle she felt as if she had an older brother, a link to home – to Kaneshigé.

So Kaneshigé had been in Kagoshima. Maybe he'd even tried to see her, though he must have realized it was impossible. He wouldn't have wanted to get her into trouble. Surely he would come again.

'And is he . . . is he in good health?' she added tremulously, keeping her voice low.

Saigo fumbled in his sleeve. 'Here,' he mumbled, avoiding her eyes. He held out a slip of paper.

Atsu's hand trembled as she took it, that same paper that Kaneshigé's fingers too had touched. She hurried away, the slip of paper burning a hole in her sleeve.

With Haru behind her she climbed a little way up Castle Hill and found a log in the shade. She sat down and unfolded the paper, then laughed softly.

'The quails cry in the long grass at dusk.' Just a single line, hastily scribbled, nothing that could incriminate or embarrass her if it was intercepted. She ran her finger across the words, pictured him grinding ink, picking up his brush. She knew the strong, boyish hand. She could feel him there in each stroke.

'The quails cry in the long grass at dusk.' He knew she loved *The Tales of Ise*, written aeons ago by the greatest lover of all, the poet Ariwara no Narihira. She murmured the famous lines that Narihira had written to the woman in Long Grass Village with whom he had spent a brief night of passion: 'Will the grass grow ever longer until the village become a tangled moor?'

The words Kaneshigé had written echoed the first three lines of the lovelorn woman's poignant reply: 'If it become a moor, still like the quails I will raise my plaintive cry as the years go by.'

Tears in her eyes, Atsu whispered the last two lines that completed the poem: 'Then will you not come back, if only briefly for the quail hunt?'

She put the paper to her lips, imagining his lips meeting hers. Narihira had been a man, he'd been in control of his own destiny, and in the end he'd gone back to the woman in Long Grass Village. Atsu didn't have that power. She doubted if she could ever go back, not for the quail hunt or for anything else. Her destiny was in the hands of Lord Nariakira.

But now everything had changed again. Kaneshigé had a very good reason to come to Kagoshima and they even had a willing go-between – Saigo. And Lord Nariakira would soon go off to Edo. Without his eagle eye watching over her, she would be much freer. They would surely find a way to meet.

8

Atsu was making her way back to the women's wing when Elder Maki rushed up to her, tripping over her skirts, her eyes bulging like a frog's. 'My lady,' she gasped, panting. 'His Lordship requires your attendance. I have been looking for you everywhere.'

'What is it, Maki-*sama*?'

'I don't know. Please hurry, my lady. His Lordship is in his chambers.'

Atsu looked around, bewildered. The grounds were full of people talking and shouting. She'd been so preoccupied thinking of Kaneshigé, running over their lives together, imagining how they might meet, repeating his words to herself, that she'd hardly noticed the riders thundering through the gates, the bells on their harnesses ringing wildly.

Retainers bearing candles strode ahead of her through a labyrinth of corridors to His Lordship's private quarters. As Atsu slid open the door she realized that this was the very room she'd been looking for, the room where she had met the old lord and his concubine. The coffered ceiling was not as high as she remembered but she recognized the paintings of tigers and leopards that seemed about to quiver into life and leap off the walls. There was an antique scroll in the alcove and a vase glazed with gold with flowers artfully arranged in it.

Lord Nariakira was pacing up and down, his forehead furrowed. He looked drawn and pale. He took a handkerchief and wiped the sweat from his face. 'Good, you are here,' he said. His voice was hoarse.

He jerked his chin and a couple of elderly maids bowed and backed out of the room on their knees.

He threw himself down on the tatami and gestured to the cushion opposite him. Atsu dropped to her knees, holding her breath. Lord Nariakira took a long pull on his pipe and wisps of smoke seeped from his nostrils. He studied the ground for a while, looked up, raised an eyebrow. 'I hear you are enjoying my concubines' company,' he began, an ironic glint in his eye. 'I am sure you are getting along famously. But I am afraid I shall have to take you away from them.'

He shuffled, crossed and recrossed his large legs. 'But not yet. You must enjoy their company a while longer. They will learn to treat you with kindness. I will make sure of it.'

Atsu bowed, gazing at him in concern. 'What is it, Father? Something has happened. Please tell me.'

Lord Nariakira took another pull on his pipe and rested it on the tobacco box. He was holding a rolled-up scroll. He scowled, smacked it down on his palm. 'There is grave news, very grave.'

He stared abstractedly through the open doors of the room to the gardens shimmering in the heat haze. The pine trees cast long shadows. He turned to Atsu. 'You will know that I was born in Edo and lived there for many years. My home is there still and my family and most of my acquaintances.' He stared at the scroll, frowning. 'We live graciously there. Edo is a city of palaces. Each of the two hundred and sixty princes of this empire has at least one palace. I have three – upper, middle and lower. The greatest palace of all is Edo Castle, in the heart of the city. It stands on a hill. You can see it wherever you go. It is a city in itself.'

He took a breath. 'The castle is the seat of His Majesty, the Great Ruler.'

In the gardens cicadas shrilled. Their piercing whine shattered the silence. A crow cawed, an ominous sound. Atsu shivered despite the heat of the evening. Her clothes clung to her and she was clammy with sweat. She opened her mouth to speak but Lord Nariakira held up his hand, frowning.

The maids crept back in with trays laden with cups and a flask of chilled barley tea and dishes of sugar cakes.

Lord Nariakira took a cup and studied the pale-brown liquid. 'There is no reason why you should know anything of the Great Ruler. Few do, here in Satsuma. I am their prince, they are my subjects. That is all they need to know. But you are different. You are my daughter.' He shook his head heavily. His eyes were puffy and rimmed with lines.

'The Great Ruler has held power since you were born – that is to say, he held power.' He paused, gave a long sigh. 'He held the realm together. He was the realm. The realm was him. He lived in Edo Castle. He never left. The council of ministers discussed and debated and made and unmade laws. But nothing could be decided without his agreement. He attended all state meetings and signed every document.'

A look of anguish crossed his face. He lowered his head. Atsu was startled to see tears in the old warrior's eyes. She sat in silence, hardly daring to breathe.

'The Great Ruler was a gentle and kind-hearted man,' he said, his voice gruff. 'I was presented at court when I was a boy. He was a young man then. He was my lord and master but he also did me the honour of regarding me as a friend and confidant. I knew his father also.' He was gazing into the distance as if he was no longer in Kagoshima but in Edo Castle, in the presence of those all-powerful princes. 'I attended the daily audiences as we are all obliged to, but I also regularly exchanged words with him in private. We discussed politics. We hunted together. He was a great falconer. I had the honour of attending duck hunts in the castle grounds.

'For many years he was heir apparent. The year after you were born, when he was forty-five, two years after I came down to Kagoshima for the first time, his revered father retired and he took on the mantle of Great Ruler. When I arrived in Edo I always visited him personally to pay my respects and we regularly exchanged letters. I was eager to hear his thoughts on the barbarian crisis. But now . . .'

Darkness was closing in. Retainers lit candles and laid out bowls of smouldering chrysanthemum petals. Lord Nariakira thrust out a hand and Toshikyo lit another pipe and gave it to him.

Atsu was frightened to see how black and tormented his face had become. He sat hunched over, staring at the ground, for a long time, then burst out, 'The world is a terrible place, my child. You can never know who to trust. Weak men do what they think is right and end up committing dreadful crimes. Others do what they know very well is wrong.'

Atsu nodded. 'Father,' she whispered. 'Please tell me what you mean. What terrible thing has happened, why do you speak of the Great Ruler in the past?'

Lord Nariakira didn't seem to hear her. He slammed his fist on the tatami so violently that Atsu started. 'I should have been there,' he roared. 'If only I'd been there none of this would have happened.' He shook his head and groaned. 'It is no surprise, that is most terrible of all. But it is a shock all the same. It brings everything to a head. And at the worst possible time, just days after the barbarians arrive on our shores, just as we need him most, my dear old friend, my revered lord . . . dead. He is dead.'

The word was like the tolling of a bell. The room was silent. All movement stopped. The servants knelt like statues. Even the cicadas had stopped their shrilling.

'Dead?' Atsu whispered. She had just learned that there was a Great Ruler, only to hear that he was dead.

Lord Nariakira looked up as if he had forgotten she was there. 'The news will be everywhere soon,' he said, breathing heavily. 'It is a disaster for the country – and at a time like this, when we are in crisis, with the barbarians breathing down our necks. Now we need a leader, as never before.'

'Did His Majesty fall ill?' Atsu asked timidly.

'They tell me he was ailing. I heard nothing of that. He was sixty, old enough, I suppose, to die. But even so.' He shook his head, thumped his fist into his palm. 'I should have been there,' he groaned. 'I could have stopped it.'

He stared around wildly, his face like thunder. 'Fools,' he shouted. 'What did they think to achieve by this?'

'But who, Father, who?'

'You will learn in time.' He picked up his cup again. 'And now we have a new ruler, a weak and sickly boy.' He breathed out sharply and looked straight at Atsu. 'I have plans for you, Atsu, plans that will excite you. The time has come. I need you to help me. They will be taking on new staff at Edo Castle.' He frowned and took a breath. 'I am going to enter you in the women's palace. They call it the Great Interior.'

Atsu raised her cup to her lips, her hand trembling, and put it down again, trying to catch her breath. 'Me? Edo Castle?' Her voice was so faint it was hardly a voice at all. It was too cruel. Just as she had discovered that Kaneshigé came to Kagoshima, just as it seemed there was a very good chance to see him at last, she was to be banished to the women's palace in Edo.

It would be like going to the moon. Edo was twenty days on horseback from Kagoshima. On foot, travelling by palanquin, it would take several months. As for the Great Interior, she imagined a vast gloomy version of the women's wing at Crane Castle, populated by sour-faced sharp-tongued women.

'But why? I thought you brought me here to be your daughter. I thought you wanted to have me close to you.'

'And so I do. But I also want you to have every possible advantage in life, which means entering Edo Castle, at least for a spell. Many families send their daughters there to complete their education. My dear girl, you are an exceptional young woman. You are very beautiful. You are clever and talented. You have a good head on your shoulders. It will be an excellent opportunity for you. You will rise through the ranks, you will learn a great deal.

'The ladies of the women's palace lead cultured lives. They paint, they write poetry, they practise tea ceremony. They also wield considerable power. They are close to the Great Ruler. That is an enormous privilege. They enjoy luxury such as you cannot imagine, my dear. They are famous for their extravagance. You will have more silks and books and trinkets than you'll know what to do with.

'I know you do not enjoy living here with my concubines. You feel stifled here. I did not adopt you just so you could sit listening to their complaints. I have a grander future in mind for you.'

Atsu's heart was beating fast. To go to Edo would be taking a huge step into the unknown. She'd leave the jealous concubines behind, but she'd be further away than ever from Kaneshigé, hopelessly far. She felt the slip of paper in her sleeve, overwhelmed with sadness and yearning.

She looked at Lord Nariakira, large and solid, frowning in determination. He was not the sort of man anyone could persuade to change his mind. But she could dig in her heels as well as anyone. She could at least try.

She remembered how Kaneshigé had told her that the Satsuma mansions in Edo were as far as they could possibly be from Edo Castle. 'But I thought the Satsuma and the Tokugawa were enemies?' she said.

He nodded. 'You are right, my dear. Our clans are indeed enemies. Of all the outside lords I am the most feared. Most women know nothing, not even something as obvious as that. My foolish concubines only know sewing and jostling for position. As I have told your father many times, you always get to the crux of the matter. You will do very well in the palace. They are as sharp-minded as you there. But think about it. We are not such enemies that I cannot be close friends with the Great Ruler. At this time of crisis, as you yourself pointed out, the clans need to unite.'

Atsu grimaced. She wished she hadn't spoken up so glibly in front of that great assembly of warriors. 'Father, it is my duty to do whatever you command,' she said, as sweetly as she could. 'But I am a country girl. The women who live in the Great Interior must be from the highest classes.'

He laughed. He was playing with her like a cat plays with a mouse. 'You are no country girl,' he said. 'You can outwit any of them.'

'And surely they come from families loyal to the Tokugawas. They'll hate me. They'll see me as their enemy. I don't even speak their language. They will refuse to accept me, refuse to let me enter the palace. Surely even you will not be able to persuade them to take someone who hasn't passed the proper vetting procedures.'

'Make no mistake,' he boomed. 'If the Prince of Satsuma wants something, it will be done.'

Atsu chewed her lip. She could see it was impossible to shake his resolve. There was something about the way he was talking – too airy, too casual. There was something he wasn't telling her. Entering the palace was no doubt a great opportunity, but why had he suddenly come up with the idea of sending her there right after hearing about the Great Ruler's death? He was her liege lord, she was his vassal. It wasn't her place to question his orders. Added to which there wasn't much hope of trying to outwit someone as brilliant and cunning and wily as Lord Nariakira. She had the feeling she was nothing but a tiny cog in some giant scheme of his. She wondered whether she would ever find out what that scheme was.

'But Father,' she said miserably, 'I'm just settling in. It's too soon to make such a big move.'

His face blackened. 'I am disappointed in you, Atsu. After all I have done to raise you in the world. You will have to trust me. I can assure you that I have your best interests in mind. You will see the great city of Edo. It's the centre of our country, a hub of culture and civilization. All you have ever known is the life of the countryside. It will be a revelation to you. You will be presented at court. You will meet the Great Ruler, maybe become close to him. Most young women would leap at the chance.'

Her spirits sank. All this time he'd led her to believe that he wanted to adopt her as his daughter, and now he was sending her away. She tried to guess what his plan might be. Was it that with her in the palace he'd have a spy in the middle of his enemies? If that was what he had in mind she'd have to be very careful. It would be a formidable task, and dangerous.

She had to ask. 'Father, do you want me to be your spy? What are you thinking of? You're sending me into a hornets' nest.' She barely breathed the words.

'Enough,' he thundered. 'I have heard enough. I appreciate your independence of mind, my girl, but I won't tolerate disagreement. Let me remind you: I am your liege lord and this is my express command. If I can arrange it, you will enter the Great Interior. Do not oppose me.'

His black eyes bored into her as if he could read her every thought.

'I cannot imagine why you are not leaping with excitement at the chance. But I have a good inkling. I wonder if you have formed an attachment that makes you want to stay here – an attachment which is forbidden. You are seventeen. It would not be surprising.'

She started, her cheeks blazing, and felt panic like a physical blow to her stomach. In a flash she saw Lord Nariakira turning his eagle eye and glancing across the dunes as she and Kaneshigé stood on the ridge. She remembered that last reckless kiss. Up to now he had said nothing but he had stored it away, kept it to use as his most potent weapon to force her to bow to his will.

She met his eye, trying to hide her confusion, the thunder of her heart. Would he order Kaneshigé's execution? Would that be the sword he would hold over her head?

His face softened. 'But we have bigger games to play. I know you understand that. We all have to put aside our personal feelings. You are a samurai. Feelings are for the lower orders, not for warriors like us.'

Atsu swallowed, her heart pounding. Tears sprang to her eyes. She realized now that she could never see Kaneshigé again. She had to leave him behind. She had responsibilities, tasks, a role to play. She would have to learn to give up her personal desires for the greater cause. Kaneshigé too understood that. In the end they both knew that duty, not personal wishes, ruled their lives. She had done her best to fight Lord Nariakira but in the end he was bound to win.

Shaking, she put her hands to the floor and bowed. 'If it's your command, Father, I have to obey.'

He grinned. He was back to his genial self. 'That is decided, then. You will not regret it.' He leaned forward and laid his big hand on hers. 'You will not be on your own. You will have allies there. And I will be close by too. You will be in touch with me.'

Atsu breathed out hard. 'You have put your trust in me, Father, and I will do my best to repay it,' she whispered.

He grinned more broadly than ever. 'Do not look so concerned, my dear,' he said, patting her hand. 'You will have plenty of time. We shall leave in a few months, after New Year, at the season when

I always depart for Edo. I want to make sure we are there when the barbarian ships return. You wanted to see the barbarians and their ships, my dear, and you will. And on the way we shall pay some visits. There are important people I wish to introduce you to. I shall make sure you are as well prepared as you can be.'

So Atsu was going to Edo. And when the barbarians arrived, she'd be there, right in the thick of it.

She wiped her eyes, her thoughts in turmoil. She knew now how she would answer Kaneshigé's note. When the poet Narihira was sent into exile he had passed Mount Fuji on his travels. Like Narihira she too would journey to the east and she too would see Mount Fuji. And if Kaneshigé was on his way to fight the barbarians, he would pass by too.

This was what she would write: 'If only we could meet . . . where the roads cross, in the shadow of Mount Fuji.'

9

First day of the second month, Year of the Tiger, Kaei 7,
a yang wood year (27 February 1854): on the road

Atsu sat up with a start. Her legs had lost all feeling. She wriggled one, then the other, wishing there was room to stretch out, grimacing as the blood came rushing back in an excruciating tingle.

Outside there were shouts, barked orders. Horses snorted, people ran back and forth. She pushed aside the bamboo blind that covered the window of her palanquin, wrinkling her nose at the pungent smell of dung and rotting radishes. There was nothing to see but trees and dried-out paddy fields. The palanquin jerked to a halt. The tramp of straw-sandalled feet, the jingle of bells, the rattle of iron staffs and the rhythmic grunts of the bearers stopped too.

Something had happened serious enough to bring the whole procession to a standstill. Local lords, merchants, petitioners regularly arrived to pay their respects to Lord Nariakira and messengers rode in from Edo and Kagoshima several times a day. But His Lordship always held audience at designated rest places or when he stopped at an inn for a meal or to spend the night. It was unheard of for the procession to come to an unscheduled halt in the middle of nowhere. It never stopped for anything.

Atsu shook the small door open. The convoy stretched as far as she could see, like a great centipede winding along between the evenly spaced trees that lined the road. The eight burly bearers who carried her palanquin gaped when they saw her and tumbled to their knees, buttocks in the air. Haru rushed over to put her straw sandals in place as she jumped out.

Atsu's breath was like smoke in the icy air. Impatient to find out what had happened, she picked up her skirts and hurried towards Lord Nariakira's section of the procession. She passed troops of samurai, porters carrying lacquered boxes and trunks, the bearer of the ornamental parasol, the bearer of the ornamental sun hat and long lines of horses led by liveried grooms. They stumbled back, wide-eyed, and dropped to their knees as she passed. Too late she remembered how unseemly it was for her to be out in public, in full view. She hurried on, oblivious.

She was panting by the time she reached the rearguard of Lord Nariakira's escort. She rushed past the palanquins carrying his senior staff. They too were climbing out anxiously to see what was going on while the horses tugged at their reins, snorting and rearing. Valets in matching livery stood with their hands tucked into their sleeves, shivering.

She heard Lord Nariakira's voice long before she passed the last of the basket carriers, pike men and bodyguards. 'You fools!' he was shouting. 'Where did you get to? Did you get lost?'

He was standing, legs wide apart, outside his magnificent black and gold palanquin, his eyes bulging and his face purple. Atsu had never seen him so enraged. Someone had offered him a camp chair as if he were a general presiding over a battle but he thrust it aside impatiently. A couple of messengers knelt before him.

He brandished a scroll. 'Can you not read?' he roared. ' "Urgent. Express message for the Prince of Satsuma". Express message – and I receive it only now? Did you stop at every whorehouse along the way?'

'I have no excuse,' moaned one of the messengers. He pressed his face into the stony ground, skinny buttocks trembling.

'We . . . we left the moment we were dispatched,' stuttered the other. 'We rode day and night. The road was crowded.'

Lord Nariakira nodded, sighed heavily. 'I understand. It is not your fault. No doubt there were many delays before the news reached the Satsuma compound.' He shook his head. 'These people want to stop me knowing what is going on. If they think they can solve this on their own, they are fools.'

Atsu was standing to one side, listening impatiently, waiting for a chance to speak. He spun round. His face softened as he saw her.

'Atsu, you are here. Good.' He waved the scroll at her, shook his head fiercely. 'The Americans. Just as we thought we had months to go, months earlier than they said – though we would be fools to trust a barbarian's word – they are back.'

'They're back?'

'The Americans are back.'

'But it's too soon,' she gasped. Her heart was pounding. 'They said they would come back in the spring.'

'Exactly. They have lied to us, taken us by surprise. We are nowhere near completing the coastal defences around Edo. We are wide open to attack. And here we are, all of us . . .' – he swung his arm in a great circle to encompass the whole vast procession – 'with another month at least before we get there.' He slapped the scroll into his large palm with a crack. 'And here is the worst of it,' he shouted. 'They have been here fifteen days already! They must have arrived even before we left Kagoshima – and it takes that long for the news to reach me.' He shook his head. 'I dare not imagine what has happened since then.'

He stared down at the scroll, scowling. 'They come in eight ships this time, not four. They are nothing if not determined. Three steam-ships, four sail ships and a supply ship, all armed to the teeth. There are more cannons on each ship – and bigger and more modern – than in our entire arsenal. According to this letter they were heading for Uraga. With luck they have stopped there, as they did last time. If they try to take Edo, we do not have the firepower to hold them off.'

He groaned and shook his head. 'I feel as if I am in a nightmare. My great-grandfather Shigehidé was a good friend to the Hollanders. He admired and respected them and their culture and they returned his respect. But these are a different breed. They know only the gun. They are interested only in conquest. They are a violent people. They snatch realms, destroy cultures as casually as if they were playing a gigantic game of Go.

'There is a Dutch ship which visits every year, regular as the change of the seasons. One year, not long before I was born, it did not appear. It did not appear the following year or the year after that. For twelve long years no ship arrived. The Hollanders were stranded. They could not discover what had happened and they had no supplies either. We had to help them, give them provisions.

'Finally a ship appeared and we learned the cause. For twelve years their country had ceased to exist. It had been swallowed up by France like a little fish swallowed by a great fish. It seems these western nations spend their time snapping up each other's territory like pieces on a Go board. Before their country regained its independence the British sent a ship flying the Dutch flag into Nagasaki harbour, thinking to deceive us, hoping to break the Dutch monopoly and trade with us. We are not so simple-minded. We repelled the foreign intruders then and we shall repel them now.'

The wind rippled the dry stalks in the paddy fields and the pine trees rustled. Horses stamped and men whispered, casting fearful glances in Lord Nariakira's direction.

'They swallow up each other's countries and now they want to swallow up ours too,' he boomed. 'They are a plague of locusts. If we do not stop them they will devour us.'

He lowered his voice. 'They know nothing of our world or our culture. This letter they were so determined to present last time they were here, from their emperor to ours. Our emperor!' He gave a snort of laughter. 'They wished to communicate with the imperial palace but that would have been to waste their time.'

'I know nothing of the emperor or the imperial palace,' Atsu said. She was proud that Lord Nariakira took a young girl like her into his confidence. His hair was turning grey as if he bore the weight of the world on his shoulders. She would do anything, she thought, to ease that burden.

He smiled. 'No one does. No one needs to. The Son of Heaven exists in his own world. He has no need of us nor we of him. You will learn as much as you need to know when we reach the imperial capital, Miyako.

'This letter the tojin addressed to the emperor arrived in the hands of Prime Minister Abé, who communicated its contents to me. It seems the intruders have a treaty they wish us to sign – they demand it. They demand to sail their whaling ships into our ports and use them as coaling stations. That is their demand. But it would be naive to imagine that that is all they intend.' He shook his head. 'This is only the beginning. Next they will be demanding to take over our port towns, sell us their tawdry goods, establish bases in our country.

'Certainly we need to trade with the western nations, that is obvious to me – but in our own way, in our own time, on our own terms. We cannot have them breathing down our necks or we shall end up like China, crushed under the barbarian yoke. This is the crux of the problem. To sign their treaty would be rank humiliation, the beginning of the end. But if we do not sign it they will attack us. They easily outgun us. If we go to war with them, we shall be destroyed. That is our dilemma – and I cannot see a solution.

'If the government has wisdom they will stall for as long as they can. That is the best we can do. Prime Minister Abé is a competent man and my close ally. But he is young. I need to be there too. I need to learn these upstart Americans' precise demands and their conditions.'

'But what about the Great Ruler?' Ever since Lord Nariakira had told Atsu about the Great Ruler she had been curious to learn more. She remembered how dismissive he had been of their new potentate, successor to the late Great Ruler. 'A weak and sickly boy,' he had called him.

'He is our leader,' she said. 'Surely he should decide what to do.'

Lord Nariakira narrowed his eyes and glanced at her, eyebrows raised. 'Quite, my dear. You always have such a clear view of things. Indeed, the Great Ruler should decide what to do. But he is young still. For the present he does not trouble himself with affairs of state. All he is required to do is sign documents. We tell him where to sign and he signs – most of the time, anyway. Best leave his ministers to make decisions.'

'But Father, you said we need a strong leader and now the barbarians have returned it's more critical than ever. He is the Great Ruler. Why does he not rule?'

Lord Nariakira grimaced, as if he had something to tell her. Atsu was struck by the look on his face. But he said nothing. He raised his hand as if to signal that the conversation was at an end, turned away, started pacing up and down, scowling. 'It is intolerable. It will be days before these messengers reach Edo with my letter. I wish we could travel faster but that is out of the question.'

That much Atsu understood. There were rules that governed every aspect of life and most particularly a great lord's journey. The timetable had to be set in stone, the highway cleared for the passage of such a vast number of people, inns booked, meals prepared.

The scribes were waiting with brush and ink. Lord Nariakira dictated a message and read it over. The scribes rolled up the scroll, sealed it, put it in the dispatch box and the messengers galloped away.

10

More than half a year had passed since Lord Nariakira had told Atsu that he was taking her to Edo. She was eighteen. Like everyone else she'd celebrated her birthday at the beginning of the year. The world was opening up before her eyes.

They'd been on the road for ten days now, travelling from dawn to dusk, stopping frequently for meals or to see some local sight or stretch their legs. They'd travelled through towns and villages, across rivers, skirted the vast volcanic cone of Mount Aso rising across the plain, passed through forests and valleys and between fields of dried-up paddy.

At least Atsu had protection from the weather. Most of the procession – some twenty thousand people, so she'd heard – had to slog through rain and snow and mud and ice on foot. There were so many people on the road that she sometimes thought that Crane Castle must be completely empty. She felt rather sorry for the two concubines, Lady Umé and Lady Také, whiling away their days in endless complaint.

Jogging along in her palanquin there was time to think, too much time. Sometimes she wept for loneliness, thinking of Kaneshigé, her parents, her brothers and sisters. She pictured her mother's gentle faded face, remembered how sad she had been when Atsu had left, how she'd turned away, dabbing her eyes. She missed those innocent days running back and forth to school, reading by the light of candles and oil lamps, sitting with her mother and sisters sewing peaceably together. It was only now that she fully understood. She'd left home for good, she'd never see any of them again. Her mother had known that all along.

She thought of Kaneshigé sparring with her brother, heard the crack of wooden practice sticks in the garden, the shouts of boyish laughter. With Saigo's help from time to time she'd managed to exchange notes with him, brimful of wistful yearning. But she hadn't tried to arrange a meeting and neither had he. They had responsibilities now. They were adults. They could no longer let themselves be ruled by their feelings as they had when they were children.

There was an exciting future ahead of her. She was to enter the women's palace at Edo Castle. She was rising in rank at a dizzying pace. Perhaps she might even catch the eye of the Great Ruler and be chosen as a concubine. It was time to look forward, not back, to forget childhood attachments.

And sometimes she puzzled over exactly why Lord Nariakira had wanted to enter her in the women's palace, what he might want her to do there, what task he might have in mind for her. She was not for a moment fooled that it was purely for her advancement. He was far too devious for that.

As soon as the messengers had gone the cavalcade lurched back into motion. Midway through the afternoon it came to a halt again.

The road ahead of them had turned into a narrow track winding up a mountain, sheer and steep. The advance guard – quartermasters, scribes, cooks, pike men and box carriers, all in crested livery – climbed upwards for as far as the eye could see. Atsu made out a zigzag line of tiny figures high on the mountainside, straggling out of the trees and disappearing into them again.

Lord Nariakira's chief elder appeared beside her palanquin. He was a tall man whose starched robes remained miraculously uncreased despite the days of travelling. 'So sorry, madam,' he said, sucking long yellow teeth. 'We have to change vehicles. The road is very bad here. They'll have to carry the palanquins up empty and the horses won't make it at all. We'll pick up new horses on the other side.'

Atsu wondered how they'd managed to get the huge cannon and crates of arms up and over the pass without horses to drag them. The baggage train and several battalions of samurai had left

Kagoshima two days before the main party set out. She remembered the commotion, the stamping of hooves as squadron after squadron lined up in the courtyard and marched out of the gates. By now they should be well on their way on the other side.

She pulled her quilted jacket close about her, glad of the chance to stretch her legs. Her breath puffed out like steam. It was going to be colder still on the mountain.

Lord Nariakira was squeezing into a flimsy-looking litter, not much more than a basket with a carrying pole. He twisted his arms and legs into knots as he crammed himself in but still managed to look lordly and dignified. He grinned when he saw her. 'This is the worst part,' he grunted. 'After this it is easy.'

Atsu remembered that he knew the road. He had made this journey many times before.

Attendants and bodyguards were setting off up the mountain track ahead of him. Lord Nariakira took a last drag on his pipe and handed it to his page, Toshikyo. Instead of the eight bearers that carried the heavy palanquins, the light litters needed only two, hardy dark-skinned mountain men, with others running alongside to take over when they got tired.

'Are you ready, my lord?' the chief elder asked.

'As ready as I can ever be.'

The bearers braced themselves, heaved the litter on to their shoulders and shouted, 'Forward!' The carrying pole bent as they lifted the bamboo basket off the ground. To Atsu's amazement they set off at full pelt, straight for the mountain. As the basket rocked wildly from side to side, Lord Nariakira sat, arms folded, solid as a Buddha, as calm and composed as if he were at home in his castle, taking tea.

Atsu watched the large figure lurch away with Toshikyo and the other valets and a second contingent of bodyguards running behind. She wished she could climb the mountain on foot. She hated having to trust herself to these men.

The chief elder presented her with her bearers, Goro and Jiro. They were surly-looking characters with wide flat faces, slanted eyes and teeth jutting at all angles like rocks on a hillside. Instead of shaved pates and hair sleekly knotted into topknots, they had thatches of thick black hair and wore coarse hempen jackets over their loincloths. Their dialect was so rough that Atsu could barely understand a word.

'They're the best in the area,' said the chief elder, hands clasped over his stomach so tightly that the bony knuckles were white. He too was preparing to ascend by litter. 'Every rock, every stone, every tree, every bend, they know it. They're the best possible hands for a precious cargo like Your Highness.'

Atsu swung her legs into the litter with as much dignity as she could muster. There was very little to stop her falling out, nothing but a small basketwork edge. Goro and Jiro put their shoulders to the carrying pole and she felt the basket give, creaking ominously as they straightened up. 'Forward!' they shouted and charged off. She grabbed for the edges of the basket. She was tossing about so violently she was sure she'd be thrown out.

The path turned sharply uphill, the basket lurching and tilting so steeply that she was forced against the back. The bearers pounded on through dense forest, leaping across rocks in their straw sandals while Atsu gritted her teeth, hanging on for dear life to anything she could find. She felt horribly vulnerable, swinging in her basket, visible for the whole world to see.

At a small village, they stopped for a rest and she dragged herself out of the litter and sat on a rock, her legs quivering. Shafts of sunlight pierced the woodsmoke that filled the glade. The men threw off their jackets and wiped the dust off their faces. They were rank with sweat while she was shivering with cold.

Replacement bearers took over. They set off and turned along a precipitous path above a chasm. Cryptomeria trees lined the slopes and distant peaks wreathed in cloud rose on the horizon.

Atsu looked around sharply. Something was wrong, very wrong. Apart from the pad of the bearers' feet on the stony path, there was utter silence. They were sprinting so fast they'd outrun the bodyguards who should have been following and there was no sign of any attendants up ahead. There was no one around at all except two more mountain men, the other replacement bearers.

Atsu wondered if the bearers had lost their way. But that was impossible. They were mountain men, they knew every tree, every bush, every path. If they'd taken a wrong turning they'd done so on purpose.

She felt a shock of fear. She was on her own with these wild men who didn't even speak her language. These were not even Goro and Jiro, they were nameless strangers.

'Stop!' she shouted. 'Wait for my escort.' Her voice blew away in the wind.

The path was little more than a shelf edging the mountain. Halfway along the bearers stopped and dropped the litter. Atsu hit the ground with a bump. The basket rocked precariously, perilously near the edge. She was high above a gorge that sliced between enormous crags. A river foamed far below. She glanced tremulously down through the trees and made out fragments of litters and boxes scattered on the banks and what looked like bodies.

A stiff wind blew through the canyon, rocking the basket closer to the edge. Atsu sat, hardly daring to breathe, with the chasm on one side and the men on the other.

The men crouched with their backs against the mountainside, wiping their brows. One picked up a stone, twirled it in bony fingers and tossed it over the edge. It bounced into the ravine and ricocheted from rock to rock. The sound echoed off the high walls. It seemed a lifetime before Atsu heard a faint clunk as it hit the bottom.

The men's eyes bored hungrily into her. The hair prickled at the back of her neck. She felt horribly conspicuous in her lavish silks, glittering with gold and silver embroidery. These thin sun-blackened men could see her white skin, see who they had in their power – the daughter of the Prince of Satsuma, the most powerful and wealthy lord in the realm. They could kill her, rape her, hold her to ransom, topple her over the edge.

Or perhaps they had been paid to abduct her. There were many people who didn't want Lord Nariakira to get to Edo and would use any means to delay him. If he sent a search party to find her that would hold him up by many days. Almost all his children had died already. She would be just one more casualty.

The men rose to their feet, their faces blank. They moved like puppets, as if driven by something outside themselves, desperation maybe or hunger. They were young, she could see that now, though their faces were as weathered as old men's from years of working in the harsh mountain air. One had teeth that jutted out like stones, another had a wall eye. They cringed like curs, afraid to attack but determined to do so anyway, waiting for the right moment.

'Keep your distance,' Atsu shouted. To her horror her voice came out in a shrill whimper. 'Put one foot wrong and your necks will feel the executioner's blade.'

The men looked at each other and laughed. Kites and buzzards circled overhead, shrieking. The wind roared through the canyon, buffeting the basket, threatening to sweep it over the edge. It blew her hair loose, made her huge sleeves flap like sails.

The men took a step towards her, then another, closing in around her. She saw the whites of their eyes gleaming in their dirt-stained faces, hungry and pitiless.

'Pretty lady,' said one, his voice thick. 'Such soft white skin. What a pity to spoil it.' He bared his teeth in a grin and licked his lips.

Then she remembered that she had a weapon – Kaneshigé's dagger, tucked in her obi. She closed her hand around the hilt, touched her fingers to the Kimotsuki crest engraved there, and felt a surge of courage.

'I warn you,' she said. Her voice was firmer now. The men were so close she could smell them, a rank odour of woodsmoke, sweat and human excrement.

Suddenly she felt entirely calm and clear and focused. These were men, she was a mere girl and there were four of them and one of her. But they were uneducated yokels and she was a samurai, trained from birth as a warrior. She had a weapon but, more importantly, she knew how to handle herself. She'd spent years learning martial arts and sparring with her halberd. If she kept her wits about her, she could take on all four easily and dispatch them. It could be that they were just taking advantage of an unexpected opportunity and wouldn't dare go through with it. The main thing she needed to do was to get out of the litter and face them standing on her own two feet.

She took a breath. Never taking her eyes off the men, she stepped cautiously out, first one foot, then the other, lifting her cumbersome skirts, keeping well away from the canyon edge. She reached for her straw sandals and tied them on and stood poised, senses alert, hand on her dagger. She narrowed her eyes. If one of them dared attack her, she should be able to duck aside and use his momentum to send him toppling over the edge – all of them if need be.

The men were blinking, backing away, their eyes widening. They'd seen her as just a frail girl. They hadn't expected a fight.

The one with the wall eye started spitting out words in a low growl – how poor they were, how many children they had, how little food, how tough it was carrying a heavy burden like her up this steep mountain.

'Give us *mon*,' he said. 'We need *mon*.' He sounded plaintive, hesitant.

Whatever terrible things they had been planning, all they dared demand now was money. With her feet planted firmly on the ground, Atsu had the upper hand. 'Nonsense,' she said. She was beginning to feel almost sorry for them. 'How dare you? You'll be in trouble for this.'

'A hundred *ryo*!' barked the one with projecting teeth defiantly. 'Or we . . .'

He took a step towards Atsu. A hundred *ryo* was more than all of them together could hope to earn in a lifetime.

The others elbowed him in the ribs. There were raised voices, footsteps racing towards them. They shuffled back nervously.

'Be very careful,' she said, without taking her eyes off them. 'Don't do anything you might regret.'

A moment later a burly man in black livery appeared, sprinting towards them along the path – the chief bodyguard. He turned pale when he saw Atsu. The other bodyguards were close behind.

'Are you all right, madam?' he shouted.

Atsu heaved a sigh of relief. Now that the crisis was past she was shaking. 'Just stretching my legs,' she said, and waited for the bearers to move the litter to the middle of the path before she climbed back in.

All the way over the pass and down the other side Atsu was thinking about what had happened. Did these men know who she was or did they just think she was some grand lady? Were they local villains, taking advantage of an opportunity? After all, the contrast between their poverty and her visible wealth was breathtaking. Or was there something more sinister behind it? Had they been paid by one of Lord Nariakira's enemies to get rid of her? She would have to ask him.

She turned as she climbed out at the bottom. They were ashen with fear. She realized that if she once mentioned the incident to Lord Nariakira they would be executed, all of them – not just the bearers but the bodyguards who had let her out of their sight too, maybe even the chief elder who hadn't vetted the mountain men thoroughly. She gazed at these stunted bow-legged men who laboured day and night carrying people richer and more fortunate than themselves up and down this back-breakingly steep mountain. She'd never seen such wretched-looking people. She couldn't help feeling sorry for them. In the end she hadn't been harmed. This time, she decided, she would keep the matter to herself.

'Give them an extra large tip,' she told Haru. 'They worked hard.'

The following day they reached Kokura Harbour at the northernmost tip of Kyushu and boarded sailing ships to cross the straits. Atsu stood in the stern as the coastline dwindled away behind her. It was the first time she had ever left her home island. A swathe of foam stretched like a road behind the ship as the wind swelled its sails and sent it cutting across the blue water.

She watched, blinking away tears. She was leaving her home, her family, Kaneshigé. She would never see any of them again. But she was also moving towards the future, a new and exciting one.

Edo. It was the biggest city on earth and Edo Castle the greatest in the land. Just to see such a place would be an unimaginable adventure. But she also knew that the world was rough and dangerous, more dangerous than she could ever have imagined when she was just Okatsu, living quietly in her cosy home in Ibusuki. And the higher she rose in status, the more visible she became, the more dangerous it would be.

11

'Tonight we shall celebrate,' boomed Lord Nariakira, leaning back and patting his stomach, now beginning to balloon after all the rich food they'd eaten.

Atsu pushed away the last of the succession of tiny dishes. She was tired of the lavish meals. Every inn they stayed at seemed to be trying to outdo the last. They'd feasted on sardines in Hiroshima, octopus in Okayama, clams in Himeji, sea bream in Akashi. That night in Fushimi they'd been served the speciality of the region – freshly made tofu. Maids brought in dish after dish – tofu raw, tofu simmered, stuffed tofu pouches, tofu tempura, bean-curd-skin rolls and, as if that wasn't enough, dishes of seafood, seaweed and mountain vegetables, all exquisitely arranged. The table groaned under the weight of it. What she wouldn't give, Atsu thought, for a dish of plain noodles or rice and pickled vegetables.

With every day that passed they moved further and further from Kagoshima and closer to Edo. At night they stayed in the mansions of local lords or at palatial inns. The rest of the procession was billeted in houses throughout the village and villages round about, though it was hard to imagine where they could put twenty thousand people even for just one night.

And every day news arrived, more and more alarming. It seemed the barbarians had not stopped at Uraga. They were in Edo Bay now with their sights trained on the castle, demanding negotiations while the government officials shuttled back and forth, desperately stalling. If the messages were to be believed, the invaders had not attacked Edo – for the time being, at least.

But no matter how disturbing the news or how impatient Lord Nariakira might be to reach Edo, they still had to jog along at the allotted pace. They were marooned in a kind of limbo.

That day they'd arrived in the southern outskirts of Miyako, the emperor's capital. They were billeted in Fushimi's most splendid hostelry, reserved for visiting dignitaries, with Atsu and her attendants in one chamber and Lord Nariakira and his in another. After dinner Atsu and Lord Nariakira sat together warming their hands over the brazier while candles sputtered, making pools of light in the dark corners of the magnificent main room.

'Let us have some more of your famous saké,' Lord Nariakira cried as the maids cleared away the last of the dishes. 'Toshikyo! What happened to my saké glasses?'

The page ran in holding a wooden box. Eyes sparkling, Lord Nariakira slid off the lid and brought out two silk-wrapped packages. Inside were a couple of cut-glass beakers.

'Master glassblower Chubei's work,' he said, beaming. 'See how crisp and sharp these lines are?' He turned the glass this way and that, sending flashes of red and blue dancing across the walls.

'Let's drink to Edo and driving away the western intruders!' he said, as the page filled their glasses.

Atsu took a sip of the liquor, feeling the warmth travel down her throat and suffuse her body.

'Do you remember Kawamoto and Matsuki?' said Lord Nariakira. 'And my "mirror with a memory"?' His face lit up.

Atsu laughed. 'How could I forget that peculiar house that stank of chemicals or that bulging-eyed barbarian in the picture? I'd be thrilled if they've managed to make a silver print. I wish I could make one myself.'

'When Kawamoto finishes translating the manuals perhaps they will finally work out how to make the contraption work. Start with something that does not move, a building or a street or a landscape,

I told them. I wish I were there. I should like to be making silver prints too. But there is much to be done before I can go back.'

'But what are we celebrating?' Atsu asked. She'd been holding back, waiting for him to tell her.

Lord Nariakira let his eyes rest on her face. 'I shall be sorry when we get to Edo,' he said, heaving a sigh. 'I have been enjoying these evenings with you. It is a privilege to have you as my daughter.'

Atsu smiled at him. She too felt wistful. Once they were in Edo they would no longer be so free or so relaxed. Secretly she wished the journey could go on for ever.

He straightened his back. 'Tomorrow we shall visit the imperial capital, Miyako. It is a short journey away.' He looked around the splendid room, at the candles along the walls. 'We are in the emperor's territory now. It is a strange world here, all rites and rituals. Imperial courtiers are a different breed. They are like priests, those courtiers. They have no money or power, but they have infinite status. They claim they speak for the gods. They do not welcome temporal rulers. Even I, the Prince of Satsuma, have to crawl on my hands and knees. I would rather be in Edo any day, arguing about the westerners, or at home in my castle in Kyushu with my retainers, not making small talk with a high and mighty member of the imperial court. But it cannot be helped.'

He gazed at the glass with its design of leaves and flowers, twirled it in his fingers, held it out to Toshikyo to refill.

'My plans are advancing,' he said. 'I know you wish me to keep you informed and I will do the best I can. You understand that I can tell you very little at present.'

He paused, looked at Atsu from under his brows. 'I have heard from my kinsman, Prince Konoé. The paperwork is all completed. The arrangements are in place for him to become your adoptive father. He professes himself delighted.'

'Prince Konoé? My father?' Atsu gasped. 'You didn't tell me . . . you had any such plan in mind.'

The room had suddenly become very quiet. The blood was pounding in her ears.

'I thought it best to keep my counsel until everything was settled, in case some unexpected hindrance cropped up. But now it is all in place we shall celebrate your elevation,' Lord Nariakira said, beaming as if he expected her to be delighted.

She stared at him, aghast. It had been understandable for him to adopt her. His sons had all died and he had known her since she was young. He was fond of her. But to be shunted on to the Konoés after only nine months as his daughter made no sense at all. Clearly he had his reasons. Everything, it seemed, was part of some convoluted scheme of his.

She gulped down the last of her saké. 'But why?' she demanded, tears springing to her eyes.

'His Highness is one of the most powerful statesmen at the imperial court and a man of great culture,' Lord Nariakira said in level tones, raising his bushy eyebrows. 'He is Minister of the Left and first cousin to he who dwells above the clouds.' He looked at her hard. 'That is what we call the Son of Heaven. Prince Konoé is also a famous calligrapher and poet and a master of the incense ceremony. He is my kinsman,' he repeated, as if that explained everything. 'Princess Konoé is my sister by adoption, you see. My father adopted her so she could marry Prince Konoé. The Shimazu and Konoé families have been bound by marriage since antiquity. She is a lady of exquisite beauty and taste.'

Atsu tried to smile but her lips were trembling. Once again she was being swept along to some unknown destination with no control over her fate. 'But . . . but I've known you all my life,' she stammered. 'You've always been like a father to me. You are my father now. Surely no imperial prince would want a girl from Ibusuki as his daughter. Even your concubines make fun of me.'

Lord Nariakira pursed his lips and scowled. 'You are indeed my daughter now,' he boomed. 'You forget what that means. You are of extremely high rank, certainly high enough to be adopted by a member of the imperial family.' His face softened. 'Do not worry. You will not have to live with them. I do not intend to leave you in Miyako. It is a pure formality, a change of name and status, that is all. As the daughter of Prince Konoé, you will be the niece of the emperor himself. You will be an imperial princess.

'I have told you that I intend to place you in the women's palace. The women there are from very grand families. Many are from Miyako. They will torment you if they guess you are from the countryside. It will be best for you to be of the highest possible rank.'

Atsu narrowed her eyes. She wondered why he felt the need to explain himself to her in such detail. She had a sudden suspicion. 'You mean you intend the Great Ruler to take me as a concubine?' she said accusingly.

She expected Lord Nariakira to laugh at such a preposterous suggestion, but he didn't. His face took on a strange look – abashed, hooded. 'Something of that sort,' he said. 'Nothing is settled yet. I shall tell you when everything is in place. Please trust me. I want to ensure that all doors will be open to you.'

She was about to speak but he raised his hand as if everything was decided. 'Tomorrow we shall go to Miyako. You will enjoy meeting Prince and Princess Konoé.'

He smiled. 'I know you love your books. And now you will see the City of Purple Hills and Crystal Streams, where Genji the Shining Prince and Ariwara no Narihira once lived. There is plenty to celebrate.'

The following day they set out in unmarked palanquins with hired bearers and just a few attendants and trusted guards. Most of the procession had been given the day off. Even Lord Nariakira's page, Toshikyo, stayed behind. Only a few of Atsu's ladies were in attendance, with Haru carrying Atsu's sandals.

Atsu was taken aback at the secrecy. Surely to visit a prince they should travel with all possible pomp? She could only assume that Lord Nariakira had his reasons.

Saigo was one of the guards. Atsu had been overjoyed to discover that he had come with them from Kagoshima. It was reassuring to have such a giant of a man to keep watch over her. He had come to feel like an older brother.

And here she was, crossing a crystal stream – though it looked more like a sluggish brown river – and glimpsing the purple hills that rose on three sides, precisely following the principles of feng shui. She pushed aside the window blind, remembering the saying that Miyako dwellers happily spend their last coins on gorgeous clothing. Women in exquisite kimonos clattered by on high clogs, long sleeves swinging. The air felt heavy and dank and she caught the waft of incense on the breeze.

Just as in the stories, the streets were laid out in a perfect grid like a Go board, mirroring the great city of Chang'an in China. Their small convoy jogged up a boulevard lined with shops and temples and crossed a street that stretched, perfectly straight, all the way to the cloud-draped hills on the horizon. Reclining in her palanquin Atsu imagined herself a court lady of Prince Genji's time, rumbling along in a golden carriage drawn by white oxen, trailing one exquisite brocade sleeve from the window.

An icy blast whistled down the avenue and shook the bamboo slats of the window blind as they turned down a side street. Dark alleys wound between wooden houses with lanterns swinging outside, no doubt teahouses where *geiko*, the famous geisha of Miyako, entertained. Atsu listened for the tinkle of a shamisen plucking out a plaintive melody but all she heard was the shrieking of birds and the barking of dogs and the pad of the bearers' feet on the rough stone street.

She felt a stab of apprehension. There were no people about. It was too quiet. Suddenly she heard yells and the clang of steel at the front of the convoy. She sat up sharply. There was a hideous yell – a battle cry. She gripped Kaneshigé's dagger, ready to draw it, as footsteps pounded towards her.

Her palanquin swerved wildly, throwing her against one thin wall, then another. Then the flimsy wooden box crashed to the ground. Atsu's head hit something hard and the world went dark. For a moment when she came to she didn't know where she was. She struggled to sit up, catching her breath. Steel clanged right outside her palanquin and men bellowed at the tops of their voices.

Her hands shaking, she pulled out her dagger, expecting a blade to come slicing through the thin wooden wall. At the very least she would try to parry it. She pushed aside the window blind to find out what was going on, just as a snarling figure with crazed eyes and a shock of wild hair came flying straight towards her. A long steel blade flashed in his hand. He let out a shriek that set the hair on the back of her neck on end.

Suddenly she was back on the mountain reliving that fearful confrontation, with four scrawny youths circling her, their eyes burning in their grimy faces. Perhaps the attacks were connected. Perhaps this man knew which palanquin she was in. Perhaps it was her he was after.

Then a huge figure stepped into his path – Saigo. With a swing of his sword he deflected the blow and his blade bit down into the man's shoulder. Blood spurted like a fountain, splashing through the blind of the palanquin. Hot drops spattered Atsu's face and she started back.

The assailant staggered, eyes popping, jaw sagging, and dropped to his knees. Saigo wrenched his sword from his hand and thrust him to the ground. There were a couple more clangs from the front of the convoy and the sound of feet running away, then an uncanny silence. It had all happened so fast Atsu had hardly had a chance to breathe.

Shuddering, she wiped her face with her sleeve. Saigo was standing over his prisoner, gripping his arm. He held him as easily as if he were a child. His eyes were shining and his cheeks were flushed.

Atsu's ladies cowered together against the bamboo trellises of the close-packed houses. Women peered down from the upper balconies, passers-by gathered round to stare.

Lord Nariakira pushed through the crowd, checking to see if his men were hurt. He stood over Saigo's captive, scowling at him as if mystified that anyone would try to attack him. 'Fool. You chose the wrong enemy. What did you think to achieve by this?' He turned away, almost as if he was sorry for the man.

Blood still poured from the man's shoulder. His sword arm hung uselessly. His pock-marked face had turned a sickly shade of grey. He screwed it up in pain, staring sullenly at the ground. He was dressed in black like a ninja. Wiry hair bristled on his head, like a priest who has given up his calling and let his hair grow back.

He stared defiantly at Lord Nariakira. 'Traitor!' he shrieked, his face contorted with fury. 'You let in the pestilence. Those devils won't give up till they've killed us all and burnt our cities to ashes. They humiliate us and defy our ancient laws. They insult our sacred land.'

Lord Nariakira was pale with rage. 'What do you know of the world?' he hissed. 'Stick to praying, priest. If you had prayed harder you would have got rid of them by now.'

A couple of uniformed men in indigo-blue hakama and heavy jackets appeared, armed with swords and sturdy iron rods. Lord Nariakira sent Saigo to talk to them. As Saigo handed over his prisoner and the officers hustled him away, Atsu jumped out of her palanquin and ran over to Lord Nariakira.

'Father, who is that man?' she asked. 'He knew who you were. Why did he attack us?'

'Never mind,' he said, his face dark. 'We have to get on our way. We are nearly there.'

Several guards had been hurt. Saigo flagged down litters and Lord Nariakira ordered them to go back to Fushimi and send replacements in time for his return journey.

The bearers examined Atsu's palanquin for damage. There were a couple of splits in the woodwork but it was still usable. Haru ran over and wiped Atsu's face and checked her skirts and Atsu climbed back in. Her legs were shaking. Two attacks so far and they still had a long way to go before they got to Edo. These people seemed to know more of Lord Nariakira and his plans than she did. The City of Purple Hills and Crystal Streams didn't seem so enchanting any more.

12

Princess Sumiko of the House of Fujiwara

The convoy, even smaller than before, wound on through a maze of narrow streets lined with dark wooden houses. Atsu took deep breaths, tried to calm herself. She reminded herself that she was to meet her new adoptive father, Prince Konoé, Lord Nariakira's kinsman, one of the most powerful dignitaries in the city. But the horror of the attack still throbbed in her head. She peeked through the window, listened for ominous silences, but the streets seemed peaceful enough.

She had assumed the prince would live in a magnificent palace, but they stopped at a modest house with sand-plastered walls and a gateway with a shiny tiled roof. A tall man in court regalia was on his knees to greet them, flanked by ancient retainers.

Atsu had never before seen such an extraordinary-looking personage. Prince Konoé's long-jawed face was covered in white make-up like a woman's. His eyebrows were shaved off and he had two sooty ovals daubed high on his forehead and a circle of rouge on each cheek. He opened his scarlet lips in a smile, revealing a mouthful of black-painted teeth. Atsu assumed that this was how imperial courtiers always dressed but it was hard not to stare all the same.

'You are indeed most welcome, most welcome. Such a long way you have come.' He spoke in a sing-song voice in language so convoluted it was hard to understand him. He gave another simpering black-toothed smile but Atsu could tell by the sharp look in his eyes that he was no fool. He had a part to play. No doubt he could act the powerbroker or statesman just as well.

'I do hope Your Highness is in good health,' said Lord Nariakira. 'So gracious of Your Highness to condescend to receive us.'

Atsu had never known Lord Nariakira behave with the slightest deference to anyone. She realized that Prince Konoé was of higher rank even than him, which His Lordship no doubt found intensely galling.

'A little soon for the cherry blossom, alas,' said Prince Konoé with a vague flutter of a white-powdered hand. 'But we do have a few early blooms. Perhaps you will see them. So happy to see that you have brought good weather with you.'

'May I offer my humble congratulations on . . .' Lord Nariakira let his voice trail off politely.

Prince Konoé completed his sentence: '. . . on our new arrival, our young prince? Indeed, we are all delighted that the succession is assured.' He smiled at Atsu. 'We have had a very auspicious birth here, a little son for the Son of Heaven!' He gave a high-pitched laugh.

Atsu waited for Lord Nariakira to say something about the priest who had attacked them but he said not a word.

'And this is our new daughter,' said the prince. 'My goodness, what a beauty. Your Lordship told me of her loveliness but she far exceeds my expectations. She will be a most welcome addition to our household.' He turned to Atsu. 'Welcome, dear child. I am indeed charmed to meet you.'

Atsu bowed. She followed the prince around the veranda, keeping her eyes on the huge trousers flapping around his bony ankles. Prince Konoé was taller than Lord Nariakira and wore a high black hat tied under his chin, which made him look even taller and thinner, like a tree trunk. Perfume floated behind him as he walked – kyara, the rarest and most expensive of fragrances.

A disdainful maid ushered her to the women's side of the house, where an elegant woman with a kindly face was waiting on her knees to receive her. Princess Konoé too was painted like a doll. She was dressed in layer upon layer of silken robes and her hair was tied in a glossy black tail which hung to the ground, bound with ribbons. Beneath it all was a gentle round face with sparkling black eyes and a warm smile. Atsu felt at ease with her immediately.

'Welcome to our family, my dear,' trilled the princess. 'I have heard so much about you. My brother sings your praises.' She looked concerned. 'I hear you had a frightful experience on your way here. There is much disturbance at the moment. You must rest for a while. Come, see our teahouse. Let me make you tea. That will restore your spirits.'

She led the way through a garden to a tea ceremony hut with wattle walls and a thatched roof. Atsu followed as the princess stooped and crept through the small square entrance. Inside, a slender cherry trunk framed an alcove containing a vase holding a sprig of plum blossom. Above it hung a scroll with a circle brushed in a single flamboyant stroke.

'Sengai!' Atsu smiled as she recognized the work of the great Zen master.

Princess Konoé put her fingertips to the tatami and bowed. 'I can see we are going to be the best of friends.'

She knelt in front of the small brazier while the maid stoked the fire and brought in the tea ceremony utensils. Then she took a silk napkin from her sash and folded it with a few crisp movements. Atsu sat quietly, letting herself relax, enjoying the meditative atmosphere – the crackle of the charcoal, the gentle bubbling of the kettle, the maid's soft-shod feet slipping back and forth.

Princess Konoé picked up the cherry-wood dipper and ladled warm water into the tea bowl. She swished the bamboo whisk around, tipped out the water and dried the bowl.

She looked around at Atsu. 'These men,' she said, shaking her head. 'We are just pawns in their schemes. We have to do our best to unravel whatever it is they are plotting.' She shaped her mouth into a conspiratorial smile. 'No need to keep up pretences. We are all women here. As we know, the best way to deal with men is to do as the geisha do. Remember their precept: "A clever woman never lets a man know how clever she is."'

Atsu looked at her wide-eyed. She'd been imagining an afternoon of small talk. She hadn't expected Princess Konoé to speak so frankly. She wondered if she dared trust her. It would be foolish to speak too freely even to someone who seemed so kind. But she yearned to unburden her heart to another woman.

The water in the iron kettle bubbled softly. Princess Konoé ladled cold water into it from the urn and the murmur stopped. She sat back on her heels. 'Has my brother told you why you are here?' she asked.

Atsu nodded uncertainly. She still wasn't sure that these grand people really intended to adopt her or why they would wish to do so. 'I understand that Your Highness . . .'

Princess Konoé nodded. She smiled at Atsu sympathetically. 'I too was plucked from nowhere and sent soaring up in the world like a skylark. I was a country girl too. And here I am, married to Prince Konoé, the emperor's cousin, no less, and mother to his children – well, some of them.' She twisted her lips. There was something icy in her black eyes. Beneath the soft exterior there was a core of steel. 'These men. They will have their women – their concubines, their passing fancies, their brief flings with geisha and serving girls. We have a whole brood of children here. But I am the official mother to all of them.'

She lifted the lid of the tiny porcelain tea jar and a fresh sweet scent wafted out. 'Uji tea,' she said brightly. 'The finest in the land. Have you ever tried it?'

Atsu shook her head.

'An urn of this same tea is sent up to the Great Ruler in Edo every year. All other traffic has to make way for it.'

She picked up the cherry-wood scoop and put two measures of the brilliant green tea into the bowl, then tapped the scoop twice on the edge.

Atsu waited till the tiny sound had faded. 'When Lord Nariakira's father took you from your home to adopt you, did anyone tell you that you were to marry Prince Konoé?' she asked hesitantly.

Princess Konoé gave a snort of laughter. 'Of course not. I just packed my bags and went where I was sent. I have been eager to meet you. I want to help you understand the future that is being planned for you.'

She smiled. 'You know there was another of us Satsuma girls who rose even higher in the world than I, right to the very top? She became the consort of the present shogun's grandfather, Lord Ienari.'

'The present shogun?' Atsu was startled at the casual reference. 'You mean . . . the Great Ruler?'

'The Great Ruler, the Nobleman, whatever you choose to call him. He has many names. He who resides at the heart of that vast labyrinthine castle in Edo.'

An image flitted through Atsu's mind of a maggot curled at the heart of a rotten persimmon. She shuddered, hoping the strange, inappropriate thought was not a premonition. In the garden birds trilled and the scent of damp earth and fresh leaves wafted into the tiny house.

'Yes, his grandfather's consort was a Satsuma girl,' Princess Konoé said with a placid smile. If she had read Atsu's thoughts, she gave no sign of it. 'She began life as a person of no consequence, far lower in status than you. She was the daughter of a priest of the third rank. But she was beautiful and clever, like you. She was adopted by our famous great-grandfather, Shigehidé, the one who spoke Dutch and admired the Hollanders and their culture. I am sure my brother has spoken to you of him.

'Then the Konoés adopted her again to make her high enough in rank to be offered to the shogun in marriage. So you see she was my great-aunt, and my brother's. She was engaged to the shogun when they were four and they slept in the same room from the age of nine. Being the father-in-law of the shogun made our great-grandfather the most powerful prince in the land. He was a wise and benevolent man. He used his power well to benefit our people.'

Atsu's heart was thumping. She could hardly breathe. The path she was treading was the mirror image of this Shimazu princess's. Could that really be what Lord Nariakira had in mind for her – to marry the Great Ruler, the shogun, in order to gain power for himself? If so, all his scheming made sense. But surely that would be flying too high. From a height like that you could only come crashing down.

She laughed in disbelief then remembered where she was and

clapped her hands to her mouth. 'But . . . but what about her? What became of her?' she quavered.

'It is a great privilege to enter the palace,' said Princess Konoé. 'You are a bird in a gilded cage. No one ever hears from you again. You forget all about those of us left outside.'

Atsu stared at her, aghast. A bird in a gilded cage. That was not what she wanted to be.

'But the family did get the occasional piece of news,' Princess Konoé continued. 'I heard she had a son, who died when he was four, and later a miscarriage. She passed away nine years ago, at the age of seventy-two. Her name was Shigeko, Midai Shigeko. Midai is the title that they use in the palace for the shogun's consort.'

Atsu could feel Kaneshigé's dagger in her sash, pressing against her stomach. It comforted her. It reminded her of home. She felt as if she was picking up the pieces of a puzzle, arranging them one way, then another, trying to work out how they fitted together.

Marry the shogun, be queen of the realm? Atsu shook her head in disbelief. 'So you think His Lordship intends . . . But the Great Ruler has a wife. He is an adult, is he not?'

'That I cannot say. Palace matters stay within the palace,' said Princess Konoé, ladling hot water into the tea bowl. She took the bamboo whisk and beat the tea to a foam.

'Do not let me raise your hopes,' she added quietly, drawing a circle in the foam with the whisk. 'It is best not to worry too much about my brother's plans. He is laying out his cards, checking his hand, working out possibilities. It would be disastrous to reveal anything until everything is settled. You did not even need to meet us. He dealt with the paperwork for your adoption by letter long ago. But he wanted us to be friends. My husband has chosen a new name for you. I'll leave him to tell you what it is.'

The maid passed the tea bowl to Atsu. Atsu raised it in both hands and bowed, inhaling the fresh aroma, then turned the bowl so as not to touch her lips to the design on the front and took a sip of the foamy liquid. It was rich and mildly bitter with a faintly musty aftertaste.

'I have had two disturbing experiences on my way here,' she said.

She felt safe with Princess Konoé. She yearned to confide in her. 'You heard about the ambush we suffered. I was attacked in Kyushu too. My bearers threatened me and tried to extort money from me. I wasn't hurt and I decided not to tell His Lordship. Do you think there may be people who want to stop us getting to Edo, even kill me? Or were those all just bandits?'

Princess Konoé wrinkled her brow. 'Who can say? At least you haven't been hurt. I will speak to my brother. He will take precautions. You are far too precious for anything to happen to you.'

The princess smiled at her. 'I am glad we are friends,' she said softly, pouring hot water into the bowl and beginning to prepare another cup. 'Now then. Supposing I could grant you a wish, just one. What would it be?'

It was the last thing Atsu was expecting her to ask. She'd blurted out the answer before she'd had time to think whether it was wise to confide in this kindly soft-spoken woman.

'There's someone in Ibusuki,' she murmured, tears in her eyes.

She gasped as she realized what she had done. She wondered if she'd been led into a trap. Princess Konoé had managed to persuade her to let down her defences. It was madness ever to reveal one's private feelings. If word got back to Lord Nariakira he could have Kaneshigé killed if he thought Atsu's feelings for him would interfere with his plans. But it was too late. She'd said the words.

The charcoal in the brazier crackled and the kettle hummed as the water began to bubble again. To Atsu's surprise a wistful look crossed Princess Konoé's face. 'When I came here to marry the prince there was someone I cared for too,' she said quietly.

Atsu breathed a sigh of relief. Perhaps she could trust her after all. Perhaps she really was an ally.

'I have not forgotten after all these years,' said Princess Konoé. Her face grew stern and she straightened her back. 'But you come to care for the person you marry far more than anyone else. When you get older you will learn that your parents know best. Whatever my brother has in mind for you will be for the best, I am sure. After all, he has made you an imperial princess now!'

Again she shaped her mouth into a conspiratorial smile. 'Now I have a surprise for you.'

She rapped on the ground with her fan and the door slid open. A woman was kneeling outside. She was the embodiment of a Miyako lady, in voluminous multi-layered robes with her hair, like Princess Konoé's, drawn back into a long tail. Everything about her was perfect – her make-up, her clothes, her hands, right down to her delicate pink nails. Her face was a smooth oval, her shaved eyebrows lifted, giving her an air of faint amusement, and her mouth delicately pursed. But what Atsu noticed most was her sharp black eyes. At first she kept them demurely lowered but when she raised them Atsu had the feeling that she could see right through her to her innermost soul.

'This is Lady Ikushima,' said Princess Konoé, beaming as if she'd pulled off the most wonderful conjuring trick. 'She is my chief lady-in-waiting. We have been together for years. She will come with you. Whatever you need to know about the imperial court and the Edo court, she will teach you. She is all packed and ready to go. I shall miss her enormously.'

She leaned forward and lowered her voice, smiling mischievously. 'Ikushima is rather famous in our household. She spends money like water. But she has the most extraordinary insight. She can fathom almost anyone's secret intentions.'

Atsu narrowed her eyes, wondering what she would have to do that would require a lady-in-waiting with such superhuman skills. At least this all-knowing lady was to be her ally. She would make a fearsome enemy. She wondered what Haru would think of the new addition to their household.

Princess Konoé ushered Atsu to the men's section of the house. As they approached they heard raised voices. 'We have had incessant ill fortune recently – bad harvests, peasant uprisings, priests stirring up disorder, not to mention all the usual gamblers and thieves and arsonists.' It sounded as if Prince Konoé was discussing the attack their convoy had suffered on the way.

'And to top it all those damned barbarians, scaring everyone half out of their wits.' It was Lord Nariakira's voice.

'Presuming to intrude on our sacred land,' snarled Prince Konoé. 'There has been serious unrest ever since they appeared. People are angry that they have not been taught a lesson and sent on their way.'

The two men fell silent as the women came in. His Lordship's gifts to the prince – glass vases, bowls and goblets, even an exquisite glass teapot – were laid out, each on its own small table. With their sharp facets and brilliant colours they lit up the musty room that smelt faintly of incense, with its muted sunlight filtering through paper screens, its glimmering candles and ancient scroll hanging on the sand-coloured wall of the alcove. The sparkling glass seemed to belong to another world.

Prince Konoé had his black-toothed smile back in place. Fluttering his long white hands he greeted Atsu with a torrent of flowery language and presented her with bolts of exquisite Miyako silk and an urn of Uji tea. Then he announced her new title. She would still be Princess Atsu of the House of Shimazu. But she was now also Her Imperial Highness Princess Sumiko of the House of Fujiwara, daughter of Prince Tadahiro Konoé and a member of the imperial family, directly related to the Son of Heaven. She too dwelt above the clouds.

Not that she felt the tiniest bit different. Inside herself she was still Atsu and would continue to be Atsu, she thought, no matter what grand title she put on. Her new title was of no more significance than a new set of clothes, she told herself. But she knew that it was.

Imperial Princess Sumiko . . . As the conversation washed over her, a smile flitted across Atsu's face. She would follow Princess Konoé's advice, ask no questions till she had a better idea of where this journey was taking her and of what Lord Nariakira intended for her. In any case she had no choice but to go along with it. It might even turn out to be an adventure.

13

The addition of Ikushima and her retinue swelled the already vast procession to bursting point, as if a snake had swallowed a pig. That lady travelled in nearly as much splendour as if she were a princess herself, in a magnificent palanquin carried on the shoulders of liveried bearers, with her ladies travelling behind her in their own palanquins and their attendants and maids walking alongside.

But Lord Nariakira seemed not remotely concerned by the enormous number of extra rooms required or the extra cost. When they had a moment together Atsu raised her eyebrows and glanced towards Ikushima's glittering palanquin. 'At least she does not insist on travelling with her own bath and bath water like an imperial princess,' His Lordship said. 'The day is not far off when you will be demanding that for yourself, my dear.'

To Atsu's surprise she soon began to feel as if she'd known Ikushima her entire life. That shrewd lady had a knack of making everyone feel comfortable. She made a point of befriending Haru and dispelling her fears of being supplanted in Atsu's affections. Soon even Haru was seeking her out and confiding in her. With Ikushima around Atsu felt nothing could go wrong.

Now, in the evenings when Atsu joined Lord Nariakira for a glass of saké, Ikushima was always there too. It seemed she and Lord Nariakira had a great deal to discuss. Atsu began to wonder if the real purpose of their detour to Miyako had not been for her to meet Prince and Princess Konoé or even to receive her new name but simply to pick up Ikushima.

There were sixteen days still to go before they arrived in Edo. From Miyako they followed the Eastern Sea Road, the great highway that led east over the mountains and along the coast, taken by lords and their cavalcades, pilgrims, travellers, artists and poets and celebrated in innumerable woodblock prints. They stopped to see sights legendary in history and literature – famous temples, battlefields, scenes which had inspired poetry – staying sometimes in a local lord's palace, sometimes at a grand inn.

As they travelled east the cherry trees burst into bloom, clothing the hills and fields and mountain slopes in pink and white blossom. The road was immaculately swept, planted with cypresses and pines at precisely measured intervals that marked the distance they'd travelled and how far they had to go. They crossed rivers where teams of men carried Atsu's palanquin, holding it high in the air, wading through fast-flowing water up to their armpits. At other rivers there were bridges or beautiful lacquered boats to ferry them across.

Atsu counted the days left on the road. She wanted to stretch out the journey, enjoy every last moment of it. She'd been so excited about going to Edo but the closer they got, the more she dreaded it.

They were high on a hillside one day, winding along a cliff. As they rounded a bend a dazzlingly white peak came into view, so huge and so bright the pale-blue sky looked dark beside it. It was almost too perfect to be real. She gasped. 'Mount Fuji!'

The whole procession stopped to gaze. Atsu had seen it many times in woodblock prints but nothing could match the sight of the sacred mountain itself. It brought tears to her eyes. She thought of Kaneshigé and the words she'd written to him: 'If only we could meet where the roads cross, in the shadow of Mount Fuji.' She looked around, half expecting to see a golden-skinned lad strolling towards her along the mountain road. For a moment the image was so real that when there was no one there she felt a shock of disappointment. She wished she could smuggle a message to him. But they were a world apart now, separated by months of travel, and getting further every day.

As the convoy moved on she glimpsed the mountain. Sometimes

it was reflected in the mirror-like surface of the water filling the flooded paddy fields, sometimes between the pine trees that lined the highway, sometimes soaring out of the plain, a solitary peak. Then they were trooping along in the foothills, right in its shadow. For a couple of days they skirted it, craning up to gaze at its gleaming white slopes.

They'd crossed the steep mountain pass at Hakoné, gone through the border post where everyone, even Lord Nariakira, had to open the door of their palanquin so the guards could check that no one was being smuggled through, and forded the river Sakawa at Odawara. There was one day left to go before they reached Edo. When Atsu pushed back the blind they were winding high above Edo Bay. She saw blue water, smelt salt, heard the cries of seagulls and the crash of waves above the tramp of the marchers' feet.

Suddenly from up ahead came a shout. It passed down the line and the whole convoy – rickety palanquins, marching samurai, nobles on horses, ladies, attendants, right down to the porters – piled into each other as they came to an abrupt halt. Atsu's palanquin hit the ground with a bone-jarring bang. She'd slid open the door and jumped out before her attendants could rush over to help.

She looked around in bewilderment. Nobles and ladies-in-waiting climbed from their palanquins, riders jumped off their horses, porters dropped their burdens. Everyone, even Ikushima, usually so composed, had completely forgotten the usual courtesies and class distinctions. They mingled together, pushing each other out of the way, charging in a great mob for the top of the headland, shouting in a wild jumble of noise.

Fumbling in her haste, Atsu tied on her straw sandals. The crowd drew back to let her pass and she picked up her skirts, eager to find out what all the fuss was about. She raced up the hillside as fast as she could, panting. The people at the top of the hill now stood silent, all staring in the same direction. Then a great hubbub burst out.

Atsu had not even reached the crest of the hill when she saw it, the strange, appalling, fearsome sight that had caused the commotion – spindly black masts flying alien flags, rising into the sky higher than the hill itself. For a moment her heart stopped. She realized what everyone had been saying, the word that had brought the entire procession to a halt: 'Tojin! Barbarians!'

She looked down on the bay, calm and blue, with the road to Edo winding along the side, lined with restaurants and teahouses. There was the harbour bobbing with boats and vessels, large and small. And there, a little way out from the shore, where the water was deepest, was a line of eight huge ships, like dragons preparing to pounce, entirely blocking the bay. They loomed over the harbour as large as mountains, casting great shadows, like vast floating cities darkening the sky. Black smoke puffed from the funnels like a dragon's fiery breath or Sakurajima's eruptions of ash.

Even though she'd heard about them, even though she'd seen them in pictures and silver prints, in her heart of hearts Atsu hadn't really believed that the western invaders and their ships existed. They might exist in some other world, like the gods, or some other country, but surely not here, not in their own sacred land. It was simply impossible. But here they were, solid and real as boulders, like eight great islands, part of the landscape. Nothing would budge them until they chose to go away.

The sight sent a shock through her. She closed her eyes and rubbed them and opened them again but the ships were still there, far larger and more menacing than she could ever have imagined. It was not just the size of them. They were not wooden like Japanese ships, they were iron monsters spouting fire. They dwarfed the flotillas of launches and boats and little ships with single sails. Even the ship Lord Nariakira was building back at Sakurajima was a child's toy in comparison.

His Lordship was standing at the top of the headland with Toshikyo and his other pages and retainers gathered around him. His face was grim but his eyes glittered with excitement. He was peering through his spy glass, his 'mirror of distant hopes'. Without a word he handed it to her and she fumbled with the end, hands shaking, panting with excitement. At first she couldn't see the ships clearly then suddenly they came into focus.

'The size of them!' she gasped, turning and beaming at Lord Nariakira.

He shook his head. 'How could we ever have imagined we could fight an enemy like that?' he growled.

Atsu put the glass to her eye again, scouring the masts, the rigging, the flags, the vast flanks of the ships. They didn't have dragon faces like the ones she'd seen in the woodblock prints Yamada had shown them, but there were huge black funnels spouting smoke. Little boats shuttled to and fro and alien sounds floated across the water – bells ringing, shouts in a foreign tongue, snatches of music, wild and rhythmic. It was frightening yet alluring. A whole new world was opening up before her eyes.

'Fools!' barked Lord Nariakira. He took off his travelling hat and threw it on the ground.

Atsu jumped. She'd been so caught up in the new vistas she was seeing she'd almost forgotten where she was.

'We are governed by fools! They should have held off till we got here. All they had to do was wait a couple more days. The fools caved in. They signed. They have spent months wrangling – those who argue for war and those who argue for caution. And now, just as I feared, the foreigners have taken us by surprise again and once again we enter negotiations unprepared and without having agreed our policy. And the result? The barbarians get their treaty. The Great Ruler himself approved it. I do not even know what we have agreed but by all accounts we have given them everything they asked for – ports to dock in, promises of more to come. Such humiliation, such disgraceful weakness. And to sign without the agreement of myself – the Prince of Satsuma – or any of the great lords. It is an outrage! These barbarians, allow them a foothold and they will sweep through our land like a plague of locusts, as they have in China. They are a pestilence wherever they go. They bring nothing but ruin. It is intolerable. They have breached the land of the gods.'

He groaned and spread his big hands. 'But now I see those monsters I concede that the so-called wise men, our government in Edo, had little choice. We cannot defeat them. You see those cannons trained on the shore? They could destroy this little town and the whole great city of Edo whenever they wanted to. With might like that we had no choice but to negotiate.'

Atsu gazed in awe at the vast ships and the cannons, huge and grey and menacing, that studded the hulls like teeth. But most of all she was interested in the creatures manning them. She wanted to see these weird inhuman beings with her own eyes. There were so many of them, running around the decks like ants and clambering up and down the rigging.

She twisted the end again and again, focused more and more tightly until she could see them perfectly – their strange clothes, red or blue, their tight white trousers, their gawky build, even the hair on their faces, some red, some straw-coloured. She watched, fascinated, as they scurried around in their garish outfits, turning the end of the spyglass yet more, trying to see if they really did have bright blue eyeballs, like demons, as everyone said. Even at this distance she could gauge how different they were from any human being she had ever seen.

'People say they smell horrible, like animals,' she whispered. 'I heard they even lift their legs like dogs when they . . .'

Lord Nariakira looked at her, slapped his hand on his thigh and burst out laughing. 'Their diet is different from ours,' he said. 'They eat cows and pigs and from what I hear almost never bathe. But Holland men, for the most part, seem quite civilized.'

His face darkened again. 'It is intolerable that they should invade our country, use the threat of violence to force us to do their bidding. They will be leaving now they have got what they want, but not for long. Now they have established a foothold they will be back, and in far greater numbers. The only way we can stand against them is if we have ships as powerful as theirs, and as big and well equipped. At least the government has seen sense on that. They will soon lift the ban on shipbuilding. They have to. It is a matter of national security now. My men are working night and day, building twelve sailing vessels and three steamers, all fully armed and equipped. I have a warship ready to launch and I have ordered a steamship from the Hollanders, the most powerful they have. How else are we to defend ourselves against an enemy like that?'

For the longest time no one could move. People stood spellbound on every rock and stone and patch of grass, gazing at the monstrous intruders. The timid crouched behind bushes and trees, peering out through the branches. Atsu stood with Lord Nariakira, staring boldly at the ships, amused that the creatures on deck could perhaps see her as clearly as she could them.

She thought of Kaneshigé and tears came to her eyes. Strange and disturbing though the sight was, it was also thrilling and amazing. She wished he could have been here, that they could have witnessed this momentous sight together.

They reached Edo the following day, travelling along the coast in full view of the ships, gazing fearfully at those great black intruders, emissaries from another world. That night they didn't go to the main Satsuma palace. It was too near the bay, too near those fearsome ships. Instead they went to His Lordship's second mansion, a safe distance away.

The mansion soon became home. Atsu had to learn to be Sumiko, princess of the imperial court at Miyako. She still hadn't fully fathomed what part she would have to play in protecting the country against the barbarian threat or the real purpose of her extraordinary promotion, from country girl to member of the imperial family. But she did know that there would be a part for her, and when Lord Nariakira was ready to reveal it she would have to perform it to the best of her ability.

From time to time she tried to persuade him to give her a few clues. But he always just smiled his blandest, most impenetrable smile and said grandly, 'In the fullness of time, my dear, when the time is ripe.'

PART II

Aboard the Jewelled Palanquin

14

Atsu's futon pitched like a raft in a maelstrom. There was a groan like thunder as if the bowels of the earth were being wrenched apart. In a trice she was wide awake. She sprang to her feet. The tatami was heaving.

'Earthquake! The brazier!' she screamed. The wooden brazier, chock-full of glowing embers, was reeling to and fro. She raced over, grabbed the iron kettle on top of it and hurled water on to it, sending an explosion of smoke hissing towards the bamboo ceiling. One of the women snuffed out the candles, plunging the room into darkness, as a tobacco box tumbled across the floor, scattering the rice-straw tatami with ash. Others grabbed precious kimonos and flung them over the cinders.

The shaking grew stronger. The walls creaked and chunks of plaster flew about like pebbles. An antique chest crashed over. Candlesticks teetered, tables jigged, bookcases toppled, spewing out books, tubs of make-up flew about.

Attendants raced for the rain doors and shoved them open. Cold night air flooded in, filling the room with smells of burning and sounds of screaming and crashing above the thunder of the earth.

Atsu snatched up her quilt and dived across the heaving floor. Cats darted under her feet, lamps and tables flew into her path, kimonos and futons tangled round her ankles. Then a lintel came crashing down on her. She struggled to escape, shoving at the heavy wood, but she couldn't make it budge. A couple of maids rushed over and lifted it and she pulled herself out.

With no time to check if she was hurt, she threw herself towards the open doors. Hands grabbed her and helped her out on to the veranda. Men and women in night robes, quilts wrapped around their shoulders, scrambled across the gardens to the bamboo grove where the ancient roots bound the soil together. Everyone knew the drill.

There were screams from inside the building. Atsu looked around sharply. She hadn't checked that all her women were safe. 'There are people still in there!' she shouted.

Her attendants snatched at her sleeve, yelling, 'To the bamboo grove, madam. Quickly, run!' She wrenched free of them and plunged back into the quaking room. In the murky light she made out a figure pinned under a beam. It was Yasu, the young attendant who did Atsu's make-up. Her face was twisted in pain.

Atsu pulled her quilt over her head and clambered towards her, tripping over futons and wooden struts and upended tatami mats. The convulsions were growing stronger and more frequent. The walls trembled and bulged. The roar was deafening. Feverishly she grabbed one end of the beam and tried to lift it, bracing herself as the floor tilted and heaved. Another beam came crashing down and Atsu frowned and took a deep breath, choking on the dust and plaster. She put her shoulder to the beam and tried to lever it up.

A bevy of firemen in leather jackets and helmets burst out of the clouds of dust. They lifted the beam, picked up Yasu as if she was a child and hustled Atsu out as the ceiling thundered down behind them.

'My lady, you forget yourself.' Ikushima was in her night robes, her oval face contorted with fury. Atsu had never before known her lose her composure. She grabbed Atsu's sleeve and pulled her on to the quaking veranda. 'What can you be thinking of? You must never put yourself at risk. That attendant is not worth your notice. She is far beneath you in rank.'

Atsu swung round. 'We're all people,' she shouted above the uproar. She couldn't control the quiver in her voice. 'Yasu's just as important as me, more so. No one else saw her. No one was going to help her.'

'After all I have tried to teach you, you put yourself at risk,' Ikushima hissed, her lips trembling. 'This is not the way a princess behaves.'

'I never asked to be a princess,' Atsu retorted.

'You have a great destiny in front of you,' snapped Ikushima. 'We cannot afford to lose you. Look at you, the state of you. Where is your dignity? Where are your maids?' She grabbed at the skirts of Atsu's nightwear, shaking off the dust. Atsu pushed her aside and turned away, close to tears.

The quake stopped as abruptly as it had started. Screams and wails filled the sudden silence. Horses neighed and whinnied, flames crackled and tiles slid off the roof and crashed to the ground, sending razor-sharp shards spinning into the air. Most of the buildings and warehouses in the compound were ablaze. Smoke billowed and huge flames leapt above the city as fire bells jangled frantically.

A blaze of light exploded behind the castle, framing it against the night sky. Atsu started, her heart pounding. Explosion followed deafening explosion in an infernal fireworks display. Somewhere nearby an entire arsenal had gone up.

Atsu squeezed Ikushima's hand. It was madness to argue at a time like this. For a moment a look of dread hollowed the older woman's face. The same thought was in both their minds. The gods were punishing them for allowing barbarians to set foot on their sacred land. In the face of such cosmic activity, human beings counted for nothing.

The veranda began to creak and heave again as the planks ground against each other and the supports snapped from their joists. The earth groaned like a wounded animal, an almost human sound. Atsu stared in horror. The ground was rippling like water. Branches flailed and a huge tree swayed and crashed down.

'Hurry, madam,' pleaded a voice. Before she could move, someone had lifted her bodily off the veranda and whisked her away from the building. A moment later the roof came slamming down like the lid of a chest. There was a boom like thunder and a whoosh of wind that sent everyone flying. Atsu landed on her back. She sprawled, gasping and breathless, smelling the soil, hearing the crackle of flames as acrid black smoke filled the sky.

By the time she had picked herself up, the elegant mansion with its verandas and rain doors and exquisite gold screens had disappeared as if there'd never been a building there at all. The roof lay flat on the ground in a cloud of dust, engulfed in a mountain of kindling and broken wood. The veranda where they'd all been standing was gone. Faint cries came from inside.

There was no time to stop and stare. The ground was writhing. Atsu realized that she hadn't seen Haru, who slept in her own chamber now with her own ladies.

'Haru, where's Haru?' she shrieked.

'Everyone's in the bamboo grove, madam,' panted one of her ladies, a bony young woman with huge eyes called Chiyo. She'd grabbed an armful of kimonos, then dropped them when the roof came down and was running around picking them up. 'Don't worry,' she added, peering over the top of an enormous pile of silks. 'The fire brigade is taking care of everything.'

Men in leather jackets and helmets swarmed over the burning buildings, pumping water from hosepipes, tearing down walls to stop the fire spreading, flapping giant fans to beat back the flames.

Atsu raced towards the bamboo grove, hoping to find Haru there. The ground rolled like jelly under her feet. A fissure gaped in front of her. She took a breath and leapt across.

The grove was crowded with people, hollow-eyed, their faces ghastly in the light of the flames. Bamboos creaked and swayed but the ground was firm. Even the tea ceremony hut in the middle of the grove was intact.

Shivering, Atsu crouched down and tugged her quilt around her. She pulled a couple of her ladies close to her and wrapped it around their shoulders too. She felt the heat from the burning buildings, saw the glare of the fires, heard the crackling and the firemen's shouts. It was too dark to see who was missing. All she could do was hope that everyone had made it safely out of the buildings.

Finally the shaking stopped and people started to venture out of the bamboo grove. They stared at the blackened ruins that had been their home. Most of the residences, warehouses, barracks and schools were charred wrecks. Even the sturdy clay-walled storehouses where the treasures were kept had crumpled. It really did look as if the world had ended. It would take months to rebuild.

One by one Lord Nariakira's concubines and their entourages appeared, bedraggled and dirty, their glossy coiffures now tangled knots, clutching dolls, obis, memorial sticks, whatever they'd managed to snatch as they'd fled the buildings. Atsu asked each one if they'd seen Haru and her ladies, but no one had.

To complete their misery it started to rain, first a few drops, then a mighty downpour. Atsu and Ikushima and their ladies-in-waiting took shelter in one of the buildings still standing. They were frozen and drenched. Messengers arrived with news that a tsunami had swept in, swallowing up huge sections of the coast.

Atsu had been in Edo for a year and a half. She was living in Lord Nariakira's middle mansion, a good way from the shore. She wondered fearfully what had happened to his main mansion on the coast and the third mansion where his consort and little Princess Teru lived. His Lordship had gone back to Kagoshima with his entourage months earlier, as he did every other year, leaving Atsu behind. He'd completed his tour of duty in Edo and was eager to oversee his shipyards and armaments factories.

No doubt the chamberlains had already sent messengers galloping off to break the news to him. He was not due to return for another six months. She wondered if he would come back early.

It had been the most dreadful of years. Everyone had thought that once the American barbarians sailed away life would return to normal. But little more than seven months had gone by when another fleet arrived, this time from Russia. At least they hadn't threatened Edo. They'd dropped anchor at Shimoda, where the fishermen lived who had first seen the black ships. While the Americans had been thin and scrawny, the Russians were giants with arms like tree trunks and big black beards. It was said that the whores of Shimoda had quadrupled their prices and were making their fortunes.

These new barbarians too had refused to leave until the government had signed a treaty, allowing them to bring in merchant ships and trade. That was when the gods had lost patience. Not long after the ships arrived, there had been two huge earthquakes that devastated the emperor's city of Miyako and unleashed a tidal wave which flattened Shimoda and destroyed the Russians' entire fleet, followed by epidemics, deadly storms, downpours and famine. The previous day water had spouted out of the earth all over Edo and there'd been ominous groans from under the ground and eerie flashes in the night sky. And now Edo too had suffered punishment. No one dared imagine what the gods would do next.

With the mansion destroyed, Atsu and Ikushima and their chief ladies were billeted in temples on higher ground, which had suffered less damage. As they wound through the city in their palanquins on their way to their new homes, Atsu stared in disbelief at the mobs filling the streets, lugging carts laden with boxes, furniture, whatever they'd managed to salvage. Others were doggedly clearing the main roads and starting to rebuild. Much of the city had been reduced to rubble. Chunks of roofs and walls and buildings were piled up like a child's toys thrown aside – and that was in the wealthy upper city, where the clan lords had their mansions. The convoy didn't pass through the crowded downtown districts. Atsu dreaded to think what had happened there. She'd heard that thousands of people had died in fires or been crushed or swept away and thousands more had been injured.

And there was still no sign of Haru. Dreadful though it was, Atsu thought, perhaps it was time to accept that she and her ladies were dead. There was nothing left but to mourn them.

15

*Nineteenth day of the second month, Year of the Dragon, Ansei 3,
a yang fire year (26 March 1856)*

'Beautiful!' cooed Ikushima. 'The white satin. Subtle, understated, perfect for spring. An excellent choice. Your taste is impeccable, my lady.'

Atsu smiled as Ikushima ran an expert hand across the quilted mantle. With its motif of plum blossoms, camellias and gold and silver clouds it was certainly gorgeous. But it was Ikushima who had chosen it, not her. She was annoyed to find herself flushing with pleasure. It was unnerving how easily she was taken in by this Miyako lady's smooth-tongued flattery.

Ever since the earthquake Ikushima had been Atsu's constant companion, always at her side, always kind and sympathetic. But there was a sliver of ice in her heart. It was her job to be kind. She was paid to be Atsu's friend.

Haru now, Haru had been like a sister. Atsu was bereft without her. She missed her smiling face, her stern frown when Atsu did something she disapproved of, her banter and merry laughter. They'd been together since Atsu was a child. Atsu had confided in her, shared her secrets with her, and she'd kept every one. She'd known about Kaneshigé from the start, had been Atsu's co-conspirator when she slipped out to see him. Ikushima and the ladies-in-waiting had only ever known Princess Sumiko. Haru had known Okatsu, the carefree daughter of the Lord of

Ibusuki. With her loss, Atsu's last link to her past was gone.

Most terrible of all was that Haru had never been found. There was no body, nothing. She and her ladies had simply disappeared, like hundreds of others in the Satsuma compound alone. Atsu couldn't bear to think of her trapped under the rubble, in pain, calling out with no one to hear. She told herself that maybe she'd escaped and run away. Whenever a letter came she unrolled it eagerly. Whenever a door slid open she jumped up, half expecting to see Haru's smiling face.

It was a fine day in early spring. More than four months had passed since the earthquake. The gods' purge, it seemed, had been effective. There'd been no more sightings of barbarians, no sign of them at all. Everyone hoped they would finally be left in peace to get on with their lives.

Lord Nariakira's three mansions had been rebuilt with impressive speed. Beams and pillars had been erected, verandas and entrance halls built, rain doors slotted in, sliding inner doors fitted, tatami mats set in place, even more splendid than before. Carved lintels shone, newly installed screens and coffered ceilings glimmered with Satsuma gold.

Atsu had moved to the main mansion, near the coast, at the Edo end of the Eastern Sea Road. Coached by Ikushima, she'd lost her southern burr. She spoke Miyako dialect with her maids and Edo court language with a fetching Miyako lilt with everyone else. She'd learned to play the blue-blooded imperial princess to perfection. She no longer ran like a tomboy but glided with tiny pigeon-toed steps. She practised tea ceremony, flower arrangement and the incense ceremony in the mannered imperial style and plucked out elegant melodies on her koto. Sometimes she even dreamed like a princess.

She had not forgotten what Princess Konoé had hinted at. She had no doubt that she was being groomed for some destiny far higher than simply to be a lady-in-waiting at the women's palace – to be a concubine at the very least. The real question was when it would happen. Living in the mansion, she still had a degree of freedom.

Despite Ikushima's best efforts, it was all too easy for Atsu to forget she was a princess and go back to being herself again. Sometimes she even managed to sneak out of the mansion for a gallop on one of Lord Nariakira's beautiful horses. And every day – more like a fiery samurai woman than a languid princess – she sparred with her halberd with its long handle and curving, razor-sharp blade.

And today Lord Nariakira was finally coming back. Everyone was excited, Atsu more than anyone. She hadn't seen him for more than a year. She was full of anticipation, yet fearful too. Perhaps he would finally tell her what all this training was for, what destiny he had lined up for her.

The vanguard of the vast procession had started arriving a couple of days earlier – quartermasters, scribes, cooks and their assistants, lower servants, upper servants, officials and hundreds of porters, some leading horses laden with baggage, others carrying trunks and boxes and baskets, with battalions of samurai in front and behind, all marching into the vast courtyard in orderly ranks. The first battalions were already settling into their barracks, the first contingents of horses being watered and stabled.

Atsu pulled a scarf over her head to conceal her face and slipped out to watch Lord Nariakira and his entourage approaching. The procession advanced in a cloud of dust, filling the road from one side to the other, the heralds strutting in front, kicking up their heels and twirling their pikes, followed by ranks of liveried porters carrying His Lordship's personal baggage in lacquered boxes on their shoulders. Atsu felt a thrill of pride to be part of such a splendid dynasty.

She'd run back before the first marchers had reached the mansion. Another couple of hours passed before Lord Nariakira arrived and the whole household – Atsu, his concubines, their entourages and the rest of the staff – lined up in order of rank to welcome him home.

He greeted them then disappeared. He needed to talk to the estate managers about the rebuilding, visit his other mansions and check the damage there and see Her Ladyship, his consort, and little

Princess Teru. It would undoubtedly be several days before he had time to visit Atsu.

So it was a shock when a message arrived that he intended to pay his respects to Princess Atsu in her quarters that very afternoon.

Outside the cherry trees were coming into bloom. The maids pushed back the paper screens and the pale spring sunshine poured in.

Atsu's ladies-in-waiting helped her into layers of kimonos, tying them in place with ribbons, then wrapped the stiff brocade obi around her waist, pulling so tight she could hardly breathe. Finally Ikushima lifted the white satin mantle from its lacquered gold stand and wrapped it around Atsu's shoulders. She tugged the collar elegantly low at the back and spread the long train in a half circle, opening the coat to show off the red lining.

Chiyo brought tea in a porcelain cup on a stand. She had become one of Atsu's favourites since the earthquake, when she'd saved several of Atsu's best kimonos. Yasu, fully recovered from her ordeal that day, tucked in a strand of Atsu's perfumed hair and brushed her lips with safflower paste.

Atsu gazed at the painted vision in the mirror, barely visible beneath all her kimonos. Only the white hands poking from the sleeves belonged to her. For a moment she was overcome by sadness. She wished she could have been back in Kyushu, sparring in the gardens of her father's modest mansion in Ibusuki, running down to the beach to hug Kaneshigé or galloping across the purple slopes of Kirishima with her hair blowing in the wind. She took a breath, drew herself up, straightened her shoulders. She was Princess Sumiko now. Whatever Lord Nariakira had in mind for her, she had to be ready.

The door slid open to reveal a chamberlain on her knees outside. 'His Lordship! In the reception room!' she announced.

In the reception room? Already? Anyone else of such high rank would have had his arrival announced well in advance so the women could line up on their knees for the formal welcome. He wouldn't just burst into Atsu's private quarters without warning. But Lord Nariakira never stood on ceremony.

The maids were all in a flurry. Even Ikushima's hands were shaking as she checked her face in the mirror and patted her immaculate hair.

His Lordship had plumped himself down cross-legged beside the brazier and was puffing on a long-stemmed silver pipe. He was alone, at home among his women, without a single male attendant, not even his page.

Atsu glided in in her regalia, taking tiny pigeon-toed steps, keeping her head demurely lowered, her hands lightly brushing her thighs, exactly as a grand lady was supposed to comport herself. He looked up, beaming, and she laughed and lifted her skirts and twirled around, took a few skipping steps. 'So what do you think? Do I look like a princess?'

'You make a perfect princess, my dear,' he said, laughing. 'You have grown up. It is a treat to see you. You are more beautiful than ever.'

He shifted on to his knees, put his hands to the ground and bowed. It was unheard of for a great lord, let alone one as proud as Lord Nariakira, to bow to a mere woman.

'Father, you're teasing me. Why such formality?' Atsu cried.

'You are an imperial princess, my dear.'

Atsu blushed hotly. 'Whatever I am, it's you who made me, Father.'

He threw back his head and gave a roar of laughter. 'Made you? No, my dear, all I did was recognize your qualities. It was excellent luck that Prince Konoé appreciated them too. You are his daughter now, not mine. You are far above me in rank. Birth has nothing to do with it. You were made to rule.'

Atsu studied his face. In the year since she'd seen him last, he'd grown older. His genial, rather pouchy features were thinner and his chin had become a little jowly. He usually wore plain cotton garments to relax at home but today he was in huge-shouldered robes with a cord looped across his broad chest and pleated hakama trousers, as if he were on a formal visit. His eyes were hooded. She could tell immediately there was something going on.

The maids carried in trays of tea in porcelain cups. Lord Nariakira took a sip. His face darkened. 'It has been a terrible time for you, my dear. So many people dead, so many people to be mourned. I hear you lost Haru too. I am very sorry to learn that.'

Atsu pictured Haru's round smiling face and dabbed her eyes, oblivious to the thick make-up that coated her cheeks.

'It's been a dreadful time for everyone,' she said with a sigh. 'We are still suffering aftershocks. And Kagoshima? Is everyone well at Crane Castle?'

'We did not feel even a tremor. Nothing. Sakurajima still sends up black ash. The plum trees were in blossom when I left.'

'And Lady Umé and Lady Také?' Atsu asked, remembering the two sour-faced concubines.

'Both well. They send greetings. Your parents send greetings too.'

'People are saying it was the barbarians that caused the earthquake,' Atsu said hesitantly. 'The gods needed to cleanse the pollution they brought.'

Lord Nariakira frowned and looked at her hard. 'But you, my dear, you do not believe such nonsense, do you? It would be madness to let down our guard. The so-called "barbarians" have not been purged or cleansed. Far from it. They have gone away to gather their forces, that is all. We have certainly not seen the last of them.

'I received disturbing news when I was in Kagoshima. Commissioner Hayashi – an excellent man – and the other four officials delegated to deal with the Americans confessed that they had signed an extra clause that they had not dared tell anyone about. They had not shown Prime Minister Abé or the Council of Elders, let alone the clan lords, the full text of the treaty. They had kept it secret for more than a year. They knew we would be outraged and indeed we are. They swear they had no choice. The Americans had threatened to turn their cannons on Edo Castle. They had to sign it.'

'An extra clause? But what does it say?' Atsu wrinkled her brow. Women were invariably excluded from discussions concerning affairs of state. But Lord Nariakira behaved towards Atsu almost as if she were a man. He respected her opinion.

More, he seemed to want her to be educated and well informed.

He reached for his pipe and took a puff, a deep furrow between his eyebrows. 'They did not simply agree to let American ships dock here to take on coal, as they told us. They also agreed to let them send an envoy to come and live here. That was the extra clause.'

'Like the envoys from China and Korea?'

'Yes. The envoy was to arrive eighteen months after the treaty was signed.'

'And has he come? They signed the treaty two years ago. That was when we saw the ships on our way here.'

'No one has arrived as yet. But we cannot afford to relax our guard, not for an instant. These westerners are cunning. They are playing some game. An envoy will assuredly come – and when he does it will be the foot in the door. First there will be one, then millions. They will swamp us, they will try to turn us into slaves as they have the Chinese. We have to be ready.'

'I saw the tojin with my own eyes,' said Atsu. 'They won't be able to live here. They're entirely different from us. They're big. This American wouldn't fit into one of our houses. He wouldn't be able to eat our food. He'd be wanting to eat animals. They probably can't even use chopsticks with their great big fingers.'

Lord Nariakira broke into a grin. Samurai always wore their faces clamped into a fierce scowl, betraying nothing. But His Lordship was far above any samurai, even the highest level. He could do as he pleased. He unfolded his legs, crossed them and settled on his cushion. 'The Hollanders live among us,' he said, chuckling. 'Though when they travel they stay in specially equipped houses with wooden furniture. They cannot bend their knees enough to sit on tatami. Imagine that! They have to have extra-long palanquins made so they can stretch their legs out. And they carry their own food.' His face grew grave again. 'The point is that they live here by our agreement and under our laws. They do not force themselves on us.'

'I hear the Americans brought gifts,' she said.

'They did. A steam engine that runs on rails and a system for transmitting messages through wires. They call it a telegraph.'

'Like the one at Crane Castle?' Atsu smiled, remembering the humming wires that transmitted messages between the gatehouse and His Lordship's private quarters. He had explained to her in great detail how it worked, though everyone else was secretly convinced it was sorcery.

'Far more extensive. I had my men make detailed sketches of their equipment. They brought gifts of firearms too, more advanced than any I have ever seen. I asked to borrow one and took it back to my mansion overnight and had my men take it apart and put it together again. They worked through the night, drawing it in the greatest of detail. The Americans brought a globe too.' He gave a roar of laughter. 'Those Americans, they think we are children. They offered their globe to our most senior officials as if they expected them to be amazed, as if they were showing them something they had never seen before, as if they thought we did not know the world was round. Our ministers pointed out America and Japan and England and Russia for good measure. Let the westerners think what they like. We know everything about them and they know practically nothing about us. That gives us the upper hand.

'I heard something else, my dear. This will make you laugh. It seems some of the American sailors were actors. They painted their faces black.'

'Black, not white?'

'Black. They do everything the opposite way to us. They put on colourful striped clothes and played music – rollicking music like our festival music, Commissioner Hayashi said – on primitive shamisens and danced.'

Atsu laughed and clapped her hands. 'Barbarians dancing! I would love to see that!'

'Hayashi said it was simple rhythmic dancing like we do at festival time. Even their leader, Perry – I do not know his precise rank but he seemed to be an admiral or some sort of envoy. He was as stiff and stern as a daimyo though he liked his drink, so I heard. But he loosened up when they had their nightly show. Hayashi said he had never laughed so much in all his life. It was then that he realized that the tojin were not as alien as he had thought. Underneath it all they are just human beings, like us. Hayashi's secretary Matsuzaki went so far as to put his arm round Perry's shoulders.'

'He touched him?' Atsu shuddered at the thought of touching smelly alien flesh, probably hairy too.

'He touched him. He had had a cup or two of saké. He wanted to show off his English. He said to Perry, "Nippon, America, all one heart." So, you see, they do have some culture, even if it is rather primitive. They do not spend their entire time fighting and developing weaponry.

'It is not all bad, you see. Those old lords, they all think it is the end of the world, westerners washing up on our shores. "Barbarians, barbarians, coming here, threatening our traditions, our culture, our world." That is all I ever hear. Stuff and nonsense! We can learn from the westerners too. There is a lot they can teach us.'

His eyes were sparkling. There was definitely something going on.

'I have something to show you.' He jerked his chin and a retainer slid forward on his knees, holding a flat package wrapped in black fabric. Lord Nariakira pushed it across to Atsu. His face was solemn but there was a smile lurking at the corners of his mouth. 'Be careful. It is delicate.'

She ran her fingers across the silk wrapping cloth. The package was thin and light, heavier than paper but not heavy or thick enough to be wood. She could feel the sharp corners. She gasped. 'It can't be!'

'Open it.' He was drumming his fingers on the tatami, beaming like a schoolboy. He couldn't conceal his glee.

Biting her lip, with infinite care she unfolded one corner of the silk wrapper, then another. Inside was a thin metal plate. It was dull and black. There was nothing to see.

'Have you forgotten?' demanded Lord Nariakira with a rumbling laugh. 'You have to turn it and keep it close to the black silk.'

Holding it by its edges, she tilted it one way, then the other. Then she caught a glimpse of a ghostly shape. She bent over the fragile plate, laughing with excitement. 'I see it! I see it! They did it, Father! Kawamoto and Matsuki succeeded!'

'What can you see?' He leaned forward, his eyes fixed on her.

'It can't be. It is. Crane Castle. The corner of your residence. That huge pine tree – I recognize it. The roof is so big! I can see the ridge, the ridge pole, the eaves – I can almost see the tiles. And the verandas, the steps, the pillars, the rain doors. It's all there. And isn't that the big stone lantern? They must have set up their equipment right beside the pond.'

'It is not their work, it is mine,' boomed Lord Nariakira, thrusting out his chest.

'But it's back to front.'

'Naturally. It is a mirror – a mirror with a memory.'

Finally she looked up, seeing Lord Nariakira through a haze of tears. 'It's beautiful, Father. It makes me yearn for home!'

'Kawamoto finished his translation,' said Lord Nariakira, beaming. 'He published his book. He calls it *Use of Novel Devices from the Distant West*. I have brought a copy for you, though it makes for rather dry reading. He and Matsuki spent years experimenting. I too worked on it. But it all fell into place once the barbarians arrived. They brought their own silver plate machine – they call it a daguerreotype camera – and we were able to get a good look at how it works.'

'You've done it, you've actually done it.' Atsu wiped her eyes and bowed. 'Congratulations!'

'Next they will make a portrait of me,' Lord Nariakira said cheerfully, rewrapping the precious silver plate. 'As you know, my dear, people are much more difficult than buildings. I shall have to sit completely still for a very long time, as you did. That will not be easy for a restless person like myself.'

'You mustn't do that, Father. It's dangerous. I know you will think it's foolish superstition but all the same, you know what people say – that anyone who has a silver print made of them will die within three years.'

He laughed. 'I told you that was all nonsense. People who make such predictions believe daguerreotypes to be magic, but you know otherwise.'

Atsu sat back on her heels, remembering the tallow-skinned

scholars and the strange little house with its chemical smells. She breathed a sigh of relief. So that had been the meaning of the secretive look on His Lordship's face. She'd been afraid he was going to banish her, send her off on the next stage of her journey. But no. The silver print had been the big surprise.

Lord Nariakira stretched out his hand. His pipe was growing cold in the tobacco box. Ikushima lifted an eyebrow and Yasu darted forward and refilled and lit it for him. He nodded ponderously, took a long slow pull on the pipe and puffed out a cloud of smoke through his nostrils, filling the air with the rich aroma.

He shifted on to his knees and took a breath. 'I have news for you, my dear. Excellent news. My dear girl, let me be the first to congratulate you.'

16

Atsu's heart thumped painfully. Her first instincts had been right. It wasn't the silver print at all. Lord Nariakira's surprise was something far more devastating. The moment had come, the moment she'd hoped to put off for ever.

She looked around the beautiful room as if it was the last time she would ever see it, at the flowers in the alcove, the sunlight filtering through the paper screens. She heard the birds in the garden singing, smelt tea, heard the chatter of women. She was happy here, she didn't want to be shunted on to perform whatever fearsome task Lord Nariakira had lined up for her. She dreaded entering a palace where she would have to be a spy, play a part, appear to be one thing while being another. Above all she had the terrible suspicion that once she entered she would never leave again.

Lord Nariakira tapped out his pipe and frowned. He was no longer the genial man she called 'Father'. On his knees with his fan in his hand, he was Lord Nariakira, Prince of Satsuma, the most powerful and feared lord in the land.

'I told you I intended to send you to Edo Castle,' he said heavily. 'It has taken time for my plans to take shape.' He fixed her with his piercing black eyes like a hawk with a field mouse in its sights.

Atsu braced herself.

'I have arranged a marriage for you.'

'A marriage?' She could hardly breathe.

'The most advantageous imaginable. You are not just going to the palace. You are to be queen.'

'Queen . . . ?'

'You are to marry the lord of the realm.'

'You mean . . . he who may not be named?' she whispered. She dared not use any less respectful term.

'The Great Ruler, the Nobleman, the Shogun, whatever you choose to call him. You will be Her Majesty the Midai, the woman behind the screens. Prime Minister Abé, no less, has arranged the match. It is an unprecedented honour and privilege.'

Atsu gaped at him. She'd always known she'd have to marry somebody, somebody she wouldn't be able to choose for herself. Again and again she had mulled over the story of Midai Shigeko, the Satsuma girl who'd been twice adopted, just as Atsu had. Shigeko had ended up the consort of the Great Ruler's grandfather.

Atsu had wondered if that was to be her fate too. But it had seemed like the craziest of dreams to imagine for a moment that she – Okatsu of Ibusuki, the daughter of the lord of an obscure town in the far south – would marry the mysterious personage who dwelt in the great emptiness at the heart of the empire, a lord before whom even Lord Nariakira trembled, so powerful no ordinary person could even know his name. 'Shogun,' Lord Nariakira called him. 'Barbarian-Quelling Generalissimo.' And she was to marry this all-powerful lord? The most she had dared imagine was that he wished to offer her to the Great Ruler as a concubine. To be his consort was another matter altogether.

She still couldn't fathom his plans. She could see that with her in the palace he'd have a spy right in the middle of his enemies. It would be a way to introduce Ikushima into the palace too. If anyone could get a message out of that gargantuan fortress, that canny lady could. But if that was all Lord Nariakira had in mind he only needed to place her in the women's palace. He didn't need to marry her to the shogun. No, he had a far bigger purpose. As the shogun's father-in-law he would be the most powerful lord in the land, as his great-grandfather had been.

She was staggered at the enormity of his ambition. How had he managed to bring about such a feat? No matter how wily and determined Lord Nariakira might be, it must have taken years of negotiation, manoeuvring, political machinations. The Satsuma and the Tokugawa were ancient enemies. How had he persuaded the custodians of the palace to allow a member of the most powerful enemy clan of all into their innermost sanctum?

And how would it be for Atsu, living under permanent suspicion and hostility? The palace women would not be fooled even if she did bear an imperial title and speak with a Miyako accent. They would know perfectly well that she was a country bumpkin – not just that but a hated Satsuma. This marriage didn't seem like a privilege at all but a punishment, a living hell. It was a mission fraught with danger.

She stared at him desperately, wondering if he could read the thoughts that pounded in her head. 'It's too huge a responsibility,' she burst out. 'I can't do it. I'm not worthy.'

He raised an eyebrow. He didn't have to say a word. She understood immediately. With a jolt she remembered that he knew about Kaneshigé. He had seen him as clearly as he had seen her that day on the beach. Lord Nariakira was entirely ruthless. He might value her, he might care for her like a daughter, like his own child, he might love her, even. But he would sacrifice her without a second thought if he needed to do so for his own ends, for what he considered the good of the realm.

She had lost Kaneshigé long ago. She had had to give him up. She would never see him again. But she couldn't bear the thought that her actions might lead to his death. She couldn't defy Lord Nariakira. She couldn't risk going against his will.

'My dear girl,' he said smoothly. 'No one could be more worthy.' Atsu recognized that tone of voice. He would bamboozle her, browbeat her, charm her, but the end was not in doubt. He would have his way. 'Ever since a shogun has ruled this country he has always made an alliance with a princess of the highest rank, an imperial princess from Miyako. And that is what you are, my dear.'

He puffed at his pipe, smiled indulgently as if she was a child. 'You call the shogun "he who may not be named". He has a name. He is His Majesty Lord Iesada, Thirteenth Shogun of the House of Tokugawa.'

Iesada, Lord Iesada. As Atsu mouthed the syllables, she could feel herself beginning to warm to the idea. At least he had a name. Now she could begin to shape his picture, imagine what kind of man he might be, this future husband of hers. Perhaps he was young, perhaps handsome, no doubt brilliant and certainly the wielder of unimaginable power.

The previous shogun had died nearly three years earlier. She remembered Lord Nariakira's grief at the news. So Lord Iesada had already been shogun for nearly three years.

'But why does he need a consort?' she asked. 'Surely he has one already.'

'No, my dear. Concubines, for sure, everyone has concubines, but no consort.'

'Why not? Is he so very young?'

'He is old enough to marry. We have been searching for the perfect wife for him and now we have found one – you.'

Atsu narrowed her eyes. 'You mean everything has been held in limbo, even the marriage of the shogun himself, until Lord Nariakira of Satsuma completed his fiendish manoeuvrings?' she said hotly.

He threw back his head and chuckled merrily. She lowered her face with a grimace. He had won. She could say anything she liked. Nothing she said would make the slightest difference. It was a bitter realization.

There was nothing for it now but to accept her fate and make the best of it. It need not be so bad. Perhaps she could find a way to be happy with this exalted husband.

'And His Majesty has heard about me and wishes to marry a girl from the backwoods of Satsuma?'

'He will consider himself the luckiest of men when he sees you. He will be struck dumb by your beauty.' He touched her cheek with a large finger. She drew back, startled at the intimacy of the gesture. 'Such skin, my dear. Such hair. Those eyes, those slanting mysterious eyes. You are peerless. And even more alluring when you are angry. He will be helpless before you.' He paused, raised an eyebrow. 'He is the shogun,' he said, shrugging. 'He will do whatever the Council of Elders decrees. He needs a wife and we have all agreed that you, my dear, are by far the best choice.'

He seemed oddly casual about such a momentous decision. But she understood that for the shogun as much as for herself marriage was a political alliance. It was no surprise that he had as little choice as she did. As Princess Konoé had pointed out, the marriage would establish Lord Nariakira as the most powerful lord in the realm. That was the whole point of it, most probably the only point.

'Do I not need more training? Does he speak a special language that I will need to learn? Is he tall or short? Is he handsome?'

'Too many questions,' Lord Nariakira growled. His jowly face softened. 'But that is why it is so appropriate that you should be Midai. You have a mind of your own. You will learn all you need when you get there. Ikushima will help you.'

Suddenly Atsu remembered something that Lord Nariakira had said when he had told her about the previous Great Ruler's death. She drew back, stared at him accusingly. 'But you told me he was a weak and sickly boy. Those were the words you used – "weak and sickly".'

His Lordship raised his eyebrows, hesitated. He seemed momentarily abashed. 'What a memory you have! Be careful, my dear, when you speak of the Great Ruler. Never use such disrespectful language when anyone is nearby to overhear.' He hesitated again. He looked a little shifty. 'His Majesty is – how shall I put it? – unusual. He is difficult. He is not like other men.'

Atsu gaped at him. 'Not like other men?'

'Of course not. He is the shogun. He has never left Edo Castle. His upbringing has been entirely different from that of other men. It will take time to get used to his ways. But I have full confidence in you. You are competent and compassionate. He has many good qualities. I will let you in on a secret,' he added. 'He is a bit too close to his mother. But do not worry. You will be able to prise him away.

'In the end it hardly matters what he is like. You will be mistress of the palace, queen of the realm. You will live in luxury such as you cannot imagine. The kimonos, the silks, the servants – when the palace women go out in their palanquins, crowds gather just to catch a glimpse of their finery. You will make a perfect Midai.'

Atsu pursed her lips. Most young women, she knew, would give anything for the most menial job at the palace. It was the best way to complete one's education and acquire polish. Those who left had an excellent chance of finding a high-ranking husband. But that was the snag. The lower ranks could leave. But to enter the palace as the Midai, His Majesty's consort . . .

Midai Shigeko had disappeared into the women's palace and never been seen again. For a moment the premonition Atsu had had, of a maggot curled at the heart of a rotten persimmon, flashed through her mind. She shuddered, told herself not to be foolish. She was to marry a prince and be queen of the grandest, most luxurious palace in the country. She should be rejoicing, not nursing qualms.

17

'I – e – sa – da.'

Atsu whispered the syllables, shaped them with her lips. That mysterious being, the Great Ruler, 'he who may not be named' – he had a name, and she, Atsu, was privileged to know it.

She closed her eyes and murmured the name like a spell, tried to conjure up the man who went with it like a vision against the darkness of her eyelids. So this was to be her husband. Lord Nariakira had said he was 'a weak and sickly boy', 'not like other men'. But he was also the shogun.

She smiled and shook her head. Women married all manner of men. All they were required to do was produce children for them. After that they need never see each other. She felt a pang of sadness. It would have been better if she had never known what it was to be close to a man. Then she could have endured a loveless marriage without regrets.

The chilly spring breeze broke into her reverie. She changed out of her heavy robes into everyday kimonos, put up her hair and ran outside. Young leaves glinted in the sun, plants were bursting into bud. The grounds were vast. She couldn't believe that Edo Castle had gardens any larger.

Absorbed in her thoughts she wandered through the herb gardens, past the moon-viewing pavilion, through the bamboo grove and into the woods. Ikushima, Chiyo and Yasu followed at a discreet distance. She turned, waved them away, gestured to them to leave her alone, but they paid no attention. It was their job to attend her.

Hoping to shake them off, she crossed the lawns to the stables and slipped her feet into a pair of the rough wooden sandals piled at the gates, then picked her way across straw and puddles to the horses' stalls, enjoying the smells of fresh wood shavings, hay, horse urine, manure. Taro, the handsome Kiso stallion, tossed his great head to greet her. He didn't care whether she was a stable girl or queen of the realm. She patted his warm flanks, buried her face in his mane and stroked his long satiny nose as he nuzzled in search of a carrot.

'I wish I could take you with me,' she whispered. 'But you wouldn't like it at Edo Castle. I doubt if they'd ever let me take you out for a gallop.'

She'd turned to leave the stables when she saw two men at the gates, engrossed in conversation. She recognized Saigo, the gentle, softly spoken giant. He'd gone back to Kagoshima with Lord Nariakira. She hadn't seen him for more than a year.

Overjoyed, she picked up her skirts and ran across the muddy ground to greet him. It was only then that she properly noticed his companion. He had his back to her and at first all she saw was a long lean figure in billowing indigo robes with the sun glinting on his oiled topknot and smooth shaved pate.

She gasped. She knew that silhouette, the way he held himself with his back very straight and his hand on his sword hilt. His shoulders looked broader. He'd been a boy before. Now he was a man.

Kaneshigé. She took a step towards him then stopped in her tracks, trembling, feeling the hairs rise on the back of her neck. He was the last person she'd ever expected to see again – not just in Edo but here, at Lord Nariakira's mansion. She knew she should turn and run, run anywhere. She was in mortal danger of doing something foolish, something that would ruin Lord Nariakira's carefully constructed plans, that might even condemn them all to death. But she couldn't. She couldn't leave, not without speaking to him.

She was frightened at how alive it made her feel just to see him, as if she had been half asleep for the last three years. She'd thought she'd put him out of her mind but she'd been wrong. She clasped her hands, tried to calm her racing heart.

Three years. Three years had gone by since that last meeting on the beach. Their secret messages had become fewer and fewer and then, when Saigo went back to Kagoshima, stopped altogether. It was better that way, she'd told herself, better to let the flame die down. And now, now that her future was decided, now that she was promised to the highest lord in the land, Kaneshigé was here in Edo. It seemed the cruellest trick that fate could play.

It made perfect sense for him to be here. Lord Nariakira was rounding up troops to defend the shogun's capital against the next barbarian incursion. He'd probably enlisted a whole contingent from Ibusuki. Kaneshigé was the bravest, most reckless of them all. He would have been the first to volunteer.

She glanced over her shoulder. Ikushima and Chiyo and Yasu were waiting on the dry ground outside the stable yard. She turned away to hide her burning cheeks from Ikushima's all-knowing gaze.

He turned. It was the face she knew so well – the tawny skin, the full-lipped mouth, the large dark eyes that seemed to gaze into the future. She looked at him, speechless. No matter how hard she'd tried to forget him, she couldn't control the yearning that swept over her. There was so much she hadn't allowed herself to remember. Now it all came flooding back – their childhoods together, their secret meetings. She felt his dagger there in her sash.

Their eyes met barely for an instant, not long enough even to blink, but enough for Atsu to see that his feelings for her had not changed. He was as shocked and thrilled as she was.

He'd opened his mouth in astonishment. Now his face grew stern. He was well aware of the peril they were in. He knew that Lord Nariakira had seen them on the beach. They were treading on hot coals. Saigo and he had been travelling from Kyushu for nearly two months. There had been plenty of time for Saigo to tell him all about the visit to Prince Konoé and Atsu's transformation into Princess Sumiko. If he hadn't been aware of all that had happened to her before, he knew now. She was entirely out of his reach.

She took a step towards him. Saigo and Kaneshigé too had flushed dark red. They were all three aware of the ladies-in-waiting watching not far away. In theory the ladies were servants who saw and heard nothing, but they were there all the same.

'Saigo-*sama*,' Atsu said, her voice shaking. 'It is good to see you. It has been a long time.' She was aware of how much she'd missed the big youth's quiet trustworthy presence.

Saigo bowed. 'I am glad you are well, Your Highness.' He gestured towards Kaneshigé. 'Let me introduce Lord Komatsu, Tatewaki Komatsu.'

Lord Komatsu? She looked from one to the other, startled. She took a breath. 'You are welcome, my lord. So you too have a new name and a new role.' It felt so strange exchanging the stiff formal platitudes.

'It is true. I no longer belong to the Kimotsuki family, Your Highness,' said Kaneshigé. He shuffled, looked up, wrinkled his brow ruefully. 'I have had the good fortune to be adopted.'

'There is no need to address me so formally,' Atsu murmured, glancing over her shoulder towards Ikushima, hoping she hadn't overheard. She couldn't bear to have him call her 'Your Highness'.

Kaneshigé bowed. To her he would always be Kaneshigé, no matter what name he went by. 'I was adopted by the Komatsu family this year, my lady. It was a great honour for me. As a Kimotsuki, I was the fourth son. I didn't have much of a future. Now I am head of the house.'

Saigo nodded. 'He's a daimyo now, an elder. He's much above me in rank.'

She turned away, utterly downcast, trying to quell the despair that swept over her. Kaneshigé didn't have to say another word. She understood. He was married. He was twenty-one, it was more than time. No doubt the Komatsu clan had lacked an heir and had chosen him for his ability. He'd probably married the eldest daughter and taken the family name to continue the family line. Maybe he even had a child on the way. The thought made her want to cry out in pain. It should have been hers, hers, not some foolish ill-educated Komatsu girl's.

She heaved a sigh, drew herself up, reminded herself she was a princess now. 'You have only just arrived,' she said. 'You must have had a long journey.'

'Nearly two months on the road,' Kaneshigé said. A smile crossed his face, that familiar beam that melted her heart. 'I don't know how many pairs of straw sandals I've been through.'

His straw sandals were in tatters and his billowing robes were dirty and stained. As a lord he was entitled to travel by palanquin if he wanted, or on horseback. He must have decided he'd rather stretch his legs and walk with his friends.

He met her eyes. 'We came by way of Mount Fuji,' he said softly. 'We walked through the foothills for days. I've never seen anything so magnificent. It made me think of Ariwara no Narihira and his journey east. You used to love his poems.'

'I remember what you wrote to me: "The quails cry in the long grass at dusk,"' she murmured.

He smiled. 'And you replied, "If only we could meet where the roads cross, in the shadow of Mount Fuji."' His voice was barely a whisper, far too soft to reach Ikushima's keen ear.

She felt tears come to her eyes. He'd understood the note she'd sent. He hadn't forgotten. He still cared. 'I miss Ibusuki, the crying of the quails at dusk,' she said in a rush, remembering the last line of Narihira's poem. 'I wish I could have been there for the quail hunt.'

There was a rustle. She caught a movement out of the corner of her eye. Ikushima was watching like a hawk, poised to intervene as soon as she judged it necessary.

Atsu turned away, frowning. She was not afraid of Ikushima. She wanted to draw their talk out for as long as she could. 'How is Ibusuki?'

'The sand is still black and it still smells of sulphur.'

'My brother and the others are here too?'

'Your brother has responsibilities. He'll be taking over soon from your father as head of the family. But a lot of the others are. We're all eager to cut down as many barbarians as we can next time they dare show their faces.'

'And my family?'

'All well. They talk about you all the time. They're very proud of you.' He took a step towards her. 'I never thought I would see you again,' he murmured. 'Saigo-*sama* showed me round the mansion. I've never seen such wealth, such culture. Do you remember I once told you that the Satsuma mansions were the most magnificent in the city?'

'I remember those days,' she murmured, breathing the scent of him. 'It was the happiest time of my life.'

'His Lordship has made me one of his aides. I have a room in the valets' quarters.'

For a moment Atsu imagined creeping out to join him one night, then reminded herself of how unthinkable the consequences would be – not for her but for him. They gazed at each other in silence. Time seemed to stop. Even if she had wanted to move away she wouldn't have been able to.

Ikushima stepped forward firmly, squelching in her silken sandals through the straw and puddles. Mud splashed the bottom of her expensive quilted hem but she paid no attention. She took up her position behind Atsu, immovable, like a sentinel. They all three – Atsu, Saigo and Kaneshigé – stiffened.

'Ikushima-*sama*,' said Saigo, bowing. Atsu bit her lip, startled at this show of defiance. He'd greeted her as one commoner to another, instead of using the title '-*dono*' to mark her vastly superior status. She was, after all, a court lady, he a mere retainer.

'Saigo-*sama*, how are you?' Ikushima replied coolly.

Kaneshigé drew himself up to his full height and bowed. 'If I may introduce myself,' he said airily. 'My name is Tatewaki of the House of Komatsu. I have the honour to be one of His Lordship's personal attendants.'

Atsu smiled to herself. He was asserting his superior rank, his right to be here and to talk to her – to Her Highness Princess Sumiko.

'I have the honour to be acquainted with Her Highness's family,' he went on. 'I bring news from them.'

'Delighted,' said Ikushima, baring her teeth in the iciest of smiles.

'You may go, Ikushima,' Atsu said. 'And Chiyo and Yasu too.'

'No need to worry about me, my lady,' said Ikushima. 'Do carry on with your conversation. I will be here in case you need anything.'

Atsu pursed her lips. Ikushima had a job to do. She was not going to leave Atsu alone with any man, let alone one that Lord Nariakira had undoubtedly told her Atsu was well acquainted with. It was unseemly ever to talk to men except to issue an order, particularly now that she was betrothed to the shogun.

She sighed. With Ikushima there she had no choice but to play the princess. She gritted her teeth, drew herself up.

'I never thought I would see Edo, Your Highness,' said Kaneshigé, ignoring Ikushima and addressing Atsu. 'Saigo-*sama* has been showing me around. I've never been anywhere so vast, so full of all manner of people. The libraries, the bookshops, the training halls, the swordsmiths. You are fortunate to live here, my lady.'

He was challenging Ikushima, testing how far he could go. After all he was a lord and one of Lord Nariakira's valets. He was not going to be cowed by a mere lady-in-waiting, even if she was from Miyako.

Ikushima said nothing.

Suddenly Atsu realized. That canny lady didn't need to say anything. Nothing any of them said or did made the slightest difference now. As Kaneshigé had pointed out that day when they'd met to say their farewells on the beach, they were mere puppets. Lord Nariakira knew perfectly well their feelings for each other. He had completed his negotiations now. He had the pieces in place ready for his next move. He could afford to bring Kaneshigé to Edo. He needed all the brave men he could find and Kaneshigé was surely the bravest. Lord Nariakira knew none of them would dare interfere with his plans. The stakes were too high. Maybe he was testing them even, testing their loyalty.

Or maybe it was his way of rewarding Atsu before she was immured in the palace for ever. If so, it felt more like torture.

'Come, Your Highness,' Ikushima said briskly. 'Please excuse us, gentlemen. Her Highness has an appointment.'

Atsu cast Kaneshigé a small sad smile. For the short time until she left, however long that was, they would breathe the same air. They might pass each other in the halls or on the verandas, maybe even exchange the occasional word. But Ikushima would always be there, watching. They'd never manage more than a couple of words of small talk. To know that he was here and she couldn't meet him or talk to him was too bitter a cup. She couldn't imagine a more exquisite agony. It was far more painful than not seeing him at all.

In any case she was no longer free. She was promised to another – to the greatest lord in the realm. She murmured the syllables of his name: 'I – e – sa – da.' But the magic didn't work any more.

18

Tenth day of the eleventh month (2 December 1856)

'I can't believe we're really going to the palace,' whispered Chiyo, her eyes wide with excitement.

'We'll get lost in all those rooms,' breathed Yasu, licking her fingers and smoothing a make-up brush to a fine point.

'The grand ladies we'll meet. We might even see he who . . .' Chiyo darted a glance at Ikushima. '. . . he who may not be named.' She barely breathed the forbidden syllables.

'We will, we surely will!' squeaked Yasu.

Ikushima swung round. 'There will be a great deal to learn,' she said crisply. The two flushed and stared at the tatami, twisting their fingers.

'I've heard the ladies there have the most beautiful clothes you'll ever see,' Chiyo burst out. 'Wealthy merchants give them gifts.'

'And why might they do that?' Ikushima asked in ominously silky tones.

The girls hesitated. 'In exchange for a favour?' Chiyo ventured.

'Exactly,' snapped Ikushima.

The pale light of dawn filtered through the narrow gaps between the rain doors, tightly closed to preserve what little warmth there was. Ghostly shadows danced across the walls in the sputtering light of the candles and oil lamps and an ember sparked and flared in the brazier.

Atsu was shivering in her underkimonos but she barely noticed the cold. Her heart was pounding so hard she could scarcely breathe. The long-awaited day had finally come. Today she would travel across the great city of Edo to the castle brooding at its heart. She was stepping into the unknown, setting off on the journey of a lifetime with only the faintest idea of what her destination would be like. The one thing she knew for sure was that she would never come back.

Ikushima held up a quilted olive-green mantle with a design of spiky snow-capped bamboo leaves zigzagging around the skirts. To Atsu it looked rather drab, more suited to a bent old grandmother than a young woman about to be married.

'I don't know, I don't know,' she murmured, running her hands distractedly through her long black hair. Yasu rushed over to her with a comb and smoothed it back into place, sucking her breath through her teeth.

'It is the style among the palace ladies, madam,' said Ikushima. 'They prefer subtle tones.'

Atsu nodded. On matters of fashion Ikushima always knew best. As Ikushima slipped the mantle over her shoulders Atsu stole a glance in the mirror. She was dressed up like a porcelain doll, hardly able to move under the weight of clothing. She looked every bit the princess. But she felt horribly empty inside. It was hard to feel any excitement about this new life she was going to. She was trapped in a gilded cage that rumbled ever onward and she could see no way to escape. She sighed. She had promised Lord Nariakira that she would do her best, and she would.

Yasu was putting the last touches to the red safflower paste on Atsu's lips when the door flew open.

'His Lordship!' shrilled the chamberlain.

A moment later Lord Nariakira swept in. He was in his finest regalia, ready to escort Imperial Princess Sumiko on her journey across the capital.

Atsu did a slow pirouette before him, swinging her heavy skirts around on the tatami.

'A princess!' He beamed. 'A true imperial princess! I am proud of you, my dear. Come. Let us go outside. I would like a few last words.'

He ushered her to the veranda. Chiyo slid back the paper screens and rain doors and laid out sandals for them.

Skeletal branches swayed in the breeze. The earth was parched and brown. Gardeners in baggy work trousers and split-toed shoes swept fallen leaves into piles, cut back the bushes and swaddled the pine trees in straw matting ready for winter. A couple of retainers ran over but Lord Nariakira raised his hand, gesturing to them to leave him alone with Atsu.

Atsu walked in silence, lifting her olive-green hem. This was the last time she would ever see His Lordship. He had been a second father to her for most of her life and her adopted father for the last three years. It was hard to imagine being on her own without him there to advise her.

They walked across stepping stones to the carp pond. There was a stone bridge across it and a small waterfall tinkling and splashing. Fat red and gold fish jostled below the surface of the water. Atsu clapped her hands and they surged over, tails thrashing, opening and shutting their huge whiskered mouths in search of food.

Lord Nariakira ran his large hand over his shaven pate. Atsu waited expectantly. He heaved a sigh.

'It is hard having two homes,' he said. 'I miss Kagoshima. I wish I were there overseeing my projects. But there is work to be done here, important work. Those Americans in Shimoda . . .'

Atsu nodded. The barbarians were back. An American ship had appeared off the coast of Shimoda two and a half months earlier and a man had disembarked. He had announced through his interpreter, a Hollander, that he was the American Consul General, as provided for by the extra clause in the treaty which the commissioners had kept secret for so long, and that the two of them had come to stay. It was exactly what Lord Nariakira had predicted and feared would happen.

For days the town fathers of Shimoda had argued and reasoned with the two foreigners, trying to persuade them to go back to their ship and leave, but they adamantly refused. Urgent messages flew back and forth between Shimoda and Edo. In the end the government had had to give way. The Shimoda governors had allocated an unused temple for the barbarian and his interpreter to live in. At least they were in Shimoda, at the far end of the Izu peninsula, a safe distance from Edo with an entire mountain range between them and the capital.

'And now they demand women,' Lord Nariakira said, raising an ironic eyebrow. 'Perry and his men were the same. No sooner were they settled in Shimoda than they had to have women.'

Atsu laughed. 'I hear the ladies of Shimoda are set up for life.' Wherever she went these days she heard the Shimoda Boatmen's Song. The maids cleaning the mansion, the grooms mucking out the stables – everyone was singing it. She hummed the last lines:

> Oh! How grateful we are to the honourable foreigner
> Who gives two *ryo* for the one-*ryo* whore.

Lord Nariakira shook his head. He wasn't laughing. 'The Russians too, and the Dutch in Nagasaki, they all want women. I suppose it shows they are just men, like us. They have appetites too. You know some of the Shimoda whores bore children after Perry's men left?'

'I wouldn't want one of those growing inside me no matter how much money I was offered,' Atsu said, screwing up her face at the thought. 'I can't imagine what they must have looked like.'

'The town elders had them smothered at birth,' said Lord Nariakira. 'They buried them on a cliff top overlooking the sea, where the barbarians had come from, so they wouldn't pollute the town. No one wants changelings anywhere nearby.'

'I hope their spirits were properly put to rest,' said Atsu. The spirits of dead babies, even changelings, would cause terrible trouble if the priests didn't conduct the necessary ceremonies.

Lord Nariakira grimaced. He was such a rationalist, Atsu was never sure whether he believed in such things or dismissed them as women's talk. But then she remembered that his children too had died, of a curse inflicted by his father's concubine.

'The American's name is Harris,' he said. 'Harris-*sama* demanded two women, one for him, one for his Dutch interpreter. He had taken a fancy to a geisha called Okichi, a beauty, I hear, just seventeen years old. The elders agreed to make a contract with her. They did not want him defiling decent women. They gave the interpreter a geisha too, one Ofuku. The two geisha are living with them now in their house.'

Atsu wrinkled her brow at the thought of the girls' plight. 'Poor things. What a terrible fate. No one will ever touch them again. Imagine sharing a bed with one of those monstrous creatures. They must be huge.' She opened her eyes wide at the thought. 'They'd tear you in half.' She lowered her head, her cheeks burning.

'They have been here two and a half months now, living on our soil,' growled Lord Nariakira, slapping his fan into his palm. A crow flapped off with a caw. 'We send incessant messages to the governors, ordering them to tell them to leave, but this Harris thinks up one condition after another. At least in Shimoda he cannot do much harm. Now he says he has a letter, another of those damned letters. He has to present it to the emperor in person. He means the Great Ruler, of course. What would the emperor know of affairs of state? In any case, it is all just a ploy. What he is really after is permission to come to Edo. He wants to insert himself into the heart of our country like a poisoned barb.

'The American speaks with a silken tongue but when the governors argue with him he roars and rages. He reminds them that his country is far mightier than ours. They can grind us under their heel whenever they choose. Every day ships from some new nation force their way into our harbours. We have made agreements with America, Russia, Britain, always with cannons pointed at our shores. The gods alone know what the end of it all will be.

'And now I hear rumours that China is under threat again. The British grabbed a toehold there, the island of Hong Kong. There has been a peace of sorts for the last fourteen years but now, so I hear, they are causing trouble again. They claim that the Chinese did not honour the terms they signed with them. That must be a warning to us too. We cannot make light of these treaties, these foolish pieces of paper they force upon us. Once we have signed, one of the barbarians will hold it like a knife to our throats. They think they can take over the world, but they will not succeed,' he roared, so loudly that

Atsu jumped. 'They will not subjugate the Land of the Rising Sun.'

He picked up a pebble and tossed it across the surface of the pond, sending the carp diving into the dark waters.

'Naturally we have spies posted throughout the American's compound – gardeners, cooks, cleaners, all excellent men. But the government is in turmoil. I meet Chief Senior Councillor Abé, I give my opinion, I offer advice, then the other lords, all two hundred and sixty of them, weigh in with their opinions too. Some say we must fight to the death, others that we must let the western barbarians have their way, others that it is to our advantage to open to trade. What we desperately need is a leader who can bind us all together, a leader who can make decisions, the right decisions. And that we do not have.'

He spread his legs wide, his hand on his sword hilt, and fixed Atsu with his eyes. A chill ran through her. 'And that is where you come in, my dear.'

Atsu looked round to make sure there was no one nearby to overhear. 'Aren't you forgetting, Father? His Majesty, my future husband.' As she said the words she felt a prickle of pride. 'He is our leader. You are not suggesting he should be deposed?'

His Lordship opened his eyes wide. 'Your future husband? His Majesty is a fine, upright man. But he is not a strong ruler. Until now we have had no need of one. Our shoguns are symbols of the state. They enjoy peaceful lives in Edo Castle, they write poetry and practise tea ceremony and disport themselves with their concubines to ensure the continuance of the Tokugawa line. But now we are under threat of barbarian attack. Now we need a shogun who can lead us.'

'You're telling me that His Majesty is dissolute, a libertine, incapable of ruling? In that case why have you arranged for me to marry him? I understand that he is weak but he is still the shogun.'

'His Majesty is indeed our ruler. But he knows nothing of the world outside the castle. Moreover he has no children and he is not in the best of health. Were he to pass away, he would have no successor. That is the point.'

'Naturally I shall bear him a child. That is my duty as his wife.'

Lord Nariakira shook his head. There was an odd look on his face. 'I am not asking you to have a child. Any child of yours would be too young to rule for many years to come. The crisis is upon us right now. We desperately need a strong leader.

'Listen to me, Atsu. Were Lord Iesada to pass away – and I pray every day for his good health – his cousin Yoshitomi, Lord of Kii, is next in line. But he is only ten years old, far too young to make vital decisions. There is, however, another contender, a very brilliant and capable young man. Lord Keiki of the House of Hitotsubashi is nineteen, but he has already shown himself a man of intellect and principle and sound judgement. He has dignity and presence and charisma. He could hold his own with the foreign envoys and negotiate with them on equal terms. He would find ways to forestall them. We would no longer have to cave in to their demands. He has an excellent claim to the throne. He would make the perfect leader.

'This is the point. If Keiki were named heir he could take over as Regent and make decisions on His Majesty's behalf.'

Atsu listened in disbelief. The more she heard, the more protective she felt of this unknown man, her future husband. She had always trusted Lord Nariakira's judgement but what he was proposing now was outrageous. 'How dare you say His Majesty is not capable of ruling! You mean this Lord Keiki is your ally while His Majesty will not be so easily manipulated?'

Lord Nariakira held up his hand. 'Let me finish. The conservatives support little Yoshitomi but what they really want is to hang on to power themselves. That will mean endless arguments between the various factions while our enemies take advantage of our indecision. A weak ruler will give them their chance to step in and grab all the concessions they can. Don't you see? That is what has happened in China. With a government of that sort we will be at their mercy. We will not be able to keep them at bay.

'Under Keiki's leadership all the clans would come together. Powerful lords like myself would have cabinet posts and make our voices heard. He would create a strong government that would save our country. Can you see now how important it is?

'This is your first task as Midai. This is what I ask of you. Once you are established in the palace, I wish you to use your influence and charm to persuade His Majesty to name Lord Keiki as his successor. As Regent, Keiki will be able to make decisions on His Majesty's behalf. We clan lords will do the best we can to hold back the barbarians till he has this power.'

Atsu was swept away by his rhetoric, grappling with everything he was telling her. 'So His Majesty is opposed to Lord Keiki?'

'His Majesty's mother is unbendingly opposed to him and she wields undue influence on her weak-willed son. Let me put it plainly. She controls him.'

'So you wish me to twist His Majesty's arm, to persuade him to do something he doesn't want to do? That is an impossible task. I am just a woman. Matters like this are for you and Prime Minister Abé to decide, not me.'

Lord Nariakira turned, gripped her hands, looked her in the eye. 'On the issue of the succession, the shogun alone decides. We men can talk and discuss, but it is impossible to manipulate him from the outside. There is a point beyond which we cannot go.' He paused. 'And that is the women's palace.'

He lowered his voice. 'The Great Interior is the shogun's private empire of women. The women there are his family. When he is among them he is at home. He is the only man who may enter, the only man of rank who ever enters. It is impossible for any man to influence what goes on there.

'The women tell him what to do.' He gave a snort of laughter. 'Think of your mother, how she runs the household. I am sure she has taught you how to run a household too. It is all I can do to stop my womenfolk running me!'

Atsu stared at him, wide-eyed. So this was what he had been planning all along, this was why he had arranged for her to enter the palace. Now he had all his pieces in place he was making his grand move, now that she was so deeply entrenched that she could not escape. Now the trap was about to snap shut. The most frightening thing was that she trusted him. She had faith that he knew what was best for the country – and she fully understood the peril they were in.

She held her breath, waiting to hear what this final move was to be.

He pinned her with his fierce black eyes. 'His Majesty has to sign every document. If the women tell him not to sign a certain paper, he will do as they say. Do you see now what an important job you have to do? As the shogun's consort, you will be able to influence him yourself. The barbarians are bursting through our gates. We need Lord Keiki to be Regent. I am on my knees, begging you. You must persuade Iesada to choose him.'

He squeezed her hands, his eyes blazing. 'I have known you all your life, ever since you were a proud, stubborn, fierce little girl. You are brave and capable and clever and wily, like me. You will twist him round your little finger. Then you can live in luxury and your son will come to the throne after Lord Keiki has sorted out the crisis and dealt with the barbarian threat.

'I beg you, do not fail. The future of our country depends on it. All these years I have always done my best for you. Now I am asking you this one small favour in return.'

She stepped back, stared at the ground. She felt the sun's warmth, heard the rush of water, the tinkle of the waterfall, branches rustling in the wintry breeze, gardeners shouting in the distance. There was a splash as a carp poked its head above the surface of the water.

She shook her head. It was not a small favour, it was a huge task. Lord Nariakira was her lord and master. He had raised her to this position, he had even arranged for Kaneshigé to be here. But she had faith that he had the interests of the nation at heart.

She bowed. 'I will do my best. If it is possible to do it, I will. I give you my word.'

'Thank you,' he said. 'I knew you would.'

She was thinking over this new mission of hers. One big piece of the puzzle was still missing. He hadn't answered her question. 'Why do you have so little faith in His Majesty? You told me he is difficult. Is he a pleasure-lover? Is he a debauchee?'

'Watch out for his mother,' he said. 'She is an old witch. You will have to be on your toes.' He smiled at her. 'But as his wife, my dear, you can become close to him.' He looked relieved. He'd cast a weight off his shoulders and placed it squarely on hers. 'I will see that you have help. You know Saigo. Giant of a lad. Entirely trustworthy, loyal to the core. He is a gardener, he does not exist as far as the palace is concerned. He will be in touch with you.'

'How will I find him?'

'He will find you. He will take messages between us. Remember, you must win the shogun's confidence first. You will not meet him until the wedding. You will have a month and a half to get to know the palace and to prepare yourself. Bide your time, plan your moves skilfully. There is no need to rush. You will have only one chance.'

'You haven't answered my question, Father. I need to know about His Majesty.' Atsu's heart was thumping.

'Ikushima will be there too. You know how astute she is. As Princess Konoé put it, Ikushima spends money like water but she can fathom practically anyone's secret intentions. She is fearsome but she is entirely loyal. She will be an invaluable ally.'

Atsu looked at Lord Nariakira desperately. 'Please, Father. Is there something I should know about His Majesty?'

He was avoiding her eyes. The carp had swum away. She could see its back flashing in the dark waters of the pond.

'It is up to you now. The future of the country is in your hands.' There was a look she'd never seen before on His Lordship's face – wistful, sentimental. She'd always thought of him as a pillar of strength. 'This is the last time I shall ever talk to Princess Sumiko,' he said. 'Next time – if there is a next time – you will be the Midai, the woman behind the screens.'

Atsu gave a start. His words struck ice into her heart. 'I'm to be hidden behind screens for the rest of my life?'

'It is just a title.' Lord Nariakira was gripping her hands still. 'I am making a sacrifice too, you know,' he said. 'I have lost most of my children. I have enjoyed having you as my daughter. You are as close to me as anyone could ever be. I shall miss you.'

Tears came to Atsu's eyes. Lord Nariakira had been more than a father to her. He'd trained her, turned her from a country girl into a woman fit to enter the shogun's castle, to become queen. And now he was releasing her, sending her out into the world to carry out her mission.

He squeezed her hands again. To her shock there were tears in the great warrior's eyes. 'I am sorry, my dear,' he muttered. His voice was hoarse. 'I am so sorry, truly sorry. I have racked my brains for some other way, any other way, to achieve this, but I cannot see any alternative.' He hesitated. 'It is true. Iesada is not like other men. You will probably not be able to have a normal marriage.'

Atsu stared at him wildly. 'What are you saying?' she asked, her voice shaking. 'What is wrong with . . . with His Majesty?'

'I told you. He is weak and sickly, a difficult boy.' He took a long breath.

'But he is the shogun. If there was something so badly wrong with him, surely he wouldn't be able to rule. And if he is so difficult, how can I influence him?'

'I am asking you to sacrifice yourself for the sake of your country. None of us can choose our destinies. We all have to work together for the common good. If you succeed it will save us all. I hope one day you will find it in your heart to forgive me.'

He let go of her, buried his face in his hands and turned away, his shoulders heaving. 'You understand the importance of your task,' he said, his voice muffled. 'I beg you to save the country. That is all that matters.'

He wiped his sleeve across his eyes, took a breath, drew himself up, thrust out his chest. He was not just her father. He was the Prince of Satsuma, the proudest, most feared daimyo in the land. 'The ladies from the palace will soon be here. They are coming to fetch you, my dear. Let me wish you farewell and all success.'

She gazed at him, taking in the contours of the face that had grown so dear to her. He was sending her away from everyone and everything she cared about, locking her up for the rest of her life, giving her a mission he knew to be impossible, using her as a pawn. But that was something she'd always known would happen. Despite it all she loved him dearly.

'I have never expressed my thanks to you,' she said. 'All you've done has been for my well-being. I can never convey my gratitude. I will do my best to be what you want me to be and do what you want me to do.'

He bowed. 'I shall leave you now. Wait here.'

She watched the large figure stride ponderously away in his huge-shouldered formal robes and stiff hakama trousers, hearing the rustle of starch and the crunch of his sandalled feet across the gravel. The gardeners had gone. There was no one around.

As he reached the corner of the veranda another figure appeared, tall and slender. Lord Nariakira greeted him and he bowed respectfully and walked towards her. Kaneshigé.

Somehow she was not surprised. His Lordship knew everything. He had all along. He didn't want her to be unhappy. After all, there was nothing either of them could do to derail his plans. It was much too late.

Kaneshigé took her hands as if careless whether anyone was watching. 'Okatsu-*san*,' he said.

The deep tones of his voice calling her by her childhood name brought tears to Atsu's eyes.

'Okatsu-*san*. Saigo and I will be there to help you. We will work together. You will see us still. Lord Nariakira has authorized it.'

Atsu gazed up at him despairingly. So this was the most she could hope for.

'We are all puppets,' he said, looking at her with his large dark eyes. 'Lord Nariakira too. We are cogs in the wheel, small parts of the whole. We all have to sacrifice our own happiness to protect our country. I told you I would be there if you needed me, and I will. We both know we can never be together but I will always be here to help you.'

Atsu wrenched her hands away. It was too cruel. 'What does Lord Nariakira think he's doing?' she groaned. 'How can I achieve my task, how can I form a bond with the shogun if you are there? He sees it as a job, a political mission. None of you have any idea how I feel.

'You will always be dear to me. But I will have to make the shogun fall in love with me, don't you see? I will have to sleep with him, fall in love with him myself. How else can I persuade him to make the decision His Lordship wants him to make? I am starting a new life. I am to be the bride of the most powerful man in the world. I can't have memories of my old life and my old love lingering on.'

It hurt her, it made her die inside but she had to say it. She had to be resolute. 'Let Saigo come,' she said, her voice shaking. 'But not you, Kaneshigé, not you. Please leave me. I am to be the shogun's wife. It will make it harder, not easier for me, if you are there.'

'It is as you choose, my lady. I will always be here to help you if you need me. You have only to say the word.'

Blinded by tears, she turned and stumbled to her rooms. She didn't look back. Yasu tidied her make-up. Ikushima was waiting to lead her to the grand audience chamber.

19

There were voices and sounds of running feet. A cry went up. 'Their ladyships! Their ladyships!'

A moment later the doors slid open. On their knees outside, attended by the chamberlains, was a group of haughty-looking women. The scent of expensive fragrance filled the air.

Atsu saw a row of faces powdered even whiter than her own, with sharp black eyes and red lips shaped into smiles. Their teeth were black, turning their mouths into dark wells, their hair looped in stiff coils. They wore lavish robes in understated colours, shimmering with gold. She was glad that she had followed Ikushima's advice and chosen the drab green mantle.

It had begun. There was no turning back. She bowed, her heart thundering. Sadness and loneliness washed over her at the thought of being wrenched from her home and taken away to the chilly halls of Edo Castle to live among women like these.

'Please excuse our intrusion,' cooed a high-pitched, fluting voice in the unmistakable tones of the castle.

'You are most welcome.' It was Her Ladyship, Lord Nariakira's consort. She too was there to see Atsu off. Even little Princess Teru, His Lordship's daughter, had come.

Atsu pressed her forehead to the ground. She needed to seem modest yet proud. These women must not think she was some untutored provincial who did not know how to behave. She was Imperial Princess Sumiko of the House of Fujiwara, above all of them in rank.

Ikushima had tutored her in what to say. She put her hands together, tips of her forefingers touching, and murmured, 'You have had to come such a long way. I am so sorry.' She bowed her head again and kept her eyes on the tatami.

'Beautiful,' said a voice that sounded kind. 'What an exquisite young woman.'

'We shall be sorry to lose Her Imperial Highness,' said Her Ladyship. 'We have been very fortunate to have her as our guest for so long.'

'Not exactly young,' muttered a rasping voice in sour tones. That would be one to watch out for, Atsu thought. She wondered how much these women knew of her origins. Everything, most likely. It was hard to keep secrets in this world.

Her Ladyship insisted that the palace ladies take tea and Atsu was called upon to show her skill at tea ceremony. As calmly as she could she measured out the brilliant green tea and whipped it to a froth. Brimming with apprehension, she hardly noticed the interminable small talk. All she could think of was the journey to come and the unknown destination.

Finally they all rose to their feet.

'Come,' said Her Ladyship. 'Let me take you to your palanquin.'

A long line of retainers, ladies, servants and staff was waiting at the main entrance to see her off. The courtyard was full of people running to and fro. There was a row of palanquins there, some belonging to the ladies who had come from the castle, adorned with the hollyhock crest of the Tokugawa, others with the peony crest of Prince Tadahiro Konoé, Atsu's official family. Yet others were decorated with His Lordship's crest, a plain cross in a circle. Outside the gates Atsu glimpsed troops of soldiers and porters laden with richly adorned lacquered trunks filling the road. A forest of spears poked above the wall. Horses snorted and neighed.

His Lordship was standing beside his charger. He'd chosen Taro, the Kiso stallion. Atsu put her lips to Taro's velvety nose and whispered goodbye to him. She threw His Lordship a quick glance, her lips trembling. It was reassuring to know that he would go with her as far as the palace. He met her eye and gave an almost imperceptible smile in return.

Retainers helped the ladies into their palanquins. In front of the main entrance was the most splendid of all, a miniature palace with a roof beam supporting a long carrying pole, lacquered in glossy black and decorated in gold leaf with the Tokugawa crest entwined with that of the Konoé. Six bearers in pale-blue livery with grey capes stood to attention before and six behind.

Atsu bowed to His Lordship for the last time. Retainers helped her in and she settled herself on her knees on the cushion inside. Everything was there to ease her journey – an armrest, a small shelf of books. Scenes from *The Tale of Genji* decorated three of the gold-leaf walls and the four symbols of long life – crane, tortoise, bamboo and pine – adorned the wall behind her.

Ikushima tucked a futon over her lap and the door slid into place with an imperceptible click. There were shouts, barked orders and the tread of innumerable feet. The bearers lifted the palanquin on to their shoulders so smoothly Atsu barely realized they'd started moving and they set off, through the gates of the Satsuma mansion and out into the teeming streets of Edo.

20

Edo Castle

Atsu swayed along in semi-darkness, watching the shadows flicker across the gilded walls and hearing the palanquin creak. She was nearly as grand as the unnameable one himself now, so grand that ordinary people could not be allowed to set eyes on her – though that meant she couldn't see anything either.

She heard the crunch of straw-sandalled feet on the earthen road as the bearers heaved her high in the air then lowered her again, rocking her back and forth as if she was in a boat on the ocean. Bells clanged, staves pounded the ground, heralds roared, 'Make way for Her Imperial Highness! Down on your knees! Down!'

As she whiled away the hours there was time enough for sadness and regret, time to think over the past and say a last farewell in her mind to all the people she was leaving behind, time – too much time – to brood over the future. Now she stared unseeingly into the gloom, wondering what kind of man she was being sent to marry. She couldn't imagine how she was going to accomplish the task Lord Nariakira had set her.

And the worst of it was that whether or not she succeeded, she would still live out the rest of her days in the palace. Her lips trembled at the thought of a lifetime of confinement, no matter how luxurious the gilded cage might be. Once a tawny face with eyes that gazed into the far distance floated into her mind. She reminded herself sternly that she would never see that face again. She had to put Kaneshigé behind her, banish him from her thoughts for ever.

It was dusk by the time they reached the castle. She peeked out. Despite herself she was eager to catch a glimpse of her new home. They were passing between the towering white walls of a gatehouse. She heard shouts and the dull thud of heavy wooden doors swinging shut. Then there was a last boom, deep and resonant, as the Great Gate, the famous cedar door that separated the women's palace from the world outside, slammed behind her.

The footsteps were lighter now and the shouts higher-pitched – women's tones. When she peeked out again, corridors beetled away into the distance. They were inside a building. Women bowed their faces to the ground, women's voices shrilled, 'Her Imperial Highness! On your knees! Make way!'

They passed gardens, walkways, vast rooms walled with exquisite painted screens. Finally the bouncing and creaking stopped and the door to the little box slid open. Ikushima was outside. She held out her hand and Atsu stepped out, straightening her legs as Ikushima tugged her kimonos into place and smoothed the skirts of her olive-green mantle.

Atsu looked around and her eyes widened. She was on a stage at the end of a huge room. Candles and oil lamps cast puddles of wan yellow light. She smelt kyara and sandalwood, musk and ambergris, mingled with camphor and a dank mustiness. Glistening heads with black hair coiled into glossy loops stretched away into the gloom. There were several hundred women on their knees but the room was totally silent. All Atsu heard was the sound of her own breathing.

Ikushima ushered her to a cushion and Atsu took her place facing the crowd, her heart thundering. These were the women among whom she was to live the rest of her life as their queen. She wondered what they thought of her.

One raised her head and Atsu saw a pinched face with piercing eyes and a prominent nose, crowned with a bouffant black wig held in place with a large hairpin. 'Your Imperial Highness is most welcome.' It was the sour voice she'd heard at Lord Nariakira's mansion.

The woman made an elaborate bow. 'If your lowly servant may take the liberty of introducing herself . . .'

Atsu tipped her head just a fraction to establish her superior rank. She was on her own now. It was time to put her training into practice.

The woman's eyes flashed. 'This unworthy person goes by the name of Anekoji. Your humble servant holds the position of Chief Elder of the Great Interior and will do her best to be of all possible assistance to Your Imperial Highness.' For all her grovelling she somehow conveyed an air of ineffable disdain. She was clearly a power to be reckoned with.

There was utter silence. Not even a kimono rustled.

'Forgive my impertinence,' said the woman, bowing again. 'There is one small formality to complete. We ask it of all who live among us, even the very highest in rank. I would be obliged if Your Imperial Highness and your ladies would graciously swear an oath of secrecy. If Your Highness would be so kind as to extend your hand, it will just be a tiny jab. It will not hurt at all.'

'You wish me to swear in blood?' Atsu opened her eyes wide. She thought she'd been fully briefed but no one had said a word of this.

Ikushima rushed forward. 'This is an unacceptable breach of protocol,' she said. 'You cannot really expect Her Imperial Highness to sign in blood!'

'A thousand thousand pardons, Your Highness,' the elder replied, addressing Atsu. 'This is our custom, established by Lord Ieyasu at the founding of the dynasty two hundred and fifty years ago. Would you deign to read this document?'

Atsu drew herself up as regally as she could and glanced at the neatly written characters: 'On my life I swear never to reveal anything of what I see or hear or witness or do behind the cedar door. The castle's secrets will go with me to my grave.'

If she was to fulfil her promise to Lord Nariakira she would have to betray many of the palace's secrets. She wondered what the penalty was for such treachery. Even as their queen she would not be above the law.

She kept her face impassive as a mask, pursed her lips as if it was the most trivial request in the world and held out her small white hand, palm up. Elder Anekoji took a needle from her sash and stabbed it into Atsu's forefinger. Atsu started. The old woman had stabbed harder than she needed to. The sting shocked her awake. She'd been half hoping that everything that had happened today had been a bad dream. But no. She was really here, in the women's palace.

The elder squeezed out a drop of blood and Atsu pressed her finger to the paper.

Her ladies followed in order of rank. Even Ikushima trembled at the solemnity of the oath.

A second woman raised her head. She had a broad motherly face with full cheeks and large wide-spaced eyes. She smiled warmly. 'Welcome, my lady. It is a great honour to have Your Highness among us. My name is Omasé. I am a Middle Elder and am assigned to be your chief attendant. I will do my best to serve you in every way I can.'

Atsu recognized her kindly tones too. This lady at least might prove an ally, she thought, returning her smile. All the same she would have to be cautious. It was impossible to be sure who she could really trust.

Elder Anekoji jerked her chin and maids filed in and served tea as the ladies of the court introduced themselves one by one.

Ikushima knelt at one side of the chamber along with Atsu's chief ladies-in-waiting, who had come with her from Kagoshima. They looked like provincials compared to the highly painted court ladies. They'd learned the palace dialect but they couldn't erase their southern twang, whereas the castle ladies spoke as if born to it. Eager, shy, uncertain of what sort of reception they were going to get, the Kagoshima women peeped at these haughty aristocrats, wondering who might turn out to be friends and who foes. And then there was Ikushima's own retinue, the grand ladies from Prince Konoé's mansion who had been assigned to Atsu in Miyako. They had a whole different set of airs and graces. It was hard to imagine how they were all going to get on.

191

Finally the introductions came to an end. Elder Anekoji smacked her fan on the tatami and the room fell silent. 'The formal welcome in the Great Hall is at the hour of the dog,' she proclaimed. 'We must begin preparations. The Lady Dowager cannot be kept waiting.'

The Lady Dowager – the shogun's mother. Atsu's heart thumped and her breath came faster. She didn't feel ready to meet this formidable woman.

Middle Elder Omasé appeared at her elbow. 'I have taken the liberty of selecting Your Highness's kimonos for this first formal meeting,' she murmured. 'I am afraid you will find you have to change many times a day here, my lady. Let me show you to your wing. We call it the Pine Rooms.'

Atsu gazed around the vast rooms at the sumptuous furnishings, the walls and screens painted with landscapes, trees and flowers. It was oddly threadbare. The tatami mats were worn and cobwebs looped the intricately carved lintels. She wrinkled her nose. The musty smell was stronger than ever.

'We shall air them out,' said Omasé. 'They will look more welcoming when Your Highness's trunks are unpacked and your trousseau laid out.'

Atsu nodded. She couldn't imagine ever feeling at home in this gloomy place. She sighed as she thought of what she'd left behind that very morning – Kaneshigé, Lord Nariakira, the sunny rooms of the Satsuma mansion. She'd never felt so alone in all her life.

In the dressing room kimonos hung on racks and there were boxes of make-up spread across the floor. Atsu stretched out her arms as the wardrobe mistress and her assistants wrapped her in thick brocade kimonos and tied them in place with elaborate obis. They draped a white satin mantle with a quilted hem around her shoulders and tied her glossy black hair into a long heavy tail that swung as she walked.

Middle Elder Omasé ushered her to a waiting room, then excused herself. Atsu breathed a sigh of relief. For a few precious moments she and Ikushima were on their own. In this hostile place Ikushima felt like a friend.

Atsu stepped closer to her. 'What do you know about the Lady Dowager?' she asked in a whisper. She glanced around, remembering the old saying that walls have ears and screens have eyes. Very little went unheard or unseen in this palace with its paper walls.

'Her Ladyship is the most powerful person in the Great Interior,' Ikushima replied in a murmur. 'She is His Majesty's mother. She was recruited with the rank of Personal Attendant and given the name O Mitsu no kata, Lady Beautiful Harbour. In her youth she was as beautiful as the moon. She was His Majesty's father's favourite concubine in his early years. She is fifty-one years of age now and has held the title of Dowager Mother for as long as anyone can remember.

'When His Majesty's father passed away three years ago, Her Ladyship cut her hair and entered holy orders. She took the Buddhist name Honju-in, Hall of Great Happiness. However, she did not go into retirement in the Western Palace as the widows and concubines of the late lords usually do. She chose to stay on in the Main Palace, close to His Majesty, her son. She is the most senior lady here. She has ruled over the palace for a long time. She will not take kindly to having you here, my lady. She will see you as a rival.'

Atsu nodded. She would need to find a way to get on with this woman at least enough to stop her stepping between Atsu and her son.

'I gather that she is difficult,' said Ikushima. 'But do not let her goad you into getting annoyed. Leave me to fight your battles for you. You need to maintain your dignity. Remember, the proper form of address for her is Lady Dowager or Dowager Mother. It is best to treat her with deference.'

Atsu nodded. Lord Nariakira had warned her about Lady Honju-in. An old witch, he had called her, who wielded undue influence over her son. But it was a hurdle she had to cross. Everything, not just her mission but her entire future, hung on how she got on with this dreaded mother-in-law-to-be.

'And what of His Majesty?' Atsu breathed. It was the question she wanted to ask more than anything.

But Ikushima held up her hand as the door slid open and Middle Elder Omasé appeared.

21

The Great Hall was larger even than the vast chamber where Atsu had first arrived. Gold glimmered on the walls and coffered ceiling. Hundreds of women knelt motionless, faces pressed to the tatami. Candles and lamps on tall gold stands flickered along the walls. But Atsu barely saw any of it. All she was aware of was the small imperious figure who knelt on the raised platform at the far end of the room, scowling and tapping her fan into her palm.

Elder Anekoji ushered Atsu through the hall between the ranks of women. There was silence apart from the swish of her kimono skirts and the insistent tap of the fan. Atsu reached the platform and the elder showed her to her place. Atsu stopped, aghast. It was on a lower level than the Lady Dowager and there was no cushion there. It was a deliberate affront.

Atsu knew she must be careful not to antagonize Lady Honju-in but she needed to make it clear that she was not to be trifled with. Still on her feet, she glanced across the hall to where Ikushima knelt at one side.

A stir ran through the assembled women when they saw that Atsu wasn't taking her place. Hundreds of heads were lifted, hundreds of eyes fixed on her and quickly lowered again.

Ikushima understood immediately. She gestured to a maid who carried over a cushion and placed it next to Lady Honju-in's so that she and Atsu were on the same level.

Atsu turned, put her fingers to the tatami and bowed to the Lady Dowager.

Lady Honju-in bowed back. She had been watching the panto-mime through hooded eyes.

It was hard to believe she had ever been as beautiful as the moon. Her flesh hung like parchment around black-rimmed eyes, her rouged cheeks sagged and her large protruding mouth was painted an intense shade of scarlet. Far from wearing a nun's drab habit, she was clad in a mantle embroidered with phoenixes and what looked like octopuses, with gold, green and red kimonos visible at the collar and cuffs. The scent of kyara, rich and pungent, hovered around her.

The Lady Dowager turned to Atsu, lifted her shaved brows, gave a flap of her fan and drawled out a sentence in language so archaic that Atsu barely understood a word. Atsu groaned inwardly in mortification. The dowager was speaking the language reserved for the shogun and his family, which not even Ikushima knew.

It didn't take much to guess that she was uttering phrases of welcome. Covering up her confusion, Atsu recited the greetings she'd been taught. 'We are so sorry to cause you trouble. We beg your indulgence.'

'Her Imperial Highness Princess Sumiko is most welcome,' Her Ladyship said in words Atsu could understand, though her accent was still archaic. 'The weather has turned cold. Please be careful of your health.'

Elder Anekoji gestured with her chin and a procession of maids filed in with arms upraised, holding low tables, followed by others carrying shallow red bowls for saké and stacks of lacquered boxes full of delicacies. Elder Anekoji served Lady Honju-in and Atsu with saké and they toasted each other.

'So delightful to have young blood among us again,' drawled Lady Honju-in. 'But you are not that young, I think. How old did you say you were, my dear?' She narrowed her eyes and held up an eyeglass. 'Twenty, was it not? A little old to be a bride. I would have preferred someone younger.' It seemed she was so old and powerful that she didn't have to be polite. She gave a shrill laugh and her women tittered sycophantically in chorus. 'You certainly have a pretty face,' she added. 'My darling son will be pleased.' She took another sip of saké. Beneath the chalky make-up her withered cheeks were beginning to flush.

'You must be tired. What a long journey you have had. What a treat to meet someone from outside.' She raised her painted eyebrows a fraction as she uttered the last words. It was another slight, a none too subtle reminder that Atsu was an interloper. For all their pretty words, the women seemed to know perfectly well that she was a Satsuma and their enemy – a cuckoo in the nest.

Atsu tipped her head to one side. 'It is a privilege for us to be here,' she said sweetly. 'We ask your indulgence. Please allow us some time to learn the ways of the palace.' She took care to use the royal 'we'. It was just as well to remind the dowager that no matter how she had started out in life she was an imperial princess now.

Lady Honju-in glanced at her out of her sharp eyes. She missed nothing. 'Of course,' she said, giving a little cough.

Atsu shifted on her cushion. 'May we tell Your Ladyship a little about what goes on outside the palace?' she said. 'We had the chance to see a great deal on our journey up from Miyako.'

Lady Honju-in narrowed her eyes to black slits. 'You say you're from Miyako, my dear? That is hardly a Miyako face. Very pretty to be sure but not in the Miyako way. Not pale and wan and sickly like a Miyako princess. More like a strapping Satsuma wench, if I'm not mistaken. Lovely white skin, of course. But the lift of the cheekbones, not at all a Miyako face.'

Atsu flushed. 'If I'm right, Your Ladyship, His Majesty's grandmother was a Satsuma,' she shot back. 'Midai Shigeko, she was called, was she not? I understand she passed away not so long ago. Perhaps Your Ladyship was acquainted with her.'

She bit her tongue. She'd spoken without thinking. There was a month and a half to go before she would even meet the shogun. Lady Honju-in had plenty of time to poison him against her. Atsu needed to do all she could to make this fearsome old woman approve of her.

Lady Honju-in leaned forward and peered at her through her eyeglass. 'I can see we're going to be good friends,' she said dryly. 'For one so young you certainly speak up for yourself. Midai Shigeko.

Yes, I remember her well. She had the Satsuma temperament and the Satsuma temper – like you, I suspect.' She tapped Atsu on the arm with her fan. 'There is no need to worry. You are here at my wish. Lord Nariakira and I have discussed it at length.'

Atsu stared in disbelief. The old woman had turned the tables on her. Lord Nariakira was the most hated of all the outside lords, the chief enemy of this nest of vipers. Yet he had managed to persuade this shrewd old lady that it was in her best interests to have Atsu in the palace without revealing that his real purpose was for Atsu to work against her. Though perhaps Lady Honju-in guessed that too. She was no innocent.

It was going to be an enormous job to unravel the political networks here. It was a mighty enough task just to fathom who were her friends and who her enemies.

'I supported your candidacy,' the old lady continued smoothly. 'With the barbarians trying to take over our country, we need to pull together – and how better than to make an alliance with the imperial family and unite all the clans under the rule of my son?' She bared her teeth in a smile. Black polish glinted in the candlelight. 'Now. Tell me a little of the news from outside.'

Atsu could guess what would interest her. 'We are sure Your Ladyship has excellent lines of communication,' she said. 'You surely know everything that goes on. But perhaps Your Ladyship has not actually seen a western barbarian with her own eyes?'

'A barbarian?' Lady Honju-in's face puffed up like a frog's. 'They aim cannons at our castle. They bring pestilence. And now they force us to let them live here, so we keep them penned in Shimoda, at the far ends of the earth.' She cackled with laughter, then scowled. Her face blackened and she slapped her fan on the tatami with such a crack that the assembled ladies jumped. 'It is a violation of our sacred territory,' she screamed. 'How dare these creatures think they can tell us what to do?'

'Your Ladyship may be curious to know what they look like.'

The women fell silent, listening.

'Hairy and smelly like animals, are they not? I hear they gorge on animal flesh.' Lady Honju-in wrinkled her nose.

'We saw eight ships anchored just outside the harbour at Kanagawa.' Atsu smiled. She was back on the hilltop, gazing through Lord Nariakira's spyglass. 'They are huge, far bigger than any ship we have ever seen, much bigger than any of our ships, with cannons like teeth poking out all around the hull. We saw westerners too, adjusting the masts or cleaning the deck. Some were eating. Even the young ones have hairy faces like Chinese sages.'

Lady Honju-in leaned forward. 'And are they as strange-looking as in the pictures?'

Atsu smiled. 'They are human, like us, but their skin is the colour of wax and their hair is the colour of straw.' It was best not to mention that Lord Nariakira knew them well and admired their technology and that she'd had a close view of them herself through his spyglass.

'We are eager to meet His Majesty,' she added. She wanted to ask more about him but she didn't know how to begin.

'Normally he'd come in for the three daily audiences,' said Lady Honju-in. 'He loves coming here. But he is indisposed again. That boy's health was never good.'

Atsu took a breath. 'His Majesty is of delicate constitution?' she asked as casually as she could.

Lady Honju-in gave an arch smile and raised a painted eyebrow. 'Indeed. We may have to postpone the wedding.'

Atsu shot a glance at her. She was smirking. The old woman was playing with her. She would never give away any clues about her son's condition. The one thing Atsu knew was that they could never postpone the wedding. The day had been set for months.

She glanced out over the crowd of withered faces and sharp black eyes under enormous wigs. Some of the women were younger than Atsu, but many looked even older than Lady Honju-in, as shrunken and shrivelled as autumn leaves, as if the slightest wind would blow them away.

One woman sat a little apart from the others, surrounded by her own retinue. She was not particularly beautiful, in fact she was rather plain, but there was something about her that drew the eye. She looked curiously at Atsu. While the other women smiled and bowed, she seemed rather aloof. She held Atsu's gaze then slowly looked down with a faint smile.

'Lady Shiga,' said Lady Honju-in. 'Let me introduce you to Her Imperial Highness.'

The woman approached the dais on her knees. 'I'm Shiga,' she said, bowing. By her accent she was of low-ranking samurai stock. She spoke like a down-to-earth soldier's daughter.

'Lady Shiga's been with us a long time,' said Lady Honju-in. 'She came in right at the bottom as a scullery maid. She was in charge of our late lord's consort's rooms, she kept the brazier burning. Then she rose through the ranks.'

Atsu was expecting Lady Shiga to cringe at this brutal revelation of her humble origins but she looked entirely composed and unconcerned. She nodded and bowed, gazing at Atsu in a way that made Atsu feel uncomfortable.

'Now she takes care of my son's suite. They're very good friends. Isn't that right, Lady Shiga?'

Atsu felt her cheeks grow hot. She hadn't even met her husband-to-be, yet she felt an unaccountable prickle of jealousy. She narrowed her eyes. So Lady Shiga was one of his concubines. There were probably plenty more in this crowd of women.

Lady Honju-in beamed. She was enjoying Atsu's discomfiture. 'We are all eager to make Your Highness's acquaintance,' she said smoothly. 'Let us begin with the most senior. My son's father, our beloved Lord Ieyoshi, loved women.' She giggled, hiding her mouth with an arthritic hand like a blushing young girl. 'Those of his concubines who survived him went to live in the Western Palace when he passed away. Lady Tsuyu has left her prayers and observances to come over here today and welcome you.'

A tiny elderly woman slid on her knees out of the crowd. She was dressed in a drab grey habit and cowled like a nun.

'Lady Tsuyu was one of Lord Ieyoshi's favourites,' purred Lady Honju-in. 'Apart, of course, from myself.'

Lady Tsuyu touched two tiny bird's-claw hands to the tatami. She was a wisp of a woman, so ancient and frail she looked like a shadow. She fixed her eyes on Atsu. 'Do you really come from outside?' she croaked. 'How I would love to visit again, just for a day! I was so young when I was brought here, younger than you are, my dear. I never guessed I would never leave again.'

Atsu cringed in horror. She felt as if she was seeing into her own future. So this was what life had in store for her – decades immured in this living tomb till she too was as frail and insubstantial as this tiny old woman.

Lady Honju-in butted in. 'Now, Lady Tsuyu, that's not entirely true. When you were young you often broke out and enjoyed yourself. Times have changed. We've all become more sober. Your life may be dull now, but you have an excellent salary.' She gave a cackle of laughter. 'You have a good life here, Tsuyu, my dear,' she added, raising her voice.

Tsuyu cupped a hand to her ear. She peered at Atsu through eyes veiled with a white film. 'In this place you reach the age of thirty and it's "No, thank you,"' she squawked defiantly. 'Wife or concubine, it makes no difference. You're finished, you're on the rubbish heap.'

Atsu stared at her aghast.

'So if a priest petitions you to support his temple, you go. What difference does it make? There's nothing to lose. Why not consort with handsome young priests when you'll spend the rest of your life locked up?' She tugged her kimono skirts open and pointed a skinny finger between her withered thighs. 'Hungry,' she rasped. 'We get hungry down here.' The old woman reached out and grasped Atsu's wrist in a claw-like hand. Atsu started and tried to pull away but her grip was unexpectedly strong.

Lady Honju-in barked an order and a troop of maids descended on Lady Tsuyu and wrenched her away from Atsu. They lifted her bodily off the ground.

'Stop!' Atsu said. 'Treat her with more respect!'

But they had already carried her out of the room. Lady Tsuyu's voice floated back. 'We were cleared of wrongdoing,' she squawked.

Lady Honju-in flapped her fan. 'Dear old soul,' she said. 'She gets confused. So tragic. She had three children but not one survived.'

Atsu frowned. She could see that Lady Honju-in had a strangle-hold over the palace as well as over her son. One thing in particular struck her as odd. She hadn't seen a single child. With so many women, surely some would have had children. So Lord Nariakira had been right. There was no heir. There were no children at all.

The door slid open. A shaven-headed figure in the black robes of a priest was on her knees outside. Ikushima had told Atsu about these 'companion priests' who dressed like men and went back and forth between the men's and women's palaces.

'His Majesty is indisposed,' the woman announced. 'There will be no evening audience tonight.'

A smug smile creased Lady Honju-in's face.

Middle Elder Omasé led Atsu back to her wing along a labyrinth of corridors. Atsu lost track of the twists and turns, the verandas and bridges and huge empty rooms. It would take a long time to find her way by herself. The palace was as vast as a city.

Futons in red silk covers had been laid out for her with a silken pillow with long red tassels at the head. There were thinner futons at a lower level for the ladies in-waiting who would sleep with Atsu. Chiyo and Yasu, Atsu's two favourites, settled down, one on each side of her.

Atsu sank into her luxurious bedding. If they hadn't been here, she thought, she would have wept for loneliness. She wished she was in her mother's house in Ibusuki or in the Satsuma mansion, anywhere that felt at least a little bit like home. She didn't know how she would ever get used to this place of dark shadows and huge cold spaces and hostile staring eyes.

Later she was woken by a noise. She thought she'd heard cries or sobbing, but there was silence. She told herself it was just the wind shaking the window frames. Lantern light seeped between the cracks in the rain doors and she heard women's voices. Even the night watch were women. Somewhere not far away a fox gave a mournful howl. She shuddered and pulled her covers over her head and tried to go back to sleep, wondering what the next day would have in store.

22

'It is half past the sixth hour, Your Highness. Time to rise.'

The soft voice broke into Atsu's dreams and she looked around, bewildered. Her heart sank as she remembered where she was.

Chiyo and Yasu knelt beside her and combed her hair. Rosy-cheeked chambermaids lugged in baskets of charcoal and the braziers began to glow. With the rain doors pushed back and the first rays of dawn filtering through the paper screens, the great rooms felt more welcoming.

The toilet was the most elegant Atsu had ever seen, with a tatami-matted floor and a carved wooden lid. There were attendants standing by with damp scented cloths to cleanse and wipe her. It seemed she would never use her own hands again except to wield chopsticks or a writing brush or pluck the strings of her koto.

'Will madam take her morning ablutions?' whispered a serious-looking young woman with a round face and prominent forehead. 'My name is Maru,' she added shyly. Atsu had noticed her large curious eyes when she had introduced herself the previous day.

The bathroom was large and splendid, filled with the scent of cedar. Attendants scrubbed Atsu till she was glowing, then she stepped into the steaming water, feeling the warmth sink into her bones.

A lavish breakfast of soup, fish, vegetables and rice had been laid out on lacquered tables. The wardrobe attendants dressed Atsu's hair as she picked at the rich food.

All this luxury filled her with misgiving. She saw her life

stretching ahead of her – waking at the same hour, being made up and dressed and fed, with no chance to think about anything. She couldn't imagine how she was going to carry out the task Lord Nariakira had assigned her when she was constantly busy, constantly surrounded by women.

A tortoiseshell kitten rubbed against her leg. It climbed on to her lap and she tickled it behind the ears and stroked its tiny body. 'What is its name?' she asked.

Middle Elder Omasé was hovering solicitously. 'Most don't have names. This one has chosen you, my lady. Please give her a name.'

'Jewel,' Atsu said, smiling. She'd had a cat called Jewel in Ibusuki. She had made one friend here, at least.

Ikushima appeared. While Chiyo and Yasu had spent the night with Atsu, she had been assigned her own apartments.

'Come, madam,' she said, smiling mysteriously. 'I have something to show you.' She led her to the dressing room. It was filled to the rafters with embroidered silks and glittering lacquerware.

'Your trousseau,' said Ikushima. 'We took the liberty of unpacking your trunks.'

Atsu gazed around, shaking her head in astonishment. Lord Nariakira had spared no expense to set her up in a manner befitting an imperial princess. There were racks of silken kimonos, exquisite brocade obis, decorative shelves, hanging scrolls painted with scenes from *The Tale of Genji* and a jewellery box encrusted with pearls. There was a lacquered make-up set, mirrors and mirror stands, a tooth-blackening set, a writing desk and ink set, a tea ceremony chest, a smoking set, utensils for the incense-guessing game together with incense pillows, poem-matching cards, drums, a koto, a Go board and two lacquered and tasselled boxes of shells for the shell-matching game. Everything was there for a lifetime of luxury and leisure.

There was also a collection of erotic paintings, books and prints. Atsu glanced at a picture of a couple energetically making love. Chiyo peeked too, her thin cheeks flushing. Atsu wondered how they were all going to survive here, herself as much as any of them. Most of her ladies were not even twenty, very young to be doomed to celibacy. They might as well have entered a convent.

Cats picked their way between the treasures. The women shooed them away but more slunk in.

Atsu's own small trunk was in a side room. It seemed a lifetime since her mother had packed her clothes and books for her. All the time she'd been travelling, to Kagoshima, then Miyako, then to the Satsuma mansion in Edo, she'd only opened it once, to take out a book. She'd always been given everything she could possibly want. She didn't open it now either. Better to leave it packed. She had the superstitious feeling that if she unpacked it she'd never leave again.

Voices floated through the paper walls that divided the rooms.

'Ara! Isn't this a child's kimono?' It sounded like Maru, the solemn young woman who had asked if Atsu wanted a bath.

'Give it to me,' said a disdainful drawl in an Edo accent. 'It's Lady Hideko's. She liked bright colours. Look at it. How terrible. It's full of moth holes.'

'This is the one Lady Hideko wore when we went boating that time,' another voice clamoured. 'And here's one of her dolls.'

'Give it to me. She was fond of me. She didn't care for you in the slightest.'

There was a clunk and a sudden silence, followed by shrieks of 'Look what you've done. It's bad luck.'

Atsu ran to the storeroom at the far end of her wing and slid open the door. 'What is going on here? What are you arguing about?'

A group of court ladies and their maids were gathered around a chest in the far corner of the dark airless room. They dropped to their knees. Trunks stood open. In the middle was a doll lying on the tatami, dressed in quilted robes like a princess. Pieces of its porcelain head were scattered about. A superstitious shudder ran down Atsu's spine. It was almost as if it was her, Atsu, lying there broken.

'Whose is this?' she asked. She had to take a breath before she could bring herself to pick up the headless doll.

An elegant young woman tilted her head. It was an attendant who had introduced herself as Hana, Flower. She had the long-jawed oval face of a classic Edo beauty, powdered floury white. She really was as lovely as a flower. 'We weren't doing anything wrong, madam,' she said. Atsu recognized the drawl. 'We were just preparing the room to put away your belongings.' She was clutching a crumpled cornflower-blue kimono. It was tiny, like a child's garment, moth-eaten and faded. Other kimonos were heaped on the floor.

'You mentioned Lady Hideko,' said Atsu. 'Why are her belongings in my apartments?'

Ikushima swept in on Atsu's heels. 'How dare you treat Her Highness with such disrespect?' she snapped.

Middle Elder Omasé appeared, took everything in with a practised glance and dropped to her knees before Atsu. 'I'm so sorry, my lady,' she said. 'This wing of the palace has been out of use for years.'

She snatched the kimono from Hana's hands and turned pale as if she'd seen a ghost. 'Lady Hideko,' she gasped.

Her hands shaking, she reached for the broken doll and the pieces of its head. 'Why are all her things still here?' she said, dabbing her eyes. 'I was sure everything had been thrown away. It's as if she's still here among us.' She shook her head. 'After she passed away we closed this wing down. We should have checked more thoroughly before you came, my lady.'

'I thought this was the consort's wing,' Atsu said. 'My wing.'

Omasé raised her shaved and painted eyebrows. 'I'm sorry, my lady,' she said again. 'I'd forgotten. What happens here never goes beyond the palace walls.' She sighed. 'Lady Hideko was His Majesty's previous consort. We never thought there'd be another.'

Atsu dropped to her knees. It was the last thing she'd expected to hear – that the shogun had had a consort before her. She'd wanted to find out more about him, but not that. So he had a concubine and he'd had a consort. By the sounds of it he was a normal man, not as weak and sickly as Lord Nariakira had made out.

There was a rustle as an imperious figure appeared in the doorway.

'Your Imperial Highness. Here you are.' It was Chief Elder

Anekoji, the sharp-featured woman who had administered the blood oath. The elder bowed with elaborate courtesy. 'It is the hour for the morning observances,' she said. 'May I take the liberty of escorting Your Highness to the shrine room? I am sure you will wish to make yourself known to His Majesty's ancestors.'

Atsu nodded. As a wife, most particularly the shogun's, praying to the ancestors would be one of her most important duties.

The shrine room was vast and cold and crammed with tier upon tier of memorial tablets, some of black marble, some of unlacquered wood. Smoke billowed from thousands of incense sticks. Atsu hugged herself, shivering.

A forest of tablets stretched into the darkness, some old and dusty, others quite new. 'His Majesty's father and grandfather had many children,' Middle Elder Omasé explained softly. 'Most died when they were just born or very small.'

Right at the front was a tablet of pale new wood with a name etched on it in Sanskrit. 'Lord Ieyoshi, His Majesty's father,' said Elder Anekoji, bowing solemnly.

Beside it were two newish-looking tablets. Atsu started as she read the name on one: 'Lady Hideko'. The identical tablet next to it read 'Princess Tadako'. She swayed, gripped the shelf to steady herself. Her head was swimming from the smell of the incense. She was suffocating from the smoke. She pulled her jacket closer around her. A chill gripped her heart.

So there had been two consorts and both had died. That meant she was the next in line. There was no escape. She could almost see the gaping grave, waiting for her to step in. She felt as if she was being buried alive.

23

Back in Atsu's wing, Middle Elder Omasé slid open the screens in one of the smaller rooms. Leafless cherry and maple trees filled the ornamental garden alongside gnarled pines, craggy rocks, an arched bridge and a pond with a small waterfall tumbling into it. The sky was an intense shade of blue. It was a perfect winter's day.

'Princess Tadako and Lady Hideko loved sitting here,' said Omasé, smiling wistfully.

Court ladies knelt discreetly along the side of the room. Hana, the elegant Edo lady, lit a long-stemmed pipe and offered it to Atsu then filled pipes for Elder Anekoji, Middle Elder Omasé and Ikushima.

Elder Anekoji took a long pull and blew out a plume of smoke. 'The gods have been cruel to His Majesty,' she said with a sigh.

'We prayed for his health and happiness,' said Omasé. 'And now you've come, my lady. Perhaps our prayers have been answered.'

Atsu cradled a cup of tea. Her hands were shaking. It was the cold, she told herself. She wished she could meet this husband-to-be. Perhaps then things would start to make sense.

'I have been in the palace for more than forty years,' said Elder Anekoji. 'When I first came, His Majesty's grandfather was shogun. There were children everywhere, romping, playing, laughing. I can't remember how many he had.' She gave a raucous laugh.

'Fifty-three,' said Middle Elder Omasé. The court ladies dimpled.

'Some died, of course. But the gods ensured that plenty lived. They are old themselves now. They will come and pay their respects to you, Your Highness, when they visit.' She took another puff on her pipe.

Atsu nodded. All she could think of was the two memorial tablets. The shogun was young. His mother, Lady Honju-in, was only fifty-one. Yet he had already had two consorts and both were dead. She looked from one to the other, at Middle Elder Omasé's bland kindly features and Elder Anekoji's sharp-nosed hostile ones. In theory they were there to serve her, but they had both been in the palace since they were children. That was where their loyalty lay. They would protect its secrets to the end.

She took a breath. 'But His Majesty, my husband-to-be, has no children?'

'We've seen a lot of sadness, Your Highness,' said Elder Anekoji, raising her sleeve to her eyes melodramatically. 'Dear Princess Tadako. I remember the day she passed away – so young, so cruelly taken from us.'

Atsu held her breath, waiting for more.

'Excuse my presumption,' said Omasé, wrinkling her broad fore-head. 'Her Imperial Highness has only just arrived. It is too early to talk about such matters.'

Atsu tapped her pipe sharply on the side of the tobacco box. 'I would like to know,' she said. 'Please tell me what happened to . . . to Princess Tadako and Lady Hideko.' For now it was best not to ask what sort of man the shogun was. She would find that out in good time.

The elders raised their eyebrows and exchanged glances.

Elder Anekoji sighed. 'You are quite right, Your Highness. You have to know.' Her sharp features softened and she gave a senti-mental smile. 'Princess Tadako was His Majesty's first consort. She was of impeccably high lineage. She was the daughter of the Imperial Chancellor in Miyako. She was betrothed to His Majesty when they were five. It was the union of the Tokugawa dynasty and the imperial family, just as it has always been through the generations.

'They married thirteen years later, when they were both eighteen. His Majesty's grandfather had died the previous year and his father,

Lord Ieyoshi, was shogun. His Majesty was heir apparent. Princess Tadako lived here, in the consort's wing.'

'She was beautiful and talented,' said Omasé. 'She played the shoulder drum and danced. In her spare time she read and wrote poetry and painted and played games and walked in the gardens. She was a gentle and lovely person.'

'You're too forgiving, Middle Elder Omasé,' Elder Anekoji butted in sternly. 'Her Imperial Highness brought in geisha to teach her dancing, a shocking breach of protocol. And she once disappeared for several days. She had to be severely disciplined for that.'

Atsu frowned. Elder Anekoji was issuing a warning that even His Majesty's consort would not be allowed to step out of line.

'She certainly got on well with His Majesty,' said Middle Elder Omasé hastily. 'When he came for the evening audience she frequently spent the night in his quarters. We call it the Little Sitting Room though it's not really little at all, as you'll see, my lady.'

'But they had no children?' Atsu persisted.

'Sadly not.' They exchanged glances. Atsu wondered what they were not telling her.

'They'd been married seven years when there was an outbreak of smallpox. Several princes and pages and maidservants came down with it. We were fearful for Her Highness. We had shrines to the smallpox demon installed throughout the palace and isolated the sick.

'The worst seemed to be over when Princess Tadako became feverish. The shogun, His Majesty's father, sent in his own doctors. They tried the Dutch method, carried out the red treatment – dressed her in red, gave her red covers and kept red lanterns burning around her. But she only got worse.

'It's eight years ago now since she passed away. She was twenty-five. No one will ever forget that day. His Majesty was quite affected.'

There was a long silence. The court ladies wiped their eyes. A chambermaid stoked the brazier and Atsu held her hands over it.

Hana offered her a fresh pipe and she pictured those tapered fingers holding the cornflower-blue kimono. She took a breath. 'And

Lady Hideko?' she whispered. She hardly dared say the name. Princess Tadako had long since gone but Lady Hideko somehow still seemed to be present.

Elder Anekoji gave a snort of laughter. 'That one certainly stepped into the jewelled palanquin and no mistake.'

'What do you mean, speaking of the shogun's late consort with such disrespect?' demanded Atsu, shocked.

Middle Elder Omasé drew her breath through her teeth. 'That is what we say when a woman of low rank is touched by the shogun,' she murmured apologetically.

'One moment she's poor and unknown, the next the shogun has plucked her off the street and installed her in the palace,' said Elder Anekoji. 'The best for her is if she can produce a son and become the mother of the next shogun.' She laughed again, revealing her blackened teeth. 'If she can manage that she'll rise to the top in rank and wealth. We have one here among us.'

Atsu opened her eyes wide. The elder could only be talking about Lady Honju-in. Middle Elder Omasé slapped her on the arm.

'If she plays her cards right she can take her whole family along with her,' Elder Anekoji continued, unperturbed. 'There are lords who are where they are thanks to the fire in their daughter's tail. We call them "firefly lords".'

Atsu lowered her head. At least Lord Nariakira had raised her in rank long before she arrived here. Not even this malevolent woman would dare suggest that she, Atsu, had jumped into the jewelled palanquin.

'My dear madam,' said Omasé hastily. 'We are eternally thankful that you have come here to be His Majesty's consort. The palace has been very dreary in the last few years. You will cheer us all up.'

Atsu frowned. 'I insist. Please tell me. What became of Lady Hideko?'

'She must have been the only virgin of suitable age in the entire city of Miyako,' said Elder Anekoji. 'I can't think of any other reason why they would have chosen her. She was not even a princess. She was the daughter of the Minister of the Left, well below a

Regent in rank. She arrived in a grand palanquin with a huge escort. But when she stepped out she just disappeared.' She laughed again. 'She was no taller than the palanquin. She was such a little thing you couldn't even see her. She always wore a child's kimono. One of her legs was twisted and shorter than the other and she walked with a limp.

'Maybe because of that she was proud and spiteful. She forced the ladies to crawl in her presence. You must remember that incident with the chambermaid, Omasé.'

'What happened?' Atsu asked. She was scandalized at the cruelty of the elder's words, shocked that these women dared speak of His Majesty's consort with so little respect. She wondered what they said about him – and about her too behind her back.

'The chambermaid broke one of her favourite plates and Lady Hideko had a screaming fit. The next day the maid disappeared. A while later they discovered her body down a well. No one ever found out whether she killed herself or was thrown in.

'As for Lady Hideko, she didn't even last out the year. She got thinner and paler and took to her bed and just faded away.'

'That must have been hard for His Majesty,' Atsu said, 'losing two consorts in such a short time.'

The women fell silent and looked at each other.

'We all knew it was a curse, them dying like that, first Princess Tadako, then Lady Hideko,' said Omasé. 'We called in exorcists to drive away the evil influences. We try to carry out the proper ceremonies for the spirits of the dead but there are so many – concubines, children, chambermaids. And then there are the children who've died in the womb. There must be some we don't even know about. With so many unhappy ghosts around, it is no wonder bad things happen. It could very well be that some have not been properly appeased.'

'How old was she when she died?' Atsu muttered, shivering. A cat pawed at her legs. It was Jewel. She lifted her on to her lap. The small warm body comforted her.

'Twenty-five, like Princess Tadako. His Majesty had not even succeeded to the throne. After that there were no more consorts

– until you, Your Highness. His Majesty is shogun now. You will be our first queen.'

Atsu's head was spinning. Perhaps Lady Hideko had conceived a child and the dead children had been jealous. Perhaps she had died in childbirth. Or perhaps it was His Majesty who was cursed, perhaps all his consorts were doomed. Perhaps Atsu too would die at the age of twenty-five.

She clenched her fists, dug her nails into her palms. Lord Nariakira must have known something of all this but he had never said a word of it to her. That must have been why he could manoeuvre her into the palace so easily – because there were no other candidates. Who else would want such a dreadful post? It was going to be a battle just to stay alive, let alone carry out the task that he had assigned her.

But the future of the country depended on it, that much she understood. She had to rise above her doubts and fears.

She swallowed hard. She wanted to run to her room, throw herself on her luxurious futons and weep with despair. But it was too late, way too late.

At least, she told herself, trying to hang on to some glimmer of sanity, His Lordship had educated her to be a modern woman. She'd seen his Kagoshima projects, she'd seen his silver print machine and his message-transmitting wires. He would have dismissed all this talk of curses as so much superstition. She took a breath and repeated to herself the words she'd been taught as a child: 'A warrior does not believe in ghosts. A warrior does not believe in ghosts.'

24

'You must not let Elder Anekoji worry you,' Middle Elder Omasé said when the older woman had gone. 'She was touched by His Majesty's grandfather when she was only thirteen.'

'Touched?'

'That's what we say, my lady. He saw her in the gardens and made her a lady of the side chamber. That's what we call the concubines. She bore him a son but the moment the child was born he was taken away and no one ever found out what became of him. Elder Anekoji suffers still from losing him.

'She thinks the dowager had her child killed to ensure that His Majesty would succeed as shogun. Of Lord Ieyoshi's twenty-seven children, he is the only one who survived. Elder Anekoji kept up a relentless campaign against the Lady Dowager and in the end the dowager had her made an elder to silence her.

'We all have sad stories. This is not a happy place. That time Elder Anekoji was touched by the shogun was the only time she ever felt the touch of a man. But you see, most of us have never been touched at all. We are pure, we are not soiled. But we are shrivelled inside.'

The door of the storeroom was standing open. Atsu thought of the cornflower-blue kimono and felt a strange tug. She wanted to look at it again, to hold it and press her face into it. The story of Princess Tadako was touching but it was Lady Hideko whose fate nagged at her – this sad little woman who had died here so young, unloved and unmourned.

On an impulse she went in. The room had been tidied up and the lids put back on the chests. There were no moth-eaten kimonos lying around now but there was still a musty smell. It was uncannily cold. It was because the brazier was not burning, she told herself sternly.

Then she noticed a birdcage in a corner with a faded cloth draped over it.

'We used to have a gold tit, a yamagara bird, a pretty little thing with bright blue legs,' said Omasé. 'Lady Hideko loved it. She trained it to do tricks. She set up a tiny shrine and taught it to hop up and ring the bell. It died soon after she did.'

'We shall get another,' said Atsu firmly. She hadn't forgotten that she had a mission. She knew that the fate of the country depended on it. But first she had to find a way to survive. She needed to reverse the fate meted out to her predecessors. She would get a bird, a yamagara bird, and this one would live.

25

A few days later Atsu came back to her rooms after her bath to hear chirping. There was a beautiful lacquered cage, freshly polished, swinging from a hook at one side of the room. Hopping about on the perch inside was a gold tit with a blue back, black cap and collar and bright blue feet. There was a dish of berries set on the floor to feed it. It threw back its head, opened its beak and chirruped.

Atsu clapped her hands. 'A yamagara bird!' Princess Tadako and Lady Hideko had haunted her dreams, she hadn't been able to get them out of her mind. The fat little bird seemed a sign that their spirits might be at rest at last.

A couple of cats were prowling around the cage. They batted at it with their paws, turning the bird into a huddle of trembling feathers.

'Away with you!' Atsu cried, shooing them away. As she spoke she realized that that was probably why the previous bird had died. It hadn't been anything supernatural, it had just been scared to death by a cat.

The cats fled and the bird twitched its tail and began to tweet again.

Sunshine bathed the paper screens, lighting up the delicately painted walls and pale tatami matting and lacquered chests that formed the furnishings. 'Your Highness is our queen,' said Middle Elder Omasé, her broad face covered in smiles. 'Whatever Your Highness wishes we'll do our best to fulfil.'

She flung open the screens and the scent of pine swirled in

from the gardens. Bamboo rustled and water rippled in the pond.

'Thought you said you was experienced,' grumbled a man's deep tones. There were gardeners outside, bundled against the winter chill, wrapping the pine trees in straw in preparation for snow. Atsu started. She hadn't had sight or sound of a man since she'd entered the palace.

'This is how we do it where I comes from.'

Atsu had to bite her lip to stop herself laughing with joy as she heard the Satsuma accent, deliberately speaking in the rough tones of a gardener. She knew that voice.

'You don't know anything about wrapping pines where you comes from,' retorted the first. 'It's the tropics down there.'

'I sent them to catch the gold tit,' said Omasé. 'I made sure they were well rewarded.'

Atsu stole a glance at the men. One of them was huge, a good head taller than the other, broad-shouldered and burly. She glimpsed a square jaw and black eyes, shiny as diamonds, through the heavy scarves wrapping his face. Saigo. Lord Nariakira had told her he would send him to her and here he was.

He made the most ridiculous undercover agent. Far from being inconspicuous, he stuck out like a nail that needed to be hammered in. But gardeners were part of the scenery, invisible and non-existent, which was precisely why Lord Nariakira had given him that job. He could come and go and no one would pay the slightest attention to him, except to order him to perform some menial task such as catching a bird.

Suddenly the palace no longer seemed so lonely. Atsu was staggered at the extent of Lord Nariakira's reach. He had installed his henchman right here in her private gardens. With Ikushima's help she would be able to get messages to him. She might even be able to sneak a message to Kaneshigé. She was ecstatic at finding a friend and ally so close at hand. But she also realized what it meant that Saigo was there. He was not just a go-between, he was Lord Nariakira's eyes and ears. It was a message from His Lordship to tell her that he hadn't forgotten her, that she wasn't completely on her own. It was a reminder that she had a job to do.

'I am glad you tipped them well. I love the bird,' she gabbled, hoping Omasé hadn't noticed her confusion. The last thing she wanted was to reveal that there was anything special about this gardener, let alone that she knew him. If the palace officials ever guessed that he was a spy, the penalty would be death and not even Her Imperial Highness Princess Sumiko would be able to save him from that.

'They are good workers,' Middle Elder Omasé said serenely. She was entirely professional. If she had noticed anything she was far too discreet to show it.

Atsu knelt beside the cage, pretending to admire the little bird. She wished she could have had a few more days to settle into her new life. She felt as if she was on the edge of a precipice. It was difficult enough to get used to being the consort-in-waiting, let alone put her mind to the task Lord Nariakira had set her.

As consort everything was done for her, even choosing the five different kimonos she had to change into and out of every day, but she still had to familiarize herself with the palace. It was a vast rambling complex of four hundred rooms housed in ranks of build-ings linked by never-ending corridors and walkways and surrounded by pleasure gardens and boating lakes.

More than three thousand women lived and worked here, Omasé had told her, with Lady Honju-in and the other high-ranking ladies at the top and below them a vast bureaucracy of elders, chamber-lains, secretaries, scribes, female pages and other officials, among them the seasoned ladies-in-waiting with their retinues whom the palace had assigned to Atsu's service.

Below these came the service staff – maids, cooks, waitresses, errand girls, cleaners and scullery maids known as 'honourable dogs', all of whom were too low in rank ever to cast eyes on her or be seen by her. Wherever Atsu went she glimpsed women dash-ing away in a flurry of tied-back sleeves and hiked-up skirts or throwing themselves to their knees and pressing their faces to the floor.

Then there was the night patrol, a couple of hundred brawny women armed with halberds who dressed in black with tall hoods.

And there were also men, even though officially men never entered the palace. A doctor had already been in to give her a check-up and other officials and menials appeared from time to time.

Atsu was finishing her breakfast one morning when she heard voices raised in excitement in one of the large rooms overlooking the gardens.

'Hurry. They'll be here soon.'

'Is my hair smooth? Does this colour suit me?'

The women fell silent as Atsu entered.

Hana, the languid Edo beauty, was checking her long oval face in the mirror, practising her smile. She'd painted her lips with iridescent green safflower paste, the height of fashion. Even solemn Maru with her unhealthy pallor and protruding forehead was bright-eyed. Two stolid middle-aged attendants were patting their cheeks to make them pink and fluttering their fans girlishly. A musky fragrance rose from their scented skirts.

Atsu glanced at them out of the corner of her eye. Of all the Edo ladies, these two were a little too ordinary, a little too helpful, a little too nice. She wondered if they were spies, reporting to Lady Honju-in on what went on in the consort's wing. Some of these women were, certainly. There were probably spies reporting back to the men's palace too. Atsu would have to take extra care. It would never do to let down her guard. Ikushima was no doubt setting up a network of her own on Atsu's behalf to keep an eye on what went on in the rest of the palace.

As the castle bells boomed out the start of the working day, a bevy of burly carpenters in baggy blue work clothes and split-toed cotton boots came tramping through the gardens. So that was what all the fuss was about – men.

The women gazed down at their sewing or their books, trying to pretend they hadn't noticed, but they sat up straighter, tilting their chins coquettishly, trembling with excitement. The cats bristled and darted from the room. Jewel wriggled out of Atsu's grasp and fled.

One of the young men, bolder than the others, sauntered up to the veranda. He seemed to be a foreman. Middle Elder Omasé stepped outside to talk to him, pointing out pillars and boards and sections of the eaves that needed repairing. He nodded deferentially then threw a glance at the ladies inside with just the hint of a grin.

Omasé came back in and the maids slid the paper screens shut. Atsu bent over her reading but it was difficult to ignore the hammering and banging and loud male voices. The women were shuffling. She could see they were all distracted.

Then Hana closed her book and rose to her feet.

Omasé's head jerked up. 'And just where do you think you're going, young lady?'

'For a stroll, to collect some camellia branches, that's all,' said Hana, pouting. 'We're not children. This isn't a prison.' She tossed her elegant head defiantly.

The Edo ladies stiffened and exchanged glances. Atsu looked around for Ikushima. That astute lady had retreated to the side of the room and was watching quietly, taking everything in.

'No,' said Omasé. 'This isn't a prison. Just don't forget what happened last year.' She emphasized every syllable.

Atsu put down her book. If she was to be queen she needed to know everything that went on here. There should be no mysteries, no more dark stories. Nothing should be hidden from her.

'Last year?' she asked.

'How can you bring that up?' Hana snapped. 'It was nothing to do with me. You did nothing to help.' She snatched up a basket and slid open one of the screens. Cold air scented with pine swirled in. The carpenters jumped back like startled deer as she flounced between them into the gardens. She reached for a camellia branch and started snipping off twigs.

Omasé slid the screens shut with a bang. The ladies bent their heads lower over their sewing.

Atsu sat back on her heels. 'I think you should tell us what happened last year.' Whatever grim secrets this palace held, she needed to know them all if she was to spend her life here.

Omasé heaved a sigh. 'Never mind, my lady,' she said. 'It is hardly a suitable topic with Your Highness's wedding coming up.'

'A bad business,' rasped a voice. The fearsome Elder Anekoji had slipped in. She seemed to be always lingering outside Atsu's rooms, listening to everything that went on. 'Nearly brought the whole palace into disrepute. You're quite right to ask, Your Highness.' She settled herself on her knees. 'You'd never have guessed it when she moved in, she was so sweet and demure. A real firefly daimyo, that brother of hers. There's a lesson there for all you women.'

Atsu stifled a groan. Elder Anekoji seemed determined to scare her with her stories. But still she was curious to hear what she had to say.

The Edo ladies shrank back and busied themselves with their sewing. The newcomers who'd arrived with Atsu gazed wide-eyed at the elder with her parchment face and shiny black wig.

'Her name was Lady Koto,' said the elder. A maid pushed over a tobacco box and lit a pipe for her. The elder took a puff and breathed a long plume of smoke through her nostrils.

She glanced around, her eyes glittering. 'Her brother stopped at nothing to get her into the palace. The family was too high-ranking for her to enter as a lady-in-waiting. So he had her adopted by a lower-ranking family, brought her down a few rungs. He was sure if His Majesty once set eyes on her he'd be caught as tight as an octopus in a trap.'

Atsu raised her eyebrows, wondering what it meant that she dared refer to His Majesty with such disrespect.

'His Late Majesty, that is,' Middle Elder Omasé said apologetically. 'His Majesty's father, our revered Lord Ieyoshi. I remember when Lady Koto arrived,' she added, smiling nostalgically. 'Such a lovely little creature, just thirteen. Such charming ways. The prettiest thing you ever saw, like a porcelain doll.'

Elder Anekoji puffed out another plume of smoke. Her face was like leather, as if dried out by all her smoking. 'She arrived at the perfect time. His Majesty's previous sweetheart had just passed away. She'd held power in the palace for years. Whoever can capture the shogun's heart can do anything she likes.'

Atsu was listening hard. The elder was only confirming what she had sensed long ago. The only way she could keep her promise to Lord Nariakira would be if she could win the shogun's heart, win him away from his mother and Lady Shiga too. That was the key. It would make her task considerably harder that she had two formidable women to contend with, not one.

'His Majesty had plenty of concubines, all eagerly competing to produce an heir for him,' said Elder Anekoji, sucking on her pipe. 'The Lady Dowager, of course, kept a keen eye on it all. She was the mother of the heir and if any of them had produced another son her position would have been threatened. It was no surprise when the boy babies died the moment they'd poked their little heads out of the womb.'

So many babies dead, so many killed. This was a graveyard of children. 'Go on,' she said. 'How did it end?'

Elder Anekoji smiled, revealing a mouthful of blackened teeth. 'His Late Majesty was distraught at the death of his favourite concubine when Lady Koto, this beautiful new attendant, arrived. She may have looked like an innocent young girl but she knew how to twist a man around her little finger. She'd had excellent training in bedroom techniques.'

'His Majesty fell head over heels in love with her,' Omasé murmured, her cheeks colouring. 'He was completely besotted.'

'Your Highness will remember what I said about jumping aboard the jewelled palanquin,' Elder Anekoji said sourly. 'His Majesty made her brother a lord – a firefly lord if ever I saw one. And the longer His Majesty favoured her, the richer and more powerful the brother became. She didn't even have to ask. She had His Majesty by the balls.'

Middle Elder Omasé shook her head and sighed. 'She made His Majesty happy for the last ten years of his life. She gave him four children, two girls and two boys. They all died when they were little.'

There were bangs and crashes, creaks and groans outside, sounds of boards being levered up or nailed down. Shadows moved about against the thin paper screens. The workmen were as close as if they had been right in the room.

Elder Anekoji took another puff on her pipe. 'Then His Majesty passed away.'

'Very suddenly,' Omasé added, turning pale under her white

make-up. 'Three and a half years ago. Right after the barbarian ships had left.'

'Fourteen days after they left,' snapped Elder Anekoji, slapping her fan on to her palm. 'Fourteen. Not a day more, not a day less.'

'No one imagined His Majesty would pass away, when he'd been so hale and hearty.' Omasé's voice was shaking.

Atsu shuddered. Suddenly she remembered the day three and a half years earlier when Lord Nariakira had told her that the Great Ruler had died. She had only just arrived in Crane Castle when she had been summoned to his chamber. She remembered how shocked he had looked, his staring eyes, his face sagging.

'I wish I'd been there. I might have prevented it,' he'd said. His words had struck her heart like a knell of doom. She'd wondered then what he'd meant but she'd never found out. And it was then that everything had started. That very same day he'd told her he was sending her to the women's palace. And here she was.

'So there was something suspicious about his death?' she asked sharply.

The two elders looked at each other.

'His Majesty was taken ill,' said Elder Anekoji. 'It was in the men's palace. We'd been expecting him to come for the afternoon audience but he didn't appear. In fact we never saw His Majesty again.'

'Had he been ill for long?' Atsu asked.

'Then everything turned upside down,' said Elder Anekoji, puffing furiously on her pipe.

'You haven't answered my question.'

'If I may be so bold, Your Highness, here in the palace we learn not to ask questions. That's the proper way. We simply follow orders. Whatever happened to His Majesty, it didn't take long. But I was telling Your Highness about Lady Koto. After His Majesty's funeral, his concubines cut their hair and took vows and moved to the Western Palace, all but one. Lady Honju-in. She stayed here with her son, the new shogun.'

'So there was Lady Koto, who'd had such a fine life, enjoyed such favour, received gifts, had parties and feasts – there she was, just twenty-three, doomed to live out the rest of her days as a nun,' said Middle Elder Omasé. The hammering outside was deafening.

'Her brother knew the life he was condemning her to, but it was no concern of his,' growled the elder. 'She was no more use to him. For a while she passed her days visiting shrines, praying at His Majesty's tomb, dropping in to the Inner Palace to see us, as nuns do. And then that carpenter appeared.' She glared around at the women hunched over their sewing, pushing their needles in and out.

'He was no mere carpenter,' said Omasé. 'He was a carpenters' agent. He was charming and handsome. He was the very picture of Sojiro Sawamura, that kabuki actor you young women love so much.'

'Maybe Lady Koto missed her nights with His Majesty,' said Elder Anekoji. 'Most of us will never even know what that's like.' She gave a thin smile and Atsu remembered that she'd been the concubine of the shogun's grandfather. She at least knew. 'Anyway, she saw this carpenter and lost all sense of right and wrong. Her life was over anyway. She was locked away for ever.'

'She started leaving the palace, saying she was going to visit temples and graves,' said Middle Elder Omasé. 'None of us knew what she was really doing. We just noticed she didn't visit us any more, that's all.'

Elder Anekoji pursed her lips. 'They probably met at a temple. That's where that sort of thing usually goes on. Eventually news of it got back to her brother, that brother who she'd raised so high. A message arrived at the Western Palace that he had been taken gravely ill. It was around the middle of last year. She was to go home immediately. And that was the last we heard of her.'

There was an even greater flurry of hammering from the veranda. Through the gap between the paper screens Atsu saw Hana chatting to the foreman, her lips glistening in the wintry sun. She was laughing, her unblackened teeth shining, waving her hands vivaciously.

'A while later her brother filed a report. She'd suddenly died, he said. We all knew what that meant. He didn't want to take responsibility for her crime. He'd punished her himself.'

Atsu looked around the room at the women in their lavish silk kimonos. They had put down their needles. Some stared, their eyes huge as saucers. Others were pale and trembling.

That was the only way that sort of story ever ended. In a world where women were foolish creatures who couldn't be held responsible for their deeds, it was their father or husband or brother who paid the price if one committed a crime. For the favourite concubine of the late shogun to behave in such a way would have been tantamount to treason. Her brother would have been ordered to cut open his own belly. He couldn't risk the government discovering her offence.

Atsu pictured the scene. He would have led Lady Koto behind the storehouse. That was where such punishments were always carried out. Then he would have drawn his dagger across her throat.

Atsu saw the blood, heard it gushing out. That was the penalty for any woman who committed a serious offence. Even she, the shogun's consort, would be punished in this way.

Elder Anekoji gazed around, enjoying the impact of her story on her audience. 'That carpenter was lucky,' she said. 'He disappeared. Not like the kabuki actor who had an affair with the chief lady-in-waiting a hundred years or so ago. He didn't get away in time.'

Elder Anekoji spoke with almost excessive glee. She was Lady Honju-in's creature, Atsu reminded herself. She was out to scare her, to make her afraid to step out of line. She wanted to warn her that no one, no matter how high-ranking, could put a foot out of place.

'Enough stories for today,' said Middle Elder Omasé, frowning.

The other elder ignored her. 'Your Highness doesn't know that story? It just shows how well we keep our secrets here. It was six generations ago. The shogun was only five at the time. The lady-in-waiting was his mother's favourite retainer – like you, my lady.'

She turned and threw a challenging glance at Ikushima, who was kneeling to one side. Ikushima gave an amused smile and fluttered her fan. Middle Elder Omasé shuffled.

'The actor was crucified,' said Elder Anekoji.

Atsu felt her heart thumping. She wondered if that would be the fate of Kaneshigé if they were ever to try anything rash. Elder Anekoji's warnings only served to make her more determined. She had given up her lover now. She would have to devote herself to winning the shogun's heart.

The elder pursed her lips and sucked in her cheeks, her eyes glittering. 'As for the lady-in-waiting, she was sent into exile and her brother had to kill himself. Not that he had known anything about her affair. It was a complete shock for him. But I'm sure none of you ladies would ever behave in such an irresponsible way.' She gathered up her skirts, rose to her feet and swept out of the room.

'Old hypocrite!' said Ikushima once the door was safely closed. 'That Elder Anekoji. She's all piety and self-righteousness now that she's old. But I've heard she was one of the wildest when you palace ladies were flocking to temples to – how shall I put it? – study the scriptures with those handsome young priests.'

Atsu stared at Ikushima, wondering what complicated game she was playing.

The women bent their heads over their sewing. Not one of them even glanced at the male silhouettes moving about on the other side of the paper screens or looked up as Hana slipped back into the room, tossing her elegant head.

Middle Elder Omasé's cheeks blazed. 'That was a long time ago,' she said and snapped her mouth shut like a turtle.

'Not much more than fifteen years ago, I heard,' said Ikushima demurely. 'Of course, it's important to have the best possible guidance when saying one's prayers.' She raised an eyebrow and turned to Atsu. 'As you'll discover, there is an ocean of stories here, my lady. There are a thousand rules too, designed to trip you up. But plenty of ladies find ways to get around them. Isn't that right, Middle Elder Omasé?'

Atsu frowned. She knew there was a warning there for all of them and for her too. She still dreamed about sending a message to Kaneshigé by way of Saigo. But the penalties of such behaviour were very stiff, even for the shogun's consort.

How many more secrets did the palace hold? How many more skeletons lurked in dark corners? She could see how hard life was for the ladies here, deprived for ever of the company of men. No wonder they were sometimes driven to reckless acts. But her own destiny, she knew, was different. In a month or so she would be the consort of the shogun, the lord of the entire realm. And then her work would really begin.

26

The yamagara bird was chirruping as Middle Elder Omasé came in one morning. 'Today I will show Your Highness the route to the Upper Bell Corridor,' she said, after she had made her formal greetings.

Atsu nodded. It was more than time. The Upper Bell Corridor led to the great double door that divided the men's palace from the women's. It was the only link between them, the only place to cross from one to the other. The women assembled there three times a day to greet the shogun when he came in.

With her train of ladies pattering behind her, Atsu followed Omasé past the shrine room and the Great Hall. In the middle of an elegant roofed walkway she stopped to look out at the landscaped gardens, at the vistas of lakes and ponds and curving bridges stretching into the distance, laid out to form a succession of exquisite pictures. On the far side of the gardens was the wall that separated the men's and women's palaces and behind it the soaring roofs of the Middle Interior, the inner section of the men's palace. Somewhere far beyond that was the Outer Palace where the clan lords came to pay homage and the shogun held court. She shivered at the thought of the immense power her future husband wielded, the vast territories he ruled over. How was she ever going to yoke such a man's will to her own, persuade him to adopt as an heir a man she didn't even know?

They passed the Bell Guard's Lodge and the uniformed guard kneeling outside and entered a long hallway walled with gold screens

and hung with lanterns and huge red tassels – the famous Upper
Bell Corridor. The sliding doors along the right-hand side were
painted with landscapes, birds and flowers.

'That is the Little Sitting Room,' said Middle Elder Omasé.

Atsu nodded. It was the name used to refer to the shogun's private
wing. She half hoped one of the doors might slide open and the
shogun himself appear. But their walk had been timed to take place
outside of the three audiences. The shogun was ensconced in the
men's palace, no doubt busy with affairs of state.

At the far end of the hallway was a pair of doors, bolted with a
huge gold padlock, with a gleaming ball of copper bells hanging
alongside. Two ladies-in-waiting knelt in attendance.

Atsu pictured the long passage full of women on their knees,
bowing to greet the shogun. The men's palace was tantalizingly
close, just on the other side of the doors. She could almost smell the
pomade that men used to oil their topknots.

On the way back she stopped to gaze at the gardens again, pulling her jacket closer around her. It was a fine clear day. The sky was
a blue dome arching overhead. In the distance bells rang. Crows
cawed and she heard the deep croak of a bullfrog. Looking back she
saw the outside wall of the Upper Bell Corridor and the pavilion
roofs of the Little Sitting Room.

Suddenly she heard a rustle. There was the sound of panting and
a stifled gasp coming from under the walkway. She noticed a very
distinctive scent. She peeked between the slats and saw a pair of
eyes. They disappeared and there was silence. Perhaps there were
children in the palace after all. Perhaps they were playing games
with her. She took a step and the rustling started again, then stopped
the moment she did.

Atsu's ladies had halted at the beginning of the walkway. Only
Middle Elder Omasé was still beside her.

'Who's there?' Atsu called.

There was a silence, then a voice blurted out, 'Go away. Leave me
alone. I did not mean to look on you!' It was a man's voice, rather
high-pitched, speaking in an archaic dialect in a jumble of formal
and childish words.

She leaned over the trellised handrail. The voice shouted in urgent tones, 'Oshiga, Oshiga. Come quickly.' He was calling for Lady Shiga, using the polite form of her name.

Atsu stopped as realization dawned. Surely this couldn't be . . . She swung round and looked at Middle Elder Omasé. Omasé was keeping her eyes averted.

There was only one man allowed in the women's palace other than gardeners and workmen and this obviously was not a servant. He was speaking in the shogun's special dialect. She hardly dared believe this shrill voice belonged to her future husband, the lord of the realm. If this really was the shogun, why was he behaving in such an odd way? Perhaps he was a tease. Or perhaps he was as curious about her as she was about him. It was certainly an extraordinary way to meet her husband-to-be.

A woman approached, walking rather slowly. She had broad hips and heavy breasts and carried herself with a swaying motion, like a ship at sea. It was Lady Shiga. She bowed to Atsu and addressed the man under the walkway. 'Come inside,' she cajoled. 'You mustn't look at her, it's not allowed.' When she spoke her face lit up, like a mother addressing her child.

'You lied to me,' shrilled the man. 'You told me she was dead but she is not. She is here. She has come back to haunt me.'

Atsu gasped in disbelief. She was horrified. Could it really be that he thought she was Lady Hideko, the most recent of his consorts to die? That made a sort of sense. Atsu too had felt haunted by the dead consorts though she hadn't even met them, and he had known them very well.

But if he thought Lady Hideko had come back to haunt him, perhaps that meant her death had not been natural. The suspicion stopped Atsu in her tracks. Perhaps he had done something terrible and it had driven him out of his mind.

'We must go, my lady,' said Middle Elder Omasé, grabbing her arm with unsuitable ferocity and trying to drag her away.

Atsu shook her off and called out, 'Don't be afraid. I am not Hideko. I am Sumiko.'

A pale face with a pointed chin and wavering eyes poked out

from under the walkway. Atsu knew by now that the shogun was a man of thirty-two but this apparition looked more like a scared little boy. 'Leave me alone,' he shrieked. 'I shall pray, I shall make offerings, anything you like. Go away! Stop bothering me!'

'Don't be afraid,' Atsu said again, trying to conceal her dismay. 'I'm not a ghost, I'm human. My name is Sumiko. What is yours?'

The man stumbled into view. He was wearing the most beautiful kimonos she had ever seen, rich and heavy with a lustrous sheen. But nothing could conceal the ungainliness of the body underneath. 'You cannot fool me,' he shrilled in a sing-song voice. He was rocking back and forth as if he was riding a horse. 'I knew you would come back.'

There was nothing wrong with him, Atsu told herself. He was just afraid, terrified half out of his wits. She would panic too if she was unexpectedly confronted by someone she thought was a ghost – not just that, but a ghost who had good cause to haunt her.

The man was staring at her with watery eyes. 'Your leg got better. You got taller,' he said. 'And oh, your face, your face changed. So beautiful, like an angel. You got prettier, much prettier.' He took on a crafty look. 'You say you are not a ghost. Prove it.'

The best thing was to humour him. 'You know how you can tell a ghost?' she asked airily. 'They have no legs. Everyone knows that. But I have legs. Look.' She pulled up the hem of her kimono skirt to reveal a stocking-clad foot and poked it through the railings. 'Ghosts float about high in the air, but I'm not floating, am I? They have long black hair right to the ground and they pull it out in clumps, but I'm not doing that either. They wail, "I hate you, I hate you." But I don't hate you, not at all. So you see, I'm definitely not a ghost.' She laughed, delighted by her own logic. Surely she'd won him over.

He tipped his head to one side and stared at her. 'You might not be that sort of ghost,' he said, sticking out his lower lip. 'Maybe you're an umbrella ghost.'

She laughed out loud. She couldn't believe that she, the future consort of the shogun, could be having this absurd conversation with a thirty-two-year-old man who, unlikely though it might be, was the shogun himself. But despite that, he was a child, and the best thing to do was to treat him like one. 'Don't be silly,' she said. 'Do I look like a rolled paper umbrella hopping around on one wooden clog?'

A look of terror flitted across his features. Adults learn to hide their feelings as she was doing, pretend to feel at ease even if they feel the opposite. But all his emotions were there to see, displayed on his face like on a child's.

The ladies had run into the gardens and fallen to their knees. The shogun swung round. 'She is a ghost, is she not? Hana, Tokiwai, Hatsusei, I am right, am I not? She is a ghost.'

They squirmed and tittered. They dared not contradict him but they were afraid to offend Atsu too.

Lady Shiga opened her mouth and yawned. 'She's not a ghost, Masa-*kun*. You can pinch her if you like, then you'll see.' She gave a snort of laughter.

Atsu stared at her. Lady Shiga was not afraid to contradict the shogun or address him in such a casual fashion.

Slowly he closed his mouth. 'I believe you,' he said. 'You are Sumiko. Mama told me . . . She told me you were coming.'

'Come along now,' said Lady Shiga. 'I thought we were playing hide-and-seek.'

He was dragging a western-style rifle. He lifted it up, pointed it at the ladies-in-waiting and stumbled towards them, shouting, 'Bang! Bang!' They scurried backwards like crabs, screaming.

'I gave them a good scare, didn't I, Oshiga?' he said with a cackle of laughter and scampered towards the shogun's wing. Atsu watched him galumphing away with his bobbing gait, wondering if he'd glance back but he didn't. Lady Shiga strolled after him.

For a moment Atsu was so thunderstruck she couldn't speak. She clenched and unclenched her fists, breathed out sharply. If this really was the shogun, it would never do to reveal a trace of the dismay and horror she felt. Yet to be yoked to such a man – no, hardly even a man – to have to marry this invalid . . . She couldn't imagine how she could ever have even the most trivial of conversations with him, let alone persuade him to take Lord Keiki as his heir, though it was all too clear he was not fit to rule. She'd been assigned an impossible task.

She waited till he had disappeared around a corner, then turned to Middle Elder Omasé. 'So that is His Majesty?' She struggled to keep her face composed, not to display a hint of emotion.

Omasé shuffled. There was a long silence. 'That is His Majesty Lord Iesada.'

Atsu turned away sharply, closed her eyes. One thing she didn't understand was the talk of his ill health. He was very strange indeed but he was not physically ill – though maybe he was ill in his head. 'He's charming,' she said at last.

She was serious. He was indeed charming, sweet, like a child. But to marry such a man – that was a different matter altogether. Would she have to sleep with him? Would that even be possible? And how could she manipulate such a wayward creature into doing what Lord Nariakira wanted?

'We have had a lot of hauntings here,' Middle Elder Omasé said, as if that explained the shogun's extraordinary behaviour. 'A lot of deaths and a lot of hauntings. Twenty-six of Lord Ieyoshi's children died, all but His Majesty, and many of Lord Ienari's children too.' She shook her head. 'People think our life is all tea ceremonies and fine food and silk kimonos, but they are wrong. This is not a happy place. There are a lot of restless spirits.'

Atsu gazed across the gardens. The lakes and pavilions and elegantly trimmed shrubs looked faded and sad now that she had learned her fate, now that she had met this strange child-man whom she was to marry.

'You must not be deceived by His Majesty,' Omasé said. 'He is testing you. He is clever and sensitive. But he is unworldly, he has never been outside the castle. He really took to you,' she added, glancing at Atsu out of the corner of her eye. 'I have never known him talk so much. You have charmed him.'

Atsu looked around for Ikushima. She would have liked to have had her opinion of this unnerving encounter. But Ikushima was lingering behind with the other ladies.

'I would like to see His Majesty happy,' said Middle Elder Omasé.

'He is lonely. It has been six years since Lady Hideko died. He needs a consort.' Her broad, rather plain face was sad. 'His father and grandfather spent most of their time amusing themselves with page-boys or concubines. That is what we are used to. But His Majesty has only ever had one concubine. Lady Shiga has been keeping him company for years.'

There was a silence. Atsu was barely listening, caught up not so much in thought as in a gnawing, wordless sense of foreboding.

'He . . . he must miss Princess Tadako and Lady Hideko,' she stammered distractedly, trying to take her mind off the image of that pale face and contorted body.

'Princess Tadako was never at home here,' said Omasé. 'Miyako was the only place she knew. She grew up in the imperial palace, then stepped into a palanquin and came here. She left one palace only to come to another. Then for months after the wedding His Majesty would not even look at her. When he came in he just went to his rooms.

'You can imagine how pleased we were when he announced one evening that he wished to spend the night with his consort. The maids laid out the bedding and we elders lay down in the neighbouring room, listening out in case Her Highness rang the bell.' She laughed merrily. 'It must have been difficult for a couple of young people like them, trying to make love when we were just outside, listening for all we were worth.'

Atsu bit her lip. It was hard to imagine the man she had met making love to anyone.

'After that, every time His Majesty spent a night with Princess Tadako, Lady Shiga insisted that he spend the next two nights with her.

'Then Her Highness's monthly bleed did not come. She was with child. We watched over her night and day. The tasters checked her meals, just as they check yours. But then there was that dreadful outbreak of smallpox. Everyone recovered but she didn't.' Omasé dabbed her eyes. 'It took her, and her unborn child too.' A tear trickled down her heavy cheek. 'She was an aristocrat, very willowy with tiny hips. She would never have survived childbirth.

'As to poor Lady Hideko, all she knew was her dolls and her sewing and her little bird. None of them had ever been out of the castle and His Majesty never has either. But you're different, my lady. You've come from outside. Princess Tadako and Lady Hideko didn't know how to cope with His Majesty's moods, but you handled him magnificently. His Majesty needs someone strong and clever, like you. Maybe you can bring an end to the bad luck – the deaths, the hauntings. Maybe you can change things.'

Atsu hardly heard a word. She understood now why Ikushima was keeping her distance. That lady had known all along what kind of man the shogun was. After all, she had worked for Princess Konoé and Lord Nariakira had taken her on to be Atsu's mentor. She was a palace insider. Atsu thought back over the time they'd spent together, close on three years. All that time Ikushima had been at her side, training her for the role she was to play. Yet she had never let slip a single hint of what Atsu was letting herself in for. That was precisely why Lord Nariakira had chosen her. She was astute, discreet and utterly loyal.

'But not loyal to me.' Atsu had to press her lips together to stop herself saying the words aloud.

And Lord Nariakira, whom Atsu had loved and trusted like a father. He'd known the shogun since His Majesty was a boy, he knew exactly what sort of person he was.

Now at long last she understood fully why Lord Nariakira had asked her to forgive him. Now she understood what he'd meant when he'd said that she wouldn't have a normal marriage. The hints, the whispers, the glances all fell into place. His Majesty was not just a weak, sickly, difficult boy. It was far, far worse than that. This was what Lord Nariakira had meant when he'd said he had sacrificed her for the sake of the country. He'd known what a terrible fate he was condemning her to.

As to the task he'd given her, he must have known that it was virtually impossible. The only glimmer of hope was that Lady Shiga seemed to be able to control the shogun. It looked as if she could twist him round her little finger. If Atsu could find a way to stir affection in him, it might be possible to carry out her task.

So that was the devil's pact Lord Nariakira had forced her into – a lifetime of luxury in a gilded cage in exchange for a travesty of a marriage.

And the castle ladies too – they had all known. Everyone except Atsu had known precisely what sort of man this was. Behind her back they must have been laughing at her, pitying her, as she studied, prepared to be queen, looked forward bright-eyed to her wedding.

And this was the man – hardly even a man – she was going to live with for the rest of her life. She'd never felt so bruised, so betrayed, so alone.

She brushed Middle Elder Omasé aside, pushed through her ladies waiting at the end of the walkway and fled to her rooms. She paced up and down, gnawing at her knuckles, tugged the hairpins from her hair and dragged her fingers through it until it hung long and wild, as if she really was a ghost. A dry emptiness engulfed her. She was too bereft, too consumed with misery even to weep.

She saw the full extent of her betrayal now – of Lord Nariakira's treachery. Here in the palace she was out of his reach. Why should she do as he asked when he had deceived her so completely?

PART III

The Woman Behind the Screens

27

Eighteenth day of the twelfth month (12 January 1857)

The day had arrived, the day Atsu had hoped would never come
– the date the priests and soothsayers had decreed as the most
auspicious for the wedding of His Majesty the Shogun to Her
Imperial Highness Princess Sumiko of the House of Fujiwara.

She pushed away the tiny dishes spread across the low table. She
wasn't hungry. She couldn't eat any of it. Soon she would no longer
be Atsu or even Princess Sumiko. She would be the Midai, the
woman behind the screens. She was caught up in a process that she
could not escape, swept along like a leaf tossed in a whirlwind.

The sun shone bright and harsh out of a cold blue sky. Snow lay
thick on the ground, bending the bamboos and etching the branches
of the pine trees.

The previous night when she'd lain down to sleep she'd heard
cries and groans and sounds of distant sobbing. Half in a dream
she'd thought she'd glimpsed a cornflower-blue kimono disappearing round a corner. She'd sat bolt upright, quivering with horror,
expecting to see a tiny limping woman no taller than a palanquin,
and heaved a sigh of relief to find Yasu and Chiyo sleeping
peacefully, one on each side of her, with Jewel curled at her feet. As
she slid back into sleep, the image of the doll with the broken head
rose before her and she shuddered again, wondering what it all
meant.

She remembered the premonition she had had of a maggot at the heart of a rotten persimmon. If only she hadn't met her husband-to-be, she thought, if only she hadn't known what kind of man he was, she might have looked forward to being queen of the realm. But now this new eminence seemed nothing but a sorry masquerade. Worst of all, she was supposed to get close enough to this pathetic creature to keep her promise to Lord Nariakira, to have Lord Keiki installed as the next shogun and as Regent. Did she even want to accomplish such a task? She still felt the sting of Lord Nariakira's betrayal. Perhaps she would just live out her days idly in the palace and let the whole country go to ruin.

The preparations began in the afternoon. Atsu's ladies bathed and perfumed her, then the chambermaids brought in a jar of ground gallnuts and iron filings, a jug of warm vinegar, a basin and a palette. Yasu mixed the bitter gall and iron with the vinegar, dipped her brush in the dark liquid and carefully painted Atsu's teeth one by one until they shone like black lacquer.

Atsu washed out her mouth, wrinkling her nose at the metallic taste. It was the taste of marriage, the taste of adulthood. From now on she would have to have her teeth blackened every day. She couldn't imagine ever getting used to it.

Yasu plucked her eyebrows till her forehead was smooth as an egg, covered Atsu's face, throat, back and breasts with thick white make-up, then dipped a brush in charcoal paste and painted two feathery smudges – 'moth's wing eyebrows' – halfway between Atsu's hairline and where her eyebrows had been. She painted Atsu's lips scarlet with safflower paste and dabbed a little at the corners of her eyes and on her nails.

Chiyo brushed and oiled Atsu's hair and tied it in a long tail bound with white ribbons. Then the wardrobe attendants dressed her in pure white robes and draped a white mantle with a thick quilted hem over her shoulders. They set the imperial gold coronet above her forehead, placed a ceremonial fan in her hands and covered her in a white silk veil.

Atsu gazed at the spectral figure in the mirror. She was white like a ghost, white from head to toe. The only colour apart from her black hair was her red lips and the red hakama trousers hidden under her robes. The poor groom would have the shock of his life, she thought.

White, as everyone knows, is the colour of death and mourning. Corpses are swaddled in white, mourners wear white to funerals. Marriage marked the death of the old Atsu. She would be erased from the records of her family as if she'd never even existed and entered into the annals of the Tokugawa clan. Hereafter the Tokugawas would be her family and the palace her home, and when she died her wedding veil would be her shroud.

She felt as if she was a ghost already. She wished she could toss her head, throw off the powder and paint and heavy robes and race through the dusty corridors out into the cold crisp air and all the way back to sunny Kyushu. She would have given anything to leave behind the splendour and beauty, the gold-encrusted ceilings and exquisitely painted screens, and run across the black sands barefoot, be an ordinary person with no duties, no responsibilities, no empty ceremonial.

Tears came to her eyes. This was far from the future she'd envisioned for herself when she'd been a young girl living in her father's house. She heaved a sigh. In this world no one could decide their destiny, she told herself sternly. She would have to do the best she could with the fate she'd been allotted.

As the Hour of the Cock struck, as dusk was falling and maids were lighting candles, a chamberlain slid open the door. Moths flittered in. 'His Majesty awaits,' she announced.

Middle Elder Omasé led her through the shadowy corridors, past the shrine room and the Great Hall to the walkway from where Atsu could see the snow-covered gardens with their clumps of trees fading into darkness. Her ladies-in-waiting followed. Some held candles, some carried Atsu's train, some bore incense burners trailing scented smoke.

They turned at the Bell Guard's Lodge and trooped into the Upper Bell Corridor. At the far end were the double doors which divided the women's palace from the men's. Incense smoke seeped through the sliding screens that walled the Little Sitting Room. Atsu's heart leapt to her throat and she trembled as she stepped into that unknown domain.

The groom was there on his knees. He was in starched indigo robes with a tall black cap tied under his chin, his fan of office upright in his hand. He sat perfectly still, his back very straight, dignified and composed. It was hard to imagine that this was the same impish character Atsu had seen bounding about waving a rifle. She took a breath. Maybe she'd been wrong. Maybe he'd just been playing tricks on her, testing her, as Omasé had said.

The splendid room with its gold-painted walls and pristine tatami was icy cold. Shivering, Atsu knelt to the shogun's left, keeping her eyes down. There was a low table in front of them with a long-spouted kettle on it and three shallow red cups, nested one inside the other.

Sharp-eyed, sharp-tongued Elder Anekoji bowed, then uttered a stream of formulaic phrases on behalf of the shogun, welcoming the bride who had come so far and was of such distinguished lineage. Middle Elder Omasé replied on Atsu's behalf that she was grateful and honoured to have been received into this great house to which she pledged her loyalty for ever more.

Companion priests – shaven-headed women dressed as men – stepped forward and waved holy mulberry branches over the young couple to purify them. Then a lady-in-waiting took the smallest cup, filled it with saké and offered it to the shogun, who drank. She filled it again and handed it to Atsu. Atsu closed her eyes as she sipped the warm liquor. For better or for worse she was crossing from one existence to another, joining a new family, becoming a new person.

The shogun and Atsu in turn drank from the middle saucer, then from the largest.

Suddenly there was a rustle. Atsu opened her eyes to see the shogun's legs twitch and his head jerk over his left shoulder. She clenched her fists, desperately willing him to keep still.

His mother, Lady Honju-in, was on her knees behind him. She leaned forward and rapped him on the arm with her fan. He started and swung round, then stuck out his lower lip and lapsed back into sullen silence.

At Omasé's bidding, Atsu turned to greet the Lady Dowager. She was in a formal black kimono with silver plovers embroidered round the skirts. Her eyes gleamed like two black diamonds. She glared at Atsu watchfully. She looked even more formidable than the first time they had met.

The two bowed and exchanged toasts and with that the formalities were over. Atsu had joined the family. Finally she could raise her head and look at her new husband.

She widened her eyes. She hadn't expected to find him beautiful but he was, in a strange ethereal way. In repose his features were uncannily perfect, fine and delicate, with long-lashed eyes that tilted up at the corners and skin like ivory. He was small and slight with a pointed chin that gave him an elfin look, quite different from the wild-eyed character she had seen in the gardens.

It was not surprising, she told herself. His mother Lady Honju-in had once been beautiful enough to win the heart of the shogun, Iesada's father, who himself had been the son of another beautiful concubine. It was not so strange that the shogun too should be beautiful in his way. Beauty flowed in the blood.

The vision lasted barely a moment. Then Iesada screwed up his face, scowled, again stuck out his lower lip in a sullen pout and hoisted one shoulder higher than the other.

He wasn't looking at her. He hardly seemed to notice she was there. He bobbed his head and rocked back and forth. 'Can we eat now?' he demanded querulously.

Lady Honju-in clipped him on the arm again and whispered sharply in his ear. 'I did behave,' he shrieked. 'I did everything you told me. I sat perfectly still. Now I want to eat.' He slumped back on his heels and stared gloomily at the floor. The ladies-in-waiting studiously ignored his behaviour. Everyone but Atsu was used to it.

In a side room Atsu's ladies helped her out of her white kimonos and into richly coloured robes, aligning the layers at the collar, cuffs and hem. Then they draped a deep-red mantle over the top, embroidered with cranes and tortoises, symbols of long life.

By the time she was ready everyone had moved to the Great Hall.

The nine auspicious gifts were laid out on trays – dried abalone, a symbolic gift of money wrapped in a red and white envelope, bonito, cuttlefish, strands of kelp symbolizing long life, a bundle of hemp to symbolize the strong threads that bound the bridal couple's lives together, a fan, a saké cask made of willow and a pair of lacquer-ware boxes containing shells for the shell-matching game to signify that the pair fitted as perfectly as the two halves of a shell.

The shogun glowered morosely as Atsu took her place next to him. The first dishes of the wedding feast were laid out tantalizingly on trays before each guest – a clear soup, rice cooked with red beans to turn it an auspicious shade of red, grilled sea bream, rolls of simmered kelp, all filling the Great Hall with mouth-watering aromas.

Finally, after endless toasts, the feasting began. As the bride, Atsu had to smile and drink but not eat.

Lady Shiga was kneeling beside the shogun, filling his saké cup. The shogun smiled and his gaze became less vacant as he looked at that dour lady. He drummed his chopsticks on the table, shifted his legs and tapped his knees on the floor as he gobbled mouthful after mouthful.

Atsu felt a pang of foreboding as she looked at the two of them. She wondered how the shogun spent his days in the men's palace. How strange it must be, she thought, to have grown up in this great castle and never once to have left it. And all this while the barbarians were digging in deeper and deeper in Shimoda, like a clam that no amount of levering will shift. The country desperately needed a leader to bind the rival clans together, to plan how best to defy the intruders. Yet all they had was this feeble child-man.

It was not just that His Majesty was not wise. He was under his mother's thumb. She expressed his wishes to the world – but they were her wishes, not his. Atsu watched as Lady Honju-in picked out the most succulent morsels from the array of tiny dishes before her. She had yet to find out what the Dowager Mother wanted but she doubted if it had anything to do with the good of the country. All she was interested in was feeding her vanity and pride and greed. And Atsu was supposed to win over this petulant child-man, force him to do her bidding.

The feasting went on late into the night. It was a relief to put off the moment when Atsu would be left alone with her new husband. She fervently wished she could put it off for ever.

Finally Elder Anekoji announced the end of the festivities. The ladies led Atsu to a dressing room where they unpinned her hair and dressed her in white silk nightwear gathered at the waist with a silken girdle. The shogun was waiting in the bedroom, also in white nightwear, his hair beautifully oiled into a topknot. For a moment, till he scowled and jutted out his lower lip and humped his shoulder, he was strikingly handsome.

The futons were even more sumptuous than in Atsu's wing, with tortoises and cranes embroidered on the red and white silk covers. The shogun's bedding was laid out on a slightly higher level than Atsu's, with a sword rest and a smoking set behind his pillow. There were lacquered kimono racks, a large shrine to the family gods and a lacquer basin for washing their faces. But the luxury just made her feel all the more empty inside.

Her eye fell on the heap of erotic books and prints scattered about on the table, left open to reveal the jewel-bright illustrations. In one a man mounted a woman, in another the woman took the lead, her eyes closed, her mouth open and her toes curled in ecstasy. Their most secret parts – his Jade Stalk, her Cinnabar Cleft – were depicted in lavish detail, vast and engorged, like a guide for the uninitiated.

Such pictures were a normal part of a bridal boudoir, designed to arouse excitement, encourage the newly-weds to cast aside their bashfulness. But to Atsu they were nothing but a bitter reminder of everything that married love might have been. She screwed up her eyes in pain as memories crowded her mind of Kaneshigé's firm body entwined with hers. She'd forbidden herself ever to think of such things again. She looked away sharply. It was too cruel to have to make-believe this was a real marriage when everyone knew it was a sham.

The shogun wailed, 'Mama, where is Oshiga?'

Lady Honju-in loomed in the doorway. 'Now then, Masa-*kun*,' she said. 'Remember what I told you. Tonight you sleep with this nice lady, your new consort.'

'I want Oshiga,' the shogun whined.

Atsu took a breath. The first step was to find a way to win his confidence. She said softly, 'Do not worry, Your Majesty. We shall just talk a little.' It was best to take things slowly.

The ladies put screens around the sleeping area and Elder Anekoji and Middle Elder Omasé retired to the next room to keep watch, leaving Atsu and her new husband alone together.

The shogun sat bolt upright. 'Where is Oshiga? I want Mama. I want Oshiga.'

Atsu pushed aside her covers and took a breath. 'Let us be friends,' she said gently. 'Call me Atsu. That is my name. Can I call you Masa?'

He ignored her. 'Mama says I have to stay here tonight with you, but I do not want to,' he said in a loud voice. 'I am the shogun. I shall do as I like.' He stuck out his lower lip, twisted his head round and looked up from under his brows at Atsu. 'You say you have legs,' he said. 'Show me.'

Atsu was startled. At least he remembered meeting her, he knew who she was. With her white skin and her black hair long and loose she must look just like a ghost, she realized. She opened her skirts to show him her small bare feet.

'You see, Masa-*kun*,' she said, wondering how he would react if she used his nickname, 'I have legs. I am a real person. I am your consort now and my name is Atsu. We shall have a happy life together.' It was obvious they would not be able to celebrate their wedding night in the usual way. She looked around and saw two ornately lacquered boxes of shells. 'Do you like the shell-matching game?'

He scowled. 'Go away,' he said. 'I shall count to ten. Make sure you are gone by then.' He put his hands over his eyes and counted aloud very slowly, pausing between each number, then peeped through his fingers. 'You are still here,' he said in tones of deep disappointment.

She burst out laughing. 'Let us go to sleep.'

Then she remembered something she'd learned when she was growing up in Ibusuki.

When she was a child her father had had many geisha concubines and there had always been geisha around the house. She called them all indiscriminately 'Auntie'. Her favourite had been Wife Number Two, an earthy woman with a loud laugh and big personality, competent and unshakeable, very different from Atsu's refined mother, Wife Number One. Wife Number Two knew an infinite number of dirty stories. No matter how elegantly she dressed, when she opened her mouth everyone knew straight away she was a carpenter's daughter.

'Men are little boys,' she'd tell Atsu. 'They need mothering. That's the best way to their hearts – mother them.' Then she'd taught her an old geisha trick for dealing with unruly guests.

Atsu laughed softly as she remembered. 'I shall sing you a song,' she said to the shogun. 'Do you know "Momotaro, the Little Peach Boy"?' It was a song he was sure to know.

' "Momotaro-*san*, Momotaro-*san* . . .",' she warbled.

He ignored her. She sang on, deliberately muddling up the words: ' "That millet dumpling on your head, won't you give me one?" '

'That is not right,' he burst out. 'You do not carry a dumpling on your head. You carry it on your hip.' He rocked back and forth, shrieking with laughter. 'It goes like this.' He sang in a thin reedy voice, ' "That millet dumpling on your hip . . ." On your hip, you see. On your hip. "That millet dumpling on your hip, won't you give me one?" '

Atsu joined in with the chorus: ' "Come with me to fight the giants and I shall give you one." ' She allowed herself a tiny smile of satisfaction. They'd found a point of contact.

Suddenly a small furry shape slunk round the screens. The shogun shrieked and pulled his covers up to his chin, cowering. Slowly he peeked out as a tortoiseshell kitten appeared, its eyes tawny gold in the candlelight. His face lit up. 'A cat, a cat. Come, come to me.'

'Her name is Jewel,' said Atsu, picking her up and stroking her. 'She always sleeps with me.'

The shogun held out his fan and the cat darted over and batted the tassel back and forth. He laughed in delight.

'Do you want her to sleep with you? She will if you like,' said Atsu, smiling.

The shogun cuddled Jewel. Atsu heard his breathing soften and he lay back in his futons and began to snuffle and snore. She gazed at him in the light of the single candle. He didn't sleep like a warrior, lying on his right side to protect his sword arm, but like a child, one skinny limb flung out. Gently Atsu tucked his covers around him.

She stared dry-eyed into the night. At least she'd made a start. She'd found some things the shogun liked, some ways to amuse him. She felt utterly overwhelmed by the enormity of her task. How was she ever going to win this poor creature round long enough to have a conversation, let alone persuade him to adopt Keiki as his successor? It would require all her ingenuity to think of a way.

Somewhere inside herself a little bit of her seemed to shrivel up and die, some faint pulse of hope, some belief she'd once had that her life might turn out differently. She felt her shoulders rise and her face crumple as her eyes filled with tears. It was Lord Nariakira. It was all his doing. She'd trusted him completely, loved him like a father, and in return he had condemned her to this living death, forced her to sacrifice herself and her happiness, and all for the good of their country. She would do what she had to do, when she was ready. But first she had to firm up her resolve, overcome her hurt and sadness, her fury and rage at how brutally she had been betrayed.

All the same she had to do it. That was terrifyingly obvious. One way or another she was going to have to get close to this pathetic child-man, close enough to win him over – for them all, for their country, for Lord Nariakira. It was a bleak prospect.

28

The shogun mumbled and burbled in his sleep. He let out a thin high-pitched wail. 'I see you! I see you!' he whimpered. 'Hideko! Hideko! No! Go away. Leave me. Leave me alone!'

Atsu patted his shoulder and shook him until he grunted and rolled over and settled down. But when she started to drift off she too imagined she saw looming faces and felt cobwebby fingers brushing against her skin. She felt the wind of spirits rushing by and a roar like the crashing of waves on the beach. It was the cries and moans of all the babies who'd died here, not just babies but women – Princess Tadako, Lady Hideko and the maids who, so she'd heard, had thrown themselves into wells. She told herself such fears were irrational – but how could one not have them in a place like this? Was it not all too likely that the dead consorts were eyeing her – the new wife, the interloper – with malevolence?

Her heart thumping, she clapped her hands to her ears and burrowed her head under her futons. It was no wonder the shogun was not like other men. All these spirits that haunted the palace – no matter how fervently the priests carried out their rites, how diligently the mothers offered up their prayers and incense and flowers, there were too many of them, too many to placate, too many without a resting place. They flitted endlessly through the hundreds of rooms, swarming under eaves and in dark corners, filling the air with whisperings and mutterings, venting their anger and jealousy on the living.

And he, Iesada – the only one of Lord Ieyoshi's twenty-seven children to survive – he was the target of that anger, he suffered the burden of those curses. She wished she could free him from the grip of all those ghosts. There was no great mystery as to what was wrong with him. She'd known others like him. Many families had children who were born different, malformed in their minds or their bodies. It could not be helped. People usually put it down to a curse. But it was a tragedy for the entire country for the man so afflicted to be the shogun.

Tears came to her eyes, tears of pity for the shogun, but she was weeping for herself as well. There was a moan from the opposite futon. She reached out and rested her hand on her husband's bony arm. The ghostly hubbub died down and his breathing calmed.

She awoke to find Jewel curled at her feet. Pale light seeped through the gaps between the rain doors. She gazed at the sleeping figure on the neighbouring futon, sprawled on his back with his mouth agape, and up at the delicately painted screens and the designs of flowers glimmering on the coffered ceiling. She'd never seen such opulence and he – her new husband – didn't even realize how extraordinary it was. It was all he'd ever known.

There was a discreet cough. Elder Anekoji, Middle Elder Omasé and a bevy of ladies had arrived to wake them. They set up screens between Atsu's futon and the shogun's. As they brought her tea and oiled and perfumed her hair she heard him grumbling, asking for Lady Shiga. She wondered if he even remembered that he had married her yesterday and spent the night with her.

And now she was the Midai. From now on her days would revolve around the three audiences and the five changes of clothing – on rising, before each audience, and at bedtime. She would see the shogun when he came in for the daily audiences. That was when she would get to know him, lay the groundwork for her assault.

But as the Hour of the Snake approached, just as her ladies were dressing her for the morning audience, a chamberlain appeared to announce that His Majesty was unwell. Atsu stared at the woman's bland, expressionless face in disbelief. He had been perfectly well a few hours earlier. Surely this was Lady Honju-in's doing or Lady Shiga's. They were keeping her away from him.

Grimacing, she stood while her ladies removed her ceremonial robes and dressed her in everyday kimonos again. She went to the main room and slumped to her knees. Through the half-open screens she saw snow falling outside. One of the ladies brought her tea and she sipped, wondering how she was ever going to achieve her task.

The ladies bustled around her. Some were organizing storage space for her trousseau, others cataloguing and putting away the wedding gifts from daimyo and high-ranking retainers, yet more beginning preparations for the New Year celebrations, just ten days away. A couple took out writing blocks and started writing, others sewed, some painted or practised dancing.

Messengers arrived to announce that there were merchants lining up at the outer gates. Sucking the end of her brush and twirling it in her dainty fingers, Hana the Edo beauty drew up a list of cosmetics, combs, hairpins, ribbons and delicacies. Other ladies too were making lists.

Atsu's trousseau was so vast that she had distributed many of the kimonos, hair ornaments and writing sets among her ladies and their staff, though it seemed they wanted still more. The maids hurried away, glad of an excuse to go out, and returned with silks and pattern books and boxes of samples exuding fragrance. The gold tit chirruped happily in its cage.

Ikushima was kneeling beside the brazier, smoking a pipe and idly stirring the ashes in the tobacco box with the metal chopsticks used to pick out embers. She was wearing a pale-green kimono with layers of mauve and gold visible at the cuffs and throat. It looked as if it had cost a fortune. She glanced up, her oval face serene. Everything about her was as perfect as ever, her make-up immaculate, a faint smile lurking at the corner of her lips.

For the last month, ever since Atsu had met the shogun in the gardens, she'd avoided Ikushima. She could hardly bear to look at her. Ikushima had betrayed her. She'd pretended to be her friend, yet she'd never even hinted what sort of man Iesada was. At least Lord Nariakira had given Atsu a few words of warning. 'A weak and sickly boy,' he'd said, 'a difficult man'. He'd even admitted that she might not be able to have a normal marriage. Ikushima could have prepared her, filled in the details of the shogun's condition, forewarned her of how serious it was, but she had said not a word.

But now Atsu was beginning to see that Ikushima had had no choice. She couldn't have hinted that there was anything even a little odd about the shogun. It would have been virtually treason, added to which it wouldn't have made the slightest difference. Nothing could have changed Atsu's fate. She needed Ikushima. In the month and a half she'd been in the palace, she'd completely lost contact with the outside world.

While Atsu couldn't leave the palace, Ikushima could. One of her duties as Atsu's chief lady-in-waiting was to take a palanquin across town to pray at the shoguns' tombs on Atsu's behalf. That gave her the chance to arrange secret meetings with Saigo or Lord Nariakira. She had gone out just a few days earlier to ask the ancestors' blessings for the wedding. And she also regularly exchanged letters with Lord Nariakira.

Atsu jumped up, ran over and dropped to her knees beside her.

Ikushima put her fingertips to the floor and bowed. 'Congratulations, my lady,' she said, as if nothing had changed, as if she hadn't even noticed that Atsu had been keeping her distance.

As always, Atsu had the uncanny feeling that Ikushima knew exactly what she was thinking. She wondered what lay behind her composure. Ikushima could read everyone else's thoughts but she was even better at concealing her own. She was the perfect servant. They had been together day in, day out, for nearly three years now, yet Atsu knew almost nothing about her.

'You have risen to the skies. You are our Midai now, our queen,' that elegant lady said, smiling. 'But with great eminence comes great responsibility,' she added in a sterner tone.

She took a puff on her pipe and lowered her gaze meaningfully towards the tobacco box. It was a particularly large, handsome one, of lacquered wood with a design of plum blossom, and a couple of drawers for tobacco. Instead of the usual pottery jar, the entire top of the box was a tray filled with fine sand mixed with ash, which Ikushima had smoothed into a flat grey slate. There were words etched there in small neat characters: 'A month and a half has passed and you have done nothing.'

Atsu recoiled, stung. It had never occurred to her that anyone might communicate in such a devious way. She wondered if it was a trap. But Princess Konoé, Lord Nariakira's sister, had appointed Ikushima to serve her and Lord Nariakira too had confidence in her. She would have to trust her.

She glanced around. In theory all her ladies were beyond suspicion, but in reality she couldn't be sure if one or other of them was not reporting back to Lady Honju-in. They all appeared to be engrossed in their silks, chattering and laughing. She could talk to Ikushima without being overheard, though she would have to keep her voice down.

Burning with indignation she put her mouth to Ikushima's ear. 'Done nothing? How could I do anything until I was married?' she demanded in a fierce whisper.

'You have been avoiding me,' Ikushima hissed, drawing back her elegant lips in a snarl. She smoothed the ashes with a spatula and picked up a metal chopstick. Words appeared one by one: 'I am in daily communication with His Lordship. To avoid me is to avoid him. That is not just stupid. It is criminal. It is treason.'

She turned her perfectly coiffed head and glanced across at the ladies bent over their silks. Voices and laughter filled the room.

Suddenly her carefully maintained mask of urbanity seemed to crack. She threw down the chopstick, leaned forward, her mouth to Atsu's ear. 'His Lordship is very disappointed in you,' she spat, her eyes flashing.

Atsu started back, stunned at the transformation. Ikushima moved closer till her thigh was pressed against Atsu's.

'He raised you from nothing,' she hissed. 'Nothing! He arranged a marriage for you with the shogun, no less, the most powerful lord in the realm. Do you think it was easy, all the humiliating discussions, all the palms he had to grease, all the compromises, all the hateful alliances he had to agree to? The shogun and his ladies are His Lordship's bitterest enemies. It took him years.

'And here you are, the daughter of the small and inconsequential lord of a tiny seaside town in the middle of nowhere, elevated to Midai, with limitless wealth and hundreds of ladies-in-waiting to do your bidding. And yet you shirk this one small task? You cost His Lordship a lot of time and effort and money and you have been no use to him, none at all. Everything he has done for you, your marriage, everything, will be meaningless if you fail in this.'

Tears stung Atsu's eyes. 'That's not true,' she whispered fiercely. 'I haven't forgotten why I'm here. But what could I do till I had married His Majesty?' She dabbed at her eyes. 'His Lordship isn't here. He's in Kagoshima. How can he know how difficult it is? None of you know His Majesty like I do – not even you, Ikushima. He's a temperamental child. He has tantrums.' No one ever spoke of the shogun this way – not his mother, not his wife, no one. It was unthinkable. But she didn't care. 'He is treated like a god,' she hissed. 'He gets whatever he wants.'

She paused for breath, her chest heaving, dropped her voice even lower. 'Until he trusts me as much as he does his mother, I shall never be able to get him to do what I want. Don't you see? That's why I have to bide my time.'

She drew herself up, glared at Ikushima. 'You forget yourself, Lady Ikushima. You are speaking to the Midai. I am owed respect. How dare you behave with such insolence? You are here to serve me.'

'I know exactly who you are and how you got here. We have raised you up and we will bring you down again if it serves our purpose.'

'You may have trained me but it is I who hold power now. It will not be so easy to depose me.'

Ikushima's elegant face twisted into a demon mask. Her eyes flashed fire. 'We've explained it to you many times. You must have understood by now. Our country is on the brink of disaster. You must focus all your attention on your task.'

That little word 'we' was bothering Atsu. There was a question on the tip of her tongue, something she had wondered about for years but never dared ask. '"We"? Who is this "we"? You are a servant – Princess Konoé's servant, Lord Nariakira's servant. Or is there more to it than that? Tell me. You communicate with His

Lordship every day. You speak with his voice, you do his work. But is it just a job or is there more to it than that? Just how close are you to His Lordship? Closer than you should be, perhaps?'

She expected Ikushima to slap her down but to her amazement that lady's smooth cheeks coloured. 'There's no need to speak of that,' she muttered, turning her face away.

Atsu lifted her shaved brows. 'I see,' she said, keeping her voice low. She smiled in triumph. At last she'd managed to pierce the woman's composure. Now that she had won this small victory she was prepared to compromise. 'I know very well that His Lordship is right,' she added. 'I will think of the best way to proceed.'

Ikushima seemed to have difficulty regaining her self-possession. She took a few deep breaths. She patted Atsu's arm with a manicured hand, composed her face into a smile. Atsu had never noticed before how calculated her smiles were. 'I will help you, my lady,' Ikushima said quietly. 'We cannot afford to wait. If you do not succeed it will be the will of the gods. But you must try.'

She sat back on her heels. 'Yesterday you were not a queen, my lady. Today you are. A queen must be wise. A queen must know and understand her realm. I trained you to be a princess. Now you are queen it is my duty to keep you informed of everything that is going on in the world. Lady Honju-in has spies everywhere. She has a finger in everything and you must too.'

She curled her lip. 'While you've been sulking a lot has happened. You may have forgotten, but Prime Minister Abé has long since resigned. He bore the brunt of the negotiations with the barbarians and the endless arguments with the clan lords. He was only thirty-seven but he was worn out, his health ruined. Lord Hotta is our Prime Minister now. He is a very cultured and brilliant and reason-able and thoughtful man.'

She smoothed the ashes and picked up the metal chopstick. Atsu leaned forward and read as Ikushima wrote, erasing the marks after every few words. 'Lord Hotta is a close ally of His Lordship. But he has no power. Every issue has to be tossed back and forth between the Council of State and the great lords, who all have different opinions and wrangle over every detail.'

She turned and looked at Atsu, checked that she was reading and absorbing everything. 'How many times do I have to repeat myself, my lady? Before the barbarians came to our shores, it didn't matter that the shogun is eccentric. Now it does. It matters enormously. No bill can pass without his sanction and, as you know, he does whatever his mother and Lady Shiga tell him. That is why it is so important that you are here. With your help he can become a real shogun, a good shogun. And you must make sure that the next shogun is a good one too.'

Atsu sighed, thinking of that stick-thin man with his pale face and wavering gaze.

Ikushima put down the chopstick and started to speak in a low urgent voice. 'If I may remind you, since the treaty with the Americans we have been forced to sign four more, with the British, the Russians, the Dutch and the French, allowing them the same privileges as the Americans – to dock in Shimoda and Hakodaté to take on supplies. But we are not fools. We are all well aware that for them that is just the foot in the door. Next they will be asking to trade. But in the end what they plan is to batter down our doors, subdue us, occupy us, colonize us as they have China. The so-called envoy skulking in Shimoda threatens us with destruction if we do not negotiate. What more proof do you need?'

Atsu shivered, feeling the cold air of the outside world blasting through the cobwebby walls of their cocooned lives.

Ikushima shook her head. 'The moment we open our doors a crack the barbarians push them wider. We give them two ports and they send a man to live on our soil. We allow him to stay in Shimoda and he demands to come to Edo. Every time we make a concession they demand more. Not even the wisest among us can imagine where it will end.

'Even the most intransigent lords accept that we will not be able to keep our country closed for much longer. We will have to agree to trade in some form or other.'

She picked up the chopstick again and wrote, 'His Lordship certainly thinks so. He has for a long time – though there are some who want to beat the war drum, issue a call to arms. Meanwhile the American grows more and more insistent. He demands permission to come to Edo. He wants to negotiate.'

Atsu was taking all this in, chewing the end of her fan. 'Who is talking to him? Who brings this news to us?'

'The governors of Shimoda send messages back and forth, relaying the barbarian's demands, asking what response they should give.'

'But if all he wants is to negotiate why does he need to come to Edo? The governors can negotiate with him in Shimoda on our behalf. All we have to do is authorize them to do so. Surely that would solve the problem.'

Ikushima sat back on her heels, nodding approvingly. 'That is precisely what Prime Minister Hotta wants, my lady. But here is the problem. Lady Honju-in stands in his path. Before he can authorize anything the shogun needs to sanction it and Lady Honju-in refuses even to show His Majesty the document. She will not tolerate any negotiations with the barbarian or any recognition of him. She wants him driven back on to his ship and sent away.'

The Lady Dowager was certainly powerful but Atsu ranked higher. She was an imperial princess already and now she was the shogun's consort. Before she could begin wooing her husband, she needed to take on her new mother-in-law.

She smoothed the ashes and held out her hand for the chopstick. 'I understand that Lady Honju-in stands between me and the shogun. I shall talk to her. She is not a child. She knows where her best interests lie. If the country is taken over by barbarians, that will be the end for her and everything she cares about – her power, her wealth, her luxury.'

She took a breath, picked up the chopstick again. 'I shall visit her this afternoon. I need to pay my respects as her new daughter-in-law. It is important to get to know her.'

Ikushima's face lightened. 'Quite right, my lady,' she murmured. 'You are the only one of high enough rank to argue with her on equal terms. You can reason with her and she will have to listen.' She took the chopstick. 'The Lady Dowager is far from stupid. She has been immured in the palace all these years but she has been in the middle of every political intrigue since the shogun was born. She has had her finger in everything that has gone on in this country.'

'You must let me take my time,' Atsu wrote in reply. 'I must be careful not to fuel suspicion or to antagonize her.'

Ikushima raised her shaved brows and wrinkled her smooth forehead. 'Beware,' she said in an undertone. 'There are snakes in the bird's nest. You will see soon enough.'

The words sent a chill down Atsu's spine. She glanced around at her ladies, laughing innocently as they sipped their tea and fingered their silks. She wondered who she could trust and who might be a spy, watching out for a chance to betray her.

She sat back on her heels. 'Lady Ikushima, I intend to pay a courtesy call on my honourable mother-in-law this afternoon,' she said in her most official voice. 'Please send a messenger to announce me.'

She spoke boldly but her heart sank at the thought. She pictured Lady Honju-in's sharp eyes and pinched mouth, heard the rap of her fan and the vinegary tone in which she'd said, 'Twenty? That's a little old to be a bride.' It was a daunting prospect but it had to be done.

29

Ikushima led the way along corridors and verandas, past snow-covered gardens, turning left and right and left again till Atsu was completely lost. They'd taken with them only a few ladies whom Atsu was sure she could trust.

Finally they came to a section of the palace that she hadn't known existed. The ceilings seemed higher, the passageways narrower, the shadows longer. Smells of incense and ancient polish seeped from behind a pair of forbidding doors.

The doors slid back. Lady Honju-in was on her knees in the entrance, voluminous skirts spread around her, withered face creased into a condescending smile. She raised an eyeglass on a stick and peered at Atsu out of sharp black eyes.

'Welcome, dear daughter,' she cooed, bowing till her nose touched the ground. 'My rooms are small and dingy but do please come in.' She gave a tight smile as she uttered the formulaic greeting.

Far from being small and dingy, Lady Honju-in's reception room was the most palatial Atsu had ever seen. The rain doors were tightly bolted but in the dim light she made out huge gold-leaf panels painted with cranes and pine trees and heavy wooden chests piled around the walls. Porcelain dolls and ornate lacquered boxes filled the shelves and racks of kimonos glimmering with gold and silver stretched out wide sleeves in the gloom like an army of scarecrows. Through the open doors at the far end she glimpsed room after room crammed with treasures – a palace within a palace.

Battalions of elderly ladies were on their knees to greet them.

Atsu looked for Lady Shiga's broad plain face but she was nowhere to be seen. With His Majesty, no doubt, Atsu thought, feeling an unexpected stab of jealousy.

'So gracious of Your Majesty to visit our humble home,' trilled Lady Honju-in. 'I am delighted to welcome my new daughter-in-law.'

'I am distressed to hear my husband is unwell. I have been offering up prayers for his rapid recovery,' Atsu said, bowing.

Lady Honju-in raised her painted eyebrows. 'He's a darling boy, so beautiful. He talks to me. He tells me everything.'

In the candlelight Lady Honju-in's eyes gleamed yellow like a cat's. Atsu shivered, thinking of all the babies this woman had had smothered. She wondered how she could sleep at night.

It had been sheer luck that Lady Honju-in's sickly son had survived and she'd taken good care to see that he was the only one who did. And now she had the power she'd wanted so badly, it was clear she would stop at nothing to hold on to it. She ruled the palace. Atsu would have to be vigilant. Lady Honju-in would be equally ruthless to her too if she thought she threatened her position. Atsu wondered what had really happened to the shogun's two previous wives, Princess Tadako and Lady Hideko. It was just as well she had tasters to check every dish before it was served to her.

Elder Anekoji ushered Atsu to a raised area at the head of the room and indicated that she should take her place on the tatami to the left of Lady Honju-in's cushion and a little below. Atsu narrowed her eyes. The sharp-nosed elder was certainly one of the snakes in the bird's nest. She stifled a sigh of exasperation. Just as when she had first met the dowager, there was no cushion at her place. It seemed the battle over precedence would never end. She cast a glance towards Ikushima.

That lady stepped forward. 'Do forgive me,' she said silkily. 'The honourable elder seems to have forgotten. Her Majesty is the representative of He Who Lives Above the Clouds and not only that, she is our queen. Your Ladyship will of course wish to show her appropriate deference.'

Lady Honju-in's face froze into a mask as Ikushima called for a cushion and placed it in the higher position to the right of the old lady. There was a long silence. The dowager jerked her chin abruptly. A couple of dwarves in richly embroidered kimonos hurried in carrying trays of pink rice and bean cakes moulded to look like plum blossoms and began setting out the utensils for tea.

'Delightful to have fresh blood among us,' said Lady Honju-in dryly, raising her painted eyebrows. 'I understand Your Majesty is an accomplished poet and tea ceremony practitioner. And goodness me, you speak so beautifully too. No one would guess you were ever anything but a princess.' She threw Atsu a poisonous glance. She had obviously been waiting for the chance to strike back.

Atsu drew a breath. 'If I may be so bold as to say so, I suspect Your Ladyship has risen in the world too,' she shot back. 'If I am not mistaken your "goodness me" had a distinctly downtown twang.'

Lady Honju-in cocked an eyebrow in a way more suited to a geisha than a court lady. 'You get all types here,' she said coyly. 'The shoguns have always had an eye for a beautiful woman. My dear son's father, Lord Ieyoshi, scoured the streets for beautiful girls whenever he was out in his palanquin. "That one," he'd say, pointing out a young lady walking along the road. The stewards would find out who she was, visit her parents, and a few days later she'd have risen from a towns girl to a court lady and be installed in the palace. He was far from the only one. The mother of one shogun was a greengrocer's daughter, another was a second-hand-clothes seller. Myself, I'm the daughter of a simple retainer. I've been here thirty-four years now. We girls of humble origins have good strong loins. We bear children who survive, while those inbred Miyako women they usually send as consorts are barren.' She stared defiantly at Atsu.

It was on the tip of Atsu's tongue to retort that it was extraordinarily good fortune that of all Lord Ieyoshi's twenty-seven children only one son had survived – Lady Honju-in's. With an effort she kept silent.

'But, goodness me,' Lady Honju-in repeated with a girlish giggle. 'I didn't mean to offend, certainly not. Now you've come to live

among us, I must tell you about our annual ceremonies and observances. It'll be New Year's Eve in a few days. That will be a good
chance for us to get to know each other. Without men here to cramp
our style we always let ourselves go. The maids screen off one end
of the hall and the senior ladies watch the festivities from there. The
elders always insist that the new ladies dance naked.'

She threw a glance at Atsu's ladies, sitting in a group to one side
of the room. They had turned pale and were hiding behind each
other, trying to make themselves inconspicuous.

'Well, not quite naked,' Lady Honju-in went on, her eyes sparkling
wickedly. 'They can wear loincloths if they want. Some tuck in a
cushion so they look as if they're pregnant. They beat buckets with
drumsticks and dance in a line and sing. It's wonderfully amusing.
There's a troupe of dwarf entertainers to run the festivities and
many of the kitchen staff are comedians or dancers. I'm sure your
ladies will want to join in.'

'I'll leave it up to them whether they participate or not,' Atsu said
dryly.

The old lady prattled on. 'At the spring festival the senior
councillors come over from the men's palace and after the ceremonial
casting of beans we grab them and bundle them up in futons and
toss them in the air. It's the only time in the entire year we manage
to see a man, let alone lay hands on one. It's most amusing, isn't it,
ladies!'

She cackled with laughter. Her ladies laughed too, rocking back
and forth, covering their mouths with their hands.

Atsu bowed. There was a momentary silence. She noticed a
rhythmic sound coming from the shadows at the far end of the
room. There was a tall box there with a pendulum and a round face
– a western timepiece. Lord Nariakira had one too. Next to it were
books, not bound in cardboard cases like ordinary books but shiny
and rounded, standing on edge – western books. Atsu wondered
how Lady Honju-in had managed to obtain such rare and priceless
items.

'You remember that demon Perry and his monster ships?' Lady
Honju-in asked, following her gaze. 'They brought gifts for the

"emperor". That's what the barbarians call my son. They don't know any better. The weapons and most of the books went to the men's palace but some came into my possession.' She gestured airily at the grandfather clock. 'The elders in the men's palace say it's for telling time. All the daimyo have them. I don't see that I need one. I know the time well enough without it. But I like the sound. It's the way life must be among the barbarians – on and on, exactly the same, monotonous, never changing. What strange creatures they are.'

'Did His Majesty like his gifts?' Atsu asked.

The old lady narrowed her eyes and looked hard at Atsu. She put a liver-spotted hand to her mouth and burst into laughter. 'He liked the gun,' she said, chuckling. 'He kept it for himself. Oh, and the machine that runs on rails, like a mechanical palanquin. They call it an "engine". He likes sitting on it, holding on for dear life, whizzing round and round.'

Suddenly Atsu remembered something Lord Nariakira had told her. 'I heard there were gifts for the "empress" too,' she said. She bit her lip. The last thing she wanted was to antagonize Lady Honju-in. But she'd said it now. In any case it was best to let Lady Honju-in know she couldn't be pushed around.

The room fell silent. There was an audible intake of breath. Lady Honju-in glared at Atsu.

Ikushima had been kneeling to one side, a little behind Atsu. She slid forward. 'Yes, the foreigners brought gifts for the "emperor" and the "empress", so I heard. But His Majesty had no consort when they came. What became of those gifts, I wonder?'

The dowager spun round in a rustle of silk and stared at her. Ikushima kept her eyes modestly lowered, her brows raised in an expression of innocent enquiry.

Atsu held her breath. This was dangerous territory. Lady Honju-in's power depended on her wealth. She was like a jackdaw, snapping up everything in her path. If she had her way, everything in the palace would end up in her wing.

Lady Honju-in pursed her large scarlet lips. 'How perspicacious,' she said in icy tones. 'What an excellent memory Your Majesty has.'

'But hadn't my lady's marriage to His Majesty already been arranged?' Ikushima persisted silkily.

'Indeed,' said Lady Honju-in. 'I wonder what gifts those might have been?' She raised her painted brows and narrowed her eyes until they disappeared into the sea of wrinkles.

'Perhaps you know, Lady Ikushima,' Atsu said. 'Is there not a record of them?'

Ikushima nodded. 'Indeed there is.' She counted them off on her fingers. 'Flowered silk embroidered dress in the western fashion, one; gilded toiletries box, western in style and content, one; containers of western-style oil-based perfume, seventy-two.'

There was a long silence. An ancient tabby cat waddled into the room, ambled creakily over to Lady Honju-in and plumped down next to her.

'Seventy-two,' said Atsu thoughtfully. 'What a strange number.'

'The westerners count in twelves,' said Ikushima.

Lady Honju-in scowled. Atsu could see that she hated the very thought of having to give up a single one of her treasures. 'We will make enquiries,' she snarled. 'We will do our best to locate them and ensure that Your Majesty receives them. The palace is large, but we will track them down.'

Atsu smiled and gave a gracious bow. She had won this round.

The dowager turned away. The exotically clad dwarves had finished the preparations for tea.

'Perhaps my dear daughter would like to try that tea the barbarians brought,' she said with exaggerated sweetness. A wisp of a woman spooned some dried black leaves into a pot, added warm water, poured out a cup and offered it in both hands to Atsu. Atsu threw a glance at Ikushima, wondering whether it was safe to drink. Ikushima nodded imperceptibly. She certainly had spies posted even in the depths of Lady Honju-in's rooms and presumably had arranged for the tea to be tasted.

The tea was pale brown with a fragrance akin to Chinese tea and a curious bitter tang, like nothing Atsu had ever tasted before. It was the tang of the wide world outside. As she sipped, it seemed to lift her. For a moment she felt as if she could breathe at last, fly away out of this stultifying palace.

She put down the cup. In her mind's eye she saw lines of characters scrolling across the tobacco ashes as Ikushima wrote them. She had to find a way to bring the subject round to the American in Shimoda. She took a breath. 'When we first met I believe Your Ladyship told me that I am here at your wish. May I ask what you expect of me?'

'No great mystery,' said the old woman. 'My son needs a formal consort and there's a tradition of a Shimazu consort in the palace. His grandmother was a Shimazu, as you know. Your coming brings together the three most powerful families in the land – the Shimazu, the Tokugawa and the imperial family. I'm sure my dear daughter understands perfectly well that that is the sole purpose of marriage – to create alliances.'

Atsu nodded thoughtfully. 'It is certainly true that we need a united front. Our enemies are installed right on our soil.'

'Those loathsome barbarians,' Lady Honju-in shrilled. 'They're a disease. They infect the entire country, no matter how carefully we pen them in. They're a gangrenous toe. They're a pollution.' Her voice had risen to a shriek.

'Come, come, Mother. They are not as bad as that,' Atsu said, laughing. 'In any case they are contained in Shimoda, for the moment, at least, though from what I hear they are shaking the bars of their cage.'

Lady Honju-in flapped her fan, her face twisted in disgust. 'An ordeal, a dreadful ordeal for those poor people down there,' she hissed. 'I don't know how they bear it. Governor Inoué, one of the Shimoda governors, travelled up to discuss it with Prime Minister Hotta and he passed on their complaints to me.'

'I have heard a great deal about Lord Hotta,' Atsu said. 'I under-stand he is a brilliant man and an excellent successor to Lord Abé. I am looking forward to meeting him.'

Lady Honju-in didn't seem to hear. Her face had puffed up and blackened. 'Those barbarians!' she exploded. 'They're foul creatures, foul! They ordered a pig from a local farmer and had it slaughtered.

Can you imagine? You could hear its screams all over town. The priests had to chant day and night to cleanse the pollution. And they stink. Their house smells of rancid animal flesh and the vile substances they make from the milk of cows. It used to be a temple, a holy place! It was the only building they could find to lodge them in at a safe distance from town. And those two geisha, forced to live with them. They're ruined for ever, no man will ever touch them again.'

The old ladies knelt like statues, holding their tea cups in trembling hands.

Atsu sipped the bitter tea and waited for her to finish. 'We can learn from the westerners too, you know, Mother,' she said. 'They have invented many extraordinary things – lenses that bring things closer, a machine that can capture the image of a person or a place as perfectly as in a mirror, ships powered by steam that go faster than the wind can blow. In fact, you have one of their inventions yourself, right here in this room.' She gestured towards the grandfather clock ticking away in the corner.

'Toys, ingenious toys,' spat Lady Honju-in. 'Those creatures are interested only in the material world, in what they can use. You can't compare their childish toys with our glorious artefacts.' She waved at the painted screens and lacquered chests and priceless tea ceremony ware glimmering in the candlelight. 'They think they can fool us with their toys. They think we're children, that we don't know what crimes they've committed in China. We're not that naive.'

'Well, no matter what we think of them, we certainly do not want to be forced into any more humiliating treaties. We need to be sure we avoid the fate of China. We cannot go to war with them. We do not have the weapons or the power. We have no choice but to negotiate with these intruders.'

'Negotiate? We must get rid of them,' screamed Lady Honju-in. 'We've lived happily for aeons. If they take one step further into our realm they'll turn everything upside down. You know what they're demanding?'

'They wish to come to Edo. We have kept them at arm's length in Shimoda for several months.'

'The nerve of it! They demand an audience with my son, no less, with His Majesty the shogun! No one sees His Majesty the shogun, no one may even know his name. He never leaves the castle. No one has ever seen his face. Only the highest-ranking lords in the land may enter his divine presence and when they do they keep their faces down and their eyes to the ground. When the Dutch barbarians enter his presence they show proper humility. If they ever dared look up at him, we have a hundred men ready to cut them into pieces.

'Half our staff never enter his presence, let alone some unwashed meat-eating barbarian. It would pollute my son to breathe the same air. They think they can cross our country, walk our roads, pass through our villages, show themselves to the peasantry in their outlandish garb, spreading pollution as they go? They want to enter Edo and walk the streets of our great capital and pass through the gates of the greatest castle in the land and enter the presence of His Majesty himself? It's outrageous. It's the most vile, impudent presumption.'

She clamped her mouth shut and glared as fiercely as if Atsu was one of those reviled barbarians herself.

Atsu nodded. So Lady Honju-in thought they could hold back the tide. She wanted nothing to change, ever. 'What does His Majesty think?' she asked.

'He thinks what I tell him to think. He thinks they should get back on their ships and leave.'

Atsu took a breath. It was time to make her move. 'Mother, you know very well we cannot fight them. They are here on our soil and we cannot get them back on their ships. They say they represent their country and they want to come to Edo to meet our leaders, to begin discussions. They insist on negotiations, so let them negotiate. They do not need to come to Edo for that. Let the Shimoda governors negotiate with them on our behalf.'

'I allow that you have a pretty face, dear daughter,' said Lady Honju-in with a curl of her lip. 'But there's no need to worry that little head of yours with matters of state. Leave that to those of us older and more experienced. You want my opinion? I'll give you my opinion. We must order them again and again and again and again to get back on their ships until they do.' Her voice had risen to a screech. She paused, looked around at her retinue of aged crones, rapped her fan on the tatami. 'Now you're my daughter-in-law it's your duty to support me. That's why I agreed to have you here.'

Atsu pictured the monstrous ships she'd seen as they rounded the bay on their way to Edo. 'I saw the black ships with my own eyes, Mother,' she said. 'They are much bigger and more powerful than you could ever imagine. We do not have ships strong enough to resist them. We are building a fleet but it will be years before we are ready to fight. Do you not see, we shall have to negotiate with them sooner or later. Surely it is better to negotiate from a position of strength than for them to bring their warships and bombard our cities and force us to negotiate on their terms, as they have done in China? If we give the Shimoda governors full authority to negotiate with them, the barbarians will have no reason to come to Edo. You must see that it is to our advantage to keep the American barbarian in Shimoda.'

Lady Honju-in stared at her with a look of hatred. The old ladies froze, waiting to see what her response would be.

'They should never have been allowed into Shimoda in the first place,' she screamed. 'We should never have let them set foot on our soil.'

'We could not stop them,' said Atsu calmly. 'And now they are here we have to find a way to deal with them.'

There was a long silence. Lady Honju-in flapped her fan furiously, stared around, her black eyes burning. She narrowed her gaze, gave a cunning smile. 'I see,' she said. 'I understand exactly what's going on. Prime Minister Hotta and your Lord Nariakira have recruited you to win me over.'

'No, my lady,' Atsu said fervently. She was desperate to make her see reason. It seemed such a small thing to ask, yet Lady Honju-in just wouldn't budge. 'It is what I myself think. The last thing we want is the western barbarians in Edo. But if we delay any longer the American will send foreign ships to attack us. We do not have the strength to oppose them. They will lay waste our country. We must give the Shimoda governors full authorization to negotiate on our behalf. It is the only way to save ourselves.'

Atsu took a breath. She hadn't realized she'd raised her voice. Lady Honju-in was staring at her.

'Open the door a crack and they'll push it wide open,' the dowager barked. She turned to the ranks of old ladies, hollow-cheeked like ghouls in the candlelight. She pursed her large scarlet lips. 'But I suppose there's nothing else we can do,' she said grudgingly. 'I'll speak to my son. Hotta asked him to put his seal to a document giving the Shimoda governors authority to negotiate on our behalf. I will make sure he does.'

The old ladies had all been leaning forward. They clucked and murmured, following Lady Honju-in's cue, nodding in approval.

Atsu had been holding her breath. She let it go, heaved a sigh of relief. 'You are quite right, my lady,' she said. 'I defer to your superior age and experience and judgement.' A little flattery did no harm, even if Lady Honju-in was far too canny to be taken in by it.

'I shall speak to my husband too,' she added. Now that Atsu was the Midai, she intended to be involved in all meetings and affairs of state. Princess Tadako and Lady Hideko might have spent their time playing with birds and worrying about clothes, but things were different now.

But the westerners would come anyway, she thought. They could put them off and put them off but they would come in the end. Sooner or later they would come to Edo. They would spread everywhere throughout the land. Trying to stop them was like trying to hold down the waves in the ocean with a piece of wood. Atsu remembered the silver plate Lord Nariakira had shown her – a daguerreotype, he had told her it was called – and the foreign street in the foreign land she'd seen there, frozen in time, different from anything she'd ever known, more different even than the dragon king's realm beneath the sea.

The barbarians were here now, they'd arrived on their shores. No one could stop time. Life would never go back to the way it had been.

She bowed her head and tears came to her eyes. She had to find a way to make the shogun listen to her. She'd given up everything she cared about for this one purpose – to fight for Lord Nariakira, for the good of their country. Only time would tell if she could possibly succeed – and if she did, if it would have been worth her sacrifice.

30

A couple of days after the meeting with Lady Honju-in Ikushima appeared, her face as composed and imperturbable as a Buddha's. She glanced around, smoothed the ashes in the tobacco box and began to scribble: 'The shogun can't really be ill. He is playing games with you. You need to see him. He must sign the letter for the Shimoda governors. If the American doesn't get an answer soon he will summon his ships and order them to attack. You cannot delay a moment longer.'

Atsu pursed her lips, tired of Ikushima and her chivvying. She wasn't even sure if she was right. 'Don't you understand?' she sighed. 'There's nothing I can do. How can I enter the men's palace and demand a meeting with him?'

She looked up. The rain doors had been flung back and winter sunshine filtered through the paper screens. 'But there is one way we can find out. Lady Ikushima,' she said, raising her voice. 'Would you be so kind as to pay a call on Lady Honju-in and enquire after my husband's health?'

Ikushima swept out and returned an hour later. 'Her Ladyship appreciates your concern. She asks me to convey to you that the palace doctors are tending to His Majesty. He is doing as well as can be expected.'

Atsu bowed her head. Perhaps the dowager was making up stories or perhaps she had received a bulletin from the men's palace. Atsu would have to make sure that in future she too was kept better informed.

Day followed day and still there was no word of Iesada. Atsu grew more and more agitated. She paced up and down her rooms, wringing her hands, or threw herself on the tatami and knelt at the brazier, staring into the distance, pretending to read.

Then early one morning a chamberlain slid open the doors. It was the day before New Year's Eve. Thanks be to the gods, she announced, His Majesty the shogun has recovered. The ladies should prepare for the first of the daily audiences.

The women flew around, winding Atsu's long hair into an oiled and perfumed loop, touching up her make-up, selecting a splendid set of kimonos. A little before the Hour of the Snake they set off. Atsu was at the front with Middle Elder Omasé and Ikushima behind her, followed by her highest-ranking ladies, spreading her kimono train in a fan as she walked.

They had passed the Great Hall when Lady Honju-in came into view at the head of her ancient retinue, rustling along the corridor in their full-skirted kimonos. It was the first time they had crossed paths since Atsu had visited her rooms. Atsu held her ground. The dowager drew herself up and bristled then gave a tight smile and gestured for Atsu to lead the way. It was another small victory.

In the Upper Bell Corridor the golden padlock on the double doors that led to the men's palace had been removed. Atsu took her place closest to the doors while her ladies knelt behind her along the right-hand side of the corridor. Lady Honju-in and her entourage lined up along the left and they waited on their knees, still as statues, fingertips touched to the tatami.

Atsu's heart thumped as she heard deep voices and the firm tread of male feet. Bolts ground on the other side of the doors. The cluster of bells jangled and the elderly heralds shouted, 'His Majesty!' The women bowed in unison as the doors slid back.

The tang of another world swirled through – rich manly perfumes mingled with pomade and starch. Atsu glimpsed shiny topknots, shaved forelocks and the crisp black hakama of pageboys and male attendants as a couple of shaven-headed companion priests – the only women allowed in the men's palace – ran out. A slight figure appeared behind them, wafting a distinctive scent. Atsu trembled and lowered her eyes, unexpectedly overcome by awe, as she saw Iesada's pale glimmering face. A retainer from the men's side passed the shogun's sword across the threshold to a lady-in-waiting who received it in both hands, and the doors closed as firmly as if they'd never opened.

Iesada stalked forward, casting a lordly glance over the ranks of women on their knees before him. His starched robes made him look large and imposing but the hand that poked from the huge sleeve, holding his fan of office, was thin and bony. Under the towering black headdress his face was pale and his skin transparent. He looked thinner and frailer, somehow changed. Atsu saw with a mixture of relief and concern that he really had been ill. His head turned from side to side, then he limped towards his mother and Lady Shiga. For a moment his eyes rested on Atsu. There was a clarity in his gaze that she hadn't seen before.

She felt the same shock of surprise that she had felt at their wedding at the ethereal beauty of his features – his full mouth, small chiselled nose, large eyes, delicate cheekbones and smooth ivory skin. Perhaps it would not be such a terrible fate to become close to such a man.

The women jumped up, gathered round him, simpering and patting their hair. Despite everything, he was a man and he was theirs.

Clucking and chattering, pulling at his sleeves, they escorted him to the shrine room. Atsu knelt beside him on the icy tatami facing tiers of dusty memorial tablets, her breath like smoke in the frosty air. The priests launched into the first sutra but they had barely droned out a couple of lines when Iesada shuffled and jerked his head. Atsu put her hand on his arm to calm him but he shook it off. Lady Honju-in rose. 'Thank you. That will do,' she snapped and hurried him out.

The ladies took their places on their knees in the Great Hall. The shogun knelt on a low stage in front of a gold screen with a pine tree painted on it, spreading its branches like a canopy over his head. Atsu knelt to his right and Lady Honju-in to his left. Candles on tall sticks blazed with huge yellow flames around the room.

Elder Anekoji bowed. 'We are so happy to see that His Majesty has recovered,' she chirruped. Her black eyes twinkled and her harsh face softened. 'If His Majesty wishes we will enjoy a tea ceremony this afternoon, or play a few rounds of the incense game. Or would His Majesty rather spend the time in less formal pursuits?'

Iesada's shoulders slumped and his face drooped. 'But it is New Year's and there is snow out there,' he whined. 'I thought you said we were going to build a snow rabbit.'

Elder Anekoji gave a high-pitched laugh. 'Don't worry, Your Majesty. Of course we will. We'll wrap up warm and go out this afternoon and build a snow rabbit.'

Atsu looked from one to the other in disbelief. The country was in peril, the westerners threatening to advance on Edo if they didn't get an answer, and here were the shogun and the ladies of the women's palace, the most powerful people in the country, behaving as if they had nothing better to do than entertain themselves.

'Masa-*kun*,' she cried. The ladies cringed. They dared not raise their heads and stare. 'Of course we will go out and enjoy the snow. But first you have important work to do. You are our shogun, our supreme lord. There is urgent business you have to attend to. After that we can enjoy ourselves.'

Iesada stuck his lower lip out in a pout. He rocked back and forth, scowling, chewing the end of his fan.

There was a mew. A cat had slipped into the Great Hall and was slinking between the rows of women. One of Lady Honju-in's elderly attendants grabbed it by the scruff of its neck and was about to toss it out of the room when the shogun's face lit up. 'Jewel!' he cried. 'Let her stay. Jewel, Jewel! Here, here!'

Atsu cast an apologetic glance towards Lady Honju-in. She'd half suspected that if Jewel could find her way to the Little Sitting Room she'd be able to find the Great Hall too.

'Come, come,' crooned the shogun. He held up his fan of office and swung the tassel. The kitten bounded over and batted at it with its golden and white paws. He beamed at Atsu.

Now was the moment. She took a breath and glanced at Lady Honju-in. She had to take care not to make the old woman think she was trying to usurp her position. 'Masa-*kun*,' she said. 'Your mother and I have an important job for you. We have a document here. We'd like you to put your seal to it.'

The dowager bared her black teeth. 'Uncle Hotta discussed it with you. Do you remember?' she said. Atsu breathed a sigh of relief. For now at least they were on the same side.

'I hate Uncle Hotta. He is fat and his breath smells,' said the shogun. He rocked to and fro, looking at Atsu as if to check her reaction, trying to show her how rebellious he was, how independent he could be. The women drew their breath through their teeth and tittered. 'I liked Uncle Abé. He told me stories.'

'Now, Masa-*kun*, you mustn't talk like that about Uncle Hotta,' said the dowager.

Atsu looked at him pleadingly. 'Your honourable mother and I have discussed this and thought about it carefully and we would like you to put your seal to it,' she said.

'Lady Shiga thinks so too, don't you, Lady Shiga?' added Lady Honju-in.

Lady Shiga was on her knees directly in front of the shogun. She looked hard at him and he quailed. She pursed her lips and gave a careless nod.

Atsu frowned. So all that was needed was Lady Shiga's approval and Iesada did whatever he was asked. It worried her that that indolent lady wielded such power over him. If Atsu was to achieve her task she would have to find a way to supplant Lady Shiga. She didn't trust her one bit. She would have to be wary.

Elder Anekoji glanced at Lady Honju-in and raised her eyebrows. She took a stick of pressed safflower and a water dropper, ground some red ink and placed the ink stone and a seal box on the low table in front of the shogun. Then she slid forward a scroll box and took out a scroll. Lady Honju-in gestured towards Atsu. Elder Anekoji handed it to her with a bow.

Atsu unrolled the scroll and spread it on the table.

The shogun jerked his head from side to side and scowled. 'I hate Uncle Hotta. I hate him,' he said. 'What does it say? I want to know what it says.'

'We need to . . .' Atsu began.

'No need to explain,' Lady Honju-in butted in. 'Here, Masa-*kun*. Just press your seal on the ink and stamp it here. And when you come in this afternoon we'll go out and build a snow rabbit.'

Iesada picked up the scroll and peered at it, running his bony white finger down the characters. '"To Inoué, landholder in the realm of Shinano, First Governor of Shimoda. Greetings." Inoué? Shimoda?' He looked up, his eyes huge and round, his face furrowed, and smacked his fan on the tatami. 'It is the barbarians, is it not?' He swung round and pointed his fan at Atsu. 'You, tell me. What do you think?'

Their eyes met and Atsu smiled. It gave her a warm glow to hear him address her so intimately as 'You'.

'That's not the way you speak to the Honourable Midai, your lady consort,' Lady Honju-in snapped.

'It is the barbarians, is it not?' Iesada said, sticking out his lower lip. 'What does it say?' He looked straight at Atsu. 'Tell me, tell me.' He seemed different today, more lucid. It didn't seem right to treat him like a child.

Atsu hesitated. She didn't want to frighten him. 'There is nothing to worry about,' she said. 'The American barbarian wants to come to Edo and have an audience with you. There are things he wants to discuss. But we shall not let him. We have told him he must stay in Shimoda. We are giving Governor Inoué full powers to negotiate with him there. That is what this letter says.'

The shogun grabbed the cat by the scruff of its tortoiseshell neck and squeezed it to his chest, his eyes swivelling from Atsu to Lady Honju-in and back. It mewed and struggled in protest.

'They will kill me,' he shouted, his breath labouring. 'They want to kill me. They came in their black ships and brought that letter for my father and then they killed him. They made him sign and then they killed him. And now they want to kill me.'

Atsu reached out and put her hand on his thin arm. He was shaking. What he was saying made no sense, but even though his words were confused, they only added to her foreboding. There had been too many hints that something terrible had happened to Iesada's father.

The audience chamber had erupted into uproar. Atsu's ladies, who knew nothing about the late shogun's death, exclaimed in horror. Lady Honju-in's retinue of wizened old crones sat stony-faced.

'Don't be stupid, Masa. You're talking nonsense,' Lady Honju-in shrieked. Her wrinkled cheeks sagged, her skin had grown waxen. 'You're upsetting yourself. You know perfectly well the barbarians didn't kill your father.'

Atsu steeled herself. The only thing that mattered for now was for the shogun to put his seal on the document. She would find out another time what had happened to his father. 'If you stamp this document it will stop the American barbarian coming, Masa-*kun*. Then he will not be able to kill you,' she said, keeping her voice calm and steady.

'She does not know,' he screamed. 'You know, Mama, and you, Elder Ané, and Oshiga, you know too. It was not the barbarians that killed him. It was them, because he signed. And now you want me to sign.'

Lady Honju-in jerked round and stared at Atsu, her eyes burning like coals. 'He doesn't know what he's saying,' she spat. 'Don't be foolish, Masa. Your father took ill, that's all. You peeped through the doors when the doctors came, remember? You brought him water and put your finger in his rice gruel to make sure it wasn't too hot.'

Atsu swallowed. She didn't know what to believe.

'You want the barbarians to get back on their ships, don't you?' barked Lady Honju-in. 'You want them to go away? Just put your seal to this and they will.'

'That is all this will do, stop them coming? No promises, no con-con-concessions?' He stammered out the difficult word. Atsu wondered if he knew what it meant or if it was something he had heard when his father was killed.

'No concessions. No promises,' she said. 'It's just a letter. They will negotiate with Governor Inoué, then they will go.'

The shogun threw a desperate glance at her. She stroked his arm. 'It is just a letter,' she repeated. 'Do not worry. Nothing bad will happen to you. I shall make sure of it. You can trust me. I shall take care of you.'

He looked at her and she held his gaze steadily. 'You promise?'
'I promise.'

He nodded. He settled back on his heels, took a breath, straightened his back, looked around at the rows of women. He was the shogun, their shogun, master of the land.

The room fell silent. He frowned, took the seal, applied it to the ink pad then pressed it firmly to the document. When he lifted it a large red square was imprinted there – his stamp.

Atsu let out a breath, weak with relief. Her hands were trembling. They'd held back the tide, stopped the implacable barbarian coming to Edo for now at least.

She looked around, wondering if anyone else even understood the magnitude of what the shogun had done. Elder Anekoji was scattering sand over the ink, rolling up the scroll, straightening the ends, putting it into its box. Iesada was playing with the cat. He'd already forgotten that for a moment he had been the shogun, ruler of the realm, and played his role to perfection.

Lady Honju-in was smoothing her skirts, examining her nails, flapping her fan.

'Congratulations, my lady,' Atsu murmured. 'You did an excellent job.'

The dowager narrowed her eyes. She was not one to be fooled by sweet talk.

Atsu frowned. They'd managed to get the shogun to put his seal to the letter. But she saw very clearly now how difficult it was going to be to achieve anything more, let alone accomplish the mission that Lord Nariakira had assigned her. She would have to find ways to be alone with Iesada, to prise him away from the poisonous influence of his mother and Lady Shiga. She would only be able to manage that at night and even then Elder Anekoji and Middle Elder Omasé would be just the other side of the screens, listening in.

Shortly afterwards the shogun left. When he came in again for the afternoon audience he was wearing thick silk robes under a quilted green and turquoise cape embroidered with flowers. Atsu's ladies helped her into a quilted jacket and she went out on to the veranda and slid her feet into geta clogs with thick wooden soles to step down into the gardens.

Snow lay deep on the ground, bathing the landscape in an unearthly glow. It crusted the gnarled branches of the plum trees and the struts of the latticework fences, bent the bamboo leaves, sat like a coolie hat on the squat stone lantern. Iesada stomped around with the younger ladies, laughing, making a trail of footprints across the pristine white.

He stumbled about trying to help as the ladies gathered a mound of snow and rolled it into a huge ball. Then they made a smaller ball for the head and pushed in berries for eyes and sculpted two large flat ears starting from the smaller ball and lying back over the rabbit's body.

'A snow rabbit!' the shogun cried, clapping his hands. Atsu laughed with delight as she looked at the huge white rabbit with its paws tucked under its chin. Iesada grinned wickedly, scooped some snow into a ball and threw it at the ladies, shrieking with laughter as they screamed and scurried away. Atsu laughed too, happy to see his bright eyes and the healthy flush on his cheeks.

He'd barely returned to the men's palace when a message arrived. He would stay in the women's palace after the third audience. He wished to spend the night with his consort.

31

Usually the order to prepare the Little Sitting Room came through several days in advance to ensure there was plenty of time to clean and tidy. But the shogun had to have his way and this was his express decree. There was panic in the women's palace.

Middle Elder Omasé and the chamberlains led Atsu through the corridors, lighting the way with candles and tapers. But all she could think of was the ghosts that had seemed to buzz around the darkness the last time she had spent the night in the shogun's bedroom. Her heart sank at the thought of those malevolent spirits wrapping the poor shogun in their arms, dragging him down. She wished she could drive them all away, mend his body and his mind so that he could have some peace.

In the Little Sitting Room everything was laid out as it had been on the wedding night, with a pile of luxurious futons for the shogun in the upper part of the room and some for Atsu on a slightly lower level and five quilts for each of them with red and white silk covers. On the covers of the topmost quilts was an auspicious design of the three New Year trees – pine, bamboo and plum. There were red pillows with big red tassels and Iesada's sword rest and smoking set at the head of his futon and erotic prints and books spread enticingly on the low table.

The room smelt of candle smoke and tallow and tobacco.

'Open the rain doors,' Atsu said. 'Let in some air.'

The shogun emerged from the dressing room in his white silk night clothes. Middle Elder Omasé and Elder Anekoji retired to the next room, servants brought tea for Atsu and saké for the shogun and they were left alone.

They sat at the open rain doors, puffing on their pipes. The huge round moon hung low in the black sky, bathing the snow-covered gardens in silvery light.

'Can you see the rabbit in the moon?' said Atsu. 'He is up there, pounding rice cakes.' The shadows on the moon's surface really did look like a rabbit on its hind legs in front of a barrel, holding up a mallet.

'It is our snow rabbit,' Iesada said. 'It is beautiful.' His voice trembled. He had tears in his eyes. Touched, she took his hand. They sat, fingers gently entwined. 'It is making rice cakes for New Year,' he whispered.

'It is the day after tomorrow,' she said, squeezing his hand. His thin fingers were cold. 'Are you excited, Masa-*kun*? There will be dancing and delicious New Year dishes. Will you spend New Year's Eve with us?'

'Perhaps I shall,' he said. 'Perhaps I shall try to dance.' He slid closer and rested his head on her shoulder.

She held her breath, hardly daring to move, afraid to scare him away, wanting to hold on to these precious moments. She couldn't believe she'd won him over, that he could be clear-minded for so long.

'Will you really take care of me?' he asked.

'Of course.' She stroked his shaven pate and smoothed the oiled hair at the sides of his head, breathing the perfume of his pomade.

'This was my father's room and my grandfather's room and my great-grandfather's room,' he said. 'And now it is my room.'

Atsu would have to find out sometime what had happened to his father but right now she wanted to keep well away from that topic. She filled his saké cup.

'I did not see my grandfather much,' he said. 'Father was stern. He always told me not to shake my head. I acted the Old Man in a Noh play once. Did you know that? Without a mask. Father told me I must not shake my head and I did not, not once, all the way through. Everyone was pleased. Everyone clapped and clapped.'

'I would love to have seen that, Masa-*kun*,' Atsu said. 'Please do it for me sometime.'

She noticed he was turning something over and over in his hand. 'What is that?' she asked.

He opened his fingers and held out his palm. On it was an ivory snail, beautifully carved, with a curved shell, scaly neck and horned head, the exact size and shape of a real snail. It was the toggle that fastened the silken cord of his tobacco pouch. She'd seen it hanging from his sash.

He pressed his mouth to her ear. 'It is my snail,' he said, as if he was sharing a precious secret. 'Did you know I have a shell too, like a snail? I creep inside when I want to be quiet and alone. Here. You may hold it if you like.'

She took it, feeling its smooth contours. It was beautiful.

He cocked his head to one side and looked up at her. 'Where did you come from?' he asked suddenly. 'Why are you here?'

It was the first time he'd shown any curiosity about her or any awareness that there might be a world outside the walls of the palace.

'You are not Hideko and you are not the other one. I forget her name. What was she called?'

'Never mind. I am Atsu. That is my name.'

'Atsu-*chan*.' He tried out the syllables. 'Atsu-*chan*.' He studied her through his large innocent eyes. 'You are beautiful,' he said, as if it was a simple matter of fact. 'I have never seen a face so beautiful. Like an angel.' He sat up sharply. 'Are you going to die and go away like those others did?' His voice quavered. 'Everyone goes away. No one stays with me.'

'I shall stay with you for ever, Masa-*kun*,' she said. 'We shall spend our whole lives together.'

Iesada's head had begun to move and his eyes to wander. Atsu wondered how long he would remain lucid. She dared not hope that it was a permanent improvement. Then she remembered that he'd said he liked stories. He'd liked the stories that Prime Minister Abé had told him.

'You asked where I came from,' she said, putting her arm round his thin shoulders. 'I grew up in a small town right beside the sea.

From my house you could hear the waves lapping on the beach. Just across the water there was a huge volcano as tall as a mountain that puffed out fire and smoke like a dragon. There were palm trees and thick green forests, cherry blossom in the springtime and maple leaves in the autumn. And the sun shone every day.'

'I have never seen the sea,' he said. 'And the only volcano I ever see is when I glimpse Mount Fuji far far away across the castle walls.'

She'd forgotten. He had never once been outside the palace. She felt a pang of sadness and pity. 'The sea is like the lakes in the palace gardens,' she said, 'but bigger, blue and deep, so big you cannot see the other side, as big as the ocean where the dragon king's daughter has her palace. Can you imagine that?'

'I should like to see that,' he said. 'I should like to see the sea.'

'And where I grew up the sand is hot and black from all the minerals. It smells like rotten eggs, but it's very good for health. People come from all around to be buried in it to absorb the minerals and be healed. You have never been to a hot spring, have you? Maybe I can take you one day.'

He was staring at her. 'Why are you so sad?' he asked abruptly.

'Sad?' He seemed such a child but she had the uncanny feeling he could see straight through her into her soul. 'What makes you think I am sad, Masa-*kun*?'

But of course, he was right. She'd been trying to keep her sadness at bay, make herself forget. But now, as she spoke of her home, in her mind she'd travelled south, back to the beautiful land of Kyushu with its volcanic sands and orange trees and sunshine, back to her family and to Kaneshigé, to those childhood days when she'd known nothing of the palace and its looming shadows and dark intrigues.

But she was sad for Iesada too – sad that he could never leave, never know any other people or any other life, sad that he was the way he was, imprisoned in his own body. He was so thin and frail, she could almost have lifted him up in her arms and carried him away with her, sneaked out of the palace with him one night and run all the way back to Kyushu.

Of course there were many people like him. All manner of children were born. It was no great mystery, not surprising that some days he should be better and some days worse. One thing she was sure of. If only she could find a way to keep him from his mother he might have a chance to grow up.

'Sometimes I miss my home,' she whispered.

'Home,' he said wistfully. 'I don't know what that means. I suppose this must be my home.' He gazed around at the gold walls and lavish furnishings. It was all his, all this splendour, yet none of it was his. He was a prisoner in the middle of all this luxury. Atsu was filled with sadness for him. She knew now that she had to stay with him. Someone had to keep him company in this hostile place.

'When you talked about your home you were far away,' he said. 'Do not go away. Do not leave me.'

'I shall never leave you,' she said.

'You promise?'

'I promise.'

He gave a contented sigh. She put her arms around him and nuzzled her face into his, feeling the warmth of his body pressing against hers. Perhaps this was a chance to get close to him, start their marriage in earnest, get to know each other as man and wife. Perhaps they could try to have a baby.

'Let us go inside and lie down,' she said softly, 'and I shall rub your back.'

She jumped up, ran inside and folded back the red silk cover of his futon. He stood up too, looked around vaguely, then ambled over to the low table where the erotic prints were scattered. He hadn't paid the slightest attention to them before. Now he started leafing through them. Atsu held her breath. Perhaps the prints would work their magic and stir excitement in him. He picked one up, held it close to his face and peered at it intently.

'Come and lie down,' she said. 'I shall make you feel nice.'

'Look at this,' he said. His voice had become shrill. He was staring at the print. 'Look at this. It is the sea but it is not the sea. It is something else.'

Atsu was on her knees beside his futon. She looked up at him, wondering what this print showed that was so fascinating. It was hard to keep up with his changes of mood.

'Never mind that,' she said. 'Come over here. Come and lie down.'

He stumbled over, his eyes huge, and thrust the print into her hands.

She stared at it and drew back with a start, her heart sinking. She had seen such pictures before. It was a visual pun, a witty depiction of Lake Biwa in the form of a bowl of water complete with miniature trees and rocks around the edges. Right in the middle, filling nearly the entire lake, was what looked at first sight like a giant whirlpool. In fact it was the reflection of a naked woman who was squatting over the bowl – Atsu could see the outline of her hips – and the whirlpool was her most secret place, the place people call the Cinnabar Cleft, vast, swollen and purple-lipped.

She shook her head, furious with Middle Elder Omasé. There was nothing extraordinary about the picture. There were plenty of punning prints purportedly depicting a completely innocent scene which actually, when looked at more closely, turned out to depict something distinctly erotic. Nevertheless Omasé should have known better than to leave a picture like this lying around. She should have known it would upset Iesada.

But then she realized. It wasn't the Middle Elder who had left it. Lady Honju-in or Lady Shiga – someone who knew him well, who knew exactly how he would respond – had left it there deliberately in order to sabotage their night together.

'It is nothing. Put it away. Come and lie down,' she said helplessly.

'Will you show me?' he said. He glanced at her out of the corner of his eye and ran a bony finger across the purple flesh depicted in the print. 'You have one of those, do you not, between your legs? I should like to see it. Will you show me?'

Atsu hesitated. It seemed an odd demand. But she'd often heard that men were curious to see what lay between a woman's legs. Perhaps it would excite him. She thought of Wife Number Two, her father's geisha concubine, and her admonishments that men were little boys at heart. She would have to pretend she was a geisha, indulge him, play a game with him.

'Show me,' he said insistently.

He was standing over her, looking down at her. In the candlelight his face was flushed, his eyes wide like a child's. She could see a protuberance – his Jade Stalk – pushing against his white night-wear. She sighed. She would have to go along with him. She might even conceive a child. In any case, she had to keep him happy.

Middle Elder Omasé and Elder Anekoji were on the other side of the screens. They could hear everything. She listened, expecting one of them to cough, but there was silence. They'd heard all this before. Perhaps this was how it was with Lady Shiga, how it had been with the other consorts. Now he was behaving just the same with Atsu. It was a breakthrough of sorts.

'Let me see,' he whined like a spoilt child. 'You have to. I am the shogun.'

Reluctantly she lay back and opened her nightwear. She could hear his breathing, shallow and rapid.

His small triangular face loomed above her in the darkness. He took a lantern and dropped to his knees. He pushed her legs apart and put his face as deep between them as he could. She felt his breath hot on her thighs, felt him shuddering with excitement. He gasped.

'So strange,' he whispered. 'Different from mine. Like a flower, a lily flower, a purple lily. No, not purple. It is aubergine, the colour of an aubergine. What is inside, I wonder? Maybe I can make it open. I wonder if I can.'

She gave a sob as he started probing her most private place, easing apart the skin and folds of flesh. It felt wrong, horribly wrong. The only person who had ever touched her there had been Kaneshigé, softly and tenderly, filling her with loving feelings. Just to think of the black sand, his strong golden body, filled her with pain. Her eyes filled with tears. This brutal tugging and pulling had nothing to do with love or passion. She felt like a fish on a slab about to be filleted.

Then a twinge of excitement set her nerves tingling. Her back arched and she gave a moan. She felt alien, detached, as if it were someone else's body responding to his fumblings, someone else's hands clenching and toes curling. Geisha must feel like this, she thought, forced to open their legs to men they cared nothing for.

He laughed. 'Like petals,' came his voice as he stroked and rubbed.

He pushed his head deeper in still and she felt his tongue, darting like a cat's. 'Salty,' he murmured ecstatically.

She looked up and saw his skinny body in the lantern light, crouched, buttocks in the air. She remembered her father's concubine, Wife Number Two, telling her that men like to drink a woman's yin juice, that they call it the elixir of life, though she couldn't imagine the shogun thinking anything as sophisticated as that.

She felt him licking, heard him slurping and sucking. Despite herself, almost against her will, pleasure began to nag, tickling the back of her throat, burning deep in her loins. She choked back tears, tried to fight the sensation until her breath became jagged and desire swept her up, turning her limbs to water.

For a moment she was free. She'd flown back to Kyushu, left the grim halls of the women's palace far behind her. She was on the beach again with Kaneshigé, feeling warm sand under her and waves lapping around her.

She heard the shogun laugh again and came back to the present with a jolt.

'Juicy. Tastes good,' he crooned.

He sat back on his thin haunches. She raised her head, panting. In the gloom she could see him fumbling, grabbing at himself. Now was the moment, now was the chance that they could have a child.

She fought off her lethargy, stretched out her arms to him. 'Come. Come and lie with me,' she said thickly, trying to catch her breath. 'Let us lie together.'

His arm was moving briskly. He gave a groan and flopped forward with his face on her stomach. He was panting. She stroked his shaved pate. His hair was coming loose. She felt the oily strands on her skin.

He pushed his face between her breasts and pressed himself on top of her, his Jade Stalk hard against her thigh. She reached down and tried to stroke it.

'Put it inside me,' she whispered. 'See if it fits.'

He was wriggling against her, hot and sticky through the silk of his nightwear. Then he groped for her nipple with his mouth and started to suck, slurping and suckling like a baby. 'Mama,' he muttered. He wriggled harder then gave a grunt and she felt something hot and wet and sticky spurt on to her leg. His head dropped on to her chest.

Tears of frustration and disappointment sprang to her eyes and she wept. Was this the best it would ever be, all she could expect for the rest of her life?

She put her arms around him and held him, staring sombrely into the darkness. She'd imagined she might have a child with him that would be her joy and consolation when she'd achieved her mission, when all this was over. But perhaps it would always be like this for him. Perhaps that was why no children had been born. At least they had made a start. Some intimacy had occurred. She was a little nearer to becoming a true woman behind the screens, a true Midai to this troubled shogun.

32

All day long the palace was a ferment of activity as the women prepared for New Year's Eve. Even the higher-ranking ladies joined in the cleaning, clattering and chattering, flicking whisks, filling the air with smells of dust and beeswax polish.

Atsu knelt in her rooms plucking at her koto, trying to concentrate. But thoughts kept jostling through her mind. There'd been no morning audience and no message from the men's palace. She thought of Iesada's warm body against hers and felt a pang of yearning.

She'd asked him to spend New Year's Eve with her but now she realized that it was not for him to decide. The elders in the men's palace decreed what he could and couldn't do. Yet she still hoped that he might find a way to come.

Late in the afternoon Middle Elder Omasé swept in. She raised her eyebrows and gave Atsu a quizzical look. She had heard every detail of the night's activity. It was her job to listen in. But she was entirely professional, as always.

'I understand Lady Honju-in explained our New Year proceedings to Your Majesty,' she said briskly, dropping to her knees beside Atsu and arranging her skirts. 'You will enjoy it. The dancing is very entertaining. Her Ladyship will have told you that the elders like to insist that the newest girls dance naked. But don't worry, I've had a word with Elder Anekoji. Your ladies will be excused. There's one precaution I should like to ask of you, my lady. Please do not touch any of the New Year's dishes. We will be preparing a

New Year's dinner for you in your own kitchens tomorrow.'

Atsu looked at her, startled. Middle Elder Omasé's broad face was serious. 'But Lady Honju-in will be offended.'

'She won't eat either. The higher-ranking ladies always leave the New Year's Eve dishes for the staff. Just drink a little saké, as you did at your wedding. We can't be too careful.'

She raised her eyebrows again and Atsu realized with a jolt what she was saying. The tasters might not have tried every dish and it would be foolish to eat anything that had not been scrupulously checked.

Omasé laid her plump hand on Atsu's. 'You should always be careful, my lady,' she said, 'careful where you walk, careful what you eat, careful at all times. But I have an extra reason for insisting on it now. You are so good with His Majesty. He is calmer than I have ever known him.' She looked over her shoulder and lowered her voice. 'But Lady Shiga cares about him too, remember that. She's known him for a long time. When Princess Tadako and Lady Hideko were among us she always insisted on spending the next two nights with him whenever he spent a night with his consort and for the last six years, since Lady Hideko died, she's had him all to herself.'

A couple of ladies scuttled by on all fours like crabs, pushing dusters across the tatami. Omasé waited till they were out of earshot, then murmured even more softly than before, 'I doubt if she expected ever to have to share him again. You never know what jealousy may drive a woman to. She may be afraid you'll lure him away – though as Midai, of course, you have every right to do so. She won't harm you herself. She would be the first to be under suspicion. But others may look for ways to curry favour with her.'

Atsu took a sharp breath. She'd suspected that Lady Shiga might be jealous if she got too close to the shogun but she'd never imagined she was in any real danger. Then she thought of all the babies who had been killed and of Princess Tadako and Lady Hideko and their untimely ends, and the hairs rose on the back of her neck. These women would stop at nothing to preserve their power and privilege.

'The ladies you're closest to will sleep in your wing from now on and make sure they go out in a group. They've sent their servants to bring clothing from their apartments. It's probably unnecessary, but it's best to take precautions.'

Middle Elder Omasé's moon-shaped face was quite bland. She spoke as quietly and calmly as if she was talking about the weather.

'And my ladies know the danger they are in?'

Omasé wrinkled her forehead. 'Please don't worry, my lady,' she said, rising to her feet. 'I am just being careful. We have had many unpleasant occurrences in recent years. We don't want any more.'

Atsu held up her hand to stop her leaving. There was a question she had to ask. 'Middle Elder Omasé!' she cried. 'I know you know what happened to His Majesty's father.'

Omasé's eyes opened wide and her eyebrows shot up. She glanced around hurriedly. 'His Late Majesty passed away in the men's palace,' she said brusquely. 'I wasn't there. I can't tell you any more.'

'But was he ill or was he . . . ? Was it as His Majesty said? Was he . . . ?' Atsu couldn't bring herself to say 'murdered'.

Omasé shook her head and closed her large mouth firmly. Atsu was the Midai, but there was a point beyond which even she could not go.

She had one more question to ask. 'Will His Majesty be attending the New Year's Eve celebrations?'

Omasé gave her a sideways glance. 'It is strictly a women's occasion. He will come in tomorrow to join the New Year's Day festivities.'

'I see.' Atsu felt oddly deflated. Without the shogun the world seemed a duller, greyer place. Could it be that she was missing him? Could she be beginning to care for this odd, unhappy man? She had to keep her mind fixed on the task Lord Nariakira had assigned her. She had to get close to Iesada for one reason and one reason only – to persuade him to nominate Lord Keiki as his successor. Yet somehow he seemed to have crept under her skin. Was she really so weak that all he had to do was create a stirring in her loins to soften her heart to him?

That evening she went with her ladies to a large hall open to the air, with a canvas roof concealing the night sky and thin straw matting spread across the floor, like the tents that fill the pleasure districts at carnival time. Yellow flames leapt from the candles that stood along the walls.

An adjoining room at a slightly higher level had been screened off for the highest-ranking ladies. Atsu took her place there along with Lady Honju-in, some of His Majesty's late father's ex-concubines and one of his grandfather's concubines. The ex-concubines were nuns and lived in the Western Palace. Lady Tsuyu, the tiny bird-like woman whom Atsu had met on her first day in the palace, was among them, even more bent than when Atsu had last seen her. Her face nearly touched the floor.

Servants plied them with saké and they were soon merry, though Atsu noticed that none of them sampled the snacks despite the mouth-watering aromas. They were eager to tell Atsu how irresistible they had been in their youth and how many children they had borne for the shoguns, though all their children, apparently, had died. Being in holy orders, it seemed they could do or say whatever they liked and they regaled the group with songs and stories. Lady Tsuyu croaked out a tune full of innuendo in her quavery old voice and even Lady Honju-in couldn't resist taking up the shamisen and warbling a ditty.

Atsu joined in the merriment but her thoughts were far away. She was the only young woman there and she felt out of place surrounded by these elderly crones reminiscing and cackling with laughter.

She heard a clamour of voices coming from the large hall and peeped from behind the screens, grateful to see without being seen. Hundreds of ladies in brilliant New Year's kimonos were swarming into the hall, as gorgeous as butterflies. She wished Masa-*kun* could have been there. He would have enjoyed seeing such a display, she thought.

She picked out some of her own ladies, standing shyly at the edge of the crowd. Then she looked around for Lady Shiga but couldn't see her anywhere. She realized where that large-breasted indolent woman must be – in the Little Sitting Room with Masa-*kun*, taking her turn, undoing everything that Atsu had managed to achieve. The thought sent a pang as sharp as a physical pain twisting through her, like a dagger cutting into her heart.

Yet Lady Shiga had never had a child. She'd surely tried to do so. To be the mother of the next shogun would give her unimaginable power, as much as Lady Honju-in wielded. Atsu wondered what had happened, why she had not succeeded. Princess Tadako had been with child when she died, so it was certainly possible – at least it had been possible then – for the shogun to father a child.

Silently, there on her knees, peeping out at the women swarming about the hall, Atsu made a vow to whichever gods happened to be listening. She would carry out her mission, that much she promised, she would do what Lord Nariakira had asked her, but she would also bear a child for the shogun, no matter what the cost. Middle Elder Omasé had said that Princess Tadako and Lady Hideko had been willowy Miyako ladies, too thin and frail to have children, and Lady Honju-in too had spoken disparagingly of the aristocratic consorts.

'But I am not an inbred Miyako princess,' Atsu admonished the gods. 'Remember that. I am a sturdy Kagoshima girl with loins made for childbirth. Even if no one has managed yet, I will.'

In the hall, music was starting up. The women drew back, clearing a large space. They cheered as a line of young girls shuffled in, glancing around shyly.

Most were naked as the day they were born. Some giggled and tried to cover themselves with their hands, others swaggered and poked their chins brazenly in the air as if they didn't care who saw them. The most timid were in cotton slips. They were all pink and steaming as newly washed babes, as if they'd come straight from the baths. They had probably been soaking in water hot enough to boil a lobster and had no doubt downed plenty of saké to fortify themselves before prancing naked on this freezing winter's night. Atsu felt thoroughly sorry for them.

She spotted one of her bath attendants, a plump girl who always scrubbed her back with particular zest. She was blushing so furiously her entire body seemed on fire, as if she could hardly bear the ladies staring at her naked flesh – though in fact, Atsu thought to herself, it was not the slightest bit different from what one saw in the bathhouse every day.

The girls started to sing, banging out a rhythm on their wooden buckets with serving spoons. They shuffled in a circle, swaying and waving their arms in unison, moving faster and faster with the tempo of the song till they were ducking, dancing, leaping, skipping and whirling, cavorting wildly in a mad frenzy, sending up whorls of dust and showers of sweat.

The women laughed and clapped their hands to the rhythm. Atsu clapped and swayed too, remembering how she used to shut her eyes and lose herself in the dancing at festival time in Kyushu. In those days there had been men to dance with them. It was strange to be sitting motionless, just watching the naked whirling limbs.

Some of the girls donned comic masks and performed skits. One played a wife chastising a faithless husband, another a servant turning the tables on a foolish lord. Then one of the dwarf entertainers pranced in dressed as a samurai with two swords swinging from her sash, while another took the role of a courtesan trying to drag him into her brothel. As the evening wore on the skits became more and more outrageous. With no men around, the women were free to throw aside all their inhibitions.

Suddenly a boom resounded through the castle, answered by another and another, making the walls and floor and canvas ceiling quiver. *Boing!* Farewell to the old year. *Boing!* A new year begins!

All over the city, all over the realm, bells were tolling, ringing out the Year of the Dragon, ringing in the Year of the Snake, the fourth year of the Ansei era.

33

Overnight everyone had become a year older. Atsu was now twenty-one and His Majesty, hard though it was to believe, a mature man of thirty-three.

Next morning her ladies put on their most splendid kimonos and finest brocade obis. The shogun was scheduled to spend the afternoon in the women's palace and they would toast the New Year together and enjoy a lavish New Year's feast. Mouth-watering smells wafted up from Atsu's private kitchens. And that night, Atsu hoped, His Majesty might spend with his consort again.

The time for the afternoon audience approached. The women hurried past the shrine room and the Great Hall and settled on their knees along both sides of the Upper Bell Corridor. The chamberlains proclaimed, 'His Majesty!', the gold-embossed doors at the far end of the hall slid back and the thirteenth shogun, His Majesty Lord Iesada, appeared on the threshold.

The blood drained from Atsu's face as she looked at him. Iesada was in his New Year finery, layer upon layer of heavy orange robes with enormous starched sleeves, but the hand that held the fan of office was shaking. The shogun was shivering. Under the tall black headdress his face was puffy and waxen and there were drops of sweat on his brow. He was tilting unsteadily. He ground his jaw and his face contorted. He shouted, 'I will go, I will. I am fine. Nothing wrong with me. I want to see them. Leave me alone. Let me go. I am the shogun!'

He took a few wobbly steps into the Upper Bell Corridor then stopped dead.

Atsu noticed that the doors behind him hadn't closed. A crowd of men in formal black hakama were clustering there, watching intently, muttering.

Iesada was blinking hard. His head was shaking. He opened and closed his mouth and muttered, 'F-feel it c-c-coming on.' He tottered forward another step.

Atsu leapt to her feet and sprang towards him, stumbling over the skirts of her kimonos. She'd sensed what was coming.

Then Iesada crashed down. Atsu heard the bang as the back of his head hit the ground. His spine arched, wrenching his head back as if something had taken him over and was twisting and tugging him. He let out a groan as his body went rigid and his arms and legs jerked and thrashed like a puppet in thrall to some mad puppeteer. The layers of his stiff starchy clothing flapped and flew about wildly as the carefully tied knots that held them in place burst apart.

Atsu was at his side in an instant. 'Keep back,' she shouted. 'Give His Majesty air.'

She pushed him on to his side, tore off her mantle, bundled it up and slipped it under his head. His eyes rolled up unseeingly. His lips were blue and he gasped for breath.

The ladies-in-waiting had backed away. They looked on help-lessly, clapping their hands to their mouths, shrieking, 'Your Majesty! Your Majesty!'

Lady Honju-in shouted, 'Doctor Taki!' as Middle Elder Omasé and Elder Anekoji rushed to Atsu's side. The shogun's headdress had flown off. Omasé picked it up and cradled it reverently in both hands.

'Restrain him,' Lady Honju-in barked. 'Hold his arms and legs. Put something in his mouth.'

Atsu gestured to them all to keep back. 'No, leave him alone,' she said fiercely. 'He will be fine. Give him time.' She loosened the tight collars and started rubbing his back and chest through the heavy clothing. 'Do not worry,' she said soothingly. 'You will be fine. We are here, we shall take care of you. You will be fine.'

Lady Shiga appeared beside her. She raised her eyebrows and glared down at Atsu with a look of contempt. 'Pull yourself together,

Masa-*kun*,' she hissed. 'Not in front of your honourable consort.' She spat out the word. 'Whatever will she think? Stop playing about. Get up.' She was as indolent as ever, entirely unconcerned, as if she'd seen such episodes a hundred times before.

There was a flurry of pleated hakama skirts as an elderly man rushed through the doors, carrying a steaming bowl that smelt of earth and bitter herbs. Atsu caught a glimpse of a white topknot above a leathery-skinned face, twinkling black eyes and a beaky nose with a pair of pince-nez resting on them as the doctor dropped to his knees beside the poor shogun, writhing and thrashing helplessly on the floor.

'Good, good,' he said reassuringly, addressing his patient. 'Nothing to worry about. It'll be over in a moment.' He turned to Atsu and bowed. 'Excellent, Your Majesty. I see you've turned him on his side and loosened his clothing. And nothing in his mouth. Good, good.'

'What ails him, Doctor?' Atsu asked, her voice high-pitched and panicky.

The doctor sat back on his heels. 'His Majesty has been afflicted since he was a boy,' he said. 'We call it *kan* or epilepsy – the shaking disease. In simple terms, the flow of Ki energy becomes obstructed from time to time. We give him the best possible treatments, both Chinese and Dutch.'

He put a large firm hand on Iesada's shoulder and the sick man heaved and shuddered. The spasm eased, then stopped and Iesada flopped like a rag doll, panting. His face was sticky with sweat and drool trickled from his mouth.

'There, there,' said Atsu, wiping it away. 'Here you are, you see, you are fine.'

Iesada opened his eyes and stared around blankly. There was a sour-sweet smell emanating from his pores.

The doctor passed Atsu the bowl and she propped Iesada's head against her chest and held it to his lips, inhaling a powerful whiff of herbs from the thick brown brew. Now the crisis was past she was beginning to wonder whether she, the Midai, should be performing such tasks. Perhaps she was demeaning herself. She might lose the respect of her ladies. She should be standing aloof, issuing orders, as Lady Honju-in and Lady Shiga were. But all she could think about was the well-being of the poor patient.

The shogun downed some of the steaming liquid, coughing and screwing up his face at the foul taste. Atsu handed the bowl to the doctor, who took over the task.

'Finish it, sire,' he said. 'To the last drop.'

Iesada was looking around as if he was beginning to grasp where he was. 'Mama. I want Mama. Oshiga, where is Oshiga?' he whimpered.

Atsu felt an icy chill of realization, a shock of horror and jealousy. She bent down so he could see her face. 'I am here, Masa-*kun*. Atsu, your consort.'

He pushed her away feebly and said again, 'Mama, Oshiga,' in a tearful voice. It was strange and terrifying to see this grown man behaving like a child.

The glance Lady Shiga threw Atsu was blazing with triumph. She knelt in front of him, held her large plain face close to his, and said in an offhand tone of voice, 'Not to worry, Masa-*kun*. I'm here.'

Atsu knew then with the force of a blow that everything she'd achieved so far was lost. She'd have to start all over again. She might never succeed in growing close to him – close enough to carry out her mission, close enough to have a child, close enough to achieve a little happiness for herself.

Even as she'd watched him thrashing about, she'd wondered if any child they had might not be similarly afflicted. She'd tried so hard but this was the material, this was the man she had to deal with. She would have to focus all her energies on accomplishing her mission, make him name Lord Keiki as his successor and as Regent, and she would have to do so as quickly as possible. The future of their country depended on it.

34

The tiny white and pink and aubergine-coloured blossoms on the gnarled plum branches had fallen and buds were bursting out on the cherry trees when Ikushima came hurrying into Atsu's rooms one day. She hadn't even bothered to remove her mantle. Anyone could see she'd been out – officially to the temple to pray to the shogun's ancestors; in reality, no doubt, to meet Lord Nariakira.

She sank to her knees, her eyes wide, her smooth brow furrowed. Atsu had never seen her so agitated.

'Dreadful news,' she gasped. 'War has broken out in China.'

'Again?' Atsu breathed.

'The rumours were all true. The British are on the move. They are on our doorstep, flexing their muscles. For all we know they will be here next. You will hear from Lord Hotta within the hour. His Lordship asks me to alert you,' she added in a whisper. 'You may trust Lord Hotta. He is His Lordship's ally and a wise and solid man.'

Atsu had been on tenterhooks, waiting to meet Lord Hotta. She had been communicating with him by letter but she was desperate to meet him face to face. Prime Minister Hotta was head of the Council of Ministers and the most powerful person in the land below the shogun. Lady Honju-in, she knew, talked to him regularly and it was essential that Atsu start doing so too.

She understood what Ikushima was telling her. She too had a part to play – a vital part – in keeping the barbarians at bay.

Over the last months she had been working hard to regain Iesada's trust, though it was a tough job, and little by little they'd become close again. These days he was nearly always calm and lucid. There had been no more physical intimacy, no more requests to see her 'lily flower'. Atsu had ordered Middle Elder Omasé to ensure there were no erotic prints or books left in the Little Sitting Room. They'd served only to upset him. And thankfully there had been no more falling episodes either.

Sometimes she played her koto and they sang together. Sometimes they wrote poems or played games – Go, the shell-matching game, the poem-card game or the incense-guessing game, which Iesada was very good at. And sometimes she told him stories.

She'd told him the story of Shining Prince Genji and epic tales from *The Tale of the Heike* and all the novels and romances and mysteries she loved to read. She'd told him folk tales, recited poems to him and told him about the poet Ariwara no Narihira and his love affairs, though she kept well away from ghost stories. She didn't want to fill his head with frightening thoughts.

One night she'd told him about her life in Kyushu, which to him was as exotic as the moon. He'd listened, rapt, lying with his head in her lap, gazing at her with his large eyes.

'No one has ever told me stories before,' he said suddenly when she'd finished. 'No one here knows any stories or if they do they never tell me. No one ever really talks to me. Maybe they think I will not understand.' He looked around and whispered as if he were telling her a deep dark secret. 'Shall I tell you something? I think they think I am stupid.'

'You are not stupid,' she cried, putting her arms round him and giving him a hug. She was shocked that anyone could treat him so cruelly. 'You are very clever. You know many things no one else does.' She meant it, too. He was not like other people but he had a wisdom no one else had. He could read people's thoughts and feelings. Sometimes he almost seemed able to see into the future.

But it was not yet time to bring the subject round to Lord Keiki. She was sure that if she did mention him it would distress Iesada and undo all her good work. It was better to follow Lord Nariakira's advice and proceed slowly.

Ikushima had barely removed her mantle when a chamberlain appeared. Prime Minister Hotta begged the honour of an audience with Her Majesty the Midai. He would be arriving in the Visitors' Audience Chambers within the hour.

Atsu shuffled impatiently as her ladies prepared her, combing her hair into a bouffant chignon that framed her face like a halo and stretched in a glossy tail down her back to the floor and binding it with red and beige ribbons. She shifted from foot to foot as the wardrobe attendants helped her into heavy ceremonial kimonos, arranging the layers at neckline, hem and cuffs. They draped a brocade mantle with a red lining over her shoulders and set a small gold crown above her forehead.

She checked herself in the mirror, feeling the garments like a weight of responsibility on her shoulders. She had to dress appropriately for her first meeting with Lord Hotta, but it was hard to stand and wait when she wanted so badly to know what had happened.

Ikushima was waiting to one side. 'In normal times you would hold audience seated behind a screen, my lady,' she murmured. 'But these are not normal times. Lord Nariakira suggested that you should kneel in full view of the state ministers. He thought my lady might wish to cast eyes on them – and they should see you too.'

Atsu nodded. She understood. The Midai was never seen in public. It enhanced her mystique. But at a time like this she was no longer a symbolic presence. She represented the shogun. She wished he could be there to represent himself but in his absence she needed to be his voice. She needed to be as strong and as visible as Lady Honju-in.

'There will be one person present that His Lordship particularly wants you to meet,' Ikushima added with her most enigmatic smile.

Atsu was still puzzling over what that might mean as Ikushima handed her her sandalwood fan of office and ushered her out of her rooms. They hurried through the gardens that bordered the court ladies' residences. The spring sun shone in the blue sky. Insects buzzed and birds sang.

Gardeners were trimming the shrubs, weeding and raking the gravel. They dropped to their knees as Atsu approached. Among them she noticed a burly broad-shouldered young man – Saigo.

She caught her breath as an image flitted through her mind of a golden youth – Kaneshigé. He and Saigo had been friends. She saw his full mouth and intense eyes, remembered his strong hands and reckless laugh. She ran her eyes across the bent backs, imagining wildly that he might be there, and felt a stab of longing.

She blinked hard. She was supposed to have forgotten him, moved beyond childish desires, but she saw now that she'd just buried the memory. It was there, lurking at the back of her mind, waiting to spring to life even at a time of crisis like this. She grimaced and turned away, furious at her own weakness. It was folly to let her thoughts drift away from her purpose even for a moment. This once, she hoped, Ikushima hadn't read her mind.

They stepped across the threshold into the Front Quarters, the section of the women's palace that male visitors were allowed to enter on official business, and walked past rooms full of pale women bent over their desks, into a hallway. The great doors at the end slid open, heralds proclaimed, 'Her Majesty!' and Atsu swept grandly into the Visitors' Audience Chambers.

She took her place on a low stage at the head of the room. The gnarled branches of a pine tree painted on the gold leaf wall behind her stretched like an awning over her. Fat candles sputtered in huge gold candlesticks.

Lady Honju-in was seated in the inferior place, to the left and a little below Atsu. The Dowager Mother was in a yellow-ochre kimono embroidered with phoenixes and dragons, as resplendent as a Chinese empress. Beneath her thick make-up her face was as shrivelled as a pickled plum and mascara pooled in the bags under her eyes. Atsu returned her bow, wondering if she would choose to be a friend or a foe today.

Apart from the two of them and their retainers, the hall was full of men, kneeling with their faces pressed to the gold-edged tatami. Most had the slumped shoulders and careworn air of government ministers weighed down with the worries of public office. They were in court dress, their starched skirts fanning out smoothly behind them, with varnished boat-shaped headdresses tied under their chins. The officials in the front row, Ikushima murmured, were the State Council, the cabinet ministers who ruled the realm. Behind them were ministers of lesser rank, their grade denoted by the colour of their broad-sleeved hempen robes, some dusty red, others pale gold.

It was months since Atsu had been in the presence of men. She felt oddly naked, kneeling there in full view of them all.

At the back of the hall was one face that didn't fit – a young man, strikingly handsome, with a regal air. While the others kept their heads down and their eyes studiously lowered, he raised his and met her gaze for a moment.

Ikushima murmured, 'Lord Keiki.' Atsu hardly needed to be told who this was. She breathed in sharply. So this was the man Lord Nariakira wanted her to meet, the man he wanted appointed as Iesada's successor and Regent. Keiki was Iesada's cousin, royal blood flowed in his veins. She noted his straight aristocratic nose, full-lipped mouth and thoughtful eyes. He was barely out of boyhood, he had scarcely a trace of shadow on his cheeks, yet he carried himself with unmistakable charisma. He held himself with pride. He sat apart from the others and Atsu noticed that the older men treated him with deference, glancing at him from time to time as if hoping for his approval.

In the entire room he and Atsu were the only young people.

A broad man in the olive-green robes and stiff black hat of prime minister put his hands to the tatami and greeted her. Atsu warmed to Lord Hotta immediately. He had a puffy jowly face, sharp black eyes and a forthright manner and reminded her of Lord Nariakira. She hadn't realized how much she'd missed the company of men. The women's palace was full of intrigue, people who said one thing and meant another, smiled at you then put a knife between your shoulders the moment you turned your back. She liked Lord Hotta's direct open gaze.

'Your Majesty, Your Ladyship,' he boomed. He ran through the usual formalities and compliments, rubbed his plump hands together and shook his head. 'Events have overtaken us, Your Eminences,' he growled, his forehead furrowed. 'China is at war again. The British have destroyed four barrier forts around Canton, breached the gates, smashed the walls, bombarded the city and shelled the palace of the Imperial Commissioner and driven him into hiding. In the war over opium with China fifteen years ago they snatched the island of Hong Kong to use as a base for their deadly trade. Now it seems they intend to grind the whole great empire of China under their heel.'

He shook his head. 'Our spies have failed in their task, Your Majesty. Four months have gone by since these events – four months! Yet we only hear now. This morning I received a communication from Opperhoofd Donker Curtius, chief executive officer of the Dutch trading post in Nagasaki. He tells us that the British threaten to march on Shanghai, seize the Grand Canal and besiege the imperial capital, Peking, that their pretext is that the Chinese reneged on the terms of the treaty the British forced them to sign, and he warns that they are poised to turn their guns on us next.

'We already have a barbarian on our soil. He is but one but he has the weight of the British fleet behind him – and as we have now learned, it is very close at hand. The only way to avoid suffering the fate of China, so the Opperhoofd tells us, is to give this intruder every concession he demands.'

Lady Honju-in slapped her fan on to her palm. She burst out, 'And you believe this barbarian monkey? He's telling us a pile of lies to persuade us to make treaties with him and with every barbarian nation in the entire world. Just because we do not want their miserable trade is no reason to exterminate us.'

The councillors muttered and whispered.

Lord Hotta gave a weary smile. 'An excellent point, my lady. But our enemies are closing in. As you know, the American now negotiates with the Governors of Shimoda. We have agreed all his demands so far – to remove the guards we posted in his compound, whom he calls spies, and to reply to his letters by written communication, not verbal, even though that is against our custom.'

'Small demands, though understandable,' Atsu said, frowning.

'Nevertheless it sounds as if we concede everything and he concedes nothing.'

Lord Hotta grimaced and bowed his head. 'Your Majesty, the dragon breathing fire at our gates is but a small threat compared to the storm brewing within. Even among the members of the Great Council it is hard to reach a unanimous decision – and then there are the great lords. Some of the most powerful, with the loudest voices, argue that we should issue a call to arms, declare war on the intruders. Others argue that we should open our ports to foreign ships and our gates to trade but as slowly as possible, hold back until the foreigners force our hand. And some believe – as I do myself – that rather than waiting for the foreigners to force us to open our gates we should do so immediately, that that way we will maintain our dignity and autonomy and, indeed, that trade will be to our advantage.

'Your Majesty, I am at my wits' end trying to cut a path through all these different factions. I am torn between the threat of barbarian attack and the demands of the lords. The one thing I am sure of is that we must avoid war at all costs. Should there be the sound of a single cannon shot, diplomatic action will already be too late.'

Atsu took a breath, gathered her thoughts. She had never before addressed such a grand assembly, never imagined she ever would. She thought of the convoluted path that had brought her, the daughter of the Lord of Ibusuki, to this gathering of the most powerful men in the land. She was aware of how young she was, how inexperienced. The councillors were as old as her father, some as old as her grandfather. She wondered what they thought as they knelt, eyes deferentially lowered. It was only because she was the Midai that she could address them. But there were things that needed to be said. Lady Honju-in should not be the only voice of the women's palace.

'My lord,' she said. Silence fell. Her voice trembled as she spoke. 'Twelve years ago our friend King Willem II of Holland sent a letter to my husband's late father warning that the western nations were sailing their ships ever closer and closer to our shores. His warnings have proved entirely true.' Her voice rose. She was gaining in confidence. 'We must trust the Opperhoofd and abide by his advice. I agree with you, my lord. We must not be pushed into a corner. We must decide our policy before the British fleet arrives. We still have the chance to open to trade willingly rather than under the threat of attack. Otherwise we will find ourselves in the position of China, forced to agree to whatever the foreigners demand.'

Lord Hotta cleared his throat. 'Your Majesty is wise beyond your years. What you say is very true. The problem is that our American "guest" keeps coming up with new demands. The Governors of Shimoda have travelled across the country to be here today to report.'

Two worried-looking men were kneeling to one side of the audience chamber, dwarfed by the giant pines painted across the gold-leaf wall. Atsu could see by their weathered faces that they were not from the city. She leaned forward, intrigued to meet these men who dealt with the westerners face to face, who breathed their air and shared their food.

The older of the two, Governor Inoué, had thick bushy eyebrows and a tooth missing on one side of his mouth. He pressed his nose to the tatami, his sun-darkened hands shaking. He glanced up at Atsu in awe, as if he could hardly believe that he was actually in the same room as her, casting eyes on her. He was trembling so violently she could hear his starched robes rustling.

Despite everything she couldn't help smiling. 'We are grateful for your dedication,' she said. 'We hear so much about Shimoda and the western barbarians. You deal with them all the time. Who are these troublesome creatures? We are eager to hear about them.'

The governor wrinkled his forehead and gave a sigh. 'Ah, Your Majesty. It used to be so easy, overseeing one little port.'

Atsu smiled again at the sound of his country burr. It filled her with nostalgia. It was not as thick as Satsuma brogue but still homely compared to the high-flown court language she heard these days.

'Drunkenness, the occasional murder. That was all we had to worry about.' The governor shook his large head. 'But now the eyes of the entire world are upon us. Shimoda, Shimoda is all anyone talks about. Your Lordships in Edo tell us this, the barbarians tell us that. They rage and shout.'

'To the point, sir,' Lord Hotta snapped.

'Forgive me, my lord,' Atsu said quietly. She turned back to the governor. 'Please continue. We need to know our enemy. I fear there will be swarms of intruders like these in the future. We shall have to get used to having them among us. Please tell us what they are like, what difficulties they cause, whether they are to be feared.'

The governor bowed. 'Giants, Your Majesty, they're giants. They're big, very big, so big they have to duck when they enter our houses so as not to bang their heads on the lintels. And their bodies – their bodies are exceedingly stiff. You wouldn't believe how stiff, Your Majesty. They can't bend their legs enough even to kneel.' Atsu could see his shoulders still trembling but he was gaining confidence as he spoke. 'We've had to have special furniture made for them to sit on and sleep on and extra-long palanquins so they can stretch out their long legs. Their minds are stiff too and their manners are brusque. They are quite uncivilized. They do not remove their shoes in the house and they seldom bathe. But they are human beings all the same. We have eaten with them, drunk with them. They enjoy saké as much as we do. They are men, like other men.'

He paused. The councillors had all been glaring, looking solemn and concerned, but now they could hardly conceal their mirth. They leaned forward, rubbed their hands, exchanged glances.

The second official, Governor Nakamura, a ruddy-faced youngish man, spoke up. 'There are two tojin, Your Majesty. The chieftain is called Harris. He is an old man of thick body, an irascible person with a hairy face and high colour. He insists we call him "Ambassador". The other is his secretary, Heusken, a Holland man. He too has a hairy face but he is younger. He has a cheerful easy-going character. Our interpreters address Heusken in the language of the Holland men, then Heusken translates into the barbarian chieftain's tongue. It takes a lot of time. Sometimes the answer we get back bears no relation to the question we asked.'

'In the whole country just two of them?' shrilled Lady Honju-in. 'And we don't have enough brave samurai to cut them down and get rid of them for good?'

'It is not that easy, my lady,' said Lord Hotta, sighing. 'We would have the whole British fleet on our backs if we did that. Our country would be in ruins. Even though they threaten us, even though they push us around, we must treat them as guests, show them how civilized people behave.'

The governor nodded. 'On Your Lordships' orders we posted spies in their compound. We told them they were guards, for their protection, but as Your Majesty heard, the barbarians insisted we remove them. Without guards to keep them away the townsfolk gather outside, watching them and sniffing the air.'

The governors exchanged glances. They were enjoying being the centre of attention, the keepers of secret knowledge, custodians of these rare creatures. They had sacrificed their tranquil lives, given up the peace of their small town to protect their country. 'They do smell rank,' said Governor Inoué, chuckling. 'It's not just their diet, it's that musty sheep's-hair fibre they wear and the smoke from the meat they roast in their kitchens. Quite nauseating.'

'Tell us what they eat,' said an elderly council member, squeezing his bony hands together gleefully, cracking the knuckles.

'Pig, mainly. Pig and pheasant,' said Governor Nakamura, assuming a look of wide-eyed innocence as if that were the most normal diet in the world. He broke into a grin.

The council members chortled and wrinkled their noses.

Again Atsu glanced at Lord Keiki. He was listening with an abstracted air.

Lord Hotta rapped his fan on the tatami. 'Gentlemen,' he said. 'To their latest demands.'

'I have listed them here, my lord,' said Governor Inoué, presenting Lord Hotta with a scroll box. 'With every day they grow more importunate. They want to add new articles to the treaty we signed with Commodore Perry. They want us to open new ports to their ships – Nagasaki as well as Shimoda and Hakodaté; and they want to install an American representative in Hakodaté. They want us to allow Americans to settle in the ports we have opened to them and to bring their women and children.'

The councillors snorted and drew their breath through their teeth. 'Rank impudence,' muttered voices. 'How dare they?'

'There is worse, my lords. When these Americans come to live here, they want them tried by a court of their own countrymen if they commit a crime, even though they are on our soil and the crime they commit is against our people. Naturally their countrymen will find them innocent.'

'They want to live among us and then impose their own rules and conditions on us – in our country?' rumbled the elderly councillors.

'There's more still. We have had endless arguments about money, about how many silver ichibubans to pay for a dollar. We calculate that one ichibuban should equal one dollar but they want to charge us three ichibubans for each dollar. They think we are children. They think we don't realize they are out to cheat us. The rate we agree on will greatly affect the price we pay for their goods and they pay for ours if we trade with them.

'But here is the snag. When we argue with them they hold the threat of the British navy like a sword over our necks. And from what the excellent Opperhoofd says too, in the end we will have no choice but to give them everything they ask. All we can do is hold them off, keep them at bay for as long as we can. We've told them that although we have full powers to negotiate we have to come to Edo for further consultation.'

'Quite right,' said Lord Hotta. 'That is all we can do – delay for as long as possible.'

Atsu was watching in despair. The barbarians' demands were outrageous but she could see that Lord Hotta and the councillors had no choice but to comply. But if they did comply would it not make their country look weak in the eyes of the world? And what of the proud lords who wanted to hold out against foreign pressure, issue a call to arms, declare war? How would they and their fiery young retainers respond? There were horrors ahead that didn't bear thinking about. It was a dreadful conundrum, a riddle that could not be solved.

She looked across the rows of councillors in their varnished head-dresses to the young man sitting at the back. She was curious to know what he thought. If he was really as brilliant as Lord Nariakira said, he would have some interesting opinions. He was frowning, pursing his lips. 'Lord Keiki,' she said. 'May we hear your thoughts?'

Lady Honju-in scowled and curled her large underlip. 'I hardly think someone so young can have anything to contribute,' she barked, her voice shrill. 'You gentlemen may have forgotten but there is a faction among us who want to install this callow youth as my son's heir, to make him Regent so that he can take over affairs of state. I tell you, we won't tolerate any impostor usurping power from His Majesty or trying to overturn the proper line of succession. That would be downright treason.

'If the plotters succeed in their villainous plans, we the women of the shogun's household will lose our voice and you the State Council will lose yours. Are you so distracted by the barbarians that you can't see the danger right at your own door?'

She shot a glance at Atsu, her eyes flashing, opened her mouth then closed it again and sat glowering.

There was a rustle from behind the painted screens, a reminder that there were guards hidden there, ready to leap out at the slightest hint of treachery. Atsu clenched her fists. She wondered if the shrewd old crone guessed that that was her entire mission, that was why Lord Nariakira had installed her here in the palace.

'Forgive me, Mother,' she said, her voice shaking. 'If I may remind you, the British threaten to engulf China. The barbarians are prac-tically at our door. We all love His Majesty. No one will tolerate treason. But there are more urgent matters to discuss. Lord Keiki's opinion is of value.'

Lady Honju-in threw her a withering glance. 'You are new here, dear daughter,' she said. 'You do not know the ins and outs of this place. Lord Keiki has no opinions of his own. All he does is speak with the voice of his father, the scheming Lord of Mito.'

Atsu held up her hand, shocked at this outburst. She looked across the rows of councillors to Lord Keiki. He sat quietly, eyebrows slightly raised. He appeared impervious to the old lady's attack, like a swordsman who knows better than to waste energy on anger; or perhaps he was simply used to being the object of Lady Honju-in's scorn.

Atsu refused to be deflected. 'Lord Keiki,' she repeated. 'Would you be so kind as to tell us your thoughts?'

All heads turned towards the youth.

Keiki bowed gravely. 'I am a loyal subject to my beloved cousin Lord Iesada. I have no desire to usurp his position or to be his heir. I ask only to serve His Majesty to the best of my ability.' His voice was boyish but his demeanour was dignified.

'The boy can certainly talk,' said Lady Honju-in, tilting her crepey chin and looking down her nose at him. 'As if my son is not perfectly capable of ruling in his own right!'

Atsu bit her tongue. She could barely stop herself retorting, 'He rules with your help and does your bidding!'

Sweat glistened on Lord Hotta's jowly cheeks. He turned to the young man. 'Lord Keiki,' he said. 'Please continue.'

Keiki laid his fan on the tatami in front of him. 'My Lord. As Her Ladyship points out, I am young and inexperienced and unqualified to speak before such an august gathering. Nevertheless, I will do my best.' He paused. All eyes were on him. 'For centuries we have maintained a policy of isolation. Our rulers deemed it best to develop our culture and civilization without interference from outside, in particular from the war-loving western nations. They banned gunpowder and the development of guns and under their wise rule we have lived in peace for two and a half centuries.

'But we cannot cling to tradition for ever. The world has changed. One country after another comes knocking at our door. There are steamships now and telegraphs. We can no longer avoid interaction with the outside world.

'I agree with Lord Hotta. It will be to our advantage to import western goods and increase our knowledge of western learning. Foreign learning is rational. Chinese learning, which we have always revered, is not. This is why the western countries have been able to develop such overwhelming material strength. And now we see the great empire of China trampled under the British heel for that very reason – that the Chinese refuse to enter the modern age. If we are to make our country strong, we must study all that the west has to teach, not just areas that are relevant to warfare but medicine, navigation, geography.

'It is not enough just to read their books. We need direct contact with foreigners. We should send envoys to purchase ships, send students to learn the ingenious techniques and machinery the west has developed, bring foreign experts to Japan as teachers. If we wish to enrich the country and strengthen the army there can be no better way than by establishing trade. I already have a daguerreo-type camera. It is a fascinating contraption.

'It is not just a question of learning from the west. We will need to overhaul our society, make sweeping changes to our system of government, do away with the princedoms, unify the country under one rule if we are to be treated as equals by the western nations.'

The elderly councillors looked at each other, nodding like bobbing Daruma dolls, repeating his phrases – 'send students to the west', 'bring in foreign experts', 'unify the country under one rule'. One by one they started to applaud. Atsu applauded too, stunned at the audacity of his vision.

Lady Honju-in gave a derisive snort. 'All this callow youth does is parrot his father. Don't you see, if we let this youth become Regent, his father will take power? Do we want the Evil Dragon of Mito pulling the strings?' Her voice had risen to a shriek. 'Our enemy is right here among us. And we worry about the barbarians in the face of such a threat?'

'You know that is not true, Mother,' Atsu cried before she could stop herself. 'From all I have heard, the Lord of Mito advocates declaring war on the barbarians, as you do. Lord Keiki thinks the opposite.'

Lord Hotta's shoulders slumped and his eyebrows rose until they disappeared under the stiff black starch of his headdress. He heaved a sigh. 'What Lord Keiki says is entirely correct,' he said in exasper-ated tones, studiously ignoring Lady Honju-in who sat glowering. 'But to make such changes we need a great and open-minded ruler. Our job as the Council of Elders is merely to be caretakers, to preserve the system handed down by generations of shoguns that has served us for two and a half centuries. We do not have the authority to make more radical changes. For that a younger, stronger man must take the helm.' His gaze fell on Keiki.

Atsu glanced at Keiki too. It was not so much his words as the intelligence in his eyes, the sharpness of his look that struck her. This was a ruler among men. She'd been prepared before to do Lord Nariakira's bidding, but it had been an abstract matter, a question of obeying orders. Now that she had met Keiki she could see it for herself. The country needed him, it needed this strong, charismatic, brilliant young man to be its leader. He had the qualities to unite the people and take the vital decisions that had to be made to save the country; and the relentless pressure of the American down in Shimoda made it all the more urgent. Lord Nariakira had been right to ensure she met Keiki. She couldn't doubt His Lordship's strategy now.

Sadness swept over her. This was how Iesada ought to have been, how she had imagined he would be when she first heard she was to marry the shogun. She pictured his pale triangular face and innocent eyes. She had to carry out Lord Nariakira's command, and quickly. But it felt like a betrayal of her frail, gentle husband even to allow such a thought to enter her mind. She understood her duty but her heart told her something else.

As the meeting came to an end and the councillors filed out, Lord Keiki approached Atsu. He was slender and muscular, fresh-faced and boyish. He bowed gracefully. 'Your Majesty, please give my regards to my dear cousin, Lord Iesada. He was lonely after both his consorts died. I am very happy that now he has you. He is a gentle and generous man but there is something troubling me. If I may confide in you, up to now he and I have always been the best of friends. I used to visit him often in the gardens of the men's palace. He would be roasting beans and would offer me some.'

Atsu nodded. She was horrified yet somehow not surprised to hear that that was how Iesada spent his time when he was in the men's palace.

'Or he would be chasing birds. But recently when I have dropped in he has refused to speak to me. When I see him in the gardens he jumps up and runs away as if I am some kind of monster. Sometimes he screams and turns white. I have racked my brains to think what I might have done to offend him but I cannot think of anything. I am aware that there are rumours that certain factions wish to depose Lord Iesada and have me named as shogun in his place, but I can assure you that that is not my hope. I love my cousin and desire only to be on good terms with him. I wish there was some way we could be friends again.'

Atsu sighed. It was all the doing of Lady Honju-in and Lady Shiga. If they'd really turned Iesada against Keiki that would make her job all the more difficult.

'Let me speak to him,' she said. 'I shall see what I can do to make peace between you.'

For a moment their eyes met, then the young man looked down, blushing. Proud though he was, this self-possessed young man was flustered. He was a man and she was a woman. They were nearly the same age, the only young blood in this palace full of dried-up old people. The air was electric. Her skin tingled from his closeness.

Hastily they both took a step back. They were cousins, almost family. There could never be anything more between them than that.

35

That afternoon a tea ceremony had been scheduled.

The women took their places on a huge platform carpeted with red felt, built out over the lake, shaded by trees. Everyone was there – Lady Shiga, Lady Honju-in and all their retinue. Everyone smiled and cooed as if they were the best of friends. One of Lady Shiga's attendants managed to spill tea on the sleeve of one of Atsu's favourite ladies, ruining her kimono. An accident, the woman said, all bows and gushing apologies.

The shogun sat under a huge red parasol, nodding and smiling, watching beneficently, holding his tea bowl with perfect deportment with his elbows a little out from his sides as if he had an egg tucked into each armpit, sipping his tea with the requisite three and a half sips.

When evening came, Atsu sat with him on the veranda of the Little Sitting Room, looking up at the stars, listening to the hoot of the owls and the flitter of the bats. Each time she saw him he seemed more beautiful. She no longer noticed his oddness, only his childlike enthusiasm, the small things that excited him, the freshness with which he saw the world.

The more time she spent with him, the more she loved him. But he was certainly not a leader. She couldn't help thinking of Keiki's commanding presence. Her husband might have been born into the role of shogun but he didn't have the qualities necessary to lead the nation, that was all too obvious.

She put her arm round him and stroked his back, gently running her hand down his bony spine and across his jutting shoulder blades. He was sitting up straighter now that he was spending more time with her, holding himself prouder, standing up for himself against his mother and Lady Shiga.

She wanted to mention Lord Keiki but she wasn't sure how to begin. Perhaps if she told him she had met him and that he had said he missed seeing Iesada, that would be a first step.

'There was a meeting today of the Council of Elders,' she said lightly. 'I have never been to a council meeting before. There were lots of people. Your lady mother was there too. I met Uncle Hotta. He seems a kind man. I am sure you often meet the councillors in the men's palace.'

He bristled, narrowed his eyes and looked at her as if he was sure she was leading up to something. She groaned inwardly. It was impossible to manipulate him. She didn't know how Lady Honju-in and Lady Shiga managed it.

'You know China is at war?' she said hesitantly. She wanted to encourage him to think about the world outside the palace.

He scowled. 'Tell me a story,' he said abruptly. 'Tell me about the old man who made the trees bloom.'

Atsu took a breath. She could be just as stubborn as him, she thought to herself. 'Masa-*kun*,' she said. 'Listen to me. I met your cousin, Lord Keiki, today. He is very fond of you. He says . . .'

Iesada was staring accusingly at Atsu, his eyes burning. The air was brittle. Sometimes she heard breathing or coughing from behind the screens, where Middle Elder Omasé and Elder Anekoji were listening to every word. But now there was not a sound.

'He hates me,' he shrieked. 'He wants me killed. He wants to be shogun instead of me.'

Atsu held her ground. She was used to his mood changes, his fits of hysteria. 'That is not true,' she said.

'I thought you were my friend,' Iesada shouted. 'I thought you cared about me but you do not. You are just like everyone else. You think I should not be shogun. You think I cannot do it. You think Keiki should be shogun instead of me.'

'That is not true,' Atsu said again, keeping her eyes averted. It was impossible to lie to him. He could read her feelings.

'You should hear what they say in the men's palace,' he said. 'Those endless meetings of theirs. Sometimes they make me attend. Uncle Mito and all the other lords . . .'

Atsu nodded. She knew who he was talking about – Keiki's father.

'They yell, they shout. Half of them want to fight the barbarians, the other half want to trade with them. Uncle Hotta tries to keep order. I sit there and play with my snail. Sometimes Keiki is there. He wants to be my friend but I do not trust him, not any more.'

'Why?' Atsu said gently. 'Why do you not trust him? He is modest and kind.'

Iesada pushed his face up to hers, frowning, his eyes bulging. 'You like him more than me!'

'You know that is not true,' Atsu said. She sat back on her heels, uncomfortably aware of the two elders lying silently on their futons on the other side of the screens, listening to every word.

There was not even the faintest rustle. She pictured Elder Anekoji holding her breath, storing up the words to report to Lady Honju-in. If Atsu was ever going to achieve her task, persuade Iesada to name Keiki as his successor, she would have to find a way to take him aside somewhere well away from these eternal snoopers.

'You do not care about me,' he said miserably. 'I thought you did but you do not. You are just the same as the others. You think I am crazy.'

Atsu was horror-struck. 'No, Masa-*kun*, that is not true. You know I love you. I think you are wise, very wise.'

He was sulking now, sticking out his lower lip, humping his back like he had when she first met him. She was frightened at how quickly he shrank back inside himself. He was like an injured animal, a stricken deer.

'I trusted you,' he moaned.

She wished she hadn't spoken. She'd breached his trust and set him back just as he was doing so well, becoming more independent, more calm, more lucid, more of a man. Now she'd have to start all over again. But she also felt despair. How on earth was she ever going to achieve her task?

'I am your friend, Masa-*kun*,' she said. 'I just wanted to say that I met Keiki and he asked me to tell you that he misses you.'

She put her arm around him, gave him a hug. 'I'll tell you the story of the old man who made the trees bloom,' she said gently.

She started telling the story but he looked around. He wasn't paying attention. 'Jewel's not here,' he said.

It was true. The tortoiseshell kitten had disappeared.

'She doesn't always come,' Atsu said, humouring him. 'I'll make sure she comes next time.'

The shogun shook his head. 'She's afraid of Princess Fumi. Princess Fumi's too old and too big.'

'Princess Fumi?' Atsu asked hesitantly.

'Hideko's cat.'

A shock ran up Atsu's spine, setting the hairs at the back of her neck tingling, as it always did when he mentioned Lady Hideko. So this was how he was going to get back at her – by bringing up the subject of Lady Hideko. She hadn't known that her tiny stunted predecessor, she of the cornflower-blue kimono, had even had a cat and she certainly didn't want to hear any more about it.

'I've seen her in the lamplight with her big face and her yellow eyes,' Iesada hissed, his eyes huge in the candlelight. 'She drinks the fish oil from the lamps. She stretches up to get it and her eyes turn into slits. Her tail's splitting too. She's growing a second tail.' His voice sank to a low growl. 'Hideko used to cut her finger and make her drink her blood. And now she's growing two tails. She's turning into a cat ghost!'

Atsu shook her head in dismay at such ramblings. She guessed he wanted to scare her because she had mentioned Keiki, met him, talked to him. He was jealous. He hated the idea of her meeting any other man. The only way he could express his anger was by frightening her with terrible stories.

'Please don't talk like that, Masa-*kun*,' she said. 'You're imagin-ing things. You're scaring yourself and me.'

Then she realized with a sigh of relief that his words were

familiar. He was not mad. He was just repeating a story he'd heard. Several of the ladies had been to see *The Cat Ghost of Nabeshima*, the kabuki drama that had been playing to packed houses at the Nakamura-za Theatre. They'd gone to pray at the shoguns' tombs and had been allowed to visit the kabuki theatre as a treat afterwards. Now they filled the chilly spring evenings by scaring everyone with details of the spectacular production. The climax had been a giant white cat ghost that rose up on its hind legs, hissing and spitting, making the audience jump nearly out of their skins.

Even more frightening, the story was true. Some hundred and fifty years ago the Lord of Nabeshima had thought a retainer was plotting to overthrow him and had had him killed. The retainer's mother had wept and sobbed and bewailed her fate but she was just a woman, she didn't have the means to raise an army great enough to avenge her son's death. So she poured out her sorrows to her cat and every day cut her finger and fed it with her blood. Finally she jumped in the river holding the cat to her bosom and drowned, taking the cat with her.

The cat had turned into a ghost and every night visited the Lord of Nabeshima. It appeared in his chamber, looming over him, growing larger each night, telling him what terrible things it would do, reminding him again and again of his cruel deed. The lord was driven to distraction and only saved when a loyal retainer managed to kill the fearsome beast.

Quite recently the story had been turned into a kabuki drama. It had barely opened when a government official arrived with orders to close it down. It turned out that the official was a Nabeshima, a direct descendant of the wicked lord – proof if ever proof were needed that the story was true, at least as far as the people of Edo were concerned. There was a huge outcry. The play reopened and was a sensation.

So that was where Iesada's cat ghost had come from. Atsu had tried so hard to keep his mind off frightening stories, but someone else – it didn't take much to guess who – was not so scrupulous.

Sounds of mewing and yowling came from the gardens, mingled with the howling of foxes. A couple of black shapes bounded towards the veranda, tumbling in the darkness, clawing at each other. Iesada shuddered and shrank back.

'Don't worry, it's not Princess Fumi,' Atsu said, jumping up and closing the screens. 'We won't let any cats in here.' She stroked his shaved pate, smooth as an egg, and his oiled hair. 'Don't pay any attention to Oshiga's stories, Masa-*kun*.'

He pressed closer to her and began to nuzzle her, as if the thought of the ghostly cat had aroused him. Or perhaps it was the knowledge that she had met Keiki that made him want to assert himself, show her who was the better man, drive all thought of his rival from her mind.

He ran his hand through her scented hair, hanging long and loose down her back. Then he pulled her down next to him, tracing the contours of her face in the gloom, running his hand across her cheekbone and the line of her jaw.

'So beautiful,' he murmured. 'And all mine.'

She shivered as he brushed his fingers across her lips. He untied her sash and opened her silken nightwear.

He was gazing at her. She could see him trembling. 'Show me your lily flower,' he said. There was a glint in his eye. Her heart sank. They'd become so close. She couldn't bear another passionless encounter. Last time when he had probed at her so clinically she hadn't cared about it. She realized with a shock that now she did.

Gently he pushed her legs apart. He knelt between them and began to explore with his fingers, uttering little cries and gasps of amazement and awe. Then he began to lick and suck, darting his tongue like a cat. She fell back, closed her eyes, let herself dissolve in the pleasure of it.

He sat back on his heels, slipped off his silk gown and she looked up at his nakedness. He was as thin as a boy. His chest was smooth and hairless, the bones of his ribcage etched on his translucent skin. He gazed down at her. Something had changed. He was focused, he knew what he wanted, what he was doing.

Their eyes met. She stroked her fingers across his stomach, wondering how he would respond. He shivered and gasped. She heard him groan and his breathing grew heavy as she ran her hand lower and lower into the thicket of coarse hair above his Jade Stalk.

There was a great emptiness inside her needing to be filled. She pulled his face down to hers and their lips and tongues touched, tentatively at first, then hungrily, greedily. Then this thin, pale man seemed to gather himself up. She gasped as he entered her, moving more and more urgently as sensation grew and seized her.

When it was over he drew back, sweat trickling down his pale face. She looked up at him, laughing in disbelief, wondering if he had planted a seed inside her, a seed that would grow into a child who would save their country.

36

Atsu had never imagined that Iesada would be such an eager lover. Every time he slept with her he was as excited as if it were the first time and his excitement infected her. His tremulousness, his timidity, the wonder with which he gazed at the world made his lovemaking all the more intense. Sometimes he fumbled clumsily but more often than not he filled her with pleasure. He no longer seemed awkward and strange to her. She saw only the beauty of his face, his wide-eyed innocence. And the more time they spent together, the more he seemed to awake from whatever dark spell held him in its grip.

Her only disappointment was that she had not conceived a child. There was no young shogun growing in her womb, though she suspected the fault lay not with her sturdy Satsuma loins but with the shogun's seed.

She knew she was straying into dangerous territory, that she risked being distracted from her task, losing her heart to this gentle otherworldly man. She had to guard against such weakness. Somehow she had to strike a balance, become close enough to influence him yet keep a distance herself.

Summer had come, filling the air with heat and moisture. The rain doors had been stored away and the paper screens pushed back and smells of damp earth and flowers – peonies, irises, morning glories – wafted through the great open rooms. The bamboo was springing up so fast Atsu could almost hear it growing. The women lay around in the shade fanning themselves, damp with sweat, heavy and lethargic, barely able to move.

One morning Ikushima appeared in a crisp linen kimono and led her outside into the gardens. They strolled across the bridge over the lake and into a secluded part of the woods. There was a bench there looking out over the gardens and they sat down side by side. Ikushima took her fan from her obi. She turned to Atsu and lifted an elegant eyebrow.

Atsu's heart sank. She knew what Ikushima wanted: to know when she was going to raise the topic of the succession.

'I am doing my best,' Atsu said pleadingly. 'But it is difficult, very difficult. I wish you understood.' She glanced at Ikushima but that lady's elegant features were as rigid as marble. 'I have to find a way to get him alone, away from Elder Anekoji. That is difficult enough. Then I have to bring the subject round to Keiki. I have tried before. It upsets him. He is not ready to discuss such delicate matters.'

She hesitated, picturing the shogun's pale boyish face, his wide vulnerable eyes. 'How can I say, "I want you to take Lord Keiki as your heir"?' she burst out. 'It would be like telling him he was going to die. He is only thirty-three, he has his whole life ahead of him. Why should he worry about an heir? He will think I have grown close to him only in order to use him.'

'Events are moving fast,' Ikushima snapped. 'The governors of Shimoda have reached agreement with the barbarian. They held off for as long as they could, they wrangled over every detail, but in the end they granted every concession he asked for. We will have American ships docking in Nagasaki soon, Americans settling with their women and children in Shimoda and Hakodaté, being tried in a court of their own countrymen. The governors even accepted the exchange rate the envoy insisted on.

'He demanded one more concession. He has been granted permission to leave Shimoda. He will come to Edo, as he has requested all along. He has agreed to delay his journey until the government approves it and sets the date. But come he will.

'Lord Nariakira is all for trade, he has no objection to that. He would like to see trade restrictions lifted so that foreign ships can visit more ports and the princedoms can all engage freely in trade. There is a treaty being negotiated along those lines with the Dutch at this moment. But a lot of the princes – the Prince of Mito, Lord Keiki's father, is the most outspoken of all – are outraged that we allow foreigners to give us orders and tread our sacred soil. If we are not careful one or other of them will issue a call to arms and we will find ourselves swept up in a deadly confrontation. I don't need to tell you. There is only one way to cut through this knot. I know that the shogun is difficult but you must try.'

Atsu clenched her fists. 'Can you not understand? I see him every few evenings. But Lady Shiga sees him too and he often spends the days with his mother. They both have plenty of chances to influence him and they fill his mind with poison. They tell him Lord Keiki is a monster and out to kill him. I promise you I am doing all I can but it is a hard task to wrest him away from them and their influence.'

She screwed her eyes shut. She wanted to scream, 'I am a human being. I have feelings. I am not an automaton, to follow orders blindly. And he, my Iesada, he is a human being too.'

She thought of those nights when he didn't summon her to the Little Sitting Room. No matter how many times she told herself that he was sleeping alone in the men's palace, she would lie consumed with jealousy, picturing his thin white limbs wrapped around Lady Shiga's heavy ones. The American envoy was a distant menace, a mythical monster, barely real. Lady Shiga was a much more immediate threat.

Nevertheless, she told herself, next time she saw him she would bring up the subject of Keiki again. She understood how urgent it was. She had to put her feelings aside.

But the following day no summons came, nor the day after that. One morning Atsu lay in her nightwear while her attendants spread her long black tresses across the tatami. She closed her eyes and tried to forget her worries as they combed and perfumed. The gold and black yamagara bird hopped around in its cage, its trilling quite eclipsed by the bush warblers in the gardens.

Suddenly there was a crash as the doors in the next room burst open. Atsu sat up sharply, her hair cascading around her, as Maru, the young earnest lady-in-waiting, raced in, her face shiny with sweat. Her eyes were wide as if she'd seen a ghost.

'Someone's been killed,' she shouted. 'They found a body in the palanquin garages.' She bent over, gasping, trying to catch her breath.

'Someone killed?' Women came running in shrieking from the other rooms.

Maru dropped to her knees. 'They found a body in the palanquin sheds,' she repeated.

Atsu gave a shudder. She felt a terrible premonition. 'Who?' she demanded. 'Who is it?'

Maru shook her head. 'I was on my way over here when I saw people running about, shouting, "Someone murdered. At the Seventh Hour Gate."'

Atsu knew the Seventh Hour Gate though she had never been through it. It led to the Outer Courtyard where men – merchants, traders, servants – came and went. Lower-ranking maids went there to haggle and buy silk for their mistresses. It was open from the Seventh Hour in the morning to the Seventh Hour in the evening and woe betide anyone who got back a moment later than that.

'One of the cleaners was sweeping the sheds when she saw blood dripping from a palanquin,' whispered Maru. 'She went closer and saw a leg, a lady's leg, a high-ranking lady.'

'But who was it?' Atsu asked fearfully. 'Has anyone been reported missing?'

'I don't know,' said Maru, shaking her head.

Middle Elder Omasé wrung her hands. 'The palanquin sheds of all places, right by the Great Gate!' she wailed. 'Merchants come in, townsfolk. There'll be gossip all over the city! I hope it wasn't one of our ladies. Some are here, some in their apartments, Hana's gone to her family – I can't keep track of them all.'

'Hurry. Dress me,' Atsu snapped.

Her attendants had barely finished putting her hair up and dressing her in a summer kimono when another lady rushed in. 'I've just come from the Seventh Hour Gate,' she said, panting. She hesitated. 'You've heard the news, madam? People are saying it might be one of us.'

'One of my ladies?' Atsu clapped her hands to her mouth, her heart pounding. 'I must go immediately.'

Middle Elder Omasé shook her head in horror at the breach of protocol. The Midai always kept to her wing, away from the hustle and bustle of the palace. Princess Tadako and Lady Hideko had never once left their quarters and even Lady Honju-in wouldn't stray far off the beaten path. They were all as much prisoners as the poor shogun.

'I'll call the bearers and have them bring your palanquin,' she said, pursing her lips at Atsu's impetuous ways.

'There is no time. We shall walk. Ikushima, show us the way.'

The palace was as big as a city and most of Atsu's women only knew the route from their apartments to Atsu's wing. Hundreds of ladies had died once when there was a fire because they hadn't been able to find their way out. But Ikushima often went through the Seventh Hour Gate to pray at the shoguns' tombs or for one of her secret meetings with Lord Nariakira.

They passed the court ladies' residences, walking faster and faster, and arrived, panting, at a gateway guarded by women in black uniforms armed with halberds.

'The Seventh Hour Gate,' said Ikushima.

37

Atsu gazed up at the beams and roof struts carved with phoenixes and dragons, glittering with copper and gold. For a moment she almost forgot the fearful news that had brought her here. The door of her prison was before her. When she stepped through she would be in a part of the palace where women could glimpse and even mingle with men. She felt the wind of freedom blowing, making her spine tingle.

Women were clamouring, demanding to pass. They fell to their knees as Atsu appeared and the guards pushed open the gates. In front was an enormous courtyard with another even more formidable gate – the Great Gate – on the opposite side.

Beyond that, like the layers of a silkworm's cocoon, stretched walls, gates, palaces, gardens all the way to the outer perimeter of the castle, many *ri* away. Then came the great city of Edo, the largest metropolis in the world, thronging with people and houses and shops right out to the distant suburbs and, many months' journey further, the golden land of Kyushu, with its beaches and smoking volcano. Atsu could barely even picture it any more.

Heat shimmered above the expanses of gravel and beat from the searing sky. She saw Elder Anekoji's oily black wig shining in the sunshine. Some women were standing beside the Great Gate in front of what looked like palanquin sheds. Atsu caught her breath as she glimpsed a flash of sky blue. There was something that looked like a bundle on the ground. A shudder ran down her spine. She picked up her skirts and ran.

The courtyard stretched in front of her. She smelt dust and perfume and something metallic that she guessed was blood. The closer she got to the bundle, the stronger the stench became. Flies buzzed, cicadas droned maddeningly. A kimono sleeve flapped, strands of long black hair dragged in the dust. Atsu caught a glimpse of an outstretched arm, a white hand as small as a child's and a great rusty stain spreading across the blue. Her legs wouldn't move any more. She was shaking.

One of the women was tucking in the arm and pulling the bundle into the palanquin sheds out of sight.

'Wait!' Atsu called out. Her voice came out as a dry croak. It seemed to die in her throat.

Elder Anekoji's eyes glittered like a hawk's. 'Your Majesty,' she rasped, bowing. 'Really no need to come all this way, no need at all. Unsavoury business, not suitable for Your Majesty's delicate eyes. Leave it to us. We have our procedures. So unfortunate that the victim happened to be a lady we'd assigned to your service. Our mistake. So sorry.'

'But . . . but who is it?' Atsu demanded. Her voice was hoarse in the silence.

Elder Anekoji raised her sleeve to her eyes and gave a loud sniff. 'So headstrong. Always had to have her own way.'

Atsu was staring at the kimono, muddied with blood and dust. She recognized it – the intense blue, blue as the sky, the design of flowers and flower baskets. She knew the perfume too, musky and subtle, mixed with impeccable care. Her mouth fell open, the blood drained from her face. Her heart leapt to her throat and she quivered with horror.

'Lady Hana . . .'

Elder Anekoji gazed at her, unblinking. There was a look almost of triumph on her face.

Behind them there was a thump. Yasu, the make-up artist, who had been fond of Hana, had crumpled to the ground. Middle Elder Omasé and the other ladies who had followed Atsu to the Outer Courtyard started to rock to and fro, wringing their hands, keening and wailing.

Atsu stared at the gravel, her heart pounding. She pictured Hana's oval face, as beautiful as a flower. Just that previous night she'd been so bright and happy. She'd been in service nine years now, she'd told Atsu, laughing with excitement, which meant she was entitled to sixteen days away. She was going to see her family. So that explained why she'd been at the palanquin sheds. But what had happened after that?

Atsu put her hands to her face and sobbed aloud. She didn't care that she was the Midai. She didn't care what anyone thought.

'Let me see her,' she whispered.

The women folded back the bright blue silk hiding the dead woman's face. Atsu took a breath and forced herself to look.

It was Hana but not Hana. She was on her back, her head flopped to one side. Her floor-length black hair that had been so smooth and glossy had come loose and lay in a matted tangle in the dust. Her eyes were staring, her mouth hanging open. Her face was bruised and scratched. One eye was blackened and her mouth a bloodied mess with the front teeth missing. Flies crawled across her waxy skin and settled on her lips and ears.

Atsu swallowed, feeling the bile rise. She turned away for a moment, fighting off the urge to retch, then looked back. Hana's kimono was loosely thrown across her. It must have been torn off. Had she been raped before being bundled into the palanquin? What kind of monster could have committed such a crime? Atsu gagged as she saw the black stain, already dry and hardening, surrounding the jagged tear in the blue silk. The smell was overwhelming.

She staggered and gripped Ikushima's arm for support. The women glanced at her deferentially and started to cover the body up again.

'Wait.' Her voice reverberated off the hot walls. She dropped to her knees and fumbled under the fabric for Hana's small hand, shuddering as she touched cold rubbery flesh. She knelt, faint with horror, wishing she could give her own life for Hana's. The dusty courtyard, shimmering in the heat, spun around her.

She looked up, narrowing her eyes, as a terrible suspicion filled her. No one had any reason to kill Hana but there were plenty who might want to hurt Atsu – or at least issue a warning to her not to overstep the mark. She pictured Lady Honju-in's malignant gaze. She knew that Atsu met Keiki from time to time and suspected her of being part of the plot to install him as Regent. Whenever Atsu tried to speak to Iesada about Keiki, whenever they made love, there was always an ominous silence from behind the screens. She was sure Elder Anekoji had conveyed every sound, every word to Lady Honju-in.

And then there was Lady Shiga, Atsu's deadly rival. She must be suffering paroxysms of jealousy now that Atsu was spending so much time in Iesada's bed. She too had good reason to warn Atsu to keep away from him.

Of course they wouldn't have done the deed themselves or even ordered it. They didn't need to. Their retainers knew precisely how they felt, how best to please them. It would have been someone working on their behalf. Atsu only had to remember how many babies Lady Honju-in had had smothered. She would certainly have had no compunction. It was exactly as Omasé had warned.

Then another thought sent an icy chill down her spine. She could hardly breathe for the horror of it. She pictured Ikushima's steely eyes. Supposing the killer had been someone from Lord Nariakira's camp, someone who thought she needed to be reminded of her duty? She tried to dismiss the idea. His Lordship loved her, he would never harm her, she told herself. But the suspicion remained at the back of her mind, nagging at her like a festering sore.

She, Atsu, bore the responsibility. She had brought down this terrible punishment on this woman. Hana had accidentally put herself in the way of the killer and they had used her to exact revenge – revenge on Atsu. Hana had been the innocent victim. Atsu clenched her fists. It was too terrible that it was beautiful Hana who had had to pay the price.

She heard scuffling, a man's voice. 'It can't be, not Lady Hana. What have you done?'

There were a couple of uniformed palace guards behind her, holding a man by the arms. By his blue cotton jacket and leggings he was a workman of some sort. He was big and broad-shouldered but they were bigger. He struggled to escape. 'Let me go. What happened to her?'

'Take a good look, my friend.'

They forced his face towards the bloodstained kimono and he retched and gasped.

'Who is this?' asked Elder Anekoji, wrinkling her long nose as if she found it distasteful to be so near a member of the underclass. The guards bowed, keeping a tight grip on their prisoner.

'Begging your pardon, my lady,' said one, square-jawed and heavy-browed. 'We were on patrol when we found him lurking outside the Great Gate. Up to no good, we thought, so we challenged him. All he'd say was that he worked in the palace. We started questioning him and he tried to run off so we arrested him.'

'Tried to run away, did he?'

'The strange thing is that he didn't run away before,' said the second guard, a sinewy character with narrow eyes and a pointed face like a fox. 'Seems like he knew the lady.'

'A rough creature like him know a lady like her?' snorted Elder Anekoji. 'Very likely.'

'Maybe he'd robbed her.'

'Someone had pushed her into a palanquin. They were trying to make off with her or hide the body.'

'Looks like she put up a fight.'

Atsu kept her eyes on the dead woman but she was listening to every word.

'Have you had the body examined, madam?' the guard asked.

'We'll take care of that,' said Elder Anekoji. 'You deal with your suspect. Give him a beating, see what you can get out of him.'

While Middle Elder Omasé and the others wailed and sobbed, Maru, the solemn young woman who had brought the news of the death to Atsu, had been staring at the captive, frowning. 'Isn't that the foreman Hana was talking to that time the carpenters came to work on the veranda last winter?' she said suddenly.

All eyes turned to her. She looked from one lady to the next, biting her lip and shuffling.

Atsu sat back on her heels. She remembered that day well. Elder

Anekoji had told them the story of Lady Koto, Iesada's father's beautiful last concubine, who had had an affair and been executed by her own brother. Hana had insisted on going outside and talking to the foreman – and now she'd suffered as terrible a fate herself.

Atsu hardly remembered the foreman. He'd seemed impudent and showily dressed, that was all she could recall. This man didn't look the same at all. His face was grey and dirt-stained. One of his eyes was purple and swollen as if the guards had already been giving him a beating.

She could see his burly shoulders quivering. He was staring at the dead woman. 'Lady Hana,' he muttered again and again.

'That's our killer,' said Elder Anekoji. 'Rapist, most likely, too.' She thrust her chest out, tossed her head, put a liver-spotted hand coquettishly to her cheek, visibly glowing in the company of the guards. Low class though they were, they were men all the same. She glared at Middle Elder Omasé and the other ladies, weeping and beating their breasts. 'There's a lesson for you all. Never break the rules. No good ever comes of it.'

The guards shuffled. 'Begging your pardon, my lady. Should we take him to the magistrates and get a confession out of him before we condemn him?' asked the square-jawed guard timidly.

'No need to bother with the magistrates,' said Elder Anekoji breezily. 'We'll take care of it ourselves. We have our own justice in the palace.'

The fox-faced guard shrugged. 'Looks like you'll be down at the execution grounds in no time, my friend,' he said with a cheerful grin. 'Splayed on a cross with ruffians poking spears in you.'

Atsu sat up sharply. 'I forbid it!' she cried. 'This man did not kill her. He cared about her. He is distraught. You can see that.'

'Begging your pardon, Your Majesty,' drawled Elder Anekoji, a sardonic note in her rasping voice. 'He probably didn't mean to kill her and now he regrets it. These affairs of the heart, always best avoided.' She turned away as if everything was settled.

Maru had been keeping back, as if she regretted implicating the foreman. Now she blurted accusingly, 'I saw him in the palace.'

'In the palace?' Atsu stared at her. Was there no end to her revelations?

'In Hana's apartment. She sneaked him in in a trunk.' She turned to Atsu, her eyes huge. She was jigging from foot to foot in excitement, bobbing her shiny coil of hair. 'She made me tell the guards it was Your Majesty's private possession and they mustn't open it. "You're so young and innocent-looking," she said. "They'll believe you. They wouldn't believe me." So I did and they brought the trunk in. When I asked her what was inside she wouldn't tell me, so I went to her rooms to have a look for myself. I slid the door open a crack. He was there, this man. I saw him with my own eyes.'

'How can you say such a terrible thing?' Atsu shouted. She shook her head in horror. It made no difference whether it was true or not. To make such an accusation now, with Hana dead in front of them, was to condemn Hana to a felon's grave and the carpenter to certain death.

'What did I tell you, Your Majesty?' said Elder Anekoji. 'Brought it on herself. You wouldn't believe what these women get up to. I don't know how she managed to get through our entry procedures in the first place.'

Maru broke in. 'If it was one of the ladies, they'd have had to lure her out to the palanquin sheds. It would be difficult to kill her then drag her all this way and there's no trail of blood between the gate and the sheds. They'd have had to lure her out before the Seventh Hour Gate closed for the night unless she was already here. Mind you, she could have sneaked out and been here after the Seventh Hour.'

Her solemn face was alive, her eyes huge and round. 'And the killer . . .' She lowered her voice to a whisper. 'The killer knew she was going to be here. He was waiting for her, dagger raised.'

It was not hard to see that Elder Anekoji was gloating. She was pleased that it was Hana who'd died, vain, pretty Hana who spent twice as long as anyone else in front of the mirror, whom the carpenters always liked, who'd been so wayward and proud and sharp-tongued. As far as she was concerned, Hana had been justly punished.

The elder's heart had dried up long ago. But Maru too was dry-eyed, treating Hana's death like a crime to be solved, blurting out secrets without thought for the consequences.

The prisoner was sobbing, great wrenching, convulsive sobs. His shoulders heaved.

'Pull yourself together, my friend,' said the square-jawed guard, giving him a kick. 'Have you no pride? Sure, you're no samurai. You can't help that. But you can still take your punishment like a man.'

'Do as you please,' the man wailed, blowing his nose on the ground. The ladies hastily stepped back. 'I didn't do it, I swear. We loved each other.' The guards raised their eyebrows, exchanged glances, guffawed. 'We were going to run away. We'd arranged to meet here. And now . . . And now . . .'

'Abducting a palace lady – a capital crime,' said Elder Anekoji gleefully.

The fox-faced guard slapped his scrawny thigh. 'I see it all now,' he said. 'If I may, Your Ladyship. She wants to run away with him, he agrees to meet her outside the gates. Why else would she have been by the gates if not to meet him? They get to the palanquins, then he has second thoughts. Got a wife, no doubt, children. Realizes he's made a mistake, they have an argument, things get out of hand. He's a big fellow, a carpenter. He has a hammer, a chisel, a knife. He could easily kill a dainty lady like that. Then he tries to make a run for it.'

'It's not true. I didn't do it,' groaned the carpenter.

'You're here, she's here and she's dead. Quite a coincidence, wouldn't you say? Who else did it if not you?'

Atsu rose to her feet. 'He must have a proper trial,' she snapped, glaring at Elder Anekoji. It was obvious the carpenter was just a scapegoat. The perpetrator was someone far wilier and cleverer, better at covering their tracks than this simple fellow could ever be. The real mystery was who that person had been working for.

The old woman didn't bat an eyelid. 'It is too late for that, Your Majesty,' she said. 'It makes no difference what he did or didn't do. He's confessed to having an affair with a palace lady and that's enough to condemn him to death. We never let people like him loose. He'd be gossiping all over the city, giving away our secrets. Once carpenters enter the women's palace they're here for life.' She laughed, an unpleasant bray. 'That's why no one wants to work here. They know it's a death sentence. Isn't that right, my friend?'

Atsu remembered the vow of secrecy Elder Anekoji had forced them all, even Atsu herself, to take when they entered the palace. That time Hana had gone to talk to the foreman she'd said to Omasé, 'This is not a prison.' She'd been wrong. It was.

'We can have him killed or we can lock him up and keep him under guard for the rest of his life,' Elder Anekoji added in jocular tones. 'It really doesn't matter.'

'What sort of place is this?' Atsu demanded fiercely. 'We talk of barbarians. We should behave like civilized people ourselves. We shall send him for trial.'

'You're new here, Your Majesty,' said Elder Anekoji unctuously. 'You'll come round to our way of thinking. Carpenters don't count for much, particularly good-looking ones. They come here, upset the ladies, so we have to get rid of them. The cesspool is brimming with them.'

Atsu stared at her in horror. Even the palace guards drew back, ashen-faced.

'It's a cruel world,' said Elder Anekoji lightly. 'It's my responsibility to protect the palace and the rules. Nothing is more important than that.'

Atsu heard the menace in her voice. She remembered Ikushima warning her to beware of serpents in the nest. If anyone knew who had killed Hana, Elder Anekoji did.

She took a breath. 'Just suppose it was not him,' she said, trying to sound unconcerned. 'We should investigate who else it might have been. I shall take a look inside the palanquin sheds. I want to see the place where Hana was found.'

'People die,' said Elder Anekoji with a shrug, putting a hand to her glossy wig. 'It can't be helped. They die in childbirth, they die of illness, they jump into wells, they push each other in. It's too bad that Hana had to die in such a public way, in the Outer Courtyard of all places. Typical of her. Palace matters are best kept well inside the palace.'

Atsu looked at her hard, wondering if it was she who had hired the killer. She would probably never find out, but she would certainly keep her eyes open. She would have to be doubly watchful from now on.

'We are meant to be civilized people, modern people,' she snapped.

A bell sounded. It was time for the morning audience. The shogun would be coming in soon. The last thing she wanted was for anything frightening or disturbing to reach his ears. It would upset him enough to hear of a death in the palace, let alone the death of one of his ladies. She wanted to break it to him in her own way.

She drew herself up and turned to Elder Anekoji. She'd never hated anyone so much. 'No need to trouble His Majesty or the Dowager Mother. No need for either of them to hear of this,' she said, trying to stop her voice from shaking. She had no faith in the old woman. She understood where her loyalties lay and in any case Lady Honju-in no doubt knew all about the affair already.

Atsu led her ladies back through the Seventh Hour Gate. The palace guards were marching their suspect away. He walked proudly, head held high, as if the knowledge of his doom had raised him higher than a mere foreman. In his heart he had become a warrior, preparing to face his death as proud as any samurai. There was something immensely touching about the neatly shaved hair at the nape of his neck.

38

By the time the Hour of the Snake came round, Atsu and her ladies were in their places in the Upper Bell Corridor. They'd been through the necessary purification rites so that His Majesty would not be polluted by contact with anyone who'd been near a corpse. They'd dabbed their eyes with cold water so they were no longer red and swollen and tidied their make-up. Their faces were composed. They knelt like statues, evenly spaced so the shogun would not notice that one lady was missing.

The bells jangled, the gilded doors slid back and Iesada appeared, a slight figure inside his bulky formal robes and towering headdress. He paused to survey his women. Atsu peeped at him anxiously. His face was beaded with sweat but serious and calm. He was holding his fan of office in a firm grip and carrying himself very straight.

The day had grown yet hotter and more humid. The bamboo screens were rolled up and there was not the slightest breeze to stir the giant red tassels. The air was heavy with moisture.

The shogun made his grand entrance, advancing along the corridor with a measured tread as the women rose one by one and snapped into place behind him.

Moving at a stately pace they passed the Little Sitting Room, crossed the walkway between the gardens, passed in front of the Great Hall and arrived at the shrine room. Shaven-headed women priests on their knees prepared to slide the doors back.

Suddenly Iesada stopped. He drew back, staring at the ground, his forehead puckered. 'What is that?' he demanded.

Atsu held her breath. There was nothing there, nothing he could possibly see.

She grimaced. Someone must have spoken to the Lady Dowager by now. Atsu dared not think what Lady Honju-in might have said to the shogun and what his response might be.

'What is that?' he said again, his voice rising shrilly.

'Nothing,' said Lady Honju-in impatiently. 'There's nothing there.'

Atsu stared at the dowager, looking for some twitch of guilt, some glint of triumph. Her withered face was imperturbable.

'There is,' he said. 'Seeping under the door.' He poked at the tatami with his toe.

Atsu held her breath, full of apprehension, hearing the hysteria in his voice. She knew he saw things other people didn't. But it couldn't be blood, not Hana's blood. That had nothing to do with the shrine room. She felt the colour drain from her cheeks. She was glad she was wearing thick white make-up to hide her pallor.

'Don't be ridiculous, Masa-*kun*. You're making things up again,' said Lady Honju-in. Was it Atsu's imagination or was there a note of panic in her voice?

He stamped his foot. 'I am not going in there,' he said.

'There, there, Masa-*kun*. Calm yourself. Don't worry. We can leave the prayers to the priests for today.' His mother pursed her lips and gave a loud sigh.

They went back to the Great Hall where the six hundred ladies high enough in rank to enter the shogun's sight were kneeling, motionless and in silence, waiting for Iesada, Atsu and Lady Honju-in to take their places.

Atsu kept her eyes on the shogun. With so many ladies present he surely wouldn't notice that one was missing – unless Lady Honju-in had whispered in his ear.

He looked around, scouring the faces. His multi-layered robes were dark with sweat.

Elder Anekoji slid forward on her knees. Her cheeks were flushed and her eyes bright. She was still glowing after the meeting with the palace guards. Atsu had always known she was a malevolent woman but she'd never realized quite how hateful.

Elder Anekoji gave Lady Honju-in a deferential bow. 'If I am correct, Your Ladyship, there are no documents for His Majesty to sign today and no annual observances to plan. As the weather is fine, perhaps we might enjoy a tea ceremony beside the lake this afternoon when His Majesty comes in for the second audience. Would you like that, sire?' Her face softened and she gave him a doting smile. She'd known him ever since he was a child, Atsu remembered. She'd bounced him on her knee. Surely even she would not do anything to harm him.

All but one of the six hundred ladies kept their eyes studiously lowered so as not to pollute the shogun with their gaze. In the entire room only one pair of eyes glittered. Lady Shiga stared boldly at Atsu, her eyes blazing with hostility. Her gaze sent a shiver down Atsu's spine. She wondered if it was Lady Shiga who had sent some-one to attack Hana.

Iesada's eyelid was twitching, just as it had before his falling fit. 'Someone missing,' he said suddenly. 'Where is she?' He had some-thing white in his hand. He was turning it round and round – his toggle, his ivory snail.

Atsu's mouth went dry and her heart pounded. She couldn't trust herself to speak. The ladies who'd come with her to the Seventh Hour Gate shrank in horror as if they wished they could disappear under the floor.

'Not now, Masa,' said Lady Honju-in. 'Let's plan this afternoon's activities. Then you can go back to the men's palace. It'll be time for your lessons on Confucian texts and history soon and then you have your martial arts, archery and horsemanship to practise.'

Atsu gazed at her in disbelief. Did she really think that was the way her beloved son spent his days? Atsu had asked him once what he did when he was in the men's palace. He'd thought for a while, then said he liked roasting beans, playing games with his courtiers and chasing after them with his gun. He liked riding on the engine the barbarians had given him too. But perhaps he was finally growing up. After all, he attended meetings of the Council of Ministers, or so he said. Perhaps he was growing into the role of shogun. She hoped and prayed that he was.

His head had started to bob, making his stiff black headdress flap. He threw the ivory snail up in the air, tried to catch it, then snatched it up as it rolled across the floor. He bounced up and down on his cushion. 'Gone with Lady Hideko,' he muttered. 'Lady Hideko took her.'

Atsu shuddered. She hated the thought of her predecessor, the tiny limping ex-consort with the cornflower-blue kimono. She stared at him. His mental state was so fragile. She couldn't bear the thought that Lady Honju-in and Lady Shiga had won, possessed him again, turned him back into a child.

'Look at me, Masa-*kun*,' she said sharply. She felt Lady Shiga's eyes boring into her but she ignored her. 'That is not possible. No one has gone with Lady Hideko. Lady Hideko is not here. The priests made her go away. She is at peace now. You do not need to worry about her ever again.'

He'd been looking around with his wavering gaze but now he fixed his eyes on her. His expression changed and he nodded gravely.

Atsu took a breath. She pictured Hana's battered face and the carpenter's shaking shoulders and the proud lift to his head as he'd been led away. There'd be no mourning, no funeral. Hana would be erased as completely as if she'd never existed. She'd probably end up in a felon's grave. Maru's revelations had ensured that. There would be two more unhappy spirits to add to the dead children and dead ladies-in-waiting that haunted the palace. As for the true killer, most likely her – or his – identity would never be discovered.

39

If Hana's murderer had meant to scare Atsu off, keep her away from Iesada, they had failed. That night Atsu was summoned to the Little Sitting Room. She hurried along the corridors and across the walkway, full of trepidation, wondering who she would find there. Would it be the lover she now knew so well or the bewildered child she had met in the gardens when she first arrived?

When the shogun came in in his white night robes she scoured his face anxiously, surveyed his smooth brow, his large innocent eyes, his ivory skin, all so familiar now. She breathed a sigh of relief. He was calm and grave, an adult man. He had regained his balance, like a rocking Daruma doll finding its centre. She was amazed and reassured at how quickly he had sprung back.

He knelt beside her and put his arms around her. 'It was Lady Hana who died,' he said softly. 'I know you feel sad. I am sad too.' He knew all the ladies. Hana had been there far longer than Atsu had.

She put her head on his shoulder and sobbed, overcome that he who had always seemed vulnerable and weak should have become so strong. In this place full of plotters and evildoers it was a comfort to be with him. If the killer's plan had been to shatter his peace of mind and turn him back into a dependent child, they had failed in that too. Atsu's and Iesada's shared sadness at Hana's loss only brought them closer.

Later they lay down and he put his hand on her stomach. 'Perhaps our son is growing inside you,' he said.

She smiled wistfully. No matter how many times they tasted the pleasures of love, she had not conceived an heir. She doubted if she ever would.

She lay gazing into the darkness, thinking about Hana, wondering who had been behind her murder. Had it been Lady Honju-in or Lady Shiga? They were the obvious suspects. But that other, darker suspicion nagged at her and wouldn't let her go – that it might have been connected to Lord Nariakira, a warning to her that she was failing in her task.

She tried to put the thought out of her mind. She knew Lord Nariakira would do whatever he thought necessary for the good of the country but she couldn't believe that even he would do such a terrible thing. But the suspicion wouldn't go away. She instructed her ladies that from now on they should keep close to her, never go out except in a group.

Early one morning Ikushima came running in. It was coming up to the Festival of Tanabata on the seventh day of the seventh month, when, if you look up to the heavens, you can see the two stars, the Weaver Princess and the Cowherd, meeting across the Milky Way. There would be dancing, singing and feasting in the palace, maybe even a chance for the lower-ranking ladies to go out to admire the paper lanterns that festooned the city.

Atsu and her ladies sat inside in the shade, fanning themselves.

'My lady,' Ikushima said, taking Atsu's sleeve and drawing her aside. 'The situation grows worse by the day. Lord Hotta has received the treaty which his negotiators have agreed with the Opperhoofd, granting the Dutch the minimum possible concessions – one extra port to dock in and the freedom to trade within certain limits. It is the most reasonable of treaties. But Lord Hotta dare not ratify it. If he does, the conservative lords who are opposed to making any concession to the barbarians may rise in revolt. And there is an even greater crisis looming on the horizon.'

She thrust a note into her hand.

Atsu gave a start as she recognized Lord Nariakira's commanding scrawl. She ran her eye down the vigorous brushstrokes:

From this old man to his adopted daughter and liege lady, Midai Sumiko, greetings. I fear you have forgotten. We are in grave danger. The barbarian demands to come to Edo to meet His Majesty the Shogun and threatens to summon a fleet if he is refused. His obduracy stirs rebellion among the lords. Lord Hotta lacks the authority to maintain control. You must not delay one moment longer. Lord Iesada must nominate Lord Keiki as his successor and he must do so now. As Regent, Keiki will be able to make decisions on His Majesty's behalf. Without him we are doomed. Do not let sentiment stand in your way. You will hear from Lord Hotta within the day. Take heed. The fate of the country is in your hands.

Atsu gasped. The words were like a shock of cold water in her face. Tears sprang to her eyes. She knew very well that she had been holding back. 'Do not let sentiment stand in your way,' Lord Nariakira had written. He was the puppet master, she the puppet. He had installed her in the palace, made her queen. But the one thing he hadn't taken into account when he made his plans was that she might come to love the pale, thin, otherworldly shogun.

She clenched her fists. She feared for Iesada. While he had no successor he had a role to play. He could not be killed. But once he named his successor he would be dispensable. He might be murdered or deposed to give Keiki full power. Lord Nariakira would certainly never let sentiment stand in the way of what he considered necessary for the country.

She held the note, her hands shaking. She didn't know what to believe. She would need to think some more. She was not ready to act yet. Ikushima snatched the paper away and held a taper to it. She turned it from corner to corner, letting the flame creep up each edge until it burnt to ashes, then crumbled the blackened fragments into the tobacco box until every last scrap had gone.

Threads of smoke were drifting in the air when the door flew back. An usher was outside, flushed and panting. Lord Hotta had arrived unannounced in the Visitors' Audience Chambers and requested an audience with Her Majesty. He had urgent business to discuss. Atsu's ladies prepared her hurriedly and she rushed through the corridors.

The councillors were waiting on their knees in the spacious reception room. Atsu saw Lord Keiki's boyish face behind them. They bowed in a ripple of varnished black caps as she took her place on the low stage in the shade of the painted pine tree. A moment later Lady Honju-in swept in and took her place next to Atsu. She was in imperial purple today.

Lord Hotta's shoulders were slumped. His jowls hung heavy. 'My lady,' he said. 'Please forgive this sudden intrusion. Governors Inoué and Nakamura have arrived this morning with urgent news. I thought it best that Your Eminences be here to advise us.'

Atsu felt a shock of sadness. It should have been the shogun discussing matters of state with the councillors at this critical time, not his mother and his consort. But he was not capable of doing so. He had matured immeasurably. He was no longer as removed from the world as he had been when Atsu first met him. But he was still not capable of leading the country. He refused to take the smallest interest in affairs of state. Atsu and Lady Honju-in wielded the power. They told Iesada what to do. Lord Nariakira was quite right. She would have to act regardless of the consequences.

Governor Inoué's face was creased and his topknot askew, as if he had just climbed out of his palanquin after a long journey. He pressed thick-knuckled hands to the floor, trembling.

'We thank you for your tireless efforts on our country's behalf, sir,' said Atsu. 'We are impatient to hear your news.'

The governor wrinkled his forehead, raised his spiky eyebrows. 'Your Majesty,' he said, bowing even lower. 'It is a privilege beyond my liveliest imagining to cast my tired old eyes on such beauty.'

There was a shocked silence. The councillors sucked their breath through their teeth in hisses of horror at such an outrageous lack of respect.

'Remember where you are, sir!' barked Lord Hotta. 'You are in the palace, addressing your queen, not in the port of Shimoda.'

Governor Inoué cringed. 'Excuse my country manners, Your Majesty,' he mumbled. He took a breath. 'Here is how it is,

Your Majesty. We can no longer contain the barbarian. We have delayed and delayed till we can delay no more. Chief Harris refuses to negotiate any longer. He has obtained all he can through us, he says. He carries a letter from his leader to ours and wishes to put his letter into His Majesty's hands. He demands, he insists, he importunes. Only His Majesty's hands will do. He will not accept any alternative. To place it in the hands of any lesser mortal, he says, would be to insult his leader.'

'He would have to cut open his own belly if he did,' added Governor Nakamura. The two men glanced up at Atsu, their faces solemn.

'He has important matters to discuss that can only be negotiated face to face with His Majesty,' said Governor Inoué.

'And what might those matters be?' snapped Lord Hotta.

'He won't say, Your Lordship,' said the governor, cowering as if, big man that he was, he wished he could make himself small. His cheeks trembled. Everyone present knew as well as he did that he too might be ordered to cut open his own belly if he made a slip. 'He won't discuss with anyone lesser. He insists he has to speak with His Majesty.'

The ample skirts of the Dowager Mother's kimono quivered. 'This presumptuous barbarian demands to enter the sacred presence of His Majesty, to breathe the same air?' she exploded. 'He dare shape the name of he who may not be named with his miserable tongue? Such insolence can't be borne!' She smacked her fan into her palm with a loud crack.

Governor Inoué started and pressed his nose deeper into the tatami.

Lord Hotta was bobbing his head, a sickly smile on his face. He glanced up, looked questioningly at Atsu. He sighed heavily. 'Your Majesty,' he said. 'We are on the verge of catastrophe. Many of the great lords think as Her Ladyship does. If we defer to the barbarian, if we let him have his way, we risk their wrath. That way lies civil war.'

Lady Honju-in snorted.

'But if we do not we risk a far greater peril – the wrath of the barbarian hordes, who will lay waste our country. The lords drag us one way, the barbarians drag us another. We are torn between two equally fearful prospects.'

There was a long silence. The young man sitting at the back of the group shuffled impatiently.

'Lord Keiki,' Atsu said. 'Perhaps you have some thoughts on the best way out of this conundrum?'

Keiki cleared his throat and placed his fan on the tatami. 'Your Majesty,' he said. 'My father is at the forefront of those who resist change. Unfilial though it be, on this issue I firmly oppose him. We can no longer avoid interaction with the outside world. The world has changed and we must too. We must ignore the complaints of those who want to keep our country mired in the past, no matter how loudly they shout.

'I say let the envoy come to Edo, let him see the splendour and nobility of our capital. Let him see that we are a proud nation, not easily trodden underfoot, that though we lack the latest weaponry we are a nation no less great than his. And let us see him. Let us know our enemy. Let us see his letter and study his terms. These honourable gentlemen, the governors of Shimoda, have done an excellent job but this is a matter that needs to be dealt with at the highest level.'

'If we open the floodgates they'll all come pouring in,' growled Lady Honju-in. 'Any fool can see that.'

Atsu rapped her fan on the tatami. 'I agree with Lord Keiki,' she said firmly. 'Let the envoy come to Edo. No matter how much it infuriates the dissident lords, we cannot stop him. Let him have his way. Let us welcome him, give him all the honour we accord the daimyo. Let him pay homage as the Dutch do.'

She turned to Lady Honju-in. 'We have no choice, Mother. If we try to mollify the lords, we enrage the barbarian. Let us receive this envoy, set a precedent, show these violent western nations that we are their equals, that we are a civilized nation, more civilized than them.'

Lord Hotta bowed. 'You are right, Your Majesty. It will enflame opinion but we have no choice. We must put our minds to when and how to receive him, what ceremonial will be appropriate. If I may offer my opinion, we should receive him not like a tributary prince, not like a daimyo, but like a representative of an equal power. Give him full honours, show that we recognize the power of his country.'

Lady Honju-in had been harrumphing. 'I don't suppose he can do much harm,' she snorted. 'It's not surprising that he wants to see our capital. All he's ever seen of our country is a miserable little seaside port. He can have no idea of the splendour we live in. He'll probably never have seen such magnificence. Only the gods know how those barbarians live in their own countries – in dreadful squalor, I have no doubt. They don't even bathe. From all I hear they stink. Let him see who he's dealing with. He will be intimidated, awe-inspired.'

'Of course, Mother. Indeed he will be,' Atsu said. Lady Honju-in spoke with the voice of all those conservative dissenting lords. Atsu hoped they could be made to see things as she did.

Lord Hotta flapped his fan cheerfully, visibly relieved.

'In that case I accept,' said Lady Honju-in. 'His Majesty will receive the barbarian envoy. He will agree, will he not, Your Majesty?'

Atsu nodded, smiling.

'Of course, he may not touch His Majesty's sacred flesh or see His Majesty's revered face,' said Lord Hotta. 'But he may enter the sacred presence. I propose that we permit him to travel across our country, breathe our air, see our sacred land, proceed into Edo Castle as the clan lords do and enter the presence of the shogun. It is not fitting for the American chief to hand his letter directly to His Majesty. Let him place his letter in my humble hands in His Majesty's presence. That should satisfy all parties.'

Lady Honju-in bridled. 'Are you suggesting His Majesty is not capable of dealing with this barbarian himself? His Majesty will receive him in the full dignity of his position.'

The councillors exchanged glances. Lord Hotta said firmly, 'I will receive the letter in the presence of His Majesty and His Majesty will greet the envoy.'

'Greet the barbarian?' Lady Honju-in repeated in tones of horror. 'He who may not be named never lowers himself to speak to anyone. He will address the barbarian as he addresses the lords when they come to pay homage – through his spokesman.'

Lord Hotta rubbed his plump hands and looked up from under his heavy brows. 'Profound apologies, Your Ladyship,' he said. 'But if you will allow me to disagree, I think on this occasion it would be appropriate for His Majesty to speak to the envoy directly. Naturally the envoy must approach His Majesty in all humility, as the clan lords do, on his knees and with his head bowed to the ground. The detailed negotiations I will conduct separately. There is no need to trouble His Majesty with such trivia. We will agree in advance the envoy's address and His Majesty's reply and each will speak in his own tongue without the need for an interpreter. I will prepare His Majesty's statement in his own unique language.'

Atsu was troubled at the thought of Iesada coming face to face with this monstrous misshapen foreigner, having to confront and address him. Thankfully there would be several months to go before the ordeal. 'He will have to learn his lines,' she said firmly. 'I shall help him.'

'We have already decided the appropriate terminology to use when referring to His Majesty in discussion with the envoy. The term is that traditionally used in diplomacy: the Taikun or Supreme Commander. This will ensure that none of the sacred names of His Majesty cross foreign lips. That is right, is it not, gentlemen?'

The two governors bowed.

'The envoy must travel with all the splendour befitting a daimyo, properly escorted by a squadron of samurai,' Lord Hotta continued. 'We will negotiate with him on the matter of who will cover his costs. Your Majesty, Your Ladyship. Are you in agreement?'

Atsu and Lady Honju-in bowed. Maids bustled in and rearranged the cushions and brought in tea utensils. The Dowager Mother was going to entertain the councillors with a tea ceremony. Her withered face crinkled into a contented smile. She was in her element.

Atsu took a breath. Her heart was heavy with foreboding. She reminded herself that Iesada regularly received the lords who came to the castle to offer homage. He led the three daily audiences, he'd even performed Noh before his father. Carrying out ceremonial was what he did. It was the role he'd been born for. It would be cruel and demeaning to doubt him. He would be proud to perform such a task.

All the same it would be touch and go. She desperately hoped he didn't have a falling fit. She feared His Majesty might not conduct himself with appropriate dignity at this vital moment when he had to appear before the eyes of the whole world. She wanted him to be proud of himself. He must not fail.

40

The hour of the afternoon audience came round. Atsu led her ladies to the Upper Bell Corridor and they took their places there, facing Lady Honju-in and her ladies who knelt haughtily along the other side. Not a breeze stirred the bamboo blinds. The giant red tassels hung limp in the heat.

As the castle bells boomed, a shaven-headed companion priest ran forward and opened the golden padlock. The ushers shouted, 'His Majesty!' and the gilded doors that divided the men's palace from the women's slid back.

Atsu fixed her eyes on the tatami as footsteps advanced along the hall.

By now Lord Hotta would have spoken to His Majesty. Iesada would know that the envoy was coming to Edo, to the castle, and that he would have to meet and speak to him. She trembled to think what his response would be. She remembered how terrified he'd been last time they'd discussed the foreign intruders with him. That time all he'd had to do was to put his seal to a document. He'd become hysterical, said his father had been killed after signing the barbarians' treaty. He'd been afraid he'd be killed too. This time they were asking far, far more. He'd have to meet the envoy face to face, greet him, talk to him. Worst of all, he couldn't refuse, he had no choice. He had to do it. She would have to calm his fears, reassure him that he wouldn't die, that she would protect him.

She glanced up. His alabaster face was perfectly composed. He held himself straight and tall with his eyebrows slightly raised. In his cream brocade robe and silver hakama, his fan upright in his hand and his hair oiled into a tight topknot, he looked positively regal. He stepped forward with a firm tread.

The women fell into place behind him and he led the way into the audience hall. Elder Anekoji ran through the day's business. There was a boating trip the following month to be arranged, an outdoor tea ceremony and a poetry-writing competition to be planned. Lady Honju-in sat in stony silence. No one mentioned the coming of the envoy.

That night Atsu was to stay in the Little Sitting Room. That would be the time to break it to him, she thought, when they were sitting on the veranda, looking at the moon and stars and the fireflies flitting in the garden. She would have to bring up the subject of Keiki too, broach the succession. Despite her fears she had to do it. She waited for him to arrive. They prepared for bed and Middle Elder Omasé and Elder Anekoji retired behind the screens.

These days Iesada seemed a different person. His eyes were clear and his gaze steady. There was colour in his thin cheeks. The more Atsu treated him like someone worthy of respect and admiration, the more he grew in stature. She felt as if she had a real husband.

She thought how wonderful it would be if he could be like this for ever. She pictured the two of them living here in the castle, growing old together, ruling over the country while the years rolled by, years of prosperity and peace. Perhaps he could take over the reins of government and maybe they'd finally have children. There'd be no need to worry about the western barbarians or installing Lord Keiki as Regent. He'd deal with all that. She sighed. It was foolish to daydream. His health was precarious. She could never be sure that his periods of calm and lucidity would last.

She smiled at him and held out her hand. 'Come,' she said. 'Shall we sit together?'

The moon had not yet risen. The night was full of noises and smells. Leaves rustled, insects shrilled and whined and an owl hooted. Flowers filled the air with fragrances. Iesada took his place cross-legged on the veranda and Atsu handed him his pipe and his saké cup and rubbed his shoulders for a while.

She took a breath. 'There is something I would like to talk to you about.'

'About the envoy, the barbarian envoy?' His voice was calm.

It was disconcerting the way he could read her mind. 'Did Uncle Hotta tell you?'

'They are here now. They came in those big ships of theirs and they will not go away. They will be everywhere soon.'

'Not everywhere,' she said, keeping her voice low. No matter how composed he seemed it was best not to alarm him. 'They are coming here, to the castle. There are two of them, the envoy and his interpreter, a Dutchman.' She remembered that he had met westerners even though she hadn't. He saw the Dutch merchants every other year when they travelled up from Nagasaki to pay homage. 'He wants to pay homage to you, like the Holland men do. He has a letter. He wants to give it to you personally, put it into your hands. Then he will go, just like the Holland men.'

'Not like the Holland men. The Holland men want to be our friends. They bow and rub their noses in the dirt. These American barbarians are not our friends. We do not order them to come. They insist on it. I hear the daimyo shouting at the councillors in those meetings of theirs, Uncle Mito saying it is a disgrace to allow the barbarians to set foot in our country, let alone walk across it. These barbarians threaten us. They say we have to receive them, just like the last ones who forced my father to sign their treaty.'

He was trembling. He reached for his tobacco pouch, slipped off the small white snail toggle and started twisting it in his fingers.

'It is true that he threatens us and wants to push deeper into our country,' Atsu said. 'But you must greet him graciously even though he forces himself on us. For now he asks only to meet you.'

She topped up his saké cup and patted his hand. 'I wish I could meet the westerner too,' she said. 'I saw the barbarians once with my own eyes. Shall I tell you what they look like?'

'Like the Holland men, I expect,' he said. He raised his eyebrows, looked down his nose with a superior air as if he saw barbarians every day. 'Hairy, with bushy red hair. Very big, like giants, with long noses, like tengu demons. They speak strange words.

They dance, they sing. Very strange creatures but quite amusing.'

She laughed.

'More will come,' he said. 'Many more.' He must have heard his mother saying that once the floodgates had been opened barbarians would come pouring in. 'We shall all meet them. They will live here among us.'

'No, they will not. They will go back to their country, back to where they belong.'

'They will be everywhere,' he said. 'They will have children with us.'

'Children?' Atsu smiled in disbelief but he looked serious. Then she remembered. After the barbarians who had arrived four years earlier in their black ships had left, changelings had been born. They'd been smothered at birth and buried in the little graveyard in Shimoda.

'They will fly here like birds,' Iesada went on in the same matter-of-fact tones. 'They will come flying in metal boxes across the sky.'

Atsu narrowed her eyes. He was telling stories again. But he was perfectly clear-eyed and lucid.

'Do not be silly. They are not birds,' she said, putting her arm round him and giving him a hug. She was afraid he'd slip back into his world of fantasies. 'They are not tengu or dragons. They do not have wings. They are people, like us.'

She sighed and shook her head. There were all sorts of strange things these days. She'd even seen woodblock prints of huge balloons that carried people up into the sky. But to fly like a bird – that was one step too far. That was fantasy, pure and simple.

Iesada was gazing out at the gardens and the night sky. Atsu wondered what he saw with his big pale eyes.

'One day this palace will not be here any more,' he said dreamily. 'There will just be grass, a field of grass where we are now. The great stone base of the tower will still be here. It has always been here. It will never go. But the rest will be gone, completely gone.'

She laughed. 'Stop imagining things, Masa,' she said. 'Where would we all live? I know there are fires and earthquakes, but we always rebuild. No one would ever let our beautiful palace disappear or be overgrown with grass. It is the residence of the Tokugawa shoguns. It is the greatest castle in the realm, the greatest castle on earth.'

'Not for much longer. There will not be many shoguns after me.' He tapped out his pipe quite casually as if unconcerned at what a momentous statement he had just made. She could feel the warmth of his body pressing against hers.

The moon was beginning to rise. Atsu gazed out at the heat haze shimmering over the gardens, at the fireflies weaving trails of light across the bushes, at the morning glories, the pond with its carpet of lotus leaves crossed by a curving red bridge. The cicadas' whine was deafening. It was impossible to imagine that this beautiful place, created with such care and thought, costing such riches, would not last for ever.

She thought for a while, then said, 'It will certainly be extraordinary to have western barbarians come to the capital. But that does not mean that the rule of the shoguns will end. That is like imagining that spring will not be followed by summer or summer by autumn or day by night. You are revered and honoured, you are he who may not be named. The blood of the shoguns flows in your veins. The Tokugawas have always governed our land. That will never end.'

He gazed across the gardens, his eyes wide. 'There will be buildings that shine in the sun, tall buildings, taller than the five-storey tower, far taller. Out there.' He gestured into the darkness where the city lay slumbering, somewhere beyond the great pine trees and cedars that surrounded the castle grounds. 'I wish I could live to see them. But we shall be gone by then, all of us.'

His words made her shiver. She knew he saw things other people didn't see, knew things other people didn't know. Maybe he was right. Maybe that really was how the future would be.

'Our children will be here,' Atsu said. 'And our children's children. And if we do not have any children . . .'

The moment had come. She took a deep breath. 'Masa-*kun*,' she said. 'We need to discuss your successor.' She was shaking.

She hated to destroy the peaceful mood of the evening. She waited, heart sinking, for his response.

There was an ominous silence on the other side of the screens. Elder Anekoji was so close she could have reached around and touched them. Atsu grimaced, thinking of Ikushima's warning about the serpent in the bird's nest.

Iesada swung round, knitting his thin brows together. His eyes gleamed yellow in the candlelight. He swivelled his head to the left and to the right. 'I know what you want to say.' His voice was brittle. 'But not now, not tonight. There are more important things to talk about. In any case,' he mumbled, twisting round and peering up at her out of the corner of his eye, 'I have a successor, I thought you knew that – Yoshitomi of the House of Kii.'

Atsu cursed herself. While she had been delaying, Lady Honju-in had been hard at work. 'You have not officially nominated him though, have you, Masa-*kun*?' she said.

'No.'

She heaved a sigh of relief. There was still room for manoeuvre.

'Don't you see? He is just a little boy,' she wailed, trying and failing to keep her voice low and even. 'He is only eleven.'

'Why should that matter? I shall not die for many years and by then he will be grown up. Or do you expect me to die soon?'

Atsu was panting hard. She tried to slow her breath. Once his successor was decided, she dreaded to think what would happen to him. He would no longer be necessary and she too would be dispensable. But it was no good worrying about such things. The world was a big place and they were just two small people. She knew Lord Nariakira was right.

She squared her shoulders. Her heart was pounding. 'Lord Keiki would make a worthy successor,' she said, keeping her voice calm. 'Many people say so.'

'He hates me,' Iesada shouted. He screwed up his eyes and twisted his mouth. His cheeks were flushing dangerously. His face was beginning to swell and turn purple. 'I-I-I told you that. He will kill me. He will take over the country, reduce us to poverty. He will not be satisfied till he has closed down the palace and turned all my women out on to the streets.'

Atsu took a deep breath. This time she would not be silenced. She refused to pander to him. No matter what the consequences, she had to give this her all. 'Listen to me, Masa. That is not true. He is your friend, your cousin, your blood relation. He is kind and gentle and devoted to you. You used to love him as he does you. You've been listening to . . .'

She groaned in frustration. She thought of all those afternoons and evenings he spent with his mother or Lady Shiga. How could she keep him balanced and happy when they filled his mind with poison, with their self-serving fantasies?

'You must not believe everything your mother and Oshiga tell you,' she said. 'I love you too and I want only the best for you.'

'You are my consort,' he growled. He was shaking. 'Why should you care? What has my successor to do with you?' He pushed her away. His shoulders were hunching, his eyes burning. She could see him closing up like a clam, retreating inside his shell. 'I know what it is. My mother told me. You do not want me to be shogun. You think I am not good enough. You are like all the others. You think Iesada is stupid. You think Iesada is an idiot.' His voice was rising, becoming shrill.

She took his hands. 'That is not true,' she said miserably. She wished she could say the words with more conviction. 'Please calm down, Masa-*kun*. Be reasonable. Listen to me. You are not interested in treaties and trade and what to do about the barbarians. You told me so yourself. Lord Keiki loves you, we all love you. No one thinks you are an idiot. But it would be good for you . . .'

'You are all the same. You want me dead. He wants me dead.' He was rocking back and forth as if at any moment he would have a falling fit. 'I thought you cared about me. How can you? When you know I have to meet the barbarian? I thought you understood. I have to be calm. I have to prepare. How can you be so cruel, so thoughtless?'

There was a loud cough. Atsu started. She'd forgotten the listeners behind the screens.

'That's enough,' Elder Anekoji barked. 'His Majesty is tired. Time to go to sleep.'

Atsu swung round, furious at the interruption. 'Be silent, Elder Anekoji,' she shouted. 'We shall sleep when we are ready.' She refused to be intimidated by this spiteful old woman.

She put her arms around Iesada and held him tight, put her lips to his cheek. 'I am sorry,' she whispered. She felt how thin and tense he was, how knotted his muscles were. She started to rub his back, knead his shoulders.

She wrinkled her brow. He was right. She'd been thoughtless. For now the important job was to prepare him to meet the barbarian envoy. After that she would deal with the succession. Somehow she had to think up arguments, find a way to win him round.

Little by little she felt him relax. He turned and smiled at her.

'Anyway,' he said, opening her robes and running his finger softly between her breasts. 'We do not need Keiki. We will have children of our own. My son will be my heir.'

Later, as she drifted into sleep, a vision rose before her eyes of the endless castle buildings with their white walls and dove-grey roofs, the towers and walkways and landscaped gardens all gone, and nothing but a bleak expanse of grass, as far as the eye could see, right here where she was lying. She heard the rustle of the wind rippling the dry stalks. She sighed and gently, so as not to wake the shogun, blew out the candles.

41

The maple trees had lost their leaves and a cold wind was blowing on the day the American envoy came to Edo Castle. The sun had barely risen when Atsu threw back her covers, flung on a quilted jacket and raced outside into the gardens. Today this interloper who had appeared uninvited on their shores, issued threat after threat until he'd worn down the negotiators – today he'd have his wish granted. Today he would meet the shogun face to face. Only time would tell what the results of this historic meeting would be.

Atsu held her breath and listened for shouts, expecting to hear a roar of excitement like the crash of breakers on the beach as the envoy made his way through the crowds to his morning appointment. But she was too far away, immured behind too many walls. Only the squawk of crows broke the silence.

In the months since that momentous council meeting, Atsu had done all she could to prepare Iesada for the moment when the whole world would be looking at him. She'd rehearsed with him tirelessly, making him repeat his lines again and again and practise sitting entirely still without jerking or twitching or jumping up and running away. She knew it would be an ordeal but she was determined that he should give the best performance of his life, a performance that he could remember for ever with pride.

She no longer even thought about Lord Keiki. She dared not risk upsetting the shogun at such an important time. She would have to wait until the envoy had left. She kept him away from his mother as much as she could and he was usually calm, though he had his ups and downs. She was painfully aware of how easily he could flip, lose touch with reality.

By now Lord Hotta had signed the commercial treaties with the Dutch and the Russians too. As he had feared, many great lords were outraged. They were even more outraged that the American envoy had been allowed to cross their sacred land and enter the great city of Edo and the palace itself, the holy of holies.

Atsu was trembling with anticipation as her ladies dressed her in the magnificent kimonos Middle Elder Omasé had laid out for the occasion, topped with a mantle with a delicate design of snowflakes and herons, appropriate for early winter. Today she and a small retinue were going to enter the men's palace. It was an unheard-of event, an extraordinary occasion, and they all wanted to look their best.

Atsu checked her face in her round bronze hand mirror and smiled at the smooth pale oval she saw there, the almond-shaped eyes accentuated with charcoal, rosebud lips painted with safflower paste and wispy moth's-wing eyebrows smudged high on her forehead. Ikushima was even haughtier and more imperturbable than usual but Atsu could tell that she too was excited.

Together they swept past the shrine room, across the walkway and entered the Upper Bell Corridor. But instead of stopping there they walked on, right up to the gold-encrusted double doors. The two shaven-headed companion priests who kept watch there jangled the bells and unlocked the padlock and the doors slid open. Atsu smelt polish and leather and men's pomade. Her ladies peered around, jigging from foot to foot with expectation.

Usually the shogun would have been waiting there to enter the women's palace. But today was different. Atsu composed her face and straightened her back and stepped boldly across the threshold. She was as thrilled as her ladies to be entering that forbidden domain.

Men in starched robes, sword hilts poking from their sashes, lined the corridor on their knees. Their topknots glistened as they bowed to the ground to welcome her. A bevy of chamberlains ushered her along corridors lined with wooden boards that creaked under her tread – 'nightingale floors', installed to ensure that not even the most light-footed of assassins could slip in unnoticed. Atsu passed halls walled with glimmering gold screens painted with scenes of snarling tigers and exotic birds. Everything here was grander and more lavish than in the women's palace, the coffered ceilings higher, the rooms larger and more splendid. Cold air blew through the huge empty spaces, retainers and servants dropped to their knees as she passed.

So this is the men's palace, Atsu thought. This is where Masa-*kun* spends his days.

They came to an enormous hall where hundreds of grandees in court dress knelt in neat rows. Their varnished black caps bent to the ground as she passed. This, murmured a tall distinguished-looking chamberlain, was the Great Hall.

Beside it was another chamber, smaller but even more lavish – the Hall of State Ceremonies. The chamberlain ushered them into a secret section alongside, partitioned off by bamboo blinds. Atsu pushed apart the slats and gasped with delight. She had a perfect view of all that went on in the hall, like being on the balcony at the kabuki theatre.

She and her ladies had barely settled themselves on their cushions when Lady Honju-in appeared, attended by some of her retinue, together with Lady Shiga. Atsu made sure to give them her most gracious smile. Several of Iesada's half-sisters and aunts, the daughters of his father and grandfather, arrived. They too had been invited for this unique event. Kimonos heavy with gold and silver rustled as they swept into the narrow room.

Somewhere in the distance Atsu caught the sound of male voices. She held her breath. Some spoke in court language but she also heard alien guttural sounds. Her heart skipped a beat. Tojin. Barbarians.

She peeked through the blinds. The members of the State Council were filing in in their pale-yellow robes, followed by other officials in green. They dropped to their knees and pressed their faces to the floor. There was total silence. No one breathed, no one rustled as Lord Hotta appeared in full regalia, ushering in an awe-inspiring figure.

Iesada was in voluminous starched robes threaded with gold with enormous sleeves and full trousers. A stiff black headdress towered above his head like a bird's plumage. His silk robes rustled as he slid one foot forward, then the other, moving slowly and solemnly, holding his fan of office, wafting a distinctive scent. He looked straight ahead, frowning, his face composed and serious. He was transformed. He exuded power and dignity. He was he who may not be named, the all-powerful, the great ruler, the barbarian-quelling generalissimo, the Taikun, His Majesty the Shogun. He had power of life or death over them all.

Trembling, Atsu dropped the blinds and lowered her head as he passed.

Suddenly she heard him stumble. She pushed the slats apart sharply as he gave a lurch. He teetered for a moment, then straightened, gathered his dignity and glared around. She breathed a sigh of relief, praying to the gods that he would perform his part without a slip.

He stepped up grandly to his throne. It was set on a platform at the end of the chamber, raised above the assembly, hung with drapes and curtains. A partially rolled bamboo blind, held in place with large silk cords with heavy tassels, hung directly above him, casting his face into shadow. Even if a petitioner had been bold enough to raise his head, it was too dark to see the all-powerful countenance.

The hush was as great as in a Shinto shrine when the god himself appears. Incense smoke scented the air.

Then a herald shouted out some syllables in an alien tongue, announcing the approach of the envoy, and a procession began to file in.

Two grandees came first, crawling on hands and knees, their extravagantly long silk trouser legs trailing behind them. Then came Governor Inoué, the older of the two Shimoda governors. His trouser legs were so long they threatened to tie themselves in knots as he too advanced on his knees, jerking swathes of fabric out of the way. His leathery face was impassive but his cheeks were trembling. Atsu could almost see him shaking. It was obvious he had never before entered the fearsome presence of the shogun. He glanced behind him, checking on his charge. If the envoy did something wrong the governor would surely have to pay with his head.

But the grandees and Governor Inoué faded into insignificance as a gigantic figure loomed into view. Atsu gasped and clapped her hands to her mouth, gazing mesmerized from her secret hiding place. She'd seen barbarians in woodblock prints and daguerreotypes, peered at them through Lord Nariakira's mirror of distant hopes, his telescope, but to see one in the flesh was entirely different. Even the councillors quivered and raised their heads to catch a glimpse of this extraordinary being before quickly lowering them again.

So this was a westerner. This was the uninvited guest who had caused so much trouble, demanded and insisted and threatened till he got his way. He was huge. He towered above the courtiers, even more so because they were on their knees and he, with breathtaking arrogance, was on his feet. He was not just tall, but burly. It was as if an elephant such as one sees at a carnival had come lumbering into the palace.

He was certainly human, he had arms and legs, but he was curious-looking all the same. Coarse grey hair bristled on his head and cheeks and around his mouth. Just as in the woodblock prints, he had a bulbous nose and round staring eyes like a pig. His skin was rough-textured and pinkish beige. From his bulk and sagging jowls he was quite old. He was sweating copiously, giving off a distinct meaty odour. Atsu could hear him breathing hard but his expression was bold. He was panting not out of fear but exertion.

He was wearing a most outlandish costume – a jacket with tubular sleeves, a high collar and gold trimmings and tight leggings like a farmer's pantaloons, dark blue with a gold stripe down the leg, all made of some dense fibre. He carried a stiff triangular hat with pointed corners and a clumsy-looking sword.

And he was wearing shoes. Atsu had been reassured that the

shoes would be brand new, not soiled with dirt, but it was not something she'd ever expected to see tramping the delicate tatami of Edo Castle. It just went to show how far removed these barbarians were from civilized beings. She wondered if he was deliberately flouting their customs, then reminded herself that it was simply ignorance. Uncultured, backward people couldn't help what they did. All the same, to see him in shoes made her feel as if everything she held precious was tumbling down around her ears.

Some of the ladies had shrunk back against the wall, pale and trembling. A couple stifled screams. The grandest of Iesada's aunts, who had married into one of the wealthiest princedoms in the realm, appeared to have fainted. Her sisters were fanning her anxiously. The Lady Dowager wrinkled her nose and covered her mouth with her hand as if afraid of catching some foul disease.

As the envoy stepped towards the shogun Atsu kept her eyes fixed on his sword arm. The courtiers were on their knees but she knew that if he took a step off the agreed path or – the gods forbid – made a lunge at the shogun, they would be on their feet in an instant with their swords unsheathed. There was also a detachment of guards armed to the teeth, hidden behind the screens on the other side of the chamber.

The envoy bowed from the waist, the kind of bow a townsman would make to greet an acquaintance, not at all the humble obeisance suited to paying homage to the lord of the realm. He took another few steps forward and gave another of his insolent bows.

Atsu smiled to herself. From where he stood it was impossible for him to see His Majesty's face. The kneeling courtiers could have seen the revered countenance had they ventured to look up, but the barbarian could not for the simple reason that he was on his feet. His head was too high. The partly rolled-up blind blocked his view, as was entirely right and proper. She glanced at the other ladies. They met her eyes, smiling and nodding, beaming in satisfaction.

Then the envoy opened his mouth and uttered a stream of guttural noises in a nasal drawl. The women had read the translation of his speech. He was offering wishes for His Majesty's health and prosperity. He had come, he said, to bind his country to theirs with ties of friendship and to deliver a letter from the leader of his people.

The hall fell silent. His Majesty would now give his blessing to the union of their two nations. This was surely the most momentous event in the entire history of their country. Iesada was the first shogun ever to grant an audience to an emissary from the west. The Dutch had come as suppliants, begging to be allowed to trade; but this was a meeting of equals. With this, their country stepped on to the world stage on equal terms with the most powerful nations on earth. From now on there would be no more talk of invasion or occupation. For this Iesada would go down in history.

Atsu's heart was thundering. She was quaking with nerves on the shogun's behalf. She prayed that their rehearsals had paid off, that he would remember his lines and play his part to his own and everyone else's satisfaction.

The silence grew. Iesada did not move. Atsu held her breath. She clenched her fists so tightly she could feel her nails digging into the palms of her hands. He was the shogun, she told herself. He had no need to bestir himself with unseemly haste. He was entitled to make this impudent petitioner wait. The courtiers shuffled and pressed their noses deeper into the straw mats of the floor.

Iesada had been sitting as still as a statue. Suddenly he jerked his head over his left shoulder.

Atsu squeezed her hands together till the knuckles were white. 'Not today,' she prayed. 'Please not today.'

Iesada jerked his head again and stamped his right foot. The thud of his stockinged foot striking the tatami echoed through the room.

The envoy turned pale and clenched his fists. Sweat sprouted on his brow. He seemed transfixed, he dared not move a muscle. Despite her anxiety Atsu could not resist a grim smile. Iesada was showing him who held power here. The envoy might have come barging in against all their wishes but here in the holy of holies, in the heart of Edo Castle, Iesada was king. Now all he had to do was say his lines.

He stamped his foot a second time. Atsu held her breath. Maybe he was doing it on purpose, like a petulant schoolboy refusing to do as he was told.

Lord Hotta was on his knees, face pressed to the tatami. He raised his head and gazed up imploringly at Iesada.

Iesada stamped a third time. Then he took a breath and spoke in a firm strong voice, the voice of a man used to wielding power: 'Pleased with the letter sent with the Ambassador from a far distant country and likewise pleased with his discourse. Intercourse shall be continued for ever.'

The words were in the language which only he could use, with no word for 'I' – for he was more than human, he was he who may not be named, lord of the universe, lord of everything.

Tears of relief sprang to Atsu's eyes. She moved her lips along with his as he enunciated the syllables slowly and precisely. She had been through this little speech with him a hundred times. She knew it as well as he did.

Laughing with pride, she turned and beamed at Middle Elder Omasé and Ikushima and the other ladies. They were all mouthing, 'He did it. He did it.' Lady Honju-in and her retinue, the shogun's aunts and half-sisters, even Lady Shiga, smiled and wiped their eyes.

The councillors' bowed backs quivered with relief.

A second barbarian, even bigger than the first, had been waiting at the door of the chamber. This Atsu took to be the Holland man, the envoy's interpreter. He seemed younger, less heavy of demeanour, though he too had a disproportionately large nose and contorted face. The hair that covered his face and head was not red, as in the woodblock prints, but pale yellow, the colour of rice straw. He was holding a box wrapped in a silken cloth with a design of stars and red and white stripes.

He glanced boldly around the room. Then to her shock his eyes swivelled to the side where the women were hiding behind the blinds. Atsu had been pushing apart the slats, peeking out between them. For a moment their eyes met. His were mesmerizingly blue – blue as the sky, blue as ice, blue as the ocean. The slats fell back into place as she started and clapped her hands to her mouth. This, she could see, was a man, tall and muscular, well built, strong. She found herself wondering what it might be like to share a bed with such a creature.

She leaned forward, opened the slats again. The barbarian was walking towards the throne, measuring his paces, advancing slowly, with respect. He bowed three times to the shogun then held out the box to the envoy, who removed the silken cloth and opened the box. Inside was not a scroll but a large piece of parchment. Atsu gazed at it in fascination. So this was the vital letter that the envoy had insisted he could place only in the hands of the shogun himself.

Lord Hotta had risen to his feet. The envoy unfolded the parchment just enough to reveal lines of writing. Then he closed the box, wrapped it in its silken cover again and handed it to Lord Hotta, who placed it on the tall lacquered table in front of the shogun's throne.

The job was done, they had succeeded, the way was clear. The courtiers, the watchers behind the blinds relaxed. An almost audible sigh of relief swept through the Hall of State Ceremonies. Nothing could go wrong now.

Then suddenly the envoy turned and stared straight at the shogun sitting motionless like a statue, like a god, in the shadows at the end of the room.

No one had ever dared turn their eyes on the shogun. Not even Lord Hotta sullied him with his gaze and Atsu, when they were alone together, was careful not to look directly at him. She gasped, horrified at such presumption.

Iesada had only to utter a word and the courtiers with their faces pressed to the ground, the hundreds of grandees filling the neighbouring hall, the guards hidden behind the panelling, would be on their feet in an instant with their swords bared to cut the insolent alien down. That would be the beginning of a cataclysm such as Atsu dared not imagine.

But Iesada didn't flinch. He straightened his back, exuding power and authority, and gave a gracious inclination of his head, indicating that the audience was over.

Atsu heaved a sigh of relief. She hadn't realized she'd been holding her breath. The other ladies were dabbing their eyes again. She glanced at the courtiers. She could see their relief, their reluctant admiration. From now on, she thought, perhaps they would take Iesada more seriously.

Lord Hotta's eyes were glistening. Iesada had proved himself worthy of his position. He had performed better than anyone had dared hope, represented his country with dignity before the eyes of the whole world. He had impressed the fearsome foreigners. He had played his part to perfection. Perhaps for now, Atsu thought, she could relax. Perhaps it was no longer so desperately urgent to install Keiki as his successor.

The envoy and his interpreter took a step back and bowed, stepped back and bowed again, then again, three times in all, and moved backwards out of the Hall of State Ceremonies.

The shogun, the members of the State Council, the ladies kneeling behind the blinds all waited in silence until the westerners were safely back in the antechamber where they had first been received.

Then Lord Hotta escorted the shogun back to his rooms. Atsu wanted to run to Iesada, tell him how proud she was of him, but she knew she would have to wait till she saw him in the women's palace at the afternoon audience.

An official opened the door to the side chamber and the women filed out. Atsu led her ladies back to the women's palace. No one uttered a word till they'd crossed into the Upper Bell Corridor. Then the women all began talking at once – about the barbarians, how hairy, how terrifying they'd been, the men's palace, the ceremony and above all how well His Majesty had done. Atsu kept silent. It was better to keep her thoughts to herself.

Ever since she'd first heard that westerners had appeared on their shores all those years ago when she'd been a young girl in Ibusuki, she'd had the unnerving sense that nothing could ever be the same again. Now that she'd seen them with her own eyes she was sure of it. She felt as if the very ground under her feet was shaking. She wondered what strange wind had blown in these alien creatures from another time and another place.

In her mind she travelled back to Kagoshima. She remembered

Lord Nariakira showing her the daguerreotypes of a western man and a ghostly street in a western country, so alien she'd felt as if she was looking down through the waves to the land of the dragon king's daughter under the sea.

And this was just the beginning. The world was changing, and changing fast. She dared not imagine what might happen next and whether it would be for better or for worse. One thing she knew. Neither she nor any of her people could turn the clock back. Maybe the shogun's imagined future really would come to pass.

PART IV

Hall of the Heavenly Jewel

42

Twenty-fourth day of the second month, Year of the Horse, Ansei 5, a yang earth year (7 April 1858)

Ikushima rushed out of the gardens up to the veranda where Atsu was standing. Her face was flushed and her hair ruffled, her usually immaculate kimono skirts stained with dew.

'My lady,' she said, panting. 'The cherry blossom is in full flower. Will you come and look?'

She was not talking about the cherry blossom.

Atsu stared at her, bewildered. She had never seen her so agitated. Without a word she picked up her skirts and followed her through the ornamental gardens. Ikushima waited till they were out of sight of the palace buildings then broke into a run. Atsu hurried behind, feeling grass and twigs snag at her hems.

They were deep in the woods when they came to a glade with a rustic teahouse with faded wooden shutters. There were chickens pecking outside and a single cherry tree heavy with blossom. A tall young man was standing in a shaft of morning sunlight, legs spread wide like a guardian deity at a temple gate.

Atsu stifled a cry of joy as she recognized the broad chest and bull-like head of her old friend Saigo. He was in baggy gardener's overalls, thrown on so hastily over his riding clothes that she could see his two swords poking out. His face was grimy with dust and sweat. He had a thatching batten in one huge hand and there was a pile of thatch and a ladder propped against the wall, but it was obvious he wasn't doing any thatching.

She ran towards him, remembering the first time she'd seen him galloping past in Kagoshima, his horse streaked with sweat, and the time he'd defended her in Miyako when their convoy had been attacked. She wanted to greet him, clasp his big rough hands in hers. Ever since she'd come to the palace Ikushima had always been their intermediary. It was the first time she had had a chance to speak to him directly.

But then she saw the stern expression on his face and stopped. Something truly terrible must have happened for him to take the extraordinary step of meeting her in person. If anyone were to see the Lady Midai talking to a lowly gardener, it would put her under suspicion and he might lose his head, like the carpenter accused of killing Lady Hana.

He looked different somehow. He'd gained weight. His forehead seemed broader and there was a growth of dark hair on his large square jaw. He'd gained in gravitas too. His eyes met hers with a sombre look.

He flushed and she remembered that although she was queen she was also a young woman and beautiful. She realized how different she must look. It was not just her lavish kimonos and the regal way she wore her hair, heavy with perfume, hanging down her back in a long tail. She'd grown up in the year and a half she'd been in the palace, finding a way to survive, weaving a path between all the people who wanted to trip her up.

She looked around. They were a long way from anywhere but they could never be sure there was no one listening in. 'You bring news from Miyako?' she asked, her voice trembling. She hardly dared frame the question.

Four months had gone by since the barbarians' momentous audience with the shogun. The American had brought with him a fully drafted trade treaty and in the days that followed Lord Hotta and his negotiators had wrangled over every clause.

Lord Hotta kept Atsu informed by message, letter and sometimes in person. The American was brusque and ill-tempered, she heard, and as for the treaty, it was far more radical than anything the negotiators had agreed with the Dutch and Russians. It opened not just one extra port but many to American ships and gave the Americans practically every freedom they demanded. The American envoy would set trade tariffs, American merchants would settle in the newly opened ports and an American representative would live in Edo. That much-hated clause – that Americans who committed crimes would be tried in a court of their own countrymen – was set in stone, twisting the knife in the wound.

It was hideously humiliating but whenever Lord Hotta and his negotiators baulked, the American wheeled out another of his warnings that British warships would soon be on their way. It was better to agree his treaty willingly, he said, and use it as a template when the British arrived than accept far worse terms with cannons aimed at their shores.

Finally everything was settled. All that remained was for the shogun to set his seal to the treaty. But that was when Lord Hotta's problems had really begun. First he had to get the approval of the most powerful lords. Many had been angry at the much less stringent treaty agreed with the Dutch and Russians and furious when they heard that the American was to cross the country, go into the castle and enter the sacred presence of the shogun. When they heard the details of this new treaty they were outraged. Lord Hotta dared not risk having it signed without their consent.

By now news had spread from the lords to their senior retainers to their vassals and into the broadsheets which served the populace, most of whom were profoundly suspicious of the foreigners on their shores. Meanwhile the American champed at the bit, issuing dire warnings that the British would soon be finished with China and on their way to unleash hell on Japan. Lord Hotta was at his wits' end.

It was then that he had thought up a breathtakingly simple way to cut through the whole knotty problem. He would appeal to the emperor, invoke the authority of the Son of Heaven, the mysterious figure who never left his rambling palace in the holy city of Miyako and spent his days writing poetry and performing rituals to keep the gods happy and the country at peace. Not only was the emperor

Atsu's adoptive uncle, he commanded boundless respect and had immense prestige. He was virtually a god. But he possessed no temporal power and never opposed the wishes of the shogun's government. To clinch it, Atsu's adoptive father and Lord Nariakira's brother-in-law and close ally, that tall, languid Miyako courtier Prince Konoé, was now Minister of the Left, the most powerful figure in the emperor's court.

When Lord Hotta told Atsu he had decided to go to Miyako in person and obtain the emperor's approval of the treaty, she laughed with relief. Not even the most powerful of the lords would dare oppose the emperor's wish. The treaty would be signed and disaster averted. It was brilliant, foolproof, a stroke of genius.

More than a month had gone by since then and Atsu had been waiting for news. Lord Hotta should have completed his work there long ago. The occasional non-committal letter had arrived but she had had no message that he had been successful. She knew the imperial court was awash with ceremonial and protocol and that everything took twice as long there. But as time passed she had grown more and more anxious.

Saigo's face was so grim it made Atsu frightened. 'I've come post haste, my lady.' He shook his head.

She gazed at him wildly. 'So Lord Hotta . . .' she faltered. 'He must have seen the emperor. Did he not . . .?'

'Matters have gone not entirely as we would have wished, my lady,' Saigo said, pronouncing the awkward phrase as if he'd memorized it. 'Lord Hotta . . .' He stared at the ground, frowning.

'You mean the emperor did not approve the treaty? That is not possible. Lord Hotta was not expecting him to raise any objections. It was a formality, that was all.'

'As you know, my lady, the Son of Heaven does not usually concern himself with temporal affairs,' said Saigo, fixing his eyes on the hens pecking around his large split-toed boots. 'The shogun's ministers do not usually see fit to consult His Imperial Majesty at all.'

Atsu pictured the broad elegant streets of the holy city where the emperor lived in seclusion. 'But why should my uncle care about something that does not concern him? What have the barbarians and their treaty to do with him?'

'My lady, it is not for me to try to guess the thoughts of the Son of Heaven. Lord Nariakira's spies tell me that the coming of the foreign barbarians has thrown everything into turmoil, even within the imperial court. The Son of Heaven is outraged that they should have been allowed to set foot on our soil. He says their presence pollutes our sacred land and angers the gods, his ancestors. To allow them to stay will imperil the divine land and blemish the national honour. He demands that they be expelled immediately. Lord Hotta explained our position again and again but not even Prince Konoé's intervention could persuade His Imperial Majesty to change his mind.'

Saigo fixed Atsu with his piercing black eyes. He was a mere retainer, the lowest of the low, yet he spoke of the most powerful lords in the land as if they were equals. Atsu could understand why Lord Nariakira trusted him to carry out his commands, no matter what they were. His thoughts were his own and he was not afraid to voice them.

'My lady, there is trouble brewing,' he said heavily. 'The imperial capital is in uproar. Supporters of the rebel lords have posted placards in nine places around the city saying, "Death to Hotta the Traitor. We will have his head and nail it on Traitors' Bridge if he goes ahead with this treaty."' He grimaced. 'His Lordship travels with a battalion of guards wherever he goes.'

Atsu dropped to her knees on the damp soil, breathless with horror. It was worse, far worse than she'd dared imagine. A flurry of cherry blossom blew through the glade. She started and looked around, fearful of spies even here. 'Assassinate Lord Hotta?' she stammered.

She swallowed, trying to understand what had happened, work out the consequences. 'So either my husband does not sign the treaty, which will infuriate the American . . .' Her heart was thundering. The future of their country was in her hands.

Saigo nodded. 'The American sends Lord Hotta letters saying the British have China firmly in their grip. They'll be sailing for our shores any day now.'

'Or if he does, it will be in direct defiance of the imperial command,' Atsu said, her voice rising in horror. 'It will drive the rebel lords mad and a lot of the other lords too. More and more will turn against us. We are in a far worse position now. It will be civil war.'

Civil war. She could hardly imagine what that might mean. She pictured the placards in Miyako calling for Lord Hotta's head. That was what it would be – violence, bloodshed, uncontrolled anarchy breaking apart this peaceful life of theirs. She couldn't bear to think of what would become of their world after that.

'The foreigners thought they were cracking open our closed doors but they are cracking our whole land apart instead,' she said, groaning.

Saigo stirred the ground with his toe, frowning. 'Do you remember that time we saw them, my lady, on our way up to Edo?'

Atsu nodded. 'Eight black ships, so huge they filled the bay. They had arrived and nothing we could do would ever make them go away again. They will be living among us soon, whether we like it or not.'

'If only they had come in peace,' said Saigo. He met Atsu's eye. 'The lords are right to distrust them and their treaty.'

'I wish they had never come!' Atsu cried. 'I wish we had never agreed to this poisonous treaty. It will be a noose around our necks. If we sign, we grant the Americans freedom to trade. But then supposing something happens that interferes with their trade – some catastrophe, an uprising, such as is all too likely? They will accuse us of not keeping our word. Then they will move in and take over, like the British in China. And even if we fend off rebellion, we will still be trading on their terms like a subject nation. They're driving us into a hole. Whichever way we turn, we can't win.'

There was a mew. The hens scuttled away in a flurry of feathers as the little cat Jewel bounded across the grove and rubbed herself against Atsu's leg. She pushed her away.

'What does His Lordship think?' she asked, grasping at straws. If anyone would know what to do it was Lord Nariakira.

'He objects to foreigners forcing their treaty on us against our will. But he says His Majesty must set his seal to it, no matter what.

The western powers will destroy us if he doesn't. The trouble is that if he does, it'll crack our whole society apart. That's the crux of it.'

Atsu sat down on the veranda of the teahouse and put her head in her hands. A bullfrog croaked in the silence and a breeze rustled the trees.

Here in the palace everything seemed so perfect. Even after the barbarians had soiled it with their presence, nothing ever really changed, nothing disturbed the peace. It was as if they had all died and been reborn in Amida Buddha's Western Paradise. It was hard to imagine that just outside the massive stone walls that protected the grounds a terrible storm was brewing. While they carried on obliviously with their daily routines, sewing, playing games, mixing perfumes, parading through the corridors to attend the audiences, the foundations of their world were splintering.

Then Masa-*kun*'s prediction swam into her mind and for a moment she saw the world as he had. She saw the palace buildings with their white walls and dove-grey roofs, the landscaped gardens and boating lakes, the groves of pines and manicured trees, the ponds full of carp, all crumbling away and a vast wilderness of grass rising where all that had once stood. She heard the wind rattling around her ears, felt dust blowing in her face. She'd imagined his words mere fantasy but now she wondered if the future might not turn out just as he had foreseen. Perhaps even the line of shoguns, who had ruled over them all for as long as anyone could remember, might come to an end.

She thought of her gentle husband, of his large innocent eyes and trusting glance. Her mouth was dry, her heart pounding. She remembered him trembling at the thought of confronting the barbarians, memorizing his lines like a schoolboy. Then she pictured Lord Keiki, calm and assured. He would have conversed with them confidently, addressed them as equals. If he had been in a position of power he could have taken over the negotiations. Lord Hotta was only Prime Minister. As Regent no one would have dared question Keiki's authority.

She knew she had been putting off her mission after the American had had his audience with the shogun. It hadn't seemed so urgent any more. Iesada had acquitted himself so brilliantly, impressed everyone with his dignity, and as Prime Minister it had been only proper for Lord Hotta to carry out the negotiations. It hadn't seemed worth troubling Iesada by nagging him about taking Keiki as his heir. Added to which, as she'd told herself, the more time they spent together, the more chance there was that he would listen to her, not his mother, when she finally brought up the subject.

There was another reason too. The thought of persuading Iesada to take Keiki as his successor sent a pang of fear through her stomach. She couldn't shake off the gnawing suspicion that once he had named his successor he would be dispensable. She dreaded to think what might happen to him then.

If Lord Hotta's mission had been successful they might all have been saved. But instead they were on the brink of disaster.

The glade was full of the scent of pine leaves and ferns and moss and dew. Crows cawed, a lark sang. In the distance Atsu could hear voices and music, laughter and the clattering of saucepans. In the palace kitchens they were preparing lunch.

She took a breath, straightened her back. She knew what she had to do. Ikushima and Saigo were watching her through narrowed eyes. Saigo stood like a bear waiting to pounce, Ikushima glowered like a hawk with its eye on a field mouse. Atsu understood now why Saigo had come here in person. It was not to deliver his news – Ikushima could have done that. It was to ensure she carried out her task – and he would stop at nothing to make sure she did.

She rose to her feet, faced them. 'There is one thing we haven't tried yet,' she said, her voice firm. 'There is one way to cut through the knot. There is one person who commands as much respect and loyalty as the emperor and that is the shogun. We need a leader who can be a true barbarian-quelling generalissimo. We all know who that is.

'I love my husband but he is not a leader. Lord Keiki is young, dynamic, forward-thinking, brilliant and able, and he is of the blood. Everyone respects him. He can unite all the lords behind him, speak to the westerners on equal terms, renegotiate the treaty in our favour. With him at the helm we can regain our dignity.

'We need to put him in a position where he can control events. You have always told me this and you are right. I will speak to my husband and make sure he names Keiki as his heir today.'

She clenched her fists. If she could convince them that she could do it then she could also convince herself.

'I know I have been delaying. But it is not an easy task. As you know, Lady Honju-in is the most powerful person in the palace. She wields enormous influence over my husband and she hates Keiki. She and Lady Shiga work incessantly against me, subverting my efforts, and Elder Anekoji works with them. She is the serpent in the nest.

'I need to win over Lady Honju-in first. That will be half the battle. She is no fool. She can see reason. She knows where her best interests lie. I need to make her see that in these desperate times we need a strong leader. I need to make sure she does not sabotage my efforts. I shall get her on my side.'

The giant gardener and the elegant lady in her brilliant kimonos stood side by side, looking at Atsu expectantly. Ikushima cocked a painted brow. 'There is a cherry blossom viewing this afternoon. Take her aside then and speak to her.'

'We need to be cautious,' said Atsu. She dared not let her voice wobble, allow a single hint of uncertainty to enter her thoughts. 'She trusts you even less than she trusts me. At least make sure she has plenty of saké.

'When I have won her over I shall work on the shogun. Recently he has started coming to my rooms in the daytime.' She smiled to herself. That was one good result of her delaying. 'As soon as I can find time with him alone, away from his mother and Lady Shiga and Elder Anekoji, I shall speak to him. I shall find a way to persuade him. Leave it to me.

'Saigo-*sama*, please reassure Lord Nariakira that I shall act today and that I shall succeed.'

Saigo bowed. 'I have faith in you, my lady. I shall deliver your message. I am here if you need any further help.'

The three exchanged glances. Somewhere in the woods a bush warbler piped its melodic tune. The delicate notes died out, then another bird took up the song.

For all her brave words, Atsu was as uncertain as they were that she would succeed. It seemed crazy that the future of their country should lie in the hands of a grasping old woman and her weak-minded son and that the most important job anyone had to do was to win them over. But she had to succeed. If she failed they would all be ruined.

'Saigo-*sama* wants to speak to you alone,' said Ikushima, moving away into the trees.

The burly youth took a step towards Atsu. 'Perhaps you remember my friend Lord Komatsu?' he said in an undertone.

Atsu started. Some long-buried memory set the hairs on the back of her neck tingling. 'Komatsu' was Kaneshigé's married name. She hadn't thought of him for months. Lord Nariakira suspected she had grown too fond of Iesada, that her feelings for him were preventing her from doing her job. Perhaps he wanted to insert a wedge between them, to prise her away. Atsu sighed. She was not to be so easily manipulated.

But as her lips shaped Kaneshigé's name she felt a surge of yearning so sharp it was like a physical pain. She pictured a handsome golden-skinned youth with a broad smile and eyes that gazed into the distance, like a ray of sunshine in the darkness of the palace. Nostalgia overwhelmed her, sweeping her back to those days when everything had been simple, everything made sense. It felt like a memory of another world.

She stepped towards Saigo. 'How is he?' she whispered, aware that her cheeks were burning. 'Is he well?'

Saigo put his hand to his sleeve and Atsu wondered if he might have a note or memento for her. Instead he took out a handkerchief and wiped his brow. 'Your humble servant is in good health,' he said quietly. 'He is in Miyako now in the service of Lord Nariakira. He sends you his greetings. I shall be sure to tell him that I saw you.'

She looked at him in silence, engulfed in memories. There was so much she wanted to ask – if Kaneshigé was happy, whether he too came to the palace sometimes, like Saigo, and played at being a gardener.

To her shock Saigo took her hands and clasped them in his large rough ones and put them to his lips. 'He misses you, my lady,' he said. 'We all do. We all know what you have given up, what a hard job you have to do. We are proud of you. We know you will succeed.'

Atsu's lips trembled. Tears clouded her eyes as she looked up at this burly man she had once known so well. He was the trusted emissary of Lord Nariakira and she – she dwelt beyond the clouds. She was the queen, the Lady Midai, married to the shogun, to he who may not be named. Who would have thought, back in those innocent days in Kagoshima, that their lives would take such unimaginable paths?

But there was no time for regrets. She had to focus her mind on the formidable task ahead of her. She knew what she had to do.

43

Atsu's palanquin lurched up Miyaké Slope and circled Plover Depths, tossing her from one side to the other. Outside the small window, cherry blossom swirled by in a sea of pink. Her ladies chatted and laughed as they ambled alongside and pungent fragrances wafted from the medicinal herb gardens. They passed the moon-viewing pavilion and circled ponds full of splashing carp and came to the Fukiagé Gardens on the far side of the castle grounds.

Servants had erected pleasure pavilions under the cherry trees. Outside were tables stacked with varnished lunch boxes and flasks of saké and benches covered in red felt shaded with huge parasols. Ladies in scented kimonos, brilliant as butterflies, wafted by fluttering fans. Cats snoozed in the shade.

Elder Anekoji was organizing games. Some of the younger ladies scampered around playing blind man's buff and others played battledore and shuttlecock while entertainers strummed shamisens and sang. Mount Fuji rose on the horizon, capped with snow, a wisp of smoke at its lip.

Atsu sighed. To her the voices and laughter seemed hollow. There was something desperate about this world of women, doing their best to enjoy themselves, unaware that their lives were crumbling around them.

She went in search of the Dowager Mother and found her seated on a low throne in a private pavilion, sipping on saké. She was wearing a pink kimono richly embroidered with cherry blossom. The girlish colours only accentuated the withered features and sagging jowls under the thick make-up. She dropped to her knees to greet Atsu, baring her blackened teeth in a smile.

'If it's not our beautiful Midai!' she gushed. 'You bring sunshine into all our lives. We are so happy that you've come to live here with us, dear daughter. Now my Masa has a young consort the sun is out every day.'

'You are too kind, Mother,' Atsu said, trying to fend off the torrent of insincere compliments. The old lady was lavish with her praises but equally ready to stick the knife in when she saw the chance. 'I too am happy and grateful that you invited me here. I have never seen cherry blossom so beautiful,' she added, eager to turn the talk away from herself. 'These must be the most magnificent groves in the country.'

'They are indeed,' said Lady Honju-in, beaming. 'Planned and laid out by the eighth Tokugawa shogun, my son's great-great-great-grandfather. He took a keen interest in these gardens. Let us take a stroll and admire the blossom.'

She handed her saké cup to an attendant and stretched out one arthritic leg, then the other. Her ladies helped her rise to her feet and she shuffled outside.

'Is that not a double cherry?' Atsu asked, gesturing towards a tree spreading its branches a little distance away. 'What an extraordinary colour.'

'A rare variety,' said Lady Honju-in. 'The blossom is several shades of pink, quite exquisite.'

She gripped Atsu's arm and they made their way slowly over to the tree. Their ladies followed, holding parasols over their heads. Ikushima kept a discreet distance. She was not her lady-in-waiting or even her confidante, Atsu realized now. She was her keeper.

Atsu pulled down a branch and gazed at the blossom. Each delicate cluster hung by the thinnest of stalks. 'As if it would drop at any moment,' she murmured.

The frail blossom which lasts barely a day and falls at the first hint of a breeze seemed to symbolize this beautiful world of theirs, on the brink of disappearing for ever. That was what she needed to make Lady Honju-in see, she thought – how perilous their situation was, how it affected her personally.

'How does it go, that poem?' Lady Honju-in said dreamily. '"Cherry blossoms, so high in the mountains they seem to dwell among the clouds . . ."'

'"Not a day goes by but I go in spirit to pluck them,"' Atsu said, completing the poem.

Lady Honju-in gave a sniff and dabbed her rheumy eyes. 'The bittersweet beauty of the cherry blossom,' she sighed. 'It lasts a day, then it falls, like a samurai at the moment of his glory. And woman's beauty too,' she added, glancing up at Atsu pointedly with a malevolent gleam in her eye. 'It lasts but a season, then it is gone.'

They walked on to a pond and stopped to admire the huge golden and red and orange carp gliding just beneath the surface of the water, opening and closing their enormous jaws. The ladies threw crumbs of tempura batter to them.

'Time passes so quickly, dear Mother,' Atsu said, squeezing the dowager's bony arm. 'It is already my second cherry blossom season here. I remember my wedding day as if it were yesterday.' She laughed gaily. 'And the New Year's Eves we've spent together and all the feasts and dancing we enjoy.' She took a breath. It was time to move on to more serious matters, prepare the ground for her assault. 'Do you remember when the barbarians came and we sat behind screens to see them? Masa-*kun* performed his part perfectly. We were all so proud of him.'

The smile disappeared from Lady Honju-in's lips. She had taken the bait. Under the thick white powder her face was as furrowed as ancient cherry bark. 'Who'd ever have thought we'd live to see the day?' she snarled, sticking out her large underlip. 'Barbarians in the palace! I could smell them all the way across the audience chamber.' She snorted. 'Shoes on tatami! What kind of creatures are those? And then they lodge in the palace grounds for three whole months. Imagine how the servants had to scrub when they left. At least they've gone now. We can get back to normal. But we're here to enjoy the cherry blossom, not make ourselves miserable.'

She clapped her hands and gave a girlish trill of laughter. The carp responded with a thrash of their tails, beating the water to a froth. Atsu tossed a handful of tempura crumbs on to the water.

'If I may venture to differ, Mother,' she said, 'I do not think the barbarians have gone at all. They returned to Shimoda. They will be back in Edo again soon. They intend to stay. It is all laid out in this treaty of theirs.'

'I know I'm just a silly woman,' squawked Lady Honju-in, fluttering her fan. 'That is way above my head. It doesn't have much to do with us here in the palace. We just want them to leave us in peace.'

'Mother, they are never going to leave us in peace,' Atsu said. She knew the old lady was not that naive. 'With every day that passes they are more firmly entrenched. Lord Hotta explained the terms of the new treaty to us. There will be tens, even hundreds coming as soon as it is signed. Lord Hotta is already having a settlement built for them a safe distance from Edo.'

'Let them come,' barked Lady Honju-in, so loudly it made Atsu jump. 'They can make us sign their vile treaty but there's one thing they haven't reckoned with. We have plenty of brave young men itching to drive them out. They're already sharpening their swords, I can assure you of that.'

'If those brave young men try to drive them out, more barbarians will arrive in their ships and turn their cannons on Edo Castle. You know that, Mother.'

Lady Honju-in narrowed her eyes. 'I saw those creatures. They're big and ugly but they're not that clever. They're not warriors. They don't have warrior spirit. We'll fight them off. We'll fight to the death.'

'You have a warrior's heart, Mother,' Atsu said. 'But I am sure you understand what a perilous position we are in. The barbarians are never going to go away. We have to find a way to reach agreement with them without losing our independence or our dignity. It is a dangerous path to tread.'

She took a breath. 'We are in a frighteningly weak position. Lord Hotta does an excellent job but we need to know who our next shogun will be to give the country stability. Masa-*kun* has still not named his successor. Lady Shiga and I do our best,' she added, trying to laugh disarmingly. 'But neither of us has succeeded in producing an heir. I know I am young, I do not know much about palace ways. I defer to your greater knowledge and wisdom. But I am sure you agree it would be to our advantage to know who our next shogun will be.'

The Dowager Mother stared at her, her black eyes pinpoints of hostility. Atsu met her gaze with what she hoped was a look of wide-eyed girlish innocence.

'There's plenty of time,' Lady Honju-in said coldly. 'Darling Masa is young. He has many years ahead of him. It's too early to start worrying about a successor. I came here to enjoy the cherry blossom,' she snapped. 'Not listen to you twisting my arm about nonsense.'

Ikushima was at Atsu's shoulder. Her elegant kimono sleeves flapped as she tossed a handful of tempura crumbs to the carp. The water was roiling with their fat shiny bodies and gaping jaws. Pink petals fluttered down like snowflakes. Women's voices, chattering and laughing, echoed through the trees. Music tinkled. It sounded as if the dancing was about to begin.

'Honoured Mother,' Atsu said. 'We both know that we are in danger of losing everything. The barbarians are forcing our hand. There are vital decisions to be made.' The dowager glared at her. She carried on regardless. 'It would make all the difference to have a strong leader, a charismatic young leader to rally the daimyo and work out a solution to the impossible situation we are in.'

She took a breath. She had to take care not to antagonize Lady Honju-in or make her suspect she was trying to undermine her son.

'And did you have someone in mind, dear daughter?' asked Lady Honju-in in tones of sugary sweetness. She was not fooled in the least by Atsu's pose of humility. 'A possible candidate for this position?' Her eyes flashed dangerously. They both knew the name that was being bandied about as the country's one hope of salvation.

Atsu met her eyes boldly. 'If Masa-*kun* were to name Lord Keiki as the next shogun he could be Regent and help Lord Hotta.'

'Keiki,' Lady Honju-in said, her voice rising. She slapped her fan on her palm with a crack. 'You say my son, a man of thirty-four, should adopt a man of twenty as his heir, that a callow youth of twenty could do better than my thirty-four-year-old son? Ridiculous.' She bared her black teeth in a malevolent smile.

Atsu thought for a moment. 'You are very wise, Mother,' she said. 'Wise enough to put your personal feelings aside. You know how capable Lord Keiki is. He is mature, thoughtful, able. He is also considered very highly in the country. Many of the lords think he would make an excellent heir.'

Lady Honju-in's mask of civility seemed to crack open, revealing the demon horns beneath. She took a step towards Atsu and her arm flew up. She was holding her fan like a dagger. Atsu flinched. She couldn't believe she would hit her.

'So that's what you think, is it?' the dowager exploded, her eyes flashing. 'And where does a young lady like you pick up such opinions? You've been talking to Lord Nariakira. I didn't welcome you into the palace for you to carry out Lord Nariakira's business. The succession is for the Tokugawas to decide. It's nothing to do with Lord Nariakira.'

She glared at her, skinny arm held high.

Atsu stood her ground. 'You were happy to take me as your daughter-in-law, dear Mother,' she said.

'I thought you would be a companion for my son and that it would be for the best to bind the clans together,' the old woman shrieked. 'I didn't expect you to be Lord Nariakira's spy.'

'Mother,' Atsu said, looking her in the eye. 'You know that Lord Hotta travelled to Miyako and has been petitioning my uncle the Son of Heaven, asking him to give his seal of approval to the treaty?'

'Of course. You think I'm a fool?' Lady Honju-in snapped. 'And I know that he has failed.'

Atsu took a breath. She'd thought that Saigo had reached her before the news had got to anyone else. She'd forgotten that everyone had spies and messengers.

'Do you not see what that means, Mother?' she said, trying to keep her voice steady. She wanted to grab this stubborn old woman by the shoulders, shout at her, shake her. 'We are on the brink of civil war. Our whole world hangs in the balance. Whether the country is destroyed by barbarians or engulfed in civil war, that will be the end for all of us – the end of our luxury, the end of our comfortable lives, the end of the palace. We need to put aside our personal likes and dislikes and take whatever course will protect us from disaster. You understood that we needed to unite the clans. That is why you agreed to a Satsuma bride. It is the only way now. We must have a strong leader to bring us all together.'

'My son is an excellent monarch. He pays heed to his advisers, as any wise monarch should; no one expects the shogun to make decisions by himself. But he is perfectly capable of ruling.' The dowager looked at Atsu and raised her painted brows. 'You're not suggesting he isn't?'

Atsu groaned. The old woman was deliberately avoiding the point. It seemed nothing Atsu could say would shake her out of her blind complacency. She refused to see that their world was in peril. She was so determined to retain control that she didn't care even if everything went up in flames around her.

Atsu felt her temper rising. 'Mother, you know very well how dear he is to me,' she snapped. 'But he takes no interest in affairs of state. Do you not understand? There is open rebellion among the clans and Lord Hotta lacks the authority to bind them together. The treaty he has agreed has been forced on him by the foreigners. Some of the followers of the most rebellious lords are threatening to kill him. Lord Keiki would wield real authority. He would bind the clans together, renegotiate the treaty, represent our nation.'

Atsu frowned, wondering if she had gone too far. She glanced at Lady Honju-in.

Lady Honju-in drew herself up, tiny and proud. She flapped her fan imperiously. 'Forgive me, I'm being too hard on you,' she purred. 'I certainly agree with you on one thing. It is high time we named my son's successor.'

Her wily old face crinkled into smiles. Atsu narrowed her eyes.

The old woman was at her most dangerous when she turned on the charm.

'So you will support me when I speak to Masa-*kun*?' she said, putting off the moment of confrontation.

'Of course,' said Lady Honju-in.

Above them cherry trees crowded the sky, an exuberant mass of pink. Tiny brilliantly coloured birds darted their beaks into the blossoms.

'As you know, the successor is already decided,' the Dowager Mother said sweetly.

Atsu eyed her warily. She could guess where she was taking this.

'By right of inheritance, by bloodline.' The old woman gave an ingenuous smile. 'We will be delighted to announce His Majesty's successor: Lord Yoshitomi of the House of Kii.'

Ikushima was at Atsu's shoulder. Atsu groaned again. This was where the battle really began but she couldn't imagine how she would ever win round Lady Honju-in. 'He is only twelve years old, Mother!' she cried, trying to control her voice. 'He is a child. He will not be able to rule or make decisions. Others will rule in the shogun's name as they do now. He will not have the strength to bind all the fractious clans together. This is deadly serious. Our whole society is falling apart. It matters hugely.'

'Yoshi-*kun* is Masa-*kun*'s first cousin, dear daughter, first cousin once removed, that is. His father is Masa-*kun*'s grandfather's seventh son.' Lady Honju-in raised her painted brows wearily as if she was explaining something very simple to a child. 'Lord Keiki, on the other hand, is the seventh son of a very distant relative of the shogun. Lord Yoshitomi has the strongest claim by blood. There's really no need for further discussion.'

'Do you not understand what danger we are in, Mother?' Atsu said desperately. She stared at the carp thrashing their muscular tails, snapping up crumbs.

'If we interfere with the succession we undermine the authority of the Tokugawas,' Lady Honju-in said grandly. 'The successor is decided by bloodline. It's not for us to choose our shogun. The lower orders may clamour for Keiki but who listens to their voice?

That would be a disaster, particularly at this time of unrest. The Tokugawa blood flows in Yoshitomi's veins and the loyal clan lords and their vassals hold the Tokugawa blood in awe. The Tokugawa have ruled this country through thirteen generations. Now is not the time to interfere with that.

'You say I do not understand, dear daughter,' she said, her voice rising to a shriek. 'I understand all too well. I know the palace. I have been a Tokugawa concubine and a Tokugawa mother for more than three decades. As for you, you are an upstart, an interloper, sent here to cause trouble, undermine everything that we believe in and stand for.'

Tears came to Atsu's eyes at the venom of her attack. 'You are mistaken,' she said fiercely. 'I have only the good of the palace in mind and the good of your son. And that depends on Lord Keiki being named as heir. I wish you could see that, Mother.'

Lady Honju-in's painted brows rose even higher and her face cracked into a condescending smile. She held the winning hand and she knew it. 'I'm sure you mean well, dear daughter,' she said smoothly. 'But my son has many years ahead of him. By the time he reaches old age Yoshitomi will be ready to take over the reins of government.' She was all smiles now. 'Yoshi-*kun* is a charming child, quite delightful. You must meet him.'

There had never been any doubt about how stubborn the old woman was but Atsu had hoped she might be able to win her over by appealing to her self-interest. But here in the palace it was impossible to imagine the turmoil outside the walls. All her talk of civil war was wasted breath. All Lady Honju-in saw was her wealth, her luxury, her fine kimonos and exquisite artefacts. All she wanted was to ensure that her son would be followed by another weak shogun so that she could maintain her iron grip over the palace, the country, everything.

Iesada had said that his father had died after setting his seal to the first treaty with the barbarians. Atsu had heard differently. She had heard that he had died simply for failing to turn them away. He was the shogun, the barbarian-quelling generalissimo, and he had failed to quell them. No matter the reason, there were many rumours that his death had been sudden and unnatural. It had certainly happened a mere fifteen days after the barbarians arrived.

However long Lord Hotta delayed, eventually Iesada would have to do something far more unpopular than his father had ever done – set his seal to this hated treaty. Supposing something happened to him as a result? Atsu hardly dared frame the thought. But if it did, it would be a disaster if the next shogun were to be a twelve-year-old. She had been afraid of what would happen to Iesada if Keiki was chosen as heir. But now she saw that it made no difference who was chosen. If Yoshitomi was named as heir and Lord Nariakira's plans were thwarted, Iesada would still be dispensable.

There was a bottomless pit of despair opening beneath her. But the battle was not lost yet. The old lady might have defeated her but in the end it was for the shogun to decide, not either of them. And the Dowager Mother was no longer the only person in the palace who could bend his ear.

There was still a chance Atsu could change the course of history. She would have to speak to Iesada straight away and this time she would not take no for an answer.

She gave what she hoped was a naive smile. The old woman wouldn't be fooled if she conceded too readily. 'I see your point, Lady Mother,' she said. 'I am proud to be a member of the Tokugawa family. I am the last person who would wish to interfere with Tokugawa tradition. And I would love to meet little Yoshi. But let us not ruin this beautiful day by squabbling.'

Ikushima was treading on her hems as they strolled away from the carp pond, fanning themselves, stopping to exclaim at the delicate blossom. Atsu let a little time pass then rejoined her ladies. Lady Honju-in went back to her magnificent pavilion to tuck into a lavish feast that looked likely to go on all afternoon.

Atsu told Ikushima that she needed some time to herself. She wanted to shake off that steely-eyed lady. She murmured to Middle Elder Omasé that she was a little tired. Her ladies must stay and enjoy themselves. Perhaps Omasé could call her palanquin and escort her back to her rooms.

She needed to get to Iesada quickly, before his mother did, and in the daytime, while Elder Anekoji was not around to interfere. She hoped he might be in her rooms. If he had stayed in the men's palace she would have to wait until the next audience to see him and all her plans would be ruined.

44

The gardens seemed to go on for ever. Atsu pressed her hands to the floor to steady herself, shouting to the bearers to run faster. She didn't have much time. Lady Honju-in would surely guess what she was going to do. They crossed one bridge after another, wove through a labyrinth of flower beds.

She held her breath as they reached her rooms. Then she heard a faint rattling and laughed with relief.

Ever since the barbarians had come to the castle Iesada had taken to visiting her apartments. He often stayed on between audiences. He liked it here, he said, away from those bossy officials in the men's palace, eternally telling him what to do.

Middle Elder Omasé had insisted they install a brazier so he could indulge in his favourite pastime of roasting dried soy beans. They had had one brought in, a fat blue earthenware urn marked with the Tokugawa crest in gold.

Atsu disapproved of Iesada wasting his time with such childish pursuits. She tried to encourage him to study his ministers' notes on current affairs or read Confucian texts or practise martial arts. But today she was delighted to hear the rattle of beans.

Iesada was on his knees on the veranda, stirring a panful of beans with a pair of long metal chopsticks. Smoke billowed from the burning charcoal, making Atsu blink and rub her eyes.

'You're back early, Atsu-*chan*,' he said, looking rather abashed at being caught indulging in his childish hobby. He was in fine pale-gold silk robes over baggy linen trousers with his hair oiled into a topknot. Atsu felt a pang as she saw his pale face and innocent eyes. She couldn't bear to think of anything bad ever happening to him.

She sat down next to him on the veranda. 'We missed you at the Fukiagé Gardens,' she said, giving him a hug and kissing his smooth cheek. 'You should have come. The blossom was lovely.'

'I should rather see it here with you. I do not like so many people.'

Atsu's gardens too were full of cherry trees with branches trained across trellises in delicate pink canopies. Mount Fuji rose majestic across the sea of pink.

A hawk soared overhead, catching the updraught on its great wings. Suddenly it swooped down, cawing, and landed on one of the poles, making the trelliswork creak and sway. It was so close they could see its scaly yellow legs, great talons and hooked beak. It glared around disdainfully. Iesada gave a delighted laugh. He jumped up to chase it, then glanced ruefully at Atsu and sat down again. The bird gave a last regal stare and flapped off.

'Two out of three,' he said. 'First we see Mount Fuji, then a hawk.'

Atsu laughed uncertainly, remembering the saying that to dream of Mount Fuji, a hawk and an aubergine on the first night of the year means a good year ahead. She had no faith in such superstitions. She couldn't imagine that the year ahead was going to be good.

'Now all sire needs is an aubergine,' said Middle Elder Omasé, beaming as a lady-in-waiting bustled out, stout and square of face, holding aloft a tray with a purple aubergine on it decorated with cherry blossom.

Iesada laughed. 'Three out of three,' he cried, tossing the aubergine in the air and catching it. The lady-in-waiting tittered obsequiously.

'You will live for ever now,' Atsu said. She gave what was meant to be a light-hearted laugh but it rang hollow. Lady Honju-in would be appearing soon. The old lady hated her son visiting Atsu's rooms. Once she got back from the cherry blossom viewing she'd be looking for him, checking that Atsu wasn't taking advantage of her absence to try to win him over. Atsu needed to speak to Masa-*kun* now and find such powerful arguments that nothing the old dragon could say would change his mind. She knew he was stubborn. If she could only manage to convince him that he should take Keiki as his heir, he would insist on it.

Her husband leaned against her. 'I am glad you came to live with me and be my consort,' he said.

The lady-in-waiting ran out again, this time with two pink rice-paste cakes shaped into cherry blossoms and two cups of tea with a pickled blossom floating in each. Atsu took a sip, enjoying the faintly sour salty taste. 'I wonder what will happen in the future,' she said, trying to think of a way to ease into the subject of the heir. She wasn't sure Iesada ever thought about the future – the distant future, maybe, when the palace had become a plain of grass, but not his own immediate future.

He pulled away from her. He sensed how tense she was.

'I hate that man,' he said, taking a bite of a fat pink cake.

'Which man?' Atsu asked, stalling for time. It was unnerving the way he could read her mind. She knew perfectly well who he was talking about.

'Keiki,' he said, taking another bite. 'I wish we did not have to talk about him. He is evil, I told you that. I know he seems so young and charming but he is fooling you. He is plotting and planning. Mama always says so. Her ladies say so too.' His voice was rising, turning into a hysterical whine.

'What makes you say that, Masa-*kun*?' Atsu said. She didn't dare accuse his mother of speaking poisonous nonsense. 'What harm has he done you?' She tried to stop the question sounding like an accusation.

Iesada narrowed his eyes and pursed his lips. 'I told you,' he whined like a sulky child. 'He wants to take over. He wants to be shogun and rule the country himself. He wants to stop us spending money and take away all our delicious food and beautiful robes and feasts and games and throw us out of the palace and make us live in poverty.'

Atsu pursed her lips and shook her head. Iesada didn't even know what money was. He had no need of money. He was surrounded by beautiful things but they all belonged to the castle, belonged to his life as shogun. He was showered with gifts. He had an endless supply of new clothes. Bolts of silk, tributes from merchants, poured into the castle daily. He never bought anything. How could he? He never left the palace.

All he was doing was parroting his mother. That was what the old woman told him. Nothing worried the dowager except holding on to her wealth and privilege and power. She didn't care what happened to the country.

'I don't think that's true, sire,' Middle Elder Omasé said soothingly. Her broad face, full and pale like the moon, crinkled into a fond smile. She'd known Iesada since he was a baby. She was not afraid to contradict him. 'Lord Keiki is kind and gentle. He likes riding his horse and practising with his sword. I don't think he even wants to live here in the palace.'

'You are quite wrong about Lord Keiki, Masa-*kun*,' Atsu said, grateful for the intervention. 'He is very clever and devoted to you. Do you not remember? You used to be like brothers. He is very sad that you no longer want to see him. He is worried that he has done something to offend you. He asked me to try to make peace between you.' She took a breath. 'You know you are always tired, Masa-*kun*. You have so much to do. He could help you.'

Iesada turned his big eyes on Atsu and she flinched under his accusing gaze. 'I thought you cared about me,' he said, pouting. He turned his back on her, turned back to his brazier and started stirring defiantly, scraping the metal chopsticks against the bottom of the pan.

At least he hadn't become hysterical. It was the first time she had brought up the subject of Keiki in the daytime, while Elder Anekoji was not around. Perhaps he felt freer without his mother's spy watching over him.

Atsu laughed. 'You know I care about you,' she said. She stroked his neck, rubbed the tense knots out of his shoulders. 'But you have a very important job to do. You need people to help you, to take over your duties when you're sick.'

'It is the barbarians,' said Iesada abruptly. He let the chopsticks fall into the pan with a clatter and swung round, glancing up at her out of the corner of his eye. 'I know about this treaty. I am supposed to set my seal to it. Half the uncles do not want me to, the other half say I have to. Uncle Hotta just dithers. He shuttles around trying to please everyone. He went to see your uncle in Miyako. They are saying he made a mess of that too. While he has been out of the way they decided to get rid of him.'

Atsu turned cold. 'Get rid of him? Who? Who has decided?'

'The other councillors, of course. They say he is too weak. They say he is making us look foolish, me too. They are going to push him out.'

'Push him out? Uncle Hotta?' Atsu gasped. She gave a shudder of fear. Without Lord Hotta she could not imagine what would become of all of them. 'That cannot be right,' she cried. 'No one can make Lord Hotta leave. You have got it wrong, Masa-*kun*.'

She had a terrible sinking feeling in her stomach. She knew he hadn't got it wrong. He knew better than anyone what went on in that hotbed of intrigue, the men's palace.

'It is true,' Iesada said. Now he was the one who was calm and grown up and she was the one who was hysterical.

She buried her head in her hands. 'It cannot be. It cannot be,' she said. She realized too that if what he said was true then he had heard about Lord Hotta's fall before Ikushima or Saigo, or even Lady Honju-in.

She groaned. 'That is dreadful news. We need Lord Hotta desperately. He is wise and good.' She bowed her head. To lose him just as they were under attack from all sides was a catastrophe. It made it all the more urgent to establish Lord Keiki in a position of power. Now she wished she'd tried harder to change Iesada's mind before all this began. She'd been relying on Lord Hotta, thinking that with him at the helm they didn't need Keiki. She could never have foreseen this disaster.

'Can you not stop them, Masa-*kun*, tell them they are wrong?'

'You know I cannot. There will be a new Prime Minister.'

'Do you know who?'

'Maybe that fat Lord Ii.' He wrinkled his nose and gave a shudder of distaste. 'I do not like him.'

'The Lord of Hikoné? But he is just a small-time clan lord. He does not even attend meetings. I have never met him.'

She tried to pull herself together, conceal her shock. 'I am sure that whoever becomes Prime Minister will agree that you need an heir,' she said, her voice shaking. 'Without Uncle Hotta you will need someone to help you even more. Lord Keiki is clever and kind. I think you should start by adopting him and making him your heir. You could teach him what to do.' She had to be tactful, not suggest that Keiki might take over or imply that Iesada might die and need a successor. 'It will be a long, long time before he actually becomes shogun but you could start,' she added reassuringly.

Iesada pulled away from her. He hunched his shoulders. 'It will not be a long, long time. Do you not know what happened to Father?'

A cloud drifted across the sun. Atsu shivered in the sudden chill. There were too many questions about how his father had died. 'Never mind that, Masa-*kun*. Let us not talk about that now,' she said hastily.

He pushed out his lower lip. 'I was there,' he said. 'They think I am stupid, they thought I did not understand. You do not think I am stupid, do you?' He didn't wait for an answer. He rocked his head from side to side and his face darkened. His lips had turned white. 'They did it right in front of me.' His voice sounded as if he were being strangled.

Atsu gripped his arm. 'Let us talk about something else,' she said in alarm. 'Let me tell you about the cherry blossom viewing.'

'I will tell you,' he said. 'Do not try to stop me. Father, Father . . .' He opened his mouth wide, took a gulp of air. 'It was Ino, Uncle Echizen's chamberlain. We were in Father's rooms. It was after the barbarians came, after they had handed over their letter, after he had . . . he had . . . he had signed the treaty. Ino came in. He held out a goblet to Father. He said, "Drink, sire!" Just like that. "Drink, sire!" Father's face turned black. He roared like a bear. "Treason!"'

He shouted the word.

'Hush, hush,' Atsu said. He shook off her hand. He was staring as if he were back there again, seeing that dreadful murder happening before his eyes.

'He grabbed the goblet and threw the drink in Ino's face and the goblet fell down on the floor. It made a crash, it made me jump. Ino wiped his hand across his face. Then he took his sword out, right then. The courtiers were there, hundreds of them, watching, watching. No one stopped him, no one said a word. Just watching, as if they were watching a Noh play, and their faces blank. No one shocked, no one afraid, just watching, watching.

'Ino took out his sword. I saw the blade flash, very long and very shiny, and I shouted. "No, no! No, no!" I shouted.'

Atsu put her arm around him but he pushed her away.

'Then he . . . he . . . shoved it into Father. Into Father's chest, right in. I wanted to cover my eyes, but I could not. I saw Father's blood spurting out like a fountain.' He put his hands over his eyes, then over his ears, then over his eyes again.

'I wanted to cover my ears, not hear that terrible crunching, but I could not,' he whispered, peering between his fingers. 'Ino said, "Idiot boy, go away. It's nothing to do with you." Father looked at me. He opened his mouth to speak but he could not. His blood was gurgling out of his mouth.'

Iesada's eyes were huge. 'Then he fell down. Someone said, "The boy, the boy saw everything." Ino said, "He understands nothing. He will not remember." Then he knelt down and pushed his sword into his own belly, all the way in, and turned it and dragged it across and pulled it up. It made a noise, a terrible wrenching noise. Blood came out, a fountain of blood, a lake of blood. Then the courtiers took me away. "Just a game," they said. "Nothing to worry about." But I knew it was not a game. And I never forgot. Never.

'He called me an idiot boy. I was not a boy. I was twenty-nine.'

'You are not an idiot either.' Atsu was gasping for breath herself, shaking in horror.

She remembered when Lord Nariakira had told her that the Great

Ruler had died, nearly five years ago. She'd been in Crane Castle. He had wept and punched his fist into his palm and shouted, 'I should have been there! I could have stopped it!' That was when he had told her he was sending her to Edo Castle. That was when it had all begun.

'You know why they did that, why they killed Father? Because he put his seal on the treaty with the barbarians. And now I will have to put my seal on a barbarian treaty too.'

Atsu clasped her hands and closed her eyes and tried to hold back the nausea sweeping over her. Masa-*kun* was wrong about one thing. His father hadn't signed any treaty. All he had done was allow them to deliver a letter. But the barbarians had arrived during his reign and for that he had had to pay the price. It must have been because he had succumbed to western pressure, because the lords thought they needed a stronger leader. She shook her head. If that was why they had killed him, they had failed. They'd ended up with her frail husband as shogun, with the Dowager Mother holding power, doing her best to maintain her grip over the palace, over the country, over everything.

And now Lord Nariakira was saying the same thing all over again – that Iesada was too weak, that they should install Keiki as Regent. If this treaty went ahead, Iesada would have to do something far more earth-shaking than just receive a letter. He would have to sign a treaty in earnest and a very unpopular one at that. She was over-whelmed with fear for him.

She turned to Omasé, expecting her too to be deathly white and wild-eyed. Surely she knew this terrible tale all too well. But her face was calm. She met Atsu's eyes and frowned and raised her eyebrows.

Atsu stared at her in shock, her mind racing, remembering the other stories she'd heard about His Late Majesty's death. Hadn't Lady Honju-in said that Iesada had given his father water when he was on his deathbed and put his finger in his soup to check the temperature? So perhaps His Late Majesty had died in his bed, quite differently from the horrific tale Iesada had just told her. Then there was Iesada's talk of seeing blood outside the shrine room after Hana died and his stories of Princess Fumi, the cat ghost with two tails. After all, he was different from other people. He was not quite right in his mind. Maybe everything he said was just so much wild prattle.

But not one of the women – not Omasé, not Lady Honju-in – had been in the men's palace when his father died. They couldn't have been. All they had to go on was hearsay. But he had been there. He'd seen everything.

Atsu heard rattling and smelt roasting beans. The motherly middle-aged lady-in-waiting had put another pan of beans on the fire and was talking soothingly to Iesada. He sat cross-legged, leaning over the brazier, moving the metal chopsticks methodically round and round, round and round. It seemed to comfort him. Maybe he'd taken a turn for the worse after his father died. Maybe that was when he had retreated into his shell, taken up roasting beans. He turned to Atsu.

'Will you take care of me?' he said. 'Will you stay here with me?'

Tears came to Atsu's eyes. She felt such an outpouring of tenderness she could hardly bear it. She swallowed. 'Of course,' she said. It seemed cruel to use him but she had to follow through on this opportunity. 'You can trust Lord Keiki too,' she added. 'He will protect you too, I promise you.'

She knew now what she had to say, how to put her argument. 'You did not like the Americans, did you? You did not like meeting them.'

'They were strange, not like the Dutch. They were very aggressive. That big hairy one who came up close to me with his big staring eyes and big nose. He frightened me, the way he stared at me. I could hear his raspy breathing and his voice was very loud and harsh. I thought he might pounce on me. The Dutch are afraid of me but he was not afraid. I could see his hands, very large and hairy with coarse skin. He smelt bad too. I wanted to pull my head inside my shell.' He was turning his ivory snail over and over in his hand like a prayer bead.

'They are certainly aggressive,' said Atsu. 'We told them they could not come to the castle but they came anyway. Soon they will be sailing here in their ships, bringing more westerners to live in our country. We have to find a way to live with them. You know the lords are angry too. It seems so peaceful here in the palace but outside there is a great deal of trouble. We must be careful or we may lose everything.'

He stared up at her, his eyes wide.

'I know you do not want to meet them again.'

'No, never. Never.'

'If Lord Keiki were here you would not have to. He could meet them instead. He could do all the jobs you do not want to do, all that extra work that is piling up now the barbarians are here. You would still be shogun, you would set your seal to documents. We would still have our three daily audiences, we would play games and have tea ceremonies and do all the delightful things we always do. It would be just the same as ever. Nothing would change except that you would have Lord Keiki to do the difficult jobs for you and we would be safe from the barbarians and he would also pacify the lords who are so angry. He would help you, just like Uncle Hotta. Now that Uncle Hotta has gone you have no one to help you. Keiki can do that.'

Iesada narrowed his eyes. 'You mean he would not take over and stop us spending money and throw us out of the palace and make us all live in poverty?'

'I do not think he is interested in that,' Atsu said gently. He was gnawing at his lip. 'And I shall make sure he does not,' she added.

He nodded. He'd heard. It seemed he trusted her. 'But what about Yoshitomi? Mama says he is to be my heir.'

'He is young still. How could he possibly do all the work that Uncle Hotta does? But Lord Keiki could. Yoshi-*kun* could take over after him.'

'I see,' he said slowly. Atsu could see him frowning, thinking it through. 'So Lord Keiki would take care of everything.'

'He would protect all of us. He would protect the country.'

Iesada looked at her with his big eyes. He'd stopped stirring the beans.

'You are the shogun,' she said. 'You must determine what to do. I have faith in you. I know you will make the right decision.'

He stared down at the beans popping in the pan. Then he drew himself up. 'I have decided,' he said.

Before he had a chance to say another word, voices erupted in Atsu's rooms. A lady-in-waiting ran out, her face pale, her eyes bulging.

'Her Ladyship the Dowager Mother,' she announced.

45

Iesada crouched low over his pan of beans, stirring frantically, his lips moving soundlessly. His face had turned the colour of chalk. The chopsticks fell from his hands and clattered off the glowing charcoals on to the veranda. The middle-aged lady-in-waiting took a cloth, picked them up and laid them back on the pan. Iesada shrank closer to the floor, peering around fearfully.

The screens between Atsu's apartments and the veranda slid back.

Atsu had been expecting Lady Honju-in to stalk out, eyes flashing fire, but the Dowager Mother came slinking out on stockinged feet, as demure as a kitten in her cherry blossom kimono. She dropped to her knees and put her knobbly hands to the planks.

'My apologies for intruding, dear daughter,' she said silkily. She turned to her son, cowering beside the brazier. 'So there you are, Masa-*kun*. Goodness me, I do hope you're not making a nuisance of yourself.'

Atsu had her smile ready. 'You are most welcome, Lady Mother. I am sorry my rooms are so small and dirty. We were not expecting such a distinguished guest,' she said, repeating the formulaic greetings.

Elder Anekoji and a small troop of aged ladies-in-waiting filed out after Lady Honju-in and knelt in a line along the veranda. Their painted faces cracked into smiles as they murmured about the loveliness of the day and of Atsu's gardens. Atsu was relieved to see that Lady Shiga was not among them.

'Goodness me, such blossom,' shrilled Lady Honju-in, shaping her mouth into a rosebud pout. 'Just look at that. So lovely. And you can see Mount Fuji too from here.'

Atsu smiled and nodded, interjecting thanks as the Dowager Mother poured out a stream of platitudes and compliments. Her nerves were on edge. She felt like a farmer who has found a fox in his chicken coop. She was waiting for her to pounce, to bring up the succession. That was the only possible reason she could be here.

The Dowager Mother turned her withered cheeks towards Iesada. She smiled triumphantly, as if delighted to find him roasting beans. Atsu grimaced. It made it look as if she too wanted him to remain eternally a child.

'What a good time you're having, darling,' Lady Honju-in twittered. 'Look at those beans, so lovely and brown. But goodness me, what a mess you've made. You've got black all over your face – and in front of the Lady Midai too. Whatever must she think of you?'

Iesada quailed, avoiding his mother's gaze. His shaved pate glistened with sweat and there were stains spreading under the armpits of his pale gold robes. Atsu glanced at him in concern. It was true. There was a smear of charcoal on his cheek. Middle Elder Omasé ran over and wiped it off.

'But Masa-*kun*, darling, you know it's not time for the afternoon audience yet.' Lady Honju-in chattered on gaily, determined to drag out his punishment for as long as she could. 'You should be at home. Come to my rooms and relax. That's your home, not here. You mustn't bother your honourable consort. You're not neglecting your old mama, are you?'

'You forget, Mother,' Atsu interjected brusquely. 'I am Masa-*kun*'s wife. This is his home.' Her words were for his ears as much as for his mother's.

Some of Atsu's ladies-in-waiting bustled out with trays of cakes and tea.

'No need to put yourself to any trouble, dear daughter,' said Lady Honju-in. 'I just came to take Masa-*kun* home. He tires so easily, don't you, darling? Come back to my rooms and take a nap.' She gripped his arm with a claw-like hand.

A breeze rustled the trees, sending showers of pink blossom fluttering down. Atsu was sure Iesada would follow his mother and all her efforts would have been wasted.

Iesada had been crouching unmoving, as if in a trance, as if the only way he could endure the storm of words was by drawing his head inside his shell. Suddenly he took hold of himself. He straightened his back and looked directly at Lady Honju-in. 'I am not a child, Mother,' he snapped, shaking off her hand. 'I shall stay here if I want.'

Atsu held her breath. She was thrilled to see him standing up for himself against the fearsome dowager, addressing her as 'Mother', not 'Mama'. His whole demeanour had changed. He was proud and dignified. He was the man she knew he could be, the man she'd grown to love, who had received the barbarians like the king he was, who looked at her clear-eyed when she spoke and paid attention to the world around him.

'You know you're not well, Masa darling,' Lady Honju-in wheedled, glancing up at him slyly. 'Don't be silly now. Come along with Mama.'

Atsu breathed in sharply. It was all she could do to stop herself shouting at her. The old woman's words only confirmed everything she had suspected. If she had her way, Lady Honju-in would keep her son a child for ever. It was only because Atsu had managed to free him from under her wing that he had been able to grow up.

The air was brittle. Iesada's shoulders were quivering as if he was reeling against the force of his mother's will. He glanced towards Atsu and she held his eye, trying to steady him.

Lady Honju-in jerked her chin towards her. 'Your honourable consort is very clever and modern, but she's not one of us,' she said, curling her thick underlip. 'She doesn't know how things are done here. I hope she hasn't been putting foolish ideas into your head.'

'I am perfectly capable of having my own ideas, Mother,' said Iesada, scowling. He took a deep breath, swung to a formal kneeling position with his knees wide apart and jutted out his lower lip. 'I have been thinking about the future. I have decided the time has come to appoint my successor.'

Lady Honju-in flung Atsu a look of undisguised loathing. Atsu quailed. She'd have to instruct Omasé to take extra care, she thought, make sure the tasters checked every dish several times from now on.

She braced herself. She knew what Lady Honju-in was going to say and how she would have to answer. It was time to fight for their country.

Lady Honju-in composed her face into a bland mask and turned back to her son. 'Of course, darling,' she purred. 'You intend to appoint little Yoshi. There's no need for any fuss. It's automatic, it's his right by line of succession. But we can certainly issue a state-ment, it only to clear up any doubts. I'll inform the State Council.' She turned to Atsu, raising a gnarled hand to cover her mouth as she bared her blackened teeth in a malevolent smile. 'Or perhaps the honourable Lady Midai would like to convey your message?'

Iesada was panting. He screwed up his face as if he had some-thing bitter in his mouth and clenched his fists. He took a breath and glared at his mother. 'Yoshitomi is a child,' he barked. 'I intend to name Lord Keiki as my heir.'

He slumped back on his heels, his eyes darting from side to side as if he saw a horde of demons swarming towards him, threatening to chop him into pieces.

Atsu quivered. A shudder rippled through the rows of women.

There was a sudden crackle. 'The beans, the beans!' shrilled the square-faced lady-in-waiting.

A coil of acrid smoke rose from the brazier. The beans were burn-ing, jumping out of the pan, blackening and turning to cinders on the red-hot charcoal. The ladies pulled their skirts out of the way as hot beans skittered across the veranda. The lady-in-waiting ran over holding a thick cloth, picked up the pan and lifted it off the fire.

Lady Honju-in drew her breath through her teeth in a hiss. She seemed totally unconcerned by the commotion. 'Of course, I'm just a silly old woman,' she snarled. She bared her teeth in a hideous smile. 'What do I know?'

Atsu stiffened, preparing herself for the onslaught.

'You don't know what you're saying, darling,' the old woman

shrilled. 'You've been spending too much time with your honourable consort. How many times do I have to tell you? Lord Keiki is a monster.' Her voice was rising to a shriek. 'His father will lay waste to the entire country, he'll dismantle the women's palace, he'll throw us all out. We'll be destitute, destitute!'

Atsu narrowed her eyes. She doubted if the old woman believed any such thing. This pretence of hysteria was simply her way of trying to manipulate her son.

Iesada took a deep breath but his eyes were firm. 'That is not true, Mother.'

The women gasped.

'You dare contradict me?' stuttered Lady Honju-in.

The shogun ignored her. 'Lord Keiki is clever and capable. This is a critical time for our country. Our lives are in danger. The barbarians are on the verge of invading and we are about to be engulfed in civil war. Yoshitomi is a little boy. He will have no idea what to do. Keiki can protect us. Now that Lord Hotta has been removed, we have no Prime Minister. I need Lord Keiki's help. He will advise me and help me govern.'

Atsu listened, nodding gravely. She was pleased to hear him restating her arguments. She had been right to have faith in him. She'd known that once he'd made his choice he would stand by his decision.

'He'll have you killed, that Keiki,' Lady Honju-in hissed. 'You mark my words. He'll have you poisoned.' She slapped her fan into her palm with a crack. 'He wants you out of the way so he can be shogun himself.'

Iesada had turned pale. He stared at the faded wooden planks of the veranda to steady himself. Then he looked up, his brow clearing. 'He will not need to if he is my successor,' he retorted calmly.

Atsu had to stifle a smile at such irrefutable logic.

'You'd bring your family, the shogunate, the whole country into disrepute? You're even more of a fool than I thought you were, letting that low-class woman push you around. I knew I'd made a mistake allowing her into the palace. The Satsuma are serpents. You can't trust them a finger span.'

Atsu knelt in silence. Iesada had to fight his own battle. She could barely contain her pride at seeing him stand up to this fearsome old woman.

Iesada steeled himself. He seemed to grow taller and straighter. He set his knees further apart and rested his fist on his thigh, holding his fan upright like a general directing a battle. He took a breath, threw his shoulders back. His face was stern, his eyes focused.

'Say what you like, Mother. I am the shogun and the decision is mine and mine alone. I name Lord Keiki. There is no need to inform the State Council. I shall do so myself.'

It took all of Atsu's self-control not to shout in triumph.

Lady Honju-in stared as if shocked at his transformation. She seemed lost for words.

Crows circled in the blue sky, their caws loud in the silence. A breeze blew, cats sauntered between the bushes and across the expanses of gravel and paving stones. A waterfall tinkled in the distance and an ornamental bamboo pipe dropped on to a stone with a melodic clunk.

The Lady Dowager took an audible breath. She pushed her face up to Iesada's. 'You will do no such thing,' she said in a menacing growl. 'How dare you disobey me?'

She straightened her back, reached into her obi and grabbed the hilt of her dagger. Before anyone could move she had pulled it out. Her pink kimono sleeve fell back as she swung her shrivelled arm above her head.

The blade flashed in the sunlight, razor sharp.

She turned on her son, her face twisted in fury, her eyes blazing and her lips bared in a snarl, and drew her arm back as if to plunge the dagger into his chest.

Iesada knelt frozen, like a statue. He stared at her, his lips pale, his eyes wide and unmoving. He swayed and lifted his chin as if bracing himself for the blow.

Atsu sprang to her feet and dived across the veranda to throw herself between the blade and the shogun. She stopped dead as Lady Honju-in brought the weapon down and pressed it not to Iesada's chest but to her own throat. A jagged red scratch appeared on the folds of withered skin and blood dropped on to the collar of her pink kimono.

She leaned forward, holding the dagger to her neck, and hissed into Iesada's ear. 'If you name Keiki as your successor I shall stab myself in the throat and die. Is that what you want? Is it?' Her voice rose to a shriek. 'Will you choose him anyway, knowing that?' Her face was black with fury.

Iesada reeled. He stared at his mother, his face white. His jaw went slack, his mouth fell open. Atsu could see his strength, his composure, his confidence, everything she'd worked so hard to help him develop, all crumbling before her eyes.

'Do not believe her, Masa-*kun*,' she shouted desperately. 'She will not do it. She will never do such a thing.'

She turned on the old lady. 'You are lying. You will never kill yourself. You love your life – your luxury, your grandeur, your wealth. You will never give it up. You are bluffing. Can you not see, Masa-*kun*? She is bluffing.'

'You think I won't? Just wait and see. I'm a samurai born and bred. I'm not afraid to die. I can kill myself whenever I choose. I'll show you.' She pressed the dagger a fraction deeper. Blood welled out. She put her hand to her scraggy throat and smeared a slash of red across her kimono collar. 'Have you forgotten, Masa-*kun*? What have I told you, a hundred times? Choose Keiki and I'll stab myself in the throat. And I will. I will.'

Iesada crumpled. He had slumped to his side as if blown over by the force of her fury. His head went slack and his eyes revolved. He was shaking.

Atsu grabbed him, put her arms around him, held him tight. He was limp, as if she were holding a doll. She drew back. 'Look at me, Masa-*kun*,' she pleaded. 'She will not kill herself. It is all right. You have me now, you do not need to worry about her.'

He looked up at her despairingly. His teeth were chattering, his breath ragged. 'I cannot do it,' he whimpered, panting. 'I cannot. Do you not see? Mama . . . Mama must not kill herself.' He groaned. 'I am sorry.'

'She is bluffing, she is lying,' Atsu said. 'Remember what I told you. I will protect you, Keiki will protect you. We need Keiki to be Regent to save the country.'

He hunched over, small and beaten.

Lady Honju-in slid the dagger back into its scabbard, her eyes ablaze with triumph.

Atsu shook her head. 'Lady Mother,' she said, 'can you not see the danger we are in?'

'There is no need to discuss any further, dear daughter,' the dowager purred. 'As you said yourself, it's for the shogun to decide. And he has decided, haven't you, darling?' She didn't wait for him to answer. 'In this time of crisis we need a strong government. The next in line must inherit. Any other course would lay us open to accusations of weakness. We can't start paying attention to what the populace want. I know you will not oppose the shogun's will, dear daughter.'

The old woman's hand was still on her dagger.

Atsu opened her mouth to argue again but her heart was not in it. There was no point. All Lady Honju-in had to do was threaten suicide. Atsu had tried, she'd done her best, but she'd been defeated.

She slumped back on her heels, reeling in shock, trying to grasp what had just happened. This was the task Lord Nariakira had installed her in the palace to achieve, the vital task that would save their country, save them all from the dreadful quandary they were in. Ever since she'd arrived in the palace this task had been on her mind, nagging at her, haunting her.

All this time she had spent getting to know Iesada, becoming close to him, trying to persuade him, then rebelling and deciding she dared not do it, all the while with Ikushima and Saigo at her back, urging her to hurry, and Lord Nariakira in the shadows. It seemed most of the nation was behind her, most of the nation wanted Keiki to be Regent.

Was it really true? Could she really have failed? Had all this really come tumbling down like a child's building blocks? She felt winded. She stared in disbelief at the veranda.

There had to be some other way. She wished she could wring the old woman's scrawny neck like a chicken's. Perhaps she should authorize Ikushima to get rid of her.

She sighed and shook her head. That would be one step too far. There would be open warfare in the palace. If the dowager's death were traced to Atsu it would implicate Lord Nariakira. That would mean civil war for sure.

And even if they managed to have Lady Honju-in killed, Iesada would be heartbroken, racked with guilt. It would make him all the more determined to carry out her last wishes. It wouldn't change anything.

There was still a glimmer of hope. Nothing would be final till the shogun had spoken to the State Council. But Atsu doubted if Lord Nariakira had any other plans up his sleeve, any other people he could use besides her. She was closest to the shogun and this decision was in his hands alone.

She shuddered, overwhelmed with despair. She'd lost, Lord Nariakira had lost, the country had lost. She could plot and plan as much as she liked. The Lady Dowager had outmanoeuvred her.

She turned to Iesada, crouching cowed and sickly beside his mother. He crept over to his pan of beans and started stirring again, whimpering like a dog that's been beaten.

There was one thing left to her still – to take care of Iesada. Better that he be shogun than a twelve-year-old child. There was another demon raising its head too – the dreaded treaty. If they were to forestall a British attack, Iesada had to put his seal to it. Atsu was not at all sure he'd agree to do so.

46

'The British are coming! The British are coming!' The words flew from mouth to mouth as panic surged through the palace like a tsunami.

The news had barely reached Atsu's apartments than she was on her feet and rushing out of the door. There was no time for protocol, no time to call for her palanquin. The American envoy had arrived post haste from Shimoda to warn that the British had set sail from China with fifty warships bristling with cannon and were heading for their shores. Regent Ii and the senior councillors were hurrying to the Visitors' Audience Chambers, bringing with them the treaty for the shogun to set his seal to.

Summer had come. Heat beat down on the palace roofs and shimmered off the paving stones. The air hung heavy. The gardens were bleached and airless, the women lay around exhausted, waving their fans, damp with sweat. And still the treaty with the Americans had not been signed.

The new chief minister, Regent Ii, had sent another secret messenger to Miyako to request the emperor's approval but there'd been no reply. Now time had run out. As the American envoy had insisted again and again, the only way to avoid total destruction was to sign his treaty.

Atsu lifted her skirts and ran, her heart pounding. Her ladies scurried behind her along the corridors, through rooms lit by shafts of early morning sunshine. Eight bearers jogged ahead of her, carrying Iesada in his golden palanquin. He'd spent the night in the Little Sitting Room.

As Atsu and her ladies arrived at the Visitors' Audience Chambers they came face to face with Lady Honju-in and her retinue. The dowager greeted Atsu with a smile and a bow, carefully modulated to convey smug superiority and the knowledge of victory.

If Ikushima had secretly tried to get rid of the old woman she certainly hadn't succeeded. Lady Honju-in was healthier than ever. Her withered cheeks were flushed under her thick white make-up and her rheumy eyes sparkled.

As soon as she'd received Iesada's assent she'd wasted no time in informing the Council of State that he had named Lord Yoshitomi of Kii as his heir. Any further discussion was a waste of breath.

Ikushima had packed away her wardrobe of magnificent kimonos and left shortly afterwards with an army of staff and a train of trunks to go back to Miyako. Her job was done. She had no further role to play. Atsu felt oddly naked without her. She was used to having Ikushima around every day, interceding for her, explaining things, making suggestions, nagging at her, writing messages in the ash, dragging her into the gardens to fill her in on the latest events in the great world outside the palace. Now she was free of her. But she was also alone.

She no longer saw Saigo either, working in the gardens, reminding her she had a mission to carry out. She'd done her best, her very best, and for a moment she'd thought she'd succeed. But Lady Honju-in with her threats of suicide had trumped her.

There'd been no further communication from Lord Nariakira and Atsu had no idea how she would receive his messages now. She really was entirely on her own. All that was left was her husband. Now her job was to concentrate on being the Midai – running the palace, carrying out her daily duties and rituals, taking care of him.

There were cushions laid out for Atsu and the Dowager Mother on the low stage at the head of the vast room. They took their places on each side of the shogun with a page kneeling and holding his swords. Daylight filtered through the paper screens that formed the walls and candles on tall candlesticks burned with huge yellow flames in the dark corners of the room. Gold leaf glimmered on the walls and coffered ceiling and the great painted pine tree curved in a majestic canopy behind them.

Atsu had barely had a chance to take a breath and smooth her skirts when the court officials began to file in, smelling of sweat and pomade. The shoulders of their sleeveless mantles jutted like wings, their pleated hakama trousers crackled with starch. Atsu was pleased to see Governor Inoué's familiar weathered face among them. She guessed he had travelled up from Shimoda with the American envoy.

Grunting and puffing, Regent Ii settled himself on his knees facing the shogun, his heavy brow furrowed. He raised a stubby finger and an attendant ran over and lit a pipe for him. He was a big man with a jowly bulldog face and a red-veined nose that suggested he enjoyed his saké. He'd taken power a couple of months ago, after Lord Hotta was ousted following his ill-fated visit to the emperor in Miyako. He was several rungs higher and a lot more powerful than Lord Hotta had been – not merely Prime Minister and head of the Council of State but with the rank of Regent, second only to the shogun. Atsu had met him several times already. He was well aware of the influence she and Lady Honju-in had over the shogun and was eager to find favour with them.

The room fell silent. Governor Inoué was on his knees beside Regent Ii, looking rather uncomfortable in his starchy robes. He coughed, bowed deeply and shuffled forward on his knees, holding a box wrapped in silk high in the air. His large seaman's hands were trembling. He laid the package on the low table in front of the shogun, unfolded the four corners of the wrapping cloth and slid out a thin book, beautifully bound. The treaty.

Atsu closed her eyes and opened them again. She hardly dared look. Here it was, this treaty that the American barbarian had sailed halfway around the world to present to them and travelled all the way to Edo to negotiate, the treaty that would bind their nations together, set in stone their relationship for generations to come. Here was this treaty that Lord Hotta and he had wrangled over for so long, that had cost Lord Hotta his job and that threatened to ignite civil war in their country – here it was in writing.

The fourteen clauses were beautifully brushed on finest mulberry paper by one of the greatest calligraphers of the age. Atsu ran her eyes across them: seven ports to be opened to American ships, American barbarians to settle and trade there, paying the bare minimum of customs dues, and to be tried by a court of their own countrymen if they committed a crime; and an American envoy installed in Edo, like a canker at the heart of an apple.

She gave a superstitious shudder. She saw anarchy ahead, the blasted wilderness Iesada had foreseen, barbarians swarming across their land, destroying their ancient culture. Once the document was sealed and signed, it would be irreversible. They would be committed to giving the barbarians all the concessions listed. She reminded herself that in exchange their country would open its gates wide to the outside world and to trade. She had to cling on to the belief that it was for the best, that their country would benefit as a result.

Regent Ii had taken the decision that Lord Hotta had dared not make – to have the treaty signed without the emperor's consent. The lords who opposed it would go mad with fury; there would be an uprising, maybe civil war. But they had to sign. There was no choice. No one could forget the British fleet surging across the water towards them, having reduced China to a place of ruins haunted by opium-addled ghosts.

Her hand shaking, Atsu turned to the page where the shogun was to put his seal. Elder Anekoji poured a few drops of water on the ink stone, took a stick of red safflower paste and began to rub. The paste gave off a faint whiff of fragrance.

The shogun stared around, his eyes huge. He was avoiding looking at the open book.

He reached deep into his capacious sleeve. Atsu thought he was reaching for his ivory snail but instead he pulled out a handkerchief. He unfolded it and brought out a couple of amulets, some dice and a small top. He looked around for a smooth surface then put the top on the low table next to the treaty and gave a twist. It spun in a blur of colour.

The court nobles watched open-mouthed in astonishment. Regent Ii was well aware of Iesada's idiosyncrasies. But Atsu doubted if news of his peculiar nature had travelled beyond the closest circle of courtiers. It would have been the gravest treason, punishable by death, even to think of spreading rumours about the shogun. Most of the court officials, and Governor Inoué too, had only ever seen Iesada sitting on his throne like a statue, receiving homage, awe-inspiring and regal. All they knew was that he had power of life and death over them. They stared at him aghast, no doubt thinking he was playing some cruel game, laying a trap, expecting him to bark a command that no one could fulfil then punish them for their disobedience.

She doubted if they had any idea what a gentle sensitive person lurked inside the huge starched robes.

Iesada followed the top with his eyes, moving his head as it spun. It keeled over and he started to hum quietly.

Atsu recognized the nursery rhyme: 'Momotaro-*san*, Momotaro-*san*. That millet dumpling on your hip, won't you give me one?'

She looked at him in horror. He was playing the fool. He knew he was going to have to sign the treaty in the end but he wanted to punish Regent Ii, drag out the agony for as long as he could.

He picked up the treaty, turned it upside down, then right side up, then upside down again and stared at it. Regent Ii and the court officials kept their eyes riveted on him, oblivious to protocol, terrified he might rip it up or put a taper to it. There was nothing they could do about it if he did. If anyone moved a muscle to try to stop him, guards would leap out from behind the screens and have their heads.

The shogun put the treaty down, still humming, 'Momotaro-*san*, Momotaro-*san*.' Then he picked up the dice and tossed them from hand to hand. He looked at Regent Ii and said in a loud, clear voice, 'Odds or evens, Uncle Ii?' There was a rustle of starch as the ranks of courtiers started in unison.

Atsu held her breath. He didn't usually speak to the Regent. He was afraid of him.

Regent Ii bared his tobacco-stained teeth in a sickly smile. His broad shaved pate was slick with sweat. He swabbed it with a hand-kerchief and took an audible breath.

'Now, now, Your Majesty. You know your uncle Inoué has to go down to the bay and get on a great big ship and sign this treaty with the barbarian,' he said in a wheedling tone as if speaking to a child. 'And he has to do it today!' The last words burst out in a ferocious bark.

Iesada bobbed his head up and down, then narrowed his eyes and gave Regent Ii a sly glance. 'Let us toss for it then, Uncle Ii,' he said. 'Let the gods decide. You win, I put my seal to it. I win, I do not.'

A vein bulged on the Regent's forehead and a muscle ticked at the side of his eye. He jigged his knee up and down frantically and glowered at Atsu from under his spiky eyebrows. She could almost hear him thinking, 'Who taught the idiot shogun this low-class game? Only the lowest of the low are gamblers, not a man born to be ruler of our country.'

He clenched his fleshy fists till the knuckles were white. 'No time for games now, sire,' he hissed. 'I beg you, just put your seal on the treaty, will you?'

Iesada raised his eyebrows haughtily and looked down his nose at the corpulent Regent. 'Odds or evens?' he piped.

Regent Ii's face swelled and turned purple. He looked as if he was about to explode. 'Odds,' he grunted through clenched teeth.

Iesada laughed shrilly. 'Odds you win and I sign. Evens I win and I do not,' he sang. He took the dice in his long white fingers, shook them, screwed up his face, shut his eyes, blew on his hands, mumbled a prayer and tossed. The dice rolled across the tatami.

Atsu tried to catch his eye, frowning. It was obvious to her he was play-acting. He was just pretending to be a simpleton to delay putting his seal on the document. She wondered if anyone else realized why he was so determined not to. She wished he could see that he was just as likely to doom himself if he carried on with this performance.

He leaned forward, studied the dice. 'A four, a three . . . and a six. One odd and two evens. That makes evens!' he shouted, bouncing up and down on his cushion in triumph. 'The gods have spoken. I do not have to put my seal to the treaty.'

Regent Ii had reached the end of his tether. 'No time for games, sire,' he bellowed.

'All right then. Let us toss again,' said Iesada. 'Best of three.'

'No,' Atsu said firmly. 'No more games, Masa-*kun*.'

Every head in the room turned towards her, then the courtiers quickly averted their gaze.

She looked at him pleadingly. 'Nothing will happen to you if you put your seal on the treaty. Please. Just put it here.'

'Don't humour him,' Lady Honju-in shrieked. 'He's doing it on purpose.' She leaned over and rapped his arm hard with her fan and he started and shrank back. 'Masa-*kun*, this just won't do. Don't be stupid. You know how important it is.'

Iesada stuck out his lower lip and wobbled his head from side to side. 'I cannot,' he said. 'The gods have spoken. He lost. You cannot make me, Mama.'

The courtiers knelt immobile, their faces pale, their eyes fixed on the tatami. They were terrified. They had no idea what was going on or what they could do about it.

'I am the shogun,' Iesada shouted. 'None of you can make me. I shall do as I please.'

The shadows moved across the rows of courtiers. The day was getting hotter. The women took out their fans and began to wave them briskly. Sweat prickled the back of Atsu's neck and ran down under her arms. She knew there were palanquins lined up at the Great Gate ready to rush Governor Inoué and Councillor Iwasé to Kanagawa Bay, where the envoy was waiting on the American ship to sign the treaty. For better or for worse they had to get this done.

Iesada had taken out his ivory snail and was tossing it in the air and catching it. She was sure he was playing the fool. He knew perfectly well what he was doing. Whether he liked it or not, he had to set his seal to the treaty. Someone had to persuade him.

She caught his eye. 'You are right, Masa-*kun*,' she said.

'Save your breath, daughter dear,' snapped Lady Honju-in. 'If he won't listen to his mother or the Regent, there's not much chance he'll listen to you.'

The old woman was about to launch into a tirade.

Atsu raised her hand to stem the flow. She held Iesada's eyes with hers. 'You are quite right,' she said quietly. 'We all know you are the shogun. You are the barbarian-quelling generalissimo, you are he who may not be named, you are the most powerful man in our land and the most important. You are our ruler. We are all devoted to you. We worship and respect you. I am proud of you, proud to be your wife. But now you have to rule in earnest. You must do what the shogun has to do. I know you do not want to put your seal to this treaty and I understand why. But you cannot think just of yourself. You are not just one person. You are greater than that. You are the country, our whole country. You are all of us.'

Iesada gazed at her, his face solemn.

'You saw the barbarians when they came to the castle. You do not want them to come here with their battleships, attack our country and plunge us into war, do you?'

He grimaced, shook his head.

'Then you must put your seal to this treaty. It is the only way we can stop them, the only way we can save ourselves. It is for the best for all of us and the best for you too. This is the most important treaty we have ever made with the barbarian nations. Once it is sealed and signed there will be many more. Our lives will change completely. And it will be your seal on this historic document.

'You know I have always taken care of you and I always will. I give you my promise. Nothing will happen to you if you put your seal to the treaty.'

As she said the words, she caught a glimpse of Regent Ii's small hard eyes glittering in his fleshy cheeks and felt a tremor. She was not sure she could keep this promise. She didn't have the power.

Iesada had turned pale. He straightened his back and nodded. 'I understand. Elder Anekoji, bring me the ink.'

He untied his seal box from his obi, took out the large marble shogunal seal and pressed it on to the ink block. His hand was shaking.

Atsu pointed to the place on the treaty where he was to put his mark. He put the seal on the treaty and pressed it down, rocking it to make an even imprint. His face was solemn. He lifted it up, sat back on his heels and looked straight past Governor Inoué to where Regent Ii squatted like a huge toad.

Iesada narrowed his eyes. She could read his mind. As far as the shogun was concerned, he'd signed his own death warrant.

Elder Anekoji blew on the ink, dusted it with sand and shook it off. Then Governor Inoué closed the book, slid it into its box and folded and knotted the silk wrapper. Holding the precious package aloft in both hands he shuffled backwards out of the room, followed by Councillor Iwasé. They both bowed at the door. Atsu heard them breaking into a trot the moment they were out of sight.

One by one, in order of precedence, Regent Ii and the court officials backed out, until only the shogun and his women were left in the vast chamber with its high coffered ceilings and gold-encrusted walls painted with pine trees.

Iesada looked at Atsu. 'I did it. I did what you wanted.' A chill ran through her.

He was not smiling. He turned away and started playing for all he was worth, spinning his top, throwing his dice, singing and bobbing his head like a child trying to wish away bad luck.

'I did what you wanted.' She knew she would never forget those words. She could only hope and pray that nothing bad happened to him now.

47

A couple of days later the weather was particularly fine. The heat had eased a little. That afternoon Elder Anekoji organized a tea ceremony on the deck beside the lake in the shade of the huge red parasols, to be followed by a boat trip. The shogun had always loved floating along the streams and through the lakes and ponds strung like a necklace around the grounds.

Richly robed boatswomen punted the craft over and lined them up along the edge of the lake. Servants lifted Iesada into the shogunal barge, settled him on cushions and arranged his robes. The barge was palatial. The railings were edged with burnished gold and there was a stack of multi-tiered tables in the middle with a teapot of chilled barley tea, matching cups and bowls of snacks. A tasselled red-silk awning stretched over all.

Atsu picked up her skirts and stepped in after him, followed by some of her favourite ladies. A few entertainers came along to tell stories, play music and sing. Lady Honju-in and the others followed in a flotilla of barges and gondolas.

There was a gorgeously liveried dwarf in the prow wielding an oar and a gaily clad boatswoman at the stern with a pole to punt them along. They glided beneath willow trees, under a half-moon bridge, around little islands dotted with stone lanterns and grotesquely shaped rocks and past teahouses and moon-viewing pavilions. Water splashed and rippled against the sides of the barge as the entertainers strummed their shamisens and warbled ditties

about the heat and lethargy of summer. The shogun joined in in his
soft baritone, a fraction out of tune.

Atsu finally felt at peace. Everything was over, there was nothing
more she had to do. The fate of the country was no longer in her
hands. The world had moved on. For better or worse the decisions
had been made – to choose Yoshitomi as Iesada's successor, to sign
the treaty. Now all they could do was wait and see what the consequences would be, what the gods had in store for them.

Her main task now was to protect her husband and keep him
happy. She was perfectly content to live out the rest of her days as
the Midai, His Majesty's consort. She asked for nothing more.

The shogun trailed his pale fingers in the water, gazing down
dreamily at the pebbles that lined the bed of the lake. Carp darted
in the shallows, their fat round backs sparkling orange and gold in
the sunlight. He clapped his hands and fish surged over and crowded
around the barge, jostling and shoving. Middle Elder Omasé
crumbled a rice cracker and he tossed the crumbs on to the water,
laughing as the carp opened their big mouths and scooped them up.
The little tortoiseshell cat, Jewel, dozed on his lap.

That evening Atsu and Iesada sat side by side on the veranda of
the Little Sitting Room, watching fireflies flitting around the
gardens, lacing the bushes with trails of light. Cicadas shrilled and
owls hooted. Later he challenged her to a game of Go. Atsu put up
a good fight but finally, with many despairing groans, conceded
defeat. Iesada clapped his hands and shouted with triumphant
laughter.

Next morning the shogun had gone back to the men's palace and
Atsu's ladies were preparing her for the first audience of the day
when an usher rushed in, pale and trembling. The audience had
been cancelled. The shogun had been having his daily check-up with
his doctor when he'd complained of chest pains and collapsed.

Atsu stared out at the gardens, her heart pounding. It was nothing serious, she told herself, just a summer cold or something he'd
eaten. He was often ill, he'd be better in no time. But she felt a
dreadful gnawing fear. His father had died just fifteen days after the
barbarians first arrived and Iesada had been sure something terrible

would happen if he too bowed to the barbarians and set his seal to their treaty. And she had made him do it. He'd signed because she had told him to. She scolded herself, told herself not to be superstitious. But she couldn't make the fear go away. She wished the fifteen days were over so she could be sure he would be all right.

The following day the audiences were cancelled again and the day after that too. Several days later the elders in the men's palace issued a bulletin.

Atsu called Middle Elder Omasé to read it to her. She was afraid to read it herself.

After the initial chest pains, it seemed, the shogun had complained of a sore throat and stomach discomfort. Then his legs and groin had swollen up and he'd been unable to pass water. He'd complained endlessly of thirst and started vomiting. The doctors had diagnosed dropsy or some sort of rheumatic illness and prescribed boiled sarsaparilla root. A bevy of specialists in both western and Chinese remedies had been summoned and messengers had been sent galloping post haste to Miyako to beg the soothsayers and astrologers to intercede with the gods.

Atsu listened, stricken with horror, unable to control her tears.

She was desperate to see Iesada. She was sure he must be calling for her. Omasé sent an urgent request to the elders of the men's palace asking permission for the Lady Midai to visit the shogun's apartments. The request was refused. Even the Midai couldn't breach protocol to that extent. The Dowager Mother too, it seemed, hadn't been allowed to see her son.

A pall hung over the palace. The ladies huddled in corners, speaking in hushed tones. None of them dared voice their fear that the shogun was not going to recover. But for Atsu the agony was greater still. She couldn't help counting the days since he had signed the treaty.

She tossed and turned all night. In the daytime she paced her apartments, wringing her hands, running her fingers through her hair till it stuck out in a tangled bird's nest like a madwoman's. Then, late in the afternoon on the fourteenth day after the shogun had put his seal to the treaty, news came that the most painful symptoms had eased. He was dying. He wished to spend his last hours in the Little Sitting Room. He wanted to say goodbye to his mother and his wife.

Atsu couldn't wait for anyone to escort her. She couldn't wait a single moment. The walls closed in around her, the corridors stretched out endlessly before her as she lifted her skirts and ran, gasping convulsively. A couple of times she tripped and fell and scrambled to her feet and raced on. She passed the shrine room, choking on the thick clouds of incense smoke that poured out. A convocation of nuns was assembled there, mumbling prayers for the shogun's safe passage to the next world. She passed the Great Hall, crossed the walkway where she had looked down into the gardens and first seen the shogun. It seemed a lifetime ago now.

By the time she reached the Upper Bell Corridor she was out of breath. The ball of bells jangled with a tinny sound, the ushers removed the padlock and the double doors slid open. Instead of the imposing figure of the shogun waiting to advance into the women's palace, a golden palanquin filled the doorway. The male bearers lowered it gently to the ground. Then women bearers picked it up and carried it into the Little Sitting Room where attendants lifted Iesada out.

Atsu gasped. Her husband was a bundle of skin and bones wrapped in futons, as insubstantial as a ghost. She hardly recognized him.

Her eyes swimming with tears, she stumbled into the lavish room with its gold-bedecked walls and ceiling painted with flowers. She knew it so well. All the memories came flooding back, the many nights they'd spent here together, so intimate, so tender, so close.

The attendants laid the shogun on his lavish futons, richly embroidered with tortoises and cranes, symbols of long life. They seemed dreadfully ironic now. Even though it was the height of summer Iesada was shivering. They heaped futons over him. Ladies-in-waiting gathered anxiously at the side of the room, keening and wailing. Atsu gestured to them to go away.

She knelt beside him and took his hand, horrified at how cold it was. He was shrivelled and shrunken. His skin was waxen, his eyes

huge in his wasted face, his hands so thin and the skin so transparent the blue veins stood out like ropes. His hair was spread
around him loosely on the pillows. He was hardly breathing. His
expression was peaceful, as if he was already at the gates of Amida
Buddha's Western Paradise. A couple of monks knelt at the side of
the room, telling their beads, reciting sutras, ready to conduct him
on the last steps of his journey.

Jewel slunk in and curled up beside him. Atsu laid the sick man's
hand on the little cat's back, hoping the feel of the warm fur would
comfort him. She wished she could think of a way to keep him with
her for ever, stop him slipping away to the Western Paradise. She
swallowed, trying to hold back her tears. She wanted to gain his
attention, make him stay with her a little longer. She started to talk,
keeping her voice calm and soothing.

'Do you remember the song I sang that time we played float the saké
cup down the river? You always liked it.' She sang a few bars softly.
'And that time we saw the harvest moon bigger and rounder than it has
ever been, and those times we went boating and wrote poems and sang
and the stories I told you? Do you remember I used to tell you about
Kyushu, where I come from – the hot black sands and the volcano
shooting sparks and ash into the sky? I wish I could take you there.
And that time we discovered a secret place in the grounds where no
one would find us?' There were so many happy times to recall.

He stirred and opened his eyes. She smiled at him. He was listening, his eyes far away.

'It was in the spring,' she said softly. 'When the cherry blossom
was out.'

'Cherry blossom,' he murmured, smiling faintly. 'I shall fall like
cherry blossom.'

'No, you will not,' she said fervently. He'd been shivering but now
he was bathed in sweat. She called for iced towels and laid them on
his forehead.

There was a flurry of silks and an overpowering smell of perfume
as Lady Honju-in hobbled in, panting and wheezing. Her withered
face was swollen, her eyes red with crying.

Atsu felt a tightening in her jaw as she saw the old woman. She was Masa-*kun*'s mother and Atsu knew he would want to see her. She knew how much she adored her son and she sympathized with her grief. But she couldn't forget how the Dowager Mother had manipulated Iesada to get what she wanted – a child shogun. Now she'd won her victory, she'd become nauseatingly sycophantic. Atsu had far preferred it when her hostility was on open display.

The old woman squeezed in beside Atsu at Iesada's pillow. 'My boy, my Masa, you're so thin, so pale,' she blubbered. 'Don't leave me. Don't leave your old mama. What will I do without you?' She clasped him to her bony bosom and rocked him, wailing, holding him so tightly that Atsu was afraid she would smother him.

As gently as she could, Atsu loosened Lady Honju-in's grip and laid Iesada back on his pillows.

'It's better not to agitate the patient, my lady,' said a man's voice.

Atsu swung round, startled. These were not the familiar tones of Doctor Taki, Iesada's official doctor. A tall man with a shiny forehead and protruding teeth and hakama trousers that smelt of starch had crept in and was kneeling behind her. He introduced himself as Doctor Moriyama.

'But where is Doctor Taki?' Atsu blurted.

The man raised his thin eyebrows. 'Doctor Taki,' he said with a curl of his fleshy lip, 'has been removed.'

'Removed?' Atsu stared at him, shocked. Big, bluff, dependable Doctor Taki had always been around. Iesada loved him.

'It was decided at the highest level that he should be replaced. Your humble servant is better qualified to deal with His Majesty's indisposition. I've made my diagnosis and applied the necessary remedies. I've made dietary adjustments, I've administered steam vapour canopies. I've used every appropriate western and Chinese treatment, but sadly His Majesty's condition is such that we could never guarantee a positive prognosis.'

Atsu listened in horror. Suspicions flooded her mind. She was desperate to know what had happened to Iesada, what had precipitated his illness, whether they were sure of the diagnosis and above all what Doctor Taki had done to bring about his removal.

'But when . . . ?' she began. 'Why . . . ?' But there was no time now to protest or ask questions. She turned away. She had no faith in this man.

Iesada's hand moved in hers. She put her ear to his mouth. 'I hope Amida Buddha will have a place for me,' he breathed. 'I have not done so many bad things.'

'You have not done anything bad,' Atsu said firmly. 'Amida Buddha will be waiting for you when your time comes, I am sure of it. But that is a long way off. Stay here with me. I need you to look after me. You cannot leave me here all alone.'

She could hear his breath rumbling in his chest. He looked up at her and opened and closed his mouth.

'There is no need to talk,' Atsu said.

'There is,' he said painfully, gasping for breath. 'You have been my good and dear consort,' he whispered. 'You changed my life. Everyone else lies to me. They say what they think I want to hear. You tell me the truth. You have given my life meaning.'

'You have accomplished so much,' Atsu said in a whisper. 'This has been the most momentous and dangerous time in our country's entire history. We have never before faced such a threat, greater than anything we could ever have imagined. We are struggling still to find a way through. But we will. And you presided over it all. This new era of contact with the barbarian nations began in your reign. You granted the barbarians an audience, you met them face to face, you spoke to them, you signed the treaty making peace with them. I am so proud of you, so proud to be your wife, to be at your side. You are a great shogun. You will never be forgotten.'

'Everything I have achieved has been due to you. You made me a better shogun,' he breathed, his voice a thin whisper. 'You care about me, not because I am the shogun like all those others, but for myself. I can die in peace now. I know you will take care of everything.'

'You are not going to die,' she said, pressing her sleeve to her eyes. She didn't want to break down in tears in front of him.

'You will be here. You will pray for me, you will take care of my spirit,' he said. 'Our country faces many dangers. You must take care of Yoshi-*kun*. He has heavy responsibilities to bear. He is only twelve. You must help him. You must care for him as you have me. He is my son now. You must be a mother to him.'

A boy was standing in the doorway. He was plainly dressed in black robes and so young that he still wore his hair like a girl, with the forelock unshaved. He held himself with dignity. He had a lively curious face. With him was a woman wearing the robes of a daimyo's wife, attended by a bevy of ladies-in-waiting.

The boy knelt beside the shogun's pillow. 'It is me, Uncle Masa,' he said.

Iesada reached out feebly and laid a thin hand on the boy's cheek. 'Yoshi-*kun*. My son,' he whispered. 'You are my successor. You will be Iemochi, the fourteenth Tokugawa shogun.' The last words trailed away.

No matter what had gone before, Atsu couldn't doubt what Iesada wanted now. She took a deep breath.

'I vow I will respect your wishes,' she said. 'Everything you have asked me to do I will carry out.'

As they knelt she wondered silently what would happen to them all when this grave child was shogun, how he would deal with the ever-growing crisis, with the encroaching barbarians and the looming civil war.

Suddenly the shogun opened his eyes and struggled to sit up. He was staring towards the far corner of the room. He shrank back, his lips quivering. 'She is here,' he whispered. 'She has come to fetch me.'

'She is not here. There is no one here,' Atsu said firmly.

'I see you with your eyes flashing fire,' he breathed. 'See how her black hair is piling up on the floor. You can pull your hair out all you like but you will not frighten me, Hideko. All those years you resented me because I was alive and you were dead. Now you have your revenge.' He sank back on to his bedding and let out a long sigh.

'Hold me. I am cold,' he whispered to Atsu. 'Stay with me. Do not leave me.' He closed his eyes.

Lady Honju-in was on her knees a little way away. She pushed in next to Atsu. 'Dear daughter, you must be tired,' she said. 'Go back to your rooms and have a rest. I'll stay with him. He'll be glad to see his old mother if he wakes up.'

'I shall stay,' said Atsu, trying to smile. 'This is our bedchamber. We have spent so many happy nights together here.' She dismissed the ladies and lay down beside him and wrapped him in her arms, trying to warm him with her body. Only the monks were left, telling their beads, mumbling sutras. She was glad they were there to dispel the malevolent spirits. Darkness filled the room. The lone candle sputtered, incense smoke spiralled.

For a long time she lay there. The night went by and the day began to dawn, the fifteenth day since Iesada had signed the treaty. She felt him breathing, felt him warm still. Then, at the moment when night turns to day, when ghosts are abroad, he gave a little sigh.

She drew in her breath. 'Masa-*kun*?' she whispered. She laid her cheek next to his cold lips and knew that he was gone.

For a long time she held him still, this bundle of skin and bones, talking to him, trying to keep him warm. Then as the realization began to strike home she gave a thin dry wail. 'Masa-*kun*!'

The small ivory snail had rolled on to the floor beside the futon. She snatched it up and tucked it in her sleeve. She would keep it for ever, this little piece of him.

And finally tears came. She bent over his body, doubled up with grief. Everything that had made her life worth living, everything she cared for was gone.

Hours passed, she had no idea how many. Then finally she rose to her feet and stumbled back to her rooms, barely aware of the women holding her arms, supporting her on each side. She only knew there was one thing she had to do.

She went over to the lacquered cage where the little gold and black yamagara bird with its bright blue legs was singing in its small tinny voice and opened the door.

Middle Elder Omasé rushed towards her.

'Madam, stop. What are you doing?' she asked in consternation.

Atsu paid no attention. 'Go, little bird,' she said. 'Go and join him. Go and keep him company.'

For a moment the little bird hesitated at the door of the cage, then it hopped out and circled the room. It flitted between the screens in a flash of black and gold. Then it flew across the veranda and out into the trees and was gone.

48

'I can't believe she doesn't know.'

The querulous tones were unmistakable. Atsu smelt musty perfume, heard the rustle of heavy silk in the vestibule. It was the second time Lady Honju-in had come to visit her. The last time she had stormed in it had been to try to forestall Atsu's attempt to win over Iesada. She wondered what the old harridan had in store for her this time. She took a deep breath, bracing herself to face this unwelcome guest.

She whisked her fan. The air was so hot and dank it was hard to move. The white chrysanthemums Middle Elder Omasé had placed in a vase in the alcove were wilting.

'Know what, my lady?' It was Omasé at her most long-suffering. She was trying to keep the old woman at bay.

'Poisoned, Omasé, poisoned. My son was poisoned!'

Atsu sat bolt upright. 'Poisoned?' she gasped, her heart pounding.

Ever since Iesada had become ill there had been only one thought searing her mind. She couldn't stop thinking about it. It was so obvious she couldn't imagine why everyone didn't see it.

He had been perfectly healthy, far stronger and fitter than when she had first met him. Suddenly to become ill, when no one else had – and then to die. She couldn't believe for one moment it was natural. The timing had been too cruelly precise. He'd died exactly fifteen days after bowing to the will of the barbarians, just as his father had before him, just as he had foreseen.

Doctor Moriyama had diagnosed dropsy or rheumatic fever. Atsu had no faith in him at all. But the only man she could ask, the only man she trusted, Doctor Taki, had disappeared. She was sure Regent Ii was behind it all. She wondered what Lady Honju-in had come to tell her, if she knew who the guilty party was. If it really had been poison someone would have to be punished. The shogun had been a king, a god. It was a crime against heaven.

Four days had passed since Iesada died. It had been at the hour of the hare, at dawn on the sixth day of the seventh month in the fifth year of Ansei. Tanabata, the great summer festival celebrated on the seventh day, had come and gone. Atsu and her ladies had been so crushed with shock and grief and horror they'd paid no attention to the date.

The women drifted about the palace in their swirling white mourning robes like an army of ghosts. Atsu's ladies-in-waiting wandered aimlessly or knelt with their sleeves to their eyes, sobbing. Atsu's gentle husband had been only thirty-five, far too young to die. She was touched by how much they'd all loved him.

Atsu had attended the cremation, carried out all the necessary observances, then retired to her rooms stupefied with grief. She hardly noticed day turning to night and back again to day. Middle Elder Omasé tended to her, brought her food, insisted she take a bath, asked her solicitously if there was anything she needed. She knew she would soon have to pull herself together, attend the funeral when Iesada would be given his posthumous name and his ashes carried in state to Kaneiji Temple to be interred next to his ancestors. She was bracing herself for that.

Now Atsu stared at herself in the mirror. She looked thin and wan and pale. Her eyes were red and swollen, her cheeks sunken, her hair uncombed. She hardly recognized the face she saw there. She felt half starved. She'd barely been able to eat.

Middle Elder Omasé ran in to announce the Dowager Mother. 'Show her to the reception room,' she said. Her voice was hoarse. 'Serve tea. Send Chiyo and Yasu to help me dress, quickly.'

Atsu was in a fever of impatience as Chiyo oiled and combed and perfumed her floor-length hair, grumbling as she eased out the knots. Her ladies helped her into white silk mourning robes and tied a white wimple around her head. They'd barely finished adjusting her obi when she brushed them aside, picked up her skirts and ran after Middle Elder Omasé into the reception room.

Lady Honju-in was pacing up and down, her bony shoulders hunched. She was in the most elaborate mourning garb Atsu had ever seen, with a raised design of white chrysanthemums embroidered across the skirts. She looked thinner, more bent. She'd aged in the few days since Atsu saw her last. Her withered face peered from her starched white wimple, small and sallow, the colour of a rotten persimmon.

Her retinue of ancient ladies knelt behind her, flapping their fans.

'Beloved daughter,' the dowager said in mellifluous tones. Her starched robes rustled as she bowed.

Atsu knelt beside her and laid her hand on her bony arm. Perhaps the wrenching grief they both felt might bring them closer. Perhaps they could finally forget their differences. 'Dearest Mother,' she said. 'Such an unbearable loss for both of us. I am glad you have come so we can grieve together.'

Lady Honju-in shot her a suspicious glance. Her eyes burnt like coals in her parchment face. There was something odd in her manner. She had something to say. She could barely contain herself.

She shook off Atsu's hand. 'They knew it straight away,' she growled, her voice harsh. 'But they only now see fit to tell us. Just as I thought – my son, my Masa, he was poisoned.'

Atsu rocked back on her heels. To have her darkest suspicions brought out into the harsh light of day sent a shudder through her. She bowed her head, clapped her hands to her mouth.

'I suspected it too,' she said shakily. 'But who? Everyone loved him. Who could have committed such a terrible crime? The tasters checked his food with the utmost care. Surely it couldn't have been one of them?'

Lady Honju-in was staring at Atsu, her brow furrowed, her painted eyebrows quivering. 'I can't believe you're that naive,' she said. 'It was that doctor, of course, that Taki.' She pulled back her lips and bared her blackened teeth.

Atsu had guessed she was going to accuse poor Doctor Taki. Why else would he have been removed? She shook her head at the enormity of the injustice.

'You are wrong, Mother, quite wrong,' she cried. 'Doctor Taki was devoted to Masa-*kun*. He loved him like his own son. He delivered him, he was there when he was born. He has taken care of him ever since he was a baby. He is a wise, good man. He would never dream of such a thing.'

She leaned forward, looked hard at Lady Honju-in. 'Who makes this accusation?' she demanded.

The old woman's eyebrows rose even higher. 'Regent Ii called in Doctor Moriyama when Masa became worse. He's studied all the latest Dutch theories and methods. It was his expert conclusion that it was poison.'

'So why did he tell us it was dropsy or rheumatic fever?'

But Lady Honju-in wasn't listening. She burst into loud sobs. 'I should never have let that murderer Taki near my baby,' she howled, rocking back and forth, swabbing her eyes with her sleeves. 'What shall I do? My baby, my baby!'

Atsu couldn't help weeping too. She was close to tears nearly all the time now that Masa was gone.

Lady Honju-in sniffed loudly. She glared at Atsu, her pupils pinpoints of black in a sea of red. 'There's only one thing now,' she hissed. 'Revenge.'

'Calm yourself, Mother,' Atsu said, drying her eyes. 'Even if it was poison, what proof is there that it was Doctor Taki? What reason could he possibly have to do such a terrible thing?'

'Money, of course,' Lady Honju-in snorted. 'They gave him more than even the shogun's personal doctor could earn in a lifetime.'

Atsu shook her head. What the Dowager Mother was saying was simply wrong, the deluded ravings of a bereaved parent. 'Who made this accusation? What proof is there?'

Lady Honju-in straightened her back and threw Atsu a look of barely concealed triumph. 'You mean you don't know? They've arrested half the men's palace while you've been keeping out of the way, supposedly wallowing in sorrow. They've had them tortured. They've all confessed, every last one of them. That so-called doctor was in irons even before my Masa passed away. They chopped his head off in the prison yard like a common criminal.'

Atsu felt the blood drain from her face. She felt sick. 'Doctor Taki – executed?' she gasped. 'But . . . but on whose authorization? Who dare authorize such a thing? He did nothing!'

Lady Honju-in jutted out her chin. She loomed over Atsu, leering at her. 'They rounded them all up, all the conspirators, the whole lot, those criminals who put him up to it.'

Atsu's hands were trembling. Her tea cup clattered in its porcelain saucer. Shaking, she put it on the floor and bowed her head, trying to catch her breath, her heart thundering. 'But who?' she whispered. 'What conspirators? Who do they say were behind it?' She was afraid to hear the answer.

The air was stifling. In the gardens a cicada set off a shrill whine. The metallic sound drilled into her brain. Mosquitoes buzzed maddeningly. Servants crept about laying out bowls of smouldering chrysanthemum petals to drive them away.

Lady Honju-in pushed her face up to Atsu's. Atsu drew back from the glaring eyes and caked make-up pooling into balls.

'What are you trembling for? What do you have to be afraid of? Don't play the innocent with me, my girl,' the old woman snarled. To Atsu's shock she grabbed her by the shoulders with her claw-like hands and gave her a shove.

Taken by surprise, Atsu lost her balance and rolled over on to the floor.

Omasé rushed forward. Atsu waved her away. 'Leave her be,' she said, picking herself up and straightening her robes. 'She is upset.'

'Who do they say it was?' Lady Honju-in crowed shrilly. 'I'll tell you who. Your precious Keiki, that's who, and that father of his, the Dragon of Mito.' She screamed out each syllable. 'I knew they were evil, I knew they'd stop at nothing, but I never thought they would sink so low as to strike at our supreme ruler, at he who may not be named, the lord of the realm, at my poor frail son.' The last words came out as a sob.

Atsu wiped the old woman's spittle slowly from her face and drew herself up. She was angry too now.

'That makes no sense, Mother,' she said, trying to keep her voice calm. She could feel her heart thumping. 'They are princes of the blood, they are great nobles, they are Masa-*kun*'s cousins. They honoured and worshipped him. They would never do any such thing.'

Lady Honju-in drew back, her nostrils flaring, her eyes bulging like a demon mask. 'You were in on it too, you miserable interloper. You worm your way in here, fool us all with your pretty face and pretty ways. I should denounce you too.'

'You cannot mean that. You cannot say Masa-*kun*'s death was anything to do with me?' Atsu cried. She tossed her head. 'I refuse to put up with such vile imputations in my own apartments – in my own palace.'

'You're in it up to your neck. You ask why they'd do such a thing? To make Keiki shogun, that's why. He wanted to overthrow the government and take power himself, you know that perfectly well. And you were in on it. You were the linchpin, right here in the palace, working on the inside. With the help of the gods you failed. But not in time to save my Masa.'

49

A harsh caw rang out. Atsu started and looked round. Outside in the gardens the branches of a pine tree swayed as a great black crow spread its wings and flapped away.

'Who makes these dreadful accusations?' she asked, overcome with foreboding. It didn't take much to guess.

'Regent Ii, no less.'

Atsu groaned. She'd thought as much.

'Lord Keiki's father bribed Doctor Taki to poison Masa to have Keiki made shogun so he could hold sway over the whole country himself. The story's all over the city. Everyone's talking about it.'

Atsu groaned. The dowager's words confirmed her worst fears. She'd suspected all along that Regent Ii was pulling the strings. With every day that passed he was consolidating his power, making sure no one could topple him. Lady Honju-in was no fool. She would never have believed such an unlikely story were it not for the fact that she hated Lord Keiki and his father and welcomed anything that would discredit them. She was visibly crowing.

'That cannot be, Mother. Think about it. Do you not see? It would not have benefited Keiki in the slightest to have my husband murdered. It was too late. Masa-*kun* had already named Yoshi-*kun* as his successor. Regent Ii himself made the proclamation. He knows it is not true. I shall speak to him. He is a reasonable man.'

Atsu's voice faltered as she uttered the last words. Regent Ii was far from reasonable. He was a tyrant.

'Too late, my dear.' Lady Honju-in's smile sent a shiver down Atsu's spine. 'Regent Ii has had them arrested already.'

Atsu gasped. 'He cannot do that. They are princes of the blood. They are Masa-*kun*'s cousins.'

'Lord Keiki and his father were put under house arrest the day after Masa passed away.' The dowager shook her head, her face darkening inside her pristine white wimple. 'I knew Keiki was a bad one. I warned Masa again and again. Didn't I say he'd have him poisoned? And he did. If he and that father of his weren't of the blood, Regent Ii would have had their heads. They're under house arrest for life. They won't be causing any trouble ever again.'

The old ladies knelt like a row of mechanical dolls in their white mourning weeds. They whisked their fans and nodded.

The room seemed to close in around Atsu. She slumped back on her heels, reeling. She could hardly breathe. It was all falling into place with terrible clarity. Lord Keiki and his father were blood relations of the shogun. Regent Ii couldn't imprison them, let alone have them beheaded, no matter how much he might want to. The worst he could do was get them out of the way, put them under house arrest. And the only way to do that was to find them guilty of treason. That was why Masa-*kun* had had to be killed – so that the Regent could accuse Keiki and his father of bribing Doctor Taki to poison him.

Only one person had good reason to want Iesada out of the way: Regent Ii himself. Someone had to take the blame for defying the emperor's wishes, signing the barbarian treaty without the imperial consent – and the obvious person to sacrifice was the shogun. Added to which, Iesada had dared stand up to the Regent, made a fool of him in front of the Council of Ministers, an unforgivable slight.

Atsu put her head in her hands. With Keiki out of action, she couldn't imagine what would become of them. It was utterly terrifying – and there was nothing she could do to change it.

She saw now too late why it had been so crucial to get Lord Keiki installed as successor, why Lord Nariakira had been so insistent. It was only because there hadn't been a strong head of state that Lord Ii had managed to grab power and make himself Regent. They certainly had a strong leader now – but the wrong one. If only she'd succeeded in putting Keiki into a position of power, none of this would have happened. With Lord Hotta gone and Lord Keiki under house arrest, there was no one at all to restrain Regent Ii. He could do anything he liked.

So in a way Atsu herself had been responsible for Iesada's death. Her indecision had helped bring it about. If only she had tried to persuade Iesada sooner or managed to make Lady Honju-in see reason. If only she hadn't given up trying, fearing that once Iesada had chosen his successor, he might be killed himself.

Atsu drew a breath, raised her head. 'How do you know all this, Mother?' she asked weakly.

Lady Honju-in beamed in triumph. 'Regent Ii told me himself. He knew I'd be delighted that he's avenged Masa-*kun*'s death – and you should be too. He's arrested all the conspirators, you'll be glad to hear. He's forced the Lord of Echizen and the Lord of Owari into retirement and sent the lower-ranking lords into exile. He's having their retainers rounded up and thrown into jail and had the ring-leaders beheaded. He's making a clean sweep of it. There'll be no more talk of civil war now.'

Atsu could hardly breathe for horror. It was getting worse and worse. In one fell swoop Regent Ii had imprisoned the leaders of both parties – Keiki the reformer and his father, the most powerful of the conservative lords. It was a terrifyingly brilliant move. He'd clamped down on all those who offered a threat to his authority, rid himself of all his enemies with a single stroke. And it left him supreme.

'All those traitors who were plotting to install Keiki as my son's successor have been put out of action. Your Lord Nariakira and his friends are well and truly out of favour. It's a new era now.'

Lord Nariakira . . . Atsu's heart pounded. She felt sick with fear for him. He was too far away and too powerful for Regent Ii to have him put under house arrest too, she told herself. Even the brazen toad-like Regent wouldn't dare do such a thing. All the same she was full of foreboding. She wondered what Lord Nariakira was planning down there. He was certainly brewing up something. He wouldn't take this lying down. She wished she could be back in Kagoshima, discussing all this with him. She yearned for his fatherly wisdom.

The Dowager Mother shot Atsu a look of loathing. 'As for you, my girl, you are the kingpin of the entire plot. You were installed here for one reason only – to promote Keiki, to deceive my poor innocent son. You plotted to replace him, to have him killed if need be.'

'That is ridiculous, Mother,' Atsu said, her voice shaking with indignation. 'I would never have hurt Masa. You know how much I loved him.'

'You are a cold-hearted callous creature. You'd put your plots before anything. Like your beloved Lord Nariakira – he'd have had you killed, or Masa-*kun*, if he thought you stood in the way of his plans.'

Atsu buckled under the violence of her attack. It was true. She had had that very same suspicion herself. She had been afraid for Iesada, had wanted to protect him and herself too. That had been one reason why she had delayed so long before trying to bend his ear.

'You say you had nothing to do with it.' Nothing would stop the old woman. 'And there you were, cosying up to my poor Masa, trying to gain his confidence, when I warned him again and again that Keiki was out to poison him. Don't deny it. Elder Anekoji kept me informed of everything.'

Atsu groaned. She had always known Elder Anekoji was the serpent in the nest.

'And I was right. If only Regent Ii could reach his long arm inside this palace you'd be under arrest like the rest of your friends. If I were you I'd lie very low indeed for the rest of your life.'

Atsu shook her head. 'You are wrong, Mother,' she said miserably. 'Utterly wrong. I wish you could see it.'

The old lady bunched her fists, her eyes blazing. 'Wrong? You're the one who's wrong. You've been wrong ever since you came here. You've caused nothing but trouble.'

Without warning she threw herself at Atsu, sending her rolling back on the floor. Then she was on top of her. Atsu crashed on to her back, suffocating under swathes of silk and dusty face powder. The old woman's breath was on her face, her stale perfume in her nostrils. The Dowager Mother was old and frail but her hatred gave her strength. Atsu tried to push her off but she jammed a sharp knee into Atsu's stomach and locked her bony fingers around her throat, squeezing tighter and tighter.

With uncanny precision the dowager knew exactly where to put her fingers. Atsu gasped for breath. She was aware of nothing but the scrawny body on top of her and the hands like pincers around her throat. Choking, she scrabbled at the bony fingers, trying to prise them off. She felt consciousness slipping away, the world growing dark, her body limp. She struggled feebly.

Atsu's ladies hesitated. To lay hands on the Dowager Mother was a capital offence.

Then Middle Elder Omasé had Lady Honju-in by the collar. She wrenched her fingers apart, lifted her like a bundle of rags and tossed her sprawling on to her back, arms and legs flailing like a tortoise. The old woman's robes came undone, her obi flew loose. Her pristine white wimple and glossy black wig tumbled off, revealing a small egg-like head scattered with grey hairs bound in a net.

The dowager's retinue scuttled around her with surprising speed, setting her upright, fitting her wig and wimple back on, pulling her skirts into place, tying her obi. She settled on her knees and glowered at Atsu, panting.

Atsu took a convulsive breath. She was shaking. Her ladies helped her up and tidied her skirts. She put her hands gingerly to her throat, stifled an urge to sob.

Middle Elder Omasé loomed over Lady Honju-in. 'It's time you left, my lady,' she shouted. Her good-natured face was contorted with fury.

Lady Honju-in picked up her fan, tossed her shoulders and rose to her feet.

'No, wait, Mother,' Atsu said. She was panting, trying to catch her breath. 'Listen to me. It was Regent Ii who signed the treaty with the barbarians in defiance of the emperor's wishes. That was not what you wanted, was it? He is welcoming the barbarians with open arms. You want them expelled. Do you not see? He has double-crossed us, my lady. The only reason we women have power is because we can intercede with the shogun. Now there is no shogun there is no need for anyone to approve Regent Ii's bills. He can do anything he wants. He is taking over the government, taking over the whole country, doing whatever he wants without consulting anyone, least of all us. He is draining away our power, Mother, making us irrelevant.'

The Dowager Mother stared at her, stony-faced. Atsu groaned. The old woman was completely obsessed with Keiki and his father. All she could think of was her hatred of them. She'd wanted so badly to see them humiliated and now they had been. She was too short-sighted to care about the terrible consequences of letting Regent Ii grab power.

Atsu started. She had suddenly remembered some extraordinary news Omasé had told her just after Masa-*kun* died. Atsu had been so caught up in grief she'd hardly even heard her. But now she realized that it proved Regent Ii's duplicity beyond a shadow of a doubt.

'Have you not heard, Mother?' she asked.

'Heard what?' Lady Honju-in snapped.

'Middle Elder Omasé, tell us that news you heard, that news I refused to believe. Tell Her Ladyship, tell us all.'

Omasé dropped to her knees, her face grim. 'My lady,' she said, addressing Lady Honju-in. 'My lady, the British came.'

Lady Honju-in's mouth fell open. 'The British?' The colour drained from her ancient face.

In the reception room there was utter silence, not even the tinkle of a tea cup against a saucer. Footsteps pattered in the neighbouring rooms. Maids tiptoed in with fresh tea but Omasé waved them away. A look of horror hollowed her motherly face. She pressed her lips together as if she was afraid to say more.

'Go on, Omasé,' Atsu said.

'The British envoy. It was two days before His Majesty passed away. We were all so caught up in His Majesty's illness, no one even informed us at first.'

Atsu held her breath, glanced at Lady Honju-in.

'The British? With . . . With fifty ships?' the dowager stuttered.

'I think we would have heard of a fleet of fifty ships sailing into Edo Bay,' Atsu said gently, 'no matter how deep in mourning we were.'

'With one ship,' said Omasé.

'One ship.' There was a long silence.

Atsu gazed at Lady Honju-in. 'But you knew about this, Mother,' she said. 'Your friend Regent Ii must have told you.'

Of course she hadn't heard. Regent Ii had told Lady Honju-in what it suited his purposes to tell her, no more. With the shogun dead, both Atsu and the dowager were sidelined, both had lost their means of communication. Atsu still had Omasé to keep her informed. Lady Honju-in was even more in the dark than Atsu was.

The dowager had fallen heavily to her knees. Her lips quivered, her brow creased, her eyes bulged out of a sea of wrinkles. Her face seemed to be crumbling before Atsu's eyes. She was struggling to maintain her composure. Despite everything, Atsu felt sorry for her.

'Do you not see, Mother? The barbarian lied,' Atsu said, 'to force us into signing his treaty. He made fools of us. Tell Her Ladyship the rest, Omasé.'

'Regent Ii is signing treaties with everyone, my lady. The Dutch, the Russians, the British, the whole world is here, waiting to sign. He's signing the Dutch treaty today. Shiploads of barbarians are already arriving. Regent Ii is finishing off the new town Lord Hotta had planned for them along the coast near Kanagawa. There's a fishing village there called Yokohama. Bevies of carpenters are turning it into a barbarian town.'

Atsu shook her head. 'So you see, all our efforts were wasted,' she said. 'After all the discussion, all the to-ing and fro-ing, Regent Ii is riding roughshod over us all. If Lord Keiki had been Regent he too might well have made treaties with the barbarian countries – but not treaties that would turn us into second-class citizens in our own land.'

Atsu felt a great lassitude creep over her. She sat back on her heels. She was exhausted. She had won, she had defeated Lady Honju-in, but it was a hollow victory. She couldn't take any pleasure in it. With Keiki locked away under house arrest, many of his allies forced into retirement, their retainers jailed or executed, above all with Iesada gone, there was nothing to celebrate. They had all lost. That great desolation he predicted had come to pass. It didn't matter what either of them thought any more. They were sidelined, irrelevant, their country taken over by ruffians and barbarians.

She shook her head. 'And you know cholera has broken out now?'

'The barbarians brought it,' whispered one of Atsu's ladies. It was Yasu, the make-up attendant whom Atsu had rescued when she was trapped in the Satsuma mansion after the earthquake. She was as slight and pretty and shy as she had been then. In her mourning weeds she looked absurdly young and innocent. She cleared her throat. 'My parents wrote and told me so. It started in Nagasaki. The barbarians brought it from China on their ships. And now it's sweeping the country, killing everyone.

'You feel ill, then you start vomiting.' Yasu twisted her small hands, her face pale. 'Your skin turns blue and your eyes go dark and sunken and your hands and feet turn freezing cold. You die in a few days. It's reached Edo already. There are people falling ill in the townsmen's district.'

All this time they'd been insulated from the great world of death and disaster outside and suddenly it had come roaring in among them.

Atsu sighed. 'Perhaps that was what killed Lord Iesada,' she murmured almost to herself.

'It was too soon,' said Omasé. 'The disease hadn't reached Edo then. Besides, no one else in the palace died, only His Majesty.

'We should take precautions,' she added. 'We're a long way from town but with merchants congregating at the gates you can never be sure. They say it's carried in the water. There are notices being posted. We should avoid watery fruits – cucumbers, melons, plums, peaches, apricots – and extremes of heat and cold. The doctors are prescribing quinine and opium.'

'This disease, this cholera, reached Edo the very day His Majesty passed away,' Yasu whispered. 'Perhaps it was an omen.'

Lady Honju-in's face had turned a sickly shade of putty. 'It's the wrath of heaven,' she intoned in the voice of an oracle. 'The gods are punishing us for killing our ruler.'

Atsu shuddered. If it really was the wrath of the gods, it was more likely to be for letting barbarians trample their sacred land, defying the emperor, leading their country into chaos.

She pictured the gentle, thoughtful shogun. Tears filled her eyes and she bowed her head and turned away. No amount of anger or recrimination would bring him back. She knew that much. She wished she was in the Little Sitting Room, on the veranda, with his warm body leaning against hers and his head resting on her shoulder, gazing out at the fireflies and the stars. How innocent those days had been, how happy. His death had unleashed such horrors. If only he'd been here they could have faced them together.

She heaved a sigh. What was done was done. Nothing they could do would bring him back. But at least they'd seen the worst of it. Even Regent Ii couldn't do any worse.

50

Tensho-in

Atsu wept as Omasé cut her beautiful floor-length hair, trimming it off at the ear into the severe bob of a nun. The tresses fell to the floor till she was kneeling in a sea of her own hair. She felt like a ghost herself.

When Omasé had cut off the last long strand Atsu dried her eyes and stared at the small shorn head in the mirror with its unbecoming cap of hair. Without her cascade of jet-black locks, she was hardly even a woman any more. She grimaced. She was in holy orders now, she reminded herself. She was supposed to put aside vanity, pray never-endingly for her husband's spirit, devote herself to meditation and study.

Her ladies draped her in dull grey robes. From now on she'd wear only drab colours. At twenty-one her life was over. She was a widow.

Forty-nine days had passed since the shogun had died and now, after his spirit's slow ascent to the heavens, he had finally passed through the gates of paradise. Now was the moment that Atsu became a nun, to pray that his soul might live for ever in bliss and never be reborn to suffer again on this earth.

She was no longer Her Majesty the Midai. She had a Buddhist name now – Lady Tensho-in, 'Hall of the Heavenly Jewel'. Like Lady Honju-in, whose name meant 'Hall of Great Happiness', she was no longer a person but a temple, dedicated to the Buddha.

She could never leave the palace or marry again. She would be a nun for the rest of her days.

She'd left the luxurious apartments reserved for the Midai. According to tradition she should have moved to the Western Palace, to live with the ancient ex-concubines of Iesada's father and grand-father. But she'd put her foot down. Lady Honju-in had insisted on staying in the women's palace after His Late Majesty died and Atsu had said that she would do the same.

Lady Honju-in's reign was over at last. Her ladies packed away her enormous wardrobe of extravagant robes and her priceless lacquer and tea ceremony ware and she moved to the Western Palace, leaving Atsu her vast gloomy suite of apartments. An army of staff ran back and forth, moving Atsu's furnishings and books.

As the shogun's mother, Lady Honju-in had ruled over the palace. Atsu would soon be in that position herself. Once Yoshi-*kun* was installed as shogun she would be the Dowager Mother. Everyone, from the lowliest petitioner to the highest lord in the land, would woo her and bow to her, present her with lavish gifts, kowtow to her every wish to ensure her favour. As Lady Honju-in had once been, she would be the intermediary between the shogun and the world. And for several years he would not even have a concubine or a consort to compete with her. She would wield even more power than Lady Honju-in ever had.

From here she would be able to wage war against Regent Ii, put a stop to his worst outrages. That would be her task from now on. The women of the women's palace wielded power and the shogun's official mother was the most powerful of all.

Atsu should have been happy. Her time had come. But all she could think about was how empty her life had become. It was hard to gather up her resolve and carry on without Iesada.

Thus far there'd been no public announcement of the shogun's demise. It had all happened too fast. Outside the palace no one even knew he was dead. As far as the rest of the world was concerned, the great ruler was still on his throne. But in reality there was a vacuum at the heart of the country. Yoshi-*kun* still had to be con-firmed as shogun, move into the palace, take his official title as

Shogun Iemochi. Meanwhile Regent Ii continued his reign of terror, arresting, banishing, sometimes executing his enemies with no one to stop him.

Outside the walls of the castle cholera raged. When Atsu walked in the gardens she saw a pall of smoke above the great pine trees that surrounded the grounds. The sky was black even though it was the height of summer.

When the wind changed clouds of smoke billowed across the castle grounds, carrying the stench of burning bodies, the rank odour of bodies waiting to be burnt. Furnaces roared night and day, but they couldn't keep up with all the bodies. People said there were coffins lined up end to end along the streets. Atsu caught the distant chanting of priests comforting the dying and heard the singing of the living, dancing to appease the gods. In the palace they placed branches and red flame-shaped paper amulets over the doorways to try to keep the deadly disease at bay. It really did seem as if the gods were angry, as if the whole world were falling apart, dying along with the shogun.

Then one evening an extraordinary star appeared, dazzlingly bright, with a flaming tail that swung out across half the sky in a great arc, like a sickle or the curved blade of a halberd. Atsu rushed into the gardens and gazed up at it in wonder. She remembered standing on the beach with Kaneshigé five and a half years earlier, gazing at the comet that had flashed across the sky. It had been not long after that that the first barbarian ships had arrived. That too had been a year of calamities. This new comet was bigger still, far more spectacular. She wondered what it meant, what it symbolized, what it portended. It seemed that even the heavens were in turmoil.

She thought of Lord Nariakira and his 'mirror of distant hopes', his huge telescope, down in Kagoshima. It was comforting to think that they were both looking at the same sight at the same time even though they were so far apart. He was probably discussing the comet with his astronomers, measuring the trajectory, calculating the orbit. He certainly wasn't wasting time on superstitious worries about whether it was or was not a portent. Knowing him, he probably had his technicians hard at work making a daguerreotype of it. If they succeeded it would surely be the first daguerreotype ever of a comet.

The comet didn't fade. It grew brighter. In the evening it filled the sky to the north-west of the city and at dawn it was still visible, arching over the north-east.

A few days after the comet first appeared, Middle Elder Omasé ran into Atsu's rooms to tell her that she had a distinguished visitor. It was a gentleman from Satsuma, a Lord Komatsu. He requested to see her. He said he had a message for her from Lord Nariakira. Omasé handed Atsu his visiting card. The name was written there in confident, manly brushstrokes: 'Tatewaki Komatsu.'

Atsu glanced at it, puzzled. There was something familiar about the hand. Then her heart gave a lurch. Kaneshigé. She'd forgotten. Tatewaki Komatsu was his name now.

'A message came that there was a gentleman at the Great Gate asking to see the Lady Midai – Lady Tensho-in. I had them conduct him to the Visitors' Audience Chambers,' said Middle Elder Omasé in the blandest of tones. Her face betrayed not a whisper of curiosity or surprise.

As a nun Atsu no longer counted as a woman. She was invisible, she could move around more freely than before, sometimes even meet with men. But although she didn't need a chaperone, she still needed attendants to mark her status.

She was annoyed to find her heart beating uncomfortably hard. She took a long breath, tried to calm herself. Then she called the two ladies who still attended her and set off at a dignified pace, as befitted a nun and a lady of high rank. But despite her efforts her feet moved faster and faster. She hurried through the narrow corridors, past the chambers smelling of incense and polish, so rapidly that her ladies had to run to keep up with her.

Atsu's mind was spinning. What could Kaneshigé be doing here? What message could he possibly have that was important enough to risk coming in person to this cholera-blighted city? It was a journey of at least twenty days, galloping hard. Lord Nariakira must have heard by now that Regent Ii had arrested Lord Keiki and his father and many other of His Lordship's closest associates. It was madness for Kaneshigé to enter Edo Castle, set foot inside the enemy camp, let alone stride boldly right up to the inner sanctum, the women's palace. If he was discovered he would be arrested, most likely executed.

And why send a lord all this way to deliver a letter? There were relays of messengers who could do that. There had to be more to it than that. There was something going on.

By the time Atsu and her ladies-in-waiting reached the Visitors' Audience Chambers they were all three panting. The two ladies slid open the doors and knelt discreetly outside in the corridor.

Atsu hesitated. She remembered a time when she used to dream of this meeting, imagine what she would do, how it would be when she saw Kaneshigé again. But that time had passed. So much had happened since then. Now he was actually here she was afraid. She wondered if the old passion might still be there. That sort of feeling was forbidden her now. She belonged to the shogun, body and soul. It would be a betrayal of his memory to let anyone else enter her heart, even for a moment.

There was a tall man sauntering up and down the vast chamber, peering up at the painted pine trees, ornate carved lintels and coffered gold-encrusted ceiling. He was in travelling clothes that billowed as he walked, very different from the stiff pleated hakama of the male courtiers she was used to seeing. With his carefree air he seemed almost more foreign even than the barbarians, utterly different from the scheming courtiers with their endless worries about rank and terminology. Even his hair was not as tightly scraped back, not as heavily oiled. His leggings were dusty as if he had just this moment alighted from his horse. He carried with him the winds of Kyushu, the sweet scent of ocean and mountains, palm trees and blue skies, purple volcanoes, the vast plains he'd galloped across to be here.

He turned. His face was boyish still – the down on his upper lip, the dark eyebrows and full mouth and intense questing eyes, narrowed as if he was looking into some unimaginable future. The shadows beneath his cheekbones had grown deeper and there was a hint of a frown between his eyebrows, but he still had that golden tinge to his skin. He'd lost his boyish awkwardness. He carried himself boldly, with confidence.

Atsu felt a jolt in her stomach, a tightening in her chest. It was as if no time at all had passed. Her childhood came rushing back, those carefree years living in her parents' house, playing on the beach in Ibusuki, growing up together, growing closer. She was that girl again, saying goodbye while a cloud of black ash stained the sky above the volcano at the end of the bay.

The yearning for home, for those days when life was simple, full of love and warmth and comfort, was so sharp it brought tears to her eyes. She struggled to resist the flood of emotion and memories but her body betrayed her. Her cheeks grew hot and she lowered her head. It was all she could do to keep her face calm and dignified.

'Your Majesty,' he said. His voice was deep and resonant. Her heart swelled as she heard the broad vowels, the Satsuma drawl.

'My lord,' she replied, trying to stop her voice from trembling.

To her shock he stepped towards her and seized her hands. According to protocol he should have dropped to his knees and bowed. He didn't have a single retainer with him. It was just the two of them alone together in this empty room.

His hands were warm. She smelt his sweet manly scent. She recognized the texture of his skin, the calluses at the base of each finger where he held his sword.

He drew her towards him. 'You,' he said softly.

She snatched her hands away. That little word, 'you', that intimate whispered syllable, was for lovers or husband and wife. It was not a term to be used between a grown man and a grown woman, a clan official and the widow of the deceased lord of the realm, the newly minted Dowager Mother of the women's palace in Edo Castle.

'You forget yourself, sir,' she snapped, drawing herself up and frowning.

'Forgive me, Your Majesty,' he said. 'Forgive my country ways.' A smile lurked on his lips. He didn't look abashed in the slightest.

It seemed like a lifetime since she last felt warmth, closeness, sympathy. Since Iesada died she had been entirely alone. She felt her anger, her cares and worries, her sadness, melting away. 'I am happy to see you, my lord,' she said. 'I never thought to see you here.'

A shadow crossed his face. 'My condolences, my lady. I heard rumours . . .'

Atsu bowed her head and allowed the tears to spill down her cheeks. 'It was so sudden,' she said, her voice breaking. 'We are deep in mourning. I am a widow. I have become a nun.' She gestured at her shorn head. It had been folly to imagine that this worldly man could ever see her as a woman now.

'I've never known you so beautiful,' he said softly. 'You are peerless. You grow more beautiful with the years.'

She drew back. She looked nothing like his childhood sweetheart, that much she knew. She was thinner, she was worn and drained, her face seamed with weeping, and with her glorious floor-length hair cut short as a boy's, she'd lost all her charm.

She frowned. She was not a geisha to be trifled with. He was a man and she knew how men lived. He had a wife, he must have concubines, mistresses, liaisons. He visited geisha houses. Perhaps it was because she was so far removed from all that now that she excited his interest. All he could possibly feel was pity.

'You mock me, sir,' she said sternly, stepping away, putting distance between them.

She looked around the Visitors' Audience Chambers – the walls with their painted pine trees, the low stage at the end where she used to sit, next to Lady Honju-in. She saw the great room bustling with people, with Lord Hotta addressing her earnestly, the members of the Council of Ministers coughing and shuffling and interrupting. She felt a terrible sadness that all that was passed, Lord Hotta returned to his ancestral domain, Lord Keiki under house arrest. Of all that, nothing was left.

She came back to the present. Kaneshigé's eyes were resting boldly on her face. 'Forgive me, my lady,' he said. 'I'm too familiar. I can't forget how well we knew each other once. You must remember our childhood days, our meetings on the beach . . .'

She frowned. Her life here had become so sad, so empty, it was not surprising that she felt her will crumbling under his blandishments. She had to remember who she was, where she was. She had to stick to business.

She glanced around, remembering the old saying that walls have ears and screens have eyes and lowered her voice to a whisper. 'You must know that Regent Ii runs the government now. He is arresting all the lords who backed Lord Keiki as our next shogun. Many have been executed.' She shook her head. 'You should never have come. You are taking a terrible risk.'

She lowered her eyes as she spoke. Then she noticed something odd and out of place. Protruding from this bold confident man's obi was the dainty handle of a fan – a sandalwood fan, a woman's fan. It was hers, the fan she'd given him when they'd parted in Ibusuki all those years ago. Tears started to her eyes as she saw it.

Despite everything, she couldn't bear to think that he would go. She wanted to keep him there a little longer, this man she'd once loved so much. She was enjoying looking at his face, breathing the same air. She wanted to eke out the precious moments. 'But how did you get here?' she asked. 'You must have come all the way through the city, past the guards, into the castle, right up to the women's palace. Saigo used to come dressed as a gardener but you are not even in disguise. Did no one challenge you?'

As she knew, lords had regularly come to the castle to pay homage to the shogun. In the old days, under the benign rule of Lord Hotta, members of the Council of Elders had often met with Atsu and Lady Honju-in in the Visitors' Audience Chambers. But now that Regent Ii was clamping down on his enemies, doing all he could to keep the shogun's death a secret, security would surely be tighter than ever.

Kaneshigé cocked an eyebrow and shrugged. 'It's chaos out there,' he said carelessly. 'The guards are afraid of catching cholera. They're not checking anyone properly. They didn't look at my papers carefully enough to notice that I was from Satsuma. I left most of my men at the outer gates. Saigo and a few others came to the entrance of the women's palace. Saigo knew exactly what to do. He asked the women at the Great Gate for Middle Elder Omasé. They were squabbling over who would take my visiting card.'

'His Lordship sent you? You have a message for me?'

Kaneshigé's handsome face changed. He'd turned pale under his tan. His cheeks sagged and he bunched his eyebrows. His jauntiness had been a facade. He looked haunted, haggard.

He took Atsu's hands again and this time she didn't resist. 'I bring bad news,' he said. 'Very bad.'

The vast chamber was silent as if they were frozen in time. Somewhere outside a cicada shrilled, a discordant whine. There were sounds of sweeping, footsteps going by. Atsu held her breath. She wanted to stop time, never hear his dreadful news. Perhaps that would mean it had never happened. She wished she could hold the whole world in suspension.

Then the realization swept over her of why he had come, why he had taken such enormous risks. Her own voice broke the spell.

'No,' she cried. 'Don't say it, please, don't tell me. Not that. Don't let it be that. Not His Lordship.'

She fell to her knees. Kaneshigé knelt too and took her in his arms. She struggled to push him away then crumpled against him. She buried her face in the rough silk of his collar, sobbing as if she'd never stop, hungry for the comfort of his body against hers, his strong arms enclosing her.

She saw the vast plain that Masa-*kun* had predicted would one day be here where the palace stood, felt the cold wind blowing across the moor, saw herself, a tiny figure in the wilderness of grass. Lord Nariakira had betrayed her, deceived her, she had feared that he might try to kill her beloved husband – yet he had been her father, her liege lord, he had been the rock on which she stood. She relied on his wisdom, she knew that he did what he did for the good of the country. She had never felt so desolate and alone.

Kaneshigé held her tight as she took a long convulsive breath.

'What happened?' she whispered shakily.

There was a long silence. He sat back on his heels. 'It must be a month ago now that His Lordship fell ill. It was the ninth day of the seventh month.'

Atsu gasped. 'Just three days after Lord Iesada passed away,' she said.

'It was sudden, very sudden. He'd been out in the heat all day. Everyone thought that was all it was. He took to his futons, but the next day he was worse. He had fever and chills and diarrhoea. It wasn't cholera. We've been lucky, it hasn't reached Kagoshima, and the symptoms were different. Everyone suspected poison immediately.'

'Poison?' Atsu breathed, trembling with horror. She'd thought Regent Ii had done his worst. She'd thought he couldn't do anything else that would hurt her as much as the shogun's death, but he had. He'd stretched his long arm all the way down to Kyushu. As Atsu knew better than anyone, Lord Nariakira had been the chief of those who'd plotted to have Keiki chosen as Iesada's successor. He'd installed her in the women's palace for that very purpose, to bend Iesada's ear. If Regent Ii wanted his enemies out of the way, Lord Nariakira would be the first to go. She was staggered at the speed with which that malevolent, all-powerful lord had worked.

'We called in the best physicians in the domain. A Dutch doctor galloped down post haste from Nagasaki. But no one could save him. Six days after he fell ill he realized he was dying. He summoned the clan elders to arrange his affairs and plan the succession. He lasted through the night. He breathed his last the next day at dawn. He hadn't even reached his fiftieth year.'

'And it was a peaceful death?' Atsu asked, her voice shaking. 'Peaceful at the end?'

Kaneshigé nodded. 'I can assure you of that.'

Atsu had never felt so friendless, so alone. She clasped her hands to her chest. She couldn't speak for tears.

'My beloved Father,' she whispered at last. 'My dearest Father. You were more than a father to me. I wish I could have seen you one last time. I wish I had had the chance to say goodbye.'

She stared bleakly around the vast room. The painted walls looked faded and the gold leaf of the coffered ceiling was peeling and tawdry. With His Lordship dead it was all just so much empty pomp.

'We need him desperately. The country needs him, I need him. I can't imagine what we'll do without him. The country is entirely ruined. He was the greatest, wisest man in the land. There is no one now to stand up against Regent Ii.'

She wiped her eyes on her sleeve and turned to Kaneshigé. 'So what did he decide? Who is his successor? Who is the new Prince of Satsuma?'

'Hisamitsu's son Tadayoshi. Hisamitsu is Regent during his minority.'

Atsu stared at him open-mouthed. 'Hisamitsu? Not His Lordship's half-brother? The son of his father's concubine?'

She remembered that dark night she had gone to Crane Castle so many years ago. In her mind she was there again, facing the old lord and his icy-eyed concubine, painted like a geisha with a white face and scarlet lips. She remembered Lord Nariakira telling her how the concubine had laid curses on his children and brought about their deaths one after the other so that her own son could become lord. And now he was. Her plots had paid off.

She burst out, 'But . . . but they hated each other! Hisamitsu will undo everything His Lordship was trying to achieve.'

'There was no one else. His Lordship's children are too young. His only son, Tetsumaru, is just two.'

He sat back on his heels and cleared his throat. 'When His Lordship knew he was dying he summoned me. He told me to give you this.' He took a package in a wrapping cloth from the low table behind him and held it out to her.

Atsu folded back the silk wrapper. Inside was a box. In it was a daguerreotype in an ornate brass frame with a piece of glass over the precious silver plate to protect it. She laid it on the table, taking care not to touch it or let tears fall on it. She didn't even need to angle it to see the image. She gazed and gazed as if she'd never stop.

'He did it. He finally did it,' she said at last, laughing and weeping at the same time. 'He wanted so much to make a portrait. And he did. It is him. It is as if he was alive still, here with us.'

The likeness was so perfect it was uncanny. It was like a ghostly visitation from another world. The image was absolutely faultless, crisp and clear, not blurred in the slightest. Lord Nariakira must have sat as still as a statue for hours. He looked sombre, pensive. He was thinner than she remembered him, regal, surprisingly boyish. His underlip jutted in that stubborn way he had. He was in formal black robes with the stiffened shoulders protruding like wings and the Satsuma crest, a cross in a circle, white on black, at each side of his collar.

'He had several made,' said Kaneshigé. 'Each different, each unique.'

Atsu clasped the picture to her heart. 'Thank you. Thank you for bringing me this. It is the most precious thing I have ever had. I shall put it in my shrine. I shall pray for his spirit every day.'

Kaneshigé bowed. He shuffled and looked around.

Suddenly she couldn't bear the thought that he would leave her here to pass the rest of her life in this echoing palace full of memories. She felt utterly desolate. She tried to stop herself but the words slipped out. 'Don't go.' Her voice was small and sad, like a sob.

She hadn't realized how lonely she felt with Iesada gone. She longed for warmth, comfort, closeness. And this lover from her childhood was here before her eyes, filling her with nostalgia for a time when life had been easy and comfortable. She gazed at him, his tawny skin, his strong hands and arms. She could see the muscles of his firm young body under his robes.

She yearned to feel close to him just once again. He had been everything she cared about, everything she'd given up to come here. At that moment she would have given anything to keep him there with her for ever.

He reached out and lifted a strand of her hair. He stroked her eyebrow, ran his finger down her cheek and across her lips. She knew she should push him away but she was transfixed by his touch. She sat like a statue, afraid that if she moved he would disappear like a ghost at daybreak.

Their eyes met. She'd lost all power in her limbs. As if in a trance, she felt herself drawn towards him. Then, hardly knowing how she got there, she was in his arms. Her lips touched his and she was lost, utterly lost in his embrace. She was back in Ibusuki, on the beach, smelling the sea, tasting the salty tang of him, feeling the sand under her feet, the sun on her head as desire rose in her.

She could hardly breathe. She let herself say it, his pet name. 'Kané-*sama*,' she whispered.

Somewhere far away a voice reminded her that this was impossible, utterly wrong, that she had to stop.

Quivering, she struggled to break free. 'Don't go,' she pleaded. 'Please, stay a little longer. Omasé will order a meal for you. You must eat before you leave.'

He sat back on his heels, knees spread, hands on his thighs. 'I have something else to say to you. I haven't told you my message yet.' He hesitated, lowered his eyes as if he was searching for the right words. 'His Lordship was already ill when he heard that His Majesty too was dying. The messenger travelled down by steamship the moment he heard that His Majesty's illness might be fatal. His Lordship gave me instructions that if, when I found you, His Majesty had passed away, I should tell you this. These are his exact words: "Your job here is over. Your work is done. You do not need to suffer any longer. You do not need to share the fate of the shoguns, whatever that may be. You have done your best and there is no more for you to do. Come back to Satsuma."'

Voices echoed in the corridor, footsteps pattered by. Incense floated in the air, mingling with the scent of chrysanthemum petals.

Atsu couldn't believe what she was hearing. 'But . . . but that is impossible,' she stammered. 'I am bound to the palace. I belong here. It is . . . it is illegal for me even to go outside.'

'Maybe while you were His Majesty's consort, but not now. His Lordship's last order was to the elders, to prepare your papers. We have authorizations for you to leave the castle and pass through every border post all the way back to Satsuma. From what I hear Regent Ii will not oppose your leaving. It'll be a relief for him if you go.'

Atsu stared at him, speechless. Of course. Regent Ii must have been well aware of the central role she'd played in the plot to install Keiki as Regent and, if he wasn't, Lady Honju-in would have made sure to inform him. She was a key member of the enemy camp. Atsu was far too high-ranking for him to take her into custody or even have her put under house arrest. It would serve his purpose perfectly if she were simply to disappear. She wouldn't be able to influence the new shogun, for a start.

'It is . . . It is so sudden,' she stammered, her heart pounding. 'I need to think.'

It would be so easy. With cholera raging, the city in chaos, everyone had too much on their minds to worry about one nun running away, even if that nun was the widow of the late shogun. Regent Ii was busy with his purge of his enemies and he would be relieved to be rid of her too. Now was her chance to slip through a crack in time, leave this golden cage where she'd been imprisoned for so long. And it was not just freedom Kaneshigé was offering, it was love, comfort, home.

Her thoughts were in turmoil. Happiness lay within her reach. All she had to do was stretch out her hand and pluck it like a flower. The chance would never come again, the combination of circumstances would never be so perfect. The door was wide open. She just had to walk through it.

It was Kaneshigé's turn to glance around and lower his voice to a whisper. 'We'll get rid of Regent Ii. We may have to lie low for a year or two but we'll put a better government in place, avenge His Majesty and Lord Nariakira, I promise you that. I've already passed a message to Middle Elder Omasé. She's waiting for your word to pack whatever you need. We must go quickly before Regent Ii changes his mind.

'Do you remember that horse you loved so much, Taro, the handsome Kiso stallion? We brought him with us from the Satsuma mansion. He's waiting for you at the outer gates.'

He gripped her hands in his and held her with his eyes, those dark liquid eyes she used to dream of and yearn for.

'Okatsu-san,' he said, using her childhood name, the name he'd always called her by. 'Come back to Satsuma. Come back with me. Our lives have grown complicated but we can find a way to be together. Leave this grim place. Leave this sadness and loneliness behind. You don't have to be a nun. Come with me, Okatsu-*san*. Come back to Satsuma.'

Atsu's heart was thundering. She stared wildly around the room. She didn't know what she wanted. She tried to imagine how it might be, wished she could see into the future as Masa-*kun* had.

51

As if in a dream Atsu meets his eyes. 'Yes,' she says. 'I will. I shall come with you back to Satsuma.'

And suddenly she's floating free, as if a weight's been lifted from her shoulders. She straightens her back and smiles. She feels as if she hasn't smiled, really smiled, since the shogun died. She's no longer Lady Tensho-in or Her Majesty the Midai or even Princess Atsu. She's Okatsu now, plain Okatsu.

Kaneshigé raises her hands to his lips. 'You won't regret it. I'll make sure of that.' He takes her in his arms and she feels as if she's home at last. Their lips meet as if nothing will ever separate them.

He releases her. 'Later,' he says. 'Later, when we're on the road. We need to leave now, and quickly. From all I hear Regent Ii will be glad to see you go, but he's capable of anything. It will be easier to arrest you once you're outside the palace. It's best to take precautions. Middle Elder Omasé will find you a pageboy's outfit and a cap.' He runs his hand through her cropped hair and buries his nose in it.

'Omasé will prepare a bag for you. She will pack the rest of your belongings in a trunk and send it on to the Satsuma mansion. They'll take it to Satsuma next time a procession goes down there with a baggage train. We must go now. This may be the only chance we'll have.'

As if in a dream Atsu allows herself to be transformed into a pageboy. As they walk through the Seventh Hour Gate, she stumbles and Kaneshigé takes her elbow to support her. She's dizzy, intoxicated with this new-found freedom. She moves like a ghost. Her feet barely brush the ground. Yet something tugs at her, something holds her back.

They cross the courtyard where she found Hana's body next to the palanquin sheds and hurry up to the Great Gate. She stops to look back at the buildings with their great carved entrance porches and white plastered walls and grey tiled roofs receding endlessly into the distance, that vast palace where she spent all those months and years. Kaneshigé urges her to hurry but it's hard to turn away. Something grips her. She can't free herself.

And then they're at the gate, jostling between merchants and ladies' maids. Atsu hears the hubbub of voices but she keeps her head lowered. All she sees is swirling hems and dusty sandal-shod feet and paving stones shimmering in the heat.

Saigo is there, solid and dependable, along with some of Kaneshigé's retainers. Casually, sauntering as if they're in no hurry at all, they walk down Tide-Viewing Slope, between the massive granite blocks, big as houses, that form the fortifications. Atsu glimpses the blue waters of the bay, crowded with masts and sails, and smells salt air. They pass the Moat of Swans and the walls and gates of the Second Palace where the shoguns' concubines and their children live. She shivers as they come to the Hundred Man Guard House, bristling with samurai who narrow their eyes and stare at them, hands on their sword hilts. As they skirt the Chief Superintendent's Post, Atsu's heart is in her mouth. She's certain they'll be challenged.

But Kaneshigé marches on, head held high. The guards bow to the ground as he and his men retrieve the swords they've stored there.

And then they're through the vast double gates and outside the castle. A troop of Kaneshigé's men is waiting on the other side of the moat. Atsu hugs Taro's huge head and buries her face in his flanks and he nuzzles her cheek with his big chestnut nose.

They trot along streets lined with coffins, between crowds of people with scarves wrapped around their faces, past hastily erected crematoria, through billowing smoke full of the stench of burning corpses. And then they're out of the city, galloping along the Eastern Sea Road, the great highway that Atsu took on her way to Edo, all those years ago. She glances behind her but there's no sign of troops coming after her in hot pursuit.

That night they stay in an inn in Kanagawa, where she saw the barbarian ships on her way up to Edo. The bay is full of vast ships now, with tarred hulls and fat funnels and towering masts, and the town is noisy with building. There are streets of ungainly new houses being built in the barbarian style and she glimpses huge large-nosed pale-skinned figures striding about.

And now finally she puts the castle out of her mind as Kaneshigé removes her robes one by one and they reacquaint themselves, give themselves up to love.

But still something tugs at her. At night she dreams of Iesada, calling out to her to come back. Without her in the castle, he cries, his spirit is lonely. He cannot be at peace. But she pushes the thought away and as the days and years go by the dreams become less frequent.

Atsu grows older. She has children and they in their turn have children. She has almost forgotten that strange sad time when she lived in Edo Castle as the Midai, the shogun's consort.

Then one day she's rummaging around in one of the distant towers of Crane Castle with her granddaughter when they come across an ancient trunk, covered in dust. It's the trunk Omasé sent back from Edo all those years ago. Atsu has never bothered to unpack it. The little girl pulls out treasures – moth-eaten obis with tarnished gold embroidery, purses, porcelain tea ceremony canisters. Then she pulls out something small and white.

'Look, Granny,' she says. 'Look what I've found.'

Atsu rubs the dust off and peers at it through eyes that have grown rheumy and dull. It's an ivory snail, quite perfect, with a horned head and scaly neck stretching out of its whorled shell.

And as she looks at it she suddenly awakes, like Urashima Taro in the folk tale who thought he had spent three days under the sea, dancing and feasting and making love with the dragon king's daughter, only to discover that three hundred years had passed; or like a guest at a geisha party bewitched by the geishas' magic who suddenly remembers he has a wife and children and has to shake himself free of their spells and flee.

She comes to herself. She remembers as if with a blow that time so long ago when she was the shogun's consort. She looks up, her eyes wild, and says, 'How could I have forgotten? How could I have betrayed him?'

52

Atsu came back to the present. The picture of Lord Nariakira was beside her on the table. But in her hand she held the little ivory snail that was tied to her obi. It was a funny little thing, not a great work of art, probably not worth much, but Iesada had loved it. She remembered how he'd always said it was like him. He'd wished he had a shell too so he could draw his head inside and hide.

And as she wrapped her fingers round it she knew she could never leave. He was here still. He was everywhere, in all the things he'd loved, all the places he'd loved. His spirit permeated the palace. He'd be lonely without her, his spirit would be lonely. The place was full of memories of their life together, of his love and his trust. She'd betrayed him too many times already. She couldn't betray him this one last time. She couldn't leave him.

She pictured his large innocent eyes, thought of him gazing at the moon, playing Go with her, laughing in delight when he won, leaning out of the shogunal barge, trailing his thin fingers in the water. She saw him looking at her with such trust, such love. She saw him on his deathbed, heard him whispering, 'You must take care of Yoshi-*kun*. You must care for him as you have me. He is my son now. You must be a mother to him.'

And she had promised, she had given her word, she had vowed to respect his dying wishes. 'Everything you have asked me to do I will carry out,' she had said. She couldn't desert him, couldn't break that solemn promise.

For a moment she'd felt as if she had nothing left. She'd thrown herself like a drowning woman into the arms of this man she'd once known, who seemed to offer salvation. Out of sheer bleak hopelessness she'd contemplated accepting his offer. But she knew now she couldn't.

She wasn't a child any longer. She had duties, responsibilities. There were important things to do here. She was the most powerful woman in the palace now, the most powerful woman in the land. She was just beginning to grasp what that meant. She needed to be here to help the new shogun, Iemochi, just as she had Iesada. It would be madness to give it all up now. It would be criminal. At this time when Regent Ii was creating havoc, she had a huge responsibility to the country.

She gazed at Kaneshigé, remembered the past they had had together, saw the future she could have enjoyed with him. But she could never forget the frail shogun who had died so young, so terribly. She remembered the words Lord Nariakira had once said to her: 'You were born to be a princess.' A princess was not a weak creature who allowed herself to be driven by feelings. A princess could rise above all that.

All these years she'd kept Kaneshigé's dagger in her obi. Sometimes, when life became unbearable, she'd wrapped her fingers round the hilt, gained strength from imagining that he was there with her. And now he really was. She took it out and gazed at it, that beautiful dagger with the hilt and scabbard marked with the crest of the Kimotsukis, his birth family – two cranes with their wings extended to form a circle.

She held it out to him in both hands and gave a formal bow. 'I thank you, sir. Your offer is very kind but I cannot come with you. My place is here. Here, with my memories and my lord.'

She placed the dagger in his hands. Then she rose to her feet and firmly, with a cool dry gaze, left the Visitors' Audience Chambers. She didn't look back. With her ladies behind her she walked through the long corridors, past her apartments, past the Great Hall to the shrine room and slid open the door. She lit an incense stick and a candle and knelt before Iesada's memorial tablet and began to pray. And as the scented smoke spiralled up to envelop her, she saw his face there and knew that she was home.

Afterword

On the second day of the third month of the seventh year of Ansei, 24 March 1860, the first Japanese diplomatic mission ever to travel abroad was on its way to San Francisco, aboard the *Kanrin Maru*. Just a year and seven months had passed since Shogun Iesada's death. Westerners were setting up businesses in Yokohama and the first British envoy, Rutherford Alcock, had been installed in his legation in Tozenji Temple in Edo for nearly a year.

That morning Regent Ii, known to history as Ii Naosuké (Naosuké Ii to put his name in the western order), squeezed his vast bulk through the small door of his palanquin and, accompanied by a train of guards and retainers, set off on his daily journey to Edo Castle for his regular meeting with Iemochi, the fourteen-year-old shogun, as little Yoshi-*kun* now was. Ii was even fatter and more self-important than ever and had accumulated vast wealth.

That day the narrow bridge, which crosses the moat at the Sakuradamon Gate of Edo Castle, was congested with palanquins. In the confusion Ii was separated from all but a few of his guards. At that moment eighteen armed men who had been lying in wait disguised as menials flung off their oil-paper cloaks and leapt forward, swinging swords and pikes. A single shot was fired straight into the palanquin and Ii was pulled out and instantaneously decapitated. One of the assailants raced off clutching what appeared to be Ii's head. Ii's retainers chased through the city after him and finally captured and killed him, only to discover that he was a decoy. The head was not Regent Ii's. The other assailants meanwhile had made off with the real head. They galloped straight to Miyako and jammed it unceremoniously on to a spike on Traitors' Bridge.

Of the assailants seventeen were Mito men, followers of Lord Keiki. The other was a Satsuma. Most committed seppuku before they could be tortured or questioned.

And thus Regent Ii met his comeuppance and Iesada was avenged along with all the loyalists who had been falsely accused and executed or – in the case of Keiki and his father – thrown under house arrest. Regent Ii's reign of terror was over.

The balance of power swung around again. Lord Keiki was released from house arrest and became guardian, then Regent of the young shogun. When Yoshitomi/Iemochi died at the age of nineteen (another deeply suspicious death), Keiki finally became shogun under the name Yoshinobu Tokugawa. But it was too late. By then Japan was engulfed in civil war.

One of the clans that had risen to the top in the growing chaos was the wealthy, powerful Satsuma. They formed an alliance with their long-time enemies, the militaristic Choshu, and together led the rebellion against the shogunate, aiming to take power and install a new government under the titular headship of the fifteen-year-old Emperor Mutsuhito (later Emperor Meiji). The great general who led the rebel troops to victory was Saigo.

As for Keiki, he has gone down in history as the fifteenth and last shogun.

Atsu was right at the heart of the epoch-making events that marked the end of the shogunate and the opening of Japan to western influence. The events of her tragic story are pretty much as I have told them – though this is a work of fiction, not history, and I have taken whatever liberties were needed to tell a gripping tale. Nevertheless I have aimed to be as accurate and true to history as possible and have researched as deeply and thoroughly as I could. History is written by the winners. It is far more difficult to unearth the long-buried stories of those on the losing side – the shogunate. But I have done my best.

Atsu was not only on the shogun's side but a woman, and as a result her story is little known. In Japan, history is an account of battles and rulers – of men. According to the Confucian precept, 'women have no business outside the home, therefore their names are not known by outsiders.' If you open a history book, you will find scant mention of her.

After Iesada's death, Atsu stayed on in the palace as the Dowager Lady Tensho-in, despite the emissaries who came from Satsuma to try to persuade her to come home. She reigned in the palace unopposed until 1863 when Princess Kazu arrived to be the young Shogun Iemochi's bride. The two women became deadly rivals. The story of Princess Kazu and of Atsu's later years forms the backdrop to *The Last Concubine*.

Atsu stepped out of the shadows to make her mark on history for a second time when Japan's civil war was coming to its bloody end. The rebels had used the brilliant ruse of flying the brocade banner of the emperor, automatically turning Keiki and his shogunal troops into traitors to the imperial throne. In the ensuing battle the shogunal forces, reluctant to fight, were routed.

Desperate to bring an end to the slaughter, Keiki came to the women's palace and requested an audience with Atsu. He begged her to use her Satsuma connections to negotiate with the imperial army – the Satsuma and their allies – on his behalf. She was able to communicate with her old friend Saigo and ensure that he met with the shogunal representative. In the end Edo Castle was peacefully surrendered to the imperial troops and a bloodbath was averted.

And thus in 1868, ten years after Iesada's death, the women's palace closed its doors for ever and Satsuma and Choshu troops strode in muddy boots across the delicate tatami to show their contempt for the losing side. For a second time an emissary came from Satsuma and for a second time asked Atsu – still only thirty-three – to come back with him. According to one story this emissary was Lord Tatewaki Komatsu. He begged her to come back and share in the victory. Her people were now the winners. There was no need for her to suffer the shame of the Tokugawas.

Atsu refused. She had no reason at all to stay now. The Tokugawas, the family she had married into, were disgraced and out of power.

But she chose to remain. When the women were given a few days to vacate the palace, Atsu dug in her heels. One by one the women packed their bags and in the end only Atsu was left to walk the huge dark halls, full of memories and ghosts, alone. The new owners had to carry her out bodily.

Who knows what inspired such stubborn loyalty to a cause that was long since lost? Was it the memory of Iesada? That is the realm of the novelist. As I said, in those days women's stories were not recorded. All we can do is guess.

Atsu spent the rest of her days as a nun, overseeing the upbringing of Iesato Tokugawa, Keiki's successor, the sixteenth head of the Tokugawa family. She died in 1883 at the age of forty-seven. She is buried in the Tokugawa family temple, Kaneiji Temple in Ueno, Tokyo, alongside her husband, Iesada.

Most of the characters in this novel really existed and their lives were largely as I've described. The biggest liberty I've taken is that we don't know if Atsu really even knew Kaneshigé. He was a year older than her and from Satsuma and moved in the same circles. As Tatewaki Komatsu he was Saigo's close friend and associate. Nariakira definitely posted Saigo to the women's palace as a spy-cum-gardener to help Atsu with her task of winning over the shogun. So she may well have known Kaneshigé too. But there's no evidence. Their relationship is pure fiction.

As Tatewaki Komatsu, the real Kaneshigé went on to become a major figure in the creation of the new Japan. The British diplomat Ernest Satow, who lived in Japan in the 1860s, knew him well. In his diaries he described him as 'one of the most charming Japanese I have ever known . . . distinguished for his political ability, excellent manners and a genial companion'. Lord Komatsu died in 1870 at the age of thirty-five, of tuberculosis. People died young in those days.

Iesada was every bit as sickly as I portray, in fact more so. No one knows exactly what was wrong with him though he probably had epilepsy and was said to be mentally unstable. There were rampant rumours of poison being involved in his death and in the death of his successor, Iemochi, and of murder in the case of Iesada's father

– though by then they were all three on the losing side and no one ever bothered to investigate.

There is also a strong suspicion that Lord Nariakira was poisoned. Certainly the Dutch doctor who attended him said so. In Satsuma Lord Nariakira is hugely revered to this day as a brilliant reformer and modernizer. The first daguerreotype in Japan, of Crane Castle, was made under his tutelage. His daguerreotype portrait is kept in the place of honour in the huge Shinto shrine building next to the castle in Kagoshima. It sends a shiver down the spine to see his thin, rather delicate face and piercing eyes gazing back at you after all these years.

There really was a cat ghost play that had audiences trembling in the 1850s, and a cholera epidemic in 1858, and comets in 1853 and 1858 that everyone was sure were portents.

And so in the end Shogun Iesada's vision of the future really did come to pass.

Edo Castle was taken over by the imperial side but soon burnt down. It is now the Imperial Palace in Tokyo. Where the women's palace once stood is parkland, an endless expanse of smooth green lawn with nothing to see of that enormous complex of buildings except the gargantuan granite foundation stones of the five-storeyed tower. You have to search to find the small sign, half-hidden inside a hedge, reading 'Site of Ohoku', indicating that the *ooku*, the women's palace, once filled this whole vast area.

I paced out the area, walked the paths, worked out where Atsu's apartments and the Great Hall must have been, tried to picture the palace with its white walls and ranks of dove-grey roofs, the sheer size of the place. From where the Great Gate once stood, you can still walk down Tide-Viewing Slope, past the Moat of Swans and the formidable fortifications to the House of a Hundred Guards. Before you, the gleaming skyscrapers of Tokyo obscure the view of the bay, just as the shogun foresaw.

Nagoya Castle in the city of Nagoya, in Central Japan, home to one of the leading branches of the Tokugawa family, has been restored and there are rooms glimmering with gold where it's easier to imagine yourself back in the glory days of the Tokugawa. Some of the extraordinary artworks and treasures collected by the Tokugawa are preserved in the museum here.

But the place where the Tokugawa legacy can be most keenly felt is Nijo Castle, once the shogun's palace in Miyako – Kyoto, as it is now called. I walked the creaky 'nightingale floors' of the men's palace, walled with splendid gold-leaf screens painted with tigers and bamboo groves and giant stylized pine trees, designed to express the shogun's prestige and authority. The women's palace, described discreetly in the guidebook as the 'shogun's living quarters', is far less showy. Peaceful and intimate in tone, its pale-gold walls are decorated with delicate black and white ink-painted scenes of Chinese landscapes.

For all its magnificence Nijo Castle was no more than the shogun's pied-à-terre in the imperial capital. Its splendour was but a pale shadow of the unimaginable riches, the high-ceilinged halls and endless corridors of Edo Castle. Padding in stockinged feet across the fragrant tatami of the 'shogun's living quarters', I tried to catch a breath of what Atsu's home at Edo Castle must have been like, with its thousands of women rustling through the corridors and across the walkways, kneeling and bowing in perfect unison to greet the shogun when he came in for his daily visits.

But for all its luxury it was also a prison. The women couldn't leave. They lived and died in splendid isolation, amid incessant scheming, wishing they could spread their wings and fly away, out of their golden cage.

Bibliography

The story as I tell it is largely based on research and historical fact, though in the end this is a work of fiction and my primary aim has been to tell a good story, even if that occasionally involves taking liberties with whatever facts are known.

The main books I used are listed below; there are many more. All translations are by me.

The women of the Great Interior took a strict vow of silence when they entered the palace and after it was closed down most kept that vow to the grave. Few ever disclosed anything of their lives or of what had gone on there. However, a small number did agree to be interviewed when they were very old. Now that Women's Studies are in vogue there are also several scholars who have produced wonderfully illuminating accounts of life in the women's palace.

To my knowledge there are only three in English, one magnificent book:

Segawa Seigle, Cecilia, and Linda H. Chance, *Ooku, The Secret World of the Shogun's Women*, Cambria Press, 2014

And two lengthy and fascinating articles:

Beerens, Anna, 'Interview with Two Ladies of the *Ooku*: A Translation from *Kyji Shimonroku*', *Monumenta Nipponica*, Volume 63, Number 2, Autumn 2008, pp. 265–324
Hata, Hisako, 'Servants of the Inner Quarters: The Women of the Shogun's Great Interior', Chapter 9 in Walthall, Anne, ed., *Servants of the Dynasty: Palace Women in World History*, University of California Press, 2008
Many wonderful books were written in the early years after Perry first

sailed into Uraga Bay. The first westerners in Japan knew they were unlocking something extraordinary – a jewel box of a country that had been largely sealed off from western influence for a quarter of a millennium. These early settlers also knew that their very presence would inevitably change Japan for ever. Most kept detailed diaries of their everyday lives which are fascinating to read. Here are some of my favourites:

Alcock, Rutherford, *The Capital of the Tycoon: A Narrative of a Three Years' Residence in Japan, Volumes I and II*, Elibron Classics, 2005 (first published 1863). Alcock was the first British envoy to Japan and reports on Japan from 1860.

Cortazzi, Hugh, *Mitford's Japan: Memories & Recollections 1866–1906*, Japan Library, 2002

Harris, Townsend, *The Complete Journal of Townsend Harris: First American Consul and Minister to Japan*, ed. Mario Emilio Cosenza, New York, Doubleday, Doran, 1930

Hawks, Francis L., *Narrative of the Expedition of an American Squadron to the China Seas and Japan: Performed in the Years 1852, 1853, and 1854, under the Command of Commodore M. C. Perry, United States Navy*, 3 vols, Washington DC, A. O. P. Nicholson, 1856. The official account.

Heusken, Henry, *Japan Journal: 1855–1861*, trans. and ed. Jeannette C. van der Corput and Robert A. Wilson, Rutgers University Press, 1964

Notehelfer, F. G., *Japan through American Eyes: The Journal of Francis Hall 1859–1866*, Westview Press, 2001. An American businessman and journalist, Hall reports on Japan from November 1859, when he arrived.

There are also fascinating works by western scholars who have looked beyond the accepted winners' version of history to examine the lives and viewpoint of the losing side. These, and more general historical sources, include:

Beasley, W. G., *The Meiji Restoration*, Stanford University Press, 1973

Beasley, W. G., *The Rise of Modern Japan*, Charles E. Tuttle Company, Tokyo, 1990

Gluckman, Dale Carolyn, and Sharon Sadako Takeda, *When Art Became Fashion: Kosode in Edo-Period Japan*, Los Angeles County Museum of Art, 1992

Hanes, W. Travis, III, and Frank Sanello, *The Opium Wars: The Addiction of One Empire and the Corruption of Another*, Sourcebooks Inc., Naperville, Illinois, 2002

Miner, Earl, *An Introduction to Japanese Court Poetry* (with translations by the author and Robert H. Brower), Stanford University Press, 1968

Miyoshi, Masao, *As We Saw Them: The First Japanese Embassy to the United States*, Kodansha International, 1994

Ravina, Mark, *The Last Samurai: The Life and Battles of Saigo Takamori*, John Wiley & Sons, Inc., Hoboken, New Jersey, 2004

Shiba Ryotaro, *The Last Shogun: The Life of Tokugawa Yoshinobu*, trans. Juliet Winters Carpenter, Kodansha International, 1998

Steele, M. William, *Alternative Narratives in Modern Japanese History*, Routledge, 2003

Totman, Conrad, *Politics in the Tokugawa Bakufu,1600–1843*, Harvard University Press, 1967

Wiley, Peter Booth, with Ichiro Korogi, *Yankees in the Land of the Gods: Commodore Perry and the Opening of Japan*, Viking, 1990

The best Japanese account of the women's palace is:

Takayanagi Kaneyoshi, *Edojo ooku no seikatsu (Life in the Women's Palace at Edo Castle)*, Tokyo Yuzankaku Shuppan, 1969

Atsu's story was made into a lavish, somewhat romanticized, fifty-episode television drama entitled *Atsuhime* (*Princess Atsu*), starring Aoi Miyazaki as Atsu. It was broadcast weekly throughout 2008 on NHK, Japan's equivalent of the BBC, and was hugely popular. Excerpts can be found on websites such as YouTube.

Much information on the Black Ships can be found in this informative and entertaining website, part of the MIT Visualizing Cultures programme by John Dower:
http://ocw.mit.edu/ans7870/21f/21f.027/black_ships_and_samurai/pdf/bss_essay.pdf

The symbol at the beginning of each part is the hollyhock crest of the Tokugawas.

Acknowledgements

The Shogun's Queen is chronologically the first of my quartet of novels set in the tumultuous period when Japan was encountering the west for the first time; but in terms of writing it is the last. I've spent nearly fifteen years immersed in this period and have enjoyed many wonderfully illuminating visits to Japan. My research has taken me from Tokyo and Kyoto to Kagoshima in the deep south and Hakodaté in Hokkaido in the far north and to Aizu Wakamatsu in Fukushima Prefecture shortly after the earthquake and tsunami of 2011.

The idea of writing a novel about Atsu was sparked by the moving and dramatic Fuji TV drama *Ooku* (*The Women's Palace*), one series of which is set at the end of the civil war. I was careful not to watch too much of the very popular NHK series *Atsuhime* (*Princess Atsu*) so as not to be unconsciously influenced by it. Nevertheless I've taken inspiration and the occasional idea from it. In particular I'm indebted to the series for the idea of taking Kaneshigé Kimotsuki as Atsu's lover. When I looked into his story I realized that he was the perfect age and a very likely candidate, though as I say in the Afterword there is no actual evidence that they knew each other.

I've tried to be as true to history as possible in the writing of this book and have drawn on contemporary sources and the work of many distinguished historians of Japan to write it. Some are listed in the Bibliography; there are many more. However, this remains a work of fiction and I've certainly taken the odd liberty in the interests of telling a good story. The facts are theirs. All mistakes and misinterpretations are entirely my own.

In recent years the British Library and other bodies have reissued many out-of-print books in photocopied form, including volumes published in the 1860s; as a result I now have one of the best libraries in the country of books on Japan in the civil-war period.

Huge thanks to my agent, Bill Hamilton, who kept my nose to the grindstone, read both drafts and made many perceptive and inspiring suggestions. Thanks too to Jennifer Custer and the rest of the indefatigable team at A. M. Heath.

Enormous thanks too to my editor, Simon Taylor, whose many brilliant and illuminating suggestions did a great deal to shape this book and keep me pointing in the right direction. I'm much indebted to him and to my copy-editor, Deborah Adams, to Sophie Christopher and Hannah Bright, my publicists, and to everyone at Transworld, who have been full of support, enthusiasm and patience when required.

Much gratitude to Gaye Rowley and Tom Harper in Tokyo whose understanding of Japan, Japanese and the *ooku* is far more than I could ever hope to have and who have shared their knowledge very generously throughout the writing of this quartet.

And thanks to Kuniko Tamai, my go-to expert for all details from Japanese ladies' underwear in the Edo period to proper forms of address, seasonal plants and everything else one could ever want to know about Edo Japan.

Thanks too to John Williams for advice on Japanese birds. He introduced me to the lovely yamagara bird, whose proper (but unpoetic) English name is 'varied tit'.

As always, my husband Arthur I. Miller shared the journey with me. He read each draft several times, made many helpful suggestions and was always ready to discuss the most abstruse matters of Japanese history while also keeping me grounded in the real world. Without his love, support, good humour and excellent cooking I couldn't possibly have written this book.

This book is dedicated to him.

Also by Lesley Downer

Fiction
The Last Concubine
The Courtesan and the Samurai
Across a Bridge of Dreams

Non-fiction
Madame Sadayakko: The Geisha Who Seduced the West
Geisha: The Secret History of a Vanishing World*
The Brothers: The Hidden World of Japan's Richest Family
On the Narrow Road to the Deep North

*Published in the United States as *Women of the Pleasure
Quarters: The Secret History of the Geisha*

For more information on Lesley Downer and her books,
see her website at www.lesleydowner.com

ABOUT THE AUTHOR

Lesley Downer's mother was Chinese and her father a professor of Chinese, so she grew up in a house full of books about Asia. But Japan was to prove more alluring than China, and Lesley lived there for some fifteen years. She has written many books about the country and its culture, including *Geisha: The Secret History of a Vanishing World*, and *Madame Sadayakko: The Geisha Who Seduced the West*, and has presented television programmes on Japan for the BBC, Channel 4 and NHK. Her debut novel was *The Last Concubine* and *The Shogun's Queen* is her fourth. Lesley Downer lives in London with her husband, the writer Arthur I. Miller, and still makes sure she goes to Japan every year.